Praise for

EVENT

"The Roswell Incident—whether legend, fact, or some combination of both—has inspired countless novels and movies over the years, but David Lynn Golemon's *Event* peels back the layers of Roswell with refreshing originality. The action is spectacularly cinematic, the characters compelling, and the story is a flat-out adrenaline rush that pits real-world, cutting-edge military technology against a literally out-of-this-world threat. Even better, the Event Group itself is one of the best fictional agencies to arise in the literature of gov̶ᵉᵣⁿᵐᵉⁿᵗ conspiracies."

̶authors
̶tevens

"Golemon puts his n̶ ̶ᵃ ̶ᵖˡᵃᶜᵉ ̶ᵗᵒ ̶ᵍᵒᵒᵈ ̶ in this promising debut sur̶ ̶ ̶ ̶ ̶ ̶ ̶ᵧ ̶ᶠᵃⁿˢ ̶ᵒᶠ *The X-Files*....the plotting and hair's-breadth escapes evoke some of the early work of Preston and Child, and the author's premise offers a rich lode of materials for the inevitable sequels."

—*Publishers Weekly*

"Fans of UFO fiction will find this a great read, and fans of military fiction won't be disappointed either."

—SFSIGNAL.COM

"Imagine mixing in a blender a Tom Clancy novel with the movie *Predator* and the television series *The X-Files*....readers who enjoy nonstop action and lots of flying bullets will enjoy Golemon's first book in a projected series."

—*Library Journal*

Also by David L. Golemon

Event

Legend

Ancients

Leviathan

Primeval

Legacy

Ripper

Carpathian

LEGEND
AN EVENT GROUP ADVENTURE

David Lynn Golemon

St. Martin's Paperbacks

LEGEND

Copyright © 2007 by David Lynn Golemon.
Excerpt from *Ancients* copyright © 2008 by David Lynn Golemon.

All rights reserved. For information address St. Martin's Press, 175 Fifth Avenue, New York, NY 10010.

Library of Congress Catalog Card Number: 2007014863

ISBN: 978-1-250-15791-1

Printed in the United States of America

St. Martin's Press hardcover edition / August 2007
St. Martin's Paperbacks edition / July 2008

St. Martin's Paperbacks are published by St. Martin's Press, 175 Fifth Avenue, New York, NY 10010.

For my family—
Steve, Scott, and Ric.
The few become fewer.

For my aunts and mother, the four sisters of the
Apocalypse, living large at the time of the Depression and
conquering at the time of war. The world has become a
lessser place in your absence.

For Katie Anne, Brandon Lynn, Shaune David,
and Cindy Michelle—my children.

ACKNOWLEDGMENTS

I would like to take time out to thank my editor, Pete Wolverton; without Pete and his guidance, all would be lost. Also to Katie at Thomas Dunne, forever answering the mundane questions of the unenlightened.

Finally, to the United States Navy, consistently setting the standard among the American armed forces for professionalism and foresight. To the blue ocean and brown water navy, without whose cooperation this book would not have been possible.

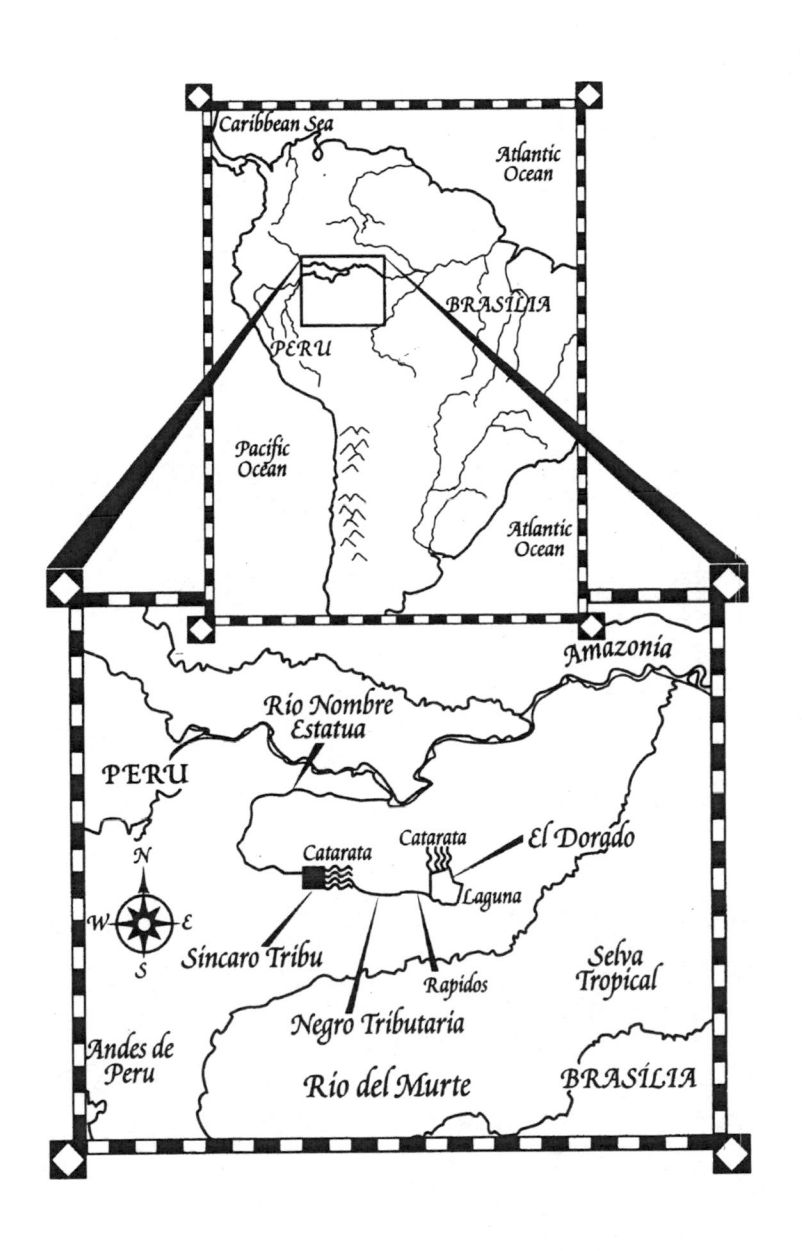

PROLOGUE
FRANCISCO PIZARRO

A quest for the riches of the earth brought them to the waters of legend and the greed of man came and destroyed the way of innocence, and the ancient one rose from the depths to consume them.

—Father Escobar Corinth,
Catholic priest to the
Francisco Pizarro expedition

AMAZONIAN RIVER BASIN
SUMMER AD 1534, 56 DAYS OUT OF PERU

THE Spaniards let loose a volley of musket fire into the end-less green of the jungle, not knowing if their lead shot struck anything more vital than fern or moss. Even before the acrid smoke was cleared by the slight breeze that reached the floor of the small valley, the soldiers had turned and continued their flight, four and five men at a time, while a like number reloaded and covered their retreat. The captain ventured a look back to make sure all of his soldiers had safely vacated their positions, then he quickly followed to catch up with them.

The deeper they fled into the surrounding jungle, the denser it became, effectively choking off their escape route with natural tangle-foot of vines and small trees. Above them, the sun was slowly being smothered by the trees that seemed to grow together, creating a false roof that offered no sanctity of protection. The river offered the only clear avenue of escape.

The captain had but two choices: stay here and stand their ground against arrow and dart while taking and losing more lives, or go into the river, where they would be more exposed yet could make better time than they would while also fighting the thickening growth around them.

"Into the water, men. Why do you delay? We must follow the river, it's our only route!"

"Look, my captain," Lieutenant Torrez said, pointing skyward.

When Captain Hernando Padilla looked up, his eyes widened at the monstrous sight. Towering above the Spaniards two sixty-foot-tall stone carvings rose above the giant trees on either side of the river. The expedition had never seen the like of them. The carvings were manlike in stature, only the heads were not that of any men or any of the Incan gods the soldiers had seen thus far. The lips were thick, and the deep etchings in the rocks depicted scales where flesh should have been. The heads of both giant figures stared down upon the intruders with the large eyes of a fish. They were ancient stone deities, guardians of the vegetation-choked waters of the darkened river beyond. Vines entered and exited the cracked and age-worn stone like snakes emerging from holes.

"They are only stone imaginings of heathen people," Padilla shouted. "Get these men into the water, Lieutenant, now."

Just as he had uttered the orders to advance, an arrow glanced off his armor from behind and ricocheted into the air. The captain almost lost his balance as he bent over, cursed, and then quickly recovered. Small darts started to strike the spit of sand and moving water around the Spaniards. The Indians were upon them once again, not only shooting their primitive arrows, but launching from long blow guns small darts tipped with the poison of exotic frogs—the very same devices the soldiers had seen the native peoples use frighteningly well during their time with the tribe. They knew it would be a slow death if even one dart pierced their exposed flesh. The men needed no more coaxing or threats. As the huge stone edifices watched on either side, they splashed into the swirling water and made their way into the shadows of the canyon.

THE SPANIARDS TRAVELED between massive trees that cut off the sky. They marched most of the late afternoon, enduring sporadic attacks from Sincaro emerging from the thick undergrowth beneath the trees. Then the Indians vanished just as abruptly into the jungle. It had been close to an hour's time since the last ambush, but the Spaniards were still expecting the next attack at any moment. As they progressed, the sky ahead of them was slowly being shut out by the jungle and towering trees from both sides of the river. They heard with ever-increasing volume the more pleasurable sounds of animal life, as a semblance of normalcy returned to their surroundings after their headlong flight. Until this point they had noticed no sound of life other than their own shouts and curses during the assaults they had endured the last few hours.

Finally they fought their way past the raging rapids that had appeared suddenly. The violence of the waters had terrified the men, who were lucky to spy a small wedge of beach along which to pass.

The captain called a halt and rested his worn body against the trunk of a large tree. The nightmare visions of the murder of so many innocents churned over and over in his mind, threatening to drive him mad. He lowered his head with shame at what they had done. The orders for the excursion into these unknown lands to the east had been given to him personally by Pizarro. The words of that order now echoed through his memory: *The Indians are not to be thought of as allies. They must be subdued with forthright action and intimidation until such a time as the source of the gold is obtained. If this course of action cannot be maintained, assistance shall be called for immediately. The location of El Dorado is paramount above all other considerations.*

But Padilla had found the Indians to be gracious and kindly toward the visiting strangers. So he had changed his tactics and tried to gain the advantage in his own manner, ignoring the orders of the madman in the east.

Padilla angrily removed his helmet and harshly rubbed the sweat from his face. The heavy iron soon slipped from his slick fingers and fell to the green jungle floor. The Spaniard ignored it as he instead looked skyward, trying desperately to penetrate the deep canopy of green for just a small glimpse of the blessed sun. But it was as hidden, removed from the world as he knew the grace of God would be forever removed from his soul.

For three months they had endured the hellishness of the Peruvian mountains and Brazilian jungle, only to find they were alone in the most godforsaken area the expedition had ever known. Only the good nature of his men, grateful to be away from the slave master Pizarro, had kept his small company in line. Then one evening they had come upon a most wondrous valley, full of exotic flowers, tall leaf-laden trees, and the blessed sun. It was here they had found the Sincaro; the dwarf Indians that inhabited the beautiful valley. The small people met them with trepidation at first. Against orders, Padilla had eventually gained their trust through trading and the honest goodwill of his men. They treated the Sincaro with respect and gentleness, and the small men and women of the village slowly welcomed the tall strangers as friends.

These prehistoric tribesmen were a hardy people and, according to their stories and legends, had been so since they had been enslaved by the empire to the west. They had gained their freedom thanks to the river gods who had dealt their Inca taskmasters a savage blow a hundred years before, which had finally freed the small people. When asked how their river gods had achieved this, the elder of the village would answer only that the Inca had gained the secret knowledge of the Sincaro through murder and slavery, and had even tried to chain their deities and turn them on the Sincaro in the Incan pursuit of earthly riches. The river gods would not become the slaves of men, and they revolted. Then the Inca were no more. The old man would smile at that point when he saw the skeptical looks of the Spaniards. The Inca had never returned to the valley, and now it was the captain who would have to gain the trust of these strange and vibrant people to learn the secret that had brought and then driven the Inca from these lands.

The short-lived harmony between Spaniard and Indian

lasted for exactly twenty days: Good days that they used to their advantage, learning the Sincaro way and their simple lifestyle. Long days of nurturing the trust he sought, and in return Padilla's men helped these industrious people learn the strange ways of their taller visitors. The soldiers amazed them with the strange black powder that made their cooking fires jump toward the heavens in a shower of smoke and sparks.

There had been smaller things, to be sure: The screaming enjoyment of young and old alike when they had been shown small mirrors. Letting the Sincaro touch and be awestruck by their armor, which the primitives thought was some sort of magical skin. The Spaniards had been patient as the children tugged and pulled on their beards and laughed as the men playfully tickled them in return. Padilla and his soldiers were also happy to share their own rations of pork and rice, and eat the strange but delicious meals the Sincaro painstakingly placed before them. It had been during one of these evening meals that the Spanish learned the Sincaro had never ventured out of the valley. Even their enslavement had been here, which indicated to the captain that what the soldiers sought was indeed close by.

A time of trust had presented itself just as Padilla had said it would. Ever so slowly, the Indians of the Sincaro village began to take the Spaniards into their confidence and soon began bringing forth small trinkets of gold they had so cautiously and painstakingly hidden during the early days of their encounter. The gold not only started to appear as small bracelets, idols, and necklaces but loose, in leather sacks around their necks that brimmed with dust from the Amazonian tributary. It had been hard to hold his men in check once they had seen that. Padilla only succeeded in doing so by promising them the El Dorado that Pizarro had rightly guessed to be hidden in this green-canopied country, despite the Incan denial. If they bided their time, these friendly people would probably share the location of the source of their gold with them without much prodding and, even more important to Padilla, without bloodshed.

Captain Padilla suspected the trouble would come from dreams of avarice, but instead it came from a man he should have been watching all along. Joaquin Suarez, a brute of a man who had worn out his welcome with the main company of conquistadors in Peru because of blackish and boorish behavior, had been attached to the expedition by Father Corinth himself, after Suarez's unholy rape and murder of an Indian child near the new Spanish town of Esposisia. The priest had sent him as far from Pizarro as he could, knowing that the big man would have been executed on the spot if word of his crime had reached the generalissimo's ears. The captain mused often how one could murder entire villages, even kidnap and kill the reigning monarch, but the single killing of a child was worth a death sentence, because nothing spawned revolt more than the deliberate murder of innocence. So the accused Suarez, a distant cousin of Father Escobar Corinth, was sent away with the only expedition to venture out this year, to keep him out of Pizarro's sight.

During those many days of travel into these forsaken parts of the world, Suarez had grumbled about how he had been treated shabbily over the murder of the Incan child; after all, he thought to himself, *It wasn't as if she had been a child of God.* But he obeyed the orders given to him. He was silent and brooding most of the time, even treading lightly among the other men of the expedition, who looked upon the large soldier as a pariah. Suarez remained well behaved even after the gold started to appear. But now Padilla rebuked himself for not remembering the brute's black heart.

Last night Suarez had taken Spanish wine with a tribal leader, against express orders to not give anything fermented to the Indians. The men could accept the strange beer that the Sincaro brewed, but the soldiers were to offer the Indians nothing of an alcoholic nature from their own stores.

After an hour of drinking, Suarez had managed to get the elder drunk. But even then it was as if the old man knew exactly the giant Spaniard's intentions, and refused to say anything about where the Sincaro mined the gold. Suarez, having been driven mad by the refusal of the elder to talk, had finally tortured him for what he knew.

Hours later, when the other tribesmen found the torn and battered body of their much-beloved leader, they viciously attacked the sleeping soldiers without warning. The raid was so fierce that the Spaniards' defense had been hurried and, in the end, futile. Padilla and his men fought back with a loss of sixteen of his best soldiers and most of their firearms. Among the casualties was Pizarro's own nephew, Dadriell. The Sincaro had lost at least forty or more, mostly women and, God forgive them all, children.

Now the survivors of his once proud and now cursed expedition were holed up in a large green basin that was fed water by a very deep tributary of the Amazon, at least ten leagues from the site of last night's massacre. This great lagoon, which for all practical description was like a small lake, lay before them. They had waded along the shore of the tributary, following the treacherous rapids to gain entrance into this hidden Eden that had trees so tall they stretched and bent over the dark waters.

This was a setting Captain Padilla had never thought to see in his lifetime. It was too beautiful, somewhere one would not wish to conclude a massacre if the small people chose to attack them here. It truly was a place God had sculpted when last upon this earth. Tree branches hung out over the water and soft grasses grew all the way to the slow-flowing lagoon. The walls of what had to be an ancient and extinct volcano rose on three sides, actually leaning out over the lagoon, creating three natural shelves.

Flowers of every variety bloomed and nourished honeybees that gently moved from species to species, never noticing or caring about the sudden invasion by the Spaniards. The strange flowers that grew with only small dapples of sunlight were large and the most fragrant Padilla had ever smelled.

The ancient volcanic bowl was not only fed by the Amazon tributary but also by a mammoth waterfall that fell from high above on the far end of the lagoon. But that was not the outstanding feature of the small valley. There, flanking either side of the tumbling waters of the falls, were pillars. They were at least 120 feet high, carved from the surrounding rock, and supported an arch that vanished into the white waterfall of the river above. Vines coursed through the cracked and weather-worn pillars; in several places they had separated the stone completely, making the columns look as if they would fall at any moment.

Now here he stood, trying to decide if he should make their last stand or continue the insanity of running deeper into the green hell beyond the lagoon. The men knew there might be something here because of those giant pillars, but they had lost all interest in riches and just wanted familiar sights. Even to return to Pizarro was preferable to this madness.

Maybe the villagers would take the decision out of his hands and just leave them be. The captain would then personally report to the fool Pizarro that the expedition had been for naught, that nothing but death awaited any man in the distant valleys of the Amazon.

While Padilla wrote his thoughts down into his personal diary, the map he had made of their travels fell from the back pages where he had placed it. As he bent over to retrieve it, he hesitated momentarily, as he was suddenly tempted to leave it to rot on the ground. Then he considered his men, picked it up, and placed it back into his journal.

His thoughts of leaving the map so no one could follow were broken by the harsh laughter of the very man who had caused so much horror in the last twelve hours. Such a display of pleasure after the spilling of so much blood seemed wrong. The captain looked over at his men. Joaquin Suarez was kneeling by the water, his hair freshly wet after washing the blood from himself and his armor. The soldiers around him looked on and shook their heads. Everyone knew now that this man was a danger to them all, because of his recklessness.

Padilla reached down and retrieved his helmet, and that

was when he caught a glimpse of a strange visitor to their makeshift rest area. Huge eyes were there for the briefest of moments before whatever it was scurried off through the thick foliage, using the jungle for cover as it slid silently into the waters of the lagoon. Captain Padilla looked around to see if his men had seen what he had, but they were busy washing and lying on the thickly carpeted grass; some of the more experienced soldiers were even kneeling in prayer. He once again peered into the thick undergrowth for some sign that the little creature had been there at all, but saw not a trace. He quickly came to the conclusion that it had been nothing but a trick of his overtaxed mind and the darkened jungle floor. Suddenly there was a rustling of bushes behind him, and his hand went to his sword.

"My captain," Ivan Rodrigo Torrez, his friend and second-in-command, stepped from the dense growth of the forest, "the Indians have disappeared." Torrez removed his helmet; his long black hair fell free as sweat poured from his face and beard. "One minute, we were watching them from a clearing about a half a league from here, and the next minute, they fell back into the jungle and were gone. Our trail into this valley was so obvious, they must know where we are." He took a breath and looked around him as he loosened his armor. "I expect them to double back this way, so I placed the men in an excellent position for ambush, but thus far they haven't come."

Padilla patted his old friend on the shoulder. "That is just as well; I can't do this any longer." He lowered his hand and looked around at the darkened area under the thick canopy of trees. "I just feel like resting here for a month before returning and reporting this horrible thing we have done." He pulled the front collar of his armor away from his soaked tunic. "Maybe I'll swim out to the only spot here that has sunlight hitting it and remain there until the Lord pulls me under." He looked at the magnificent waterfall and then back toward the center of the large lagoon and the bright dapples of sunlight that lit the blue waters and made them sparkle.

"I, like most of the men, feel like cutting Suarez's throat for bringing this evil to our doorstep," Torrez said angrily.

"I can't think on that now, my old friend, I am weary to my very bones. Besides, in the end, it is I who will be judged for this debacle, not Suarez."

"Surely Commander Pizarro will not blame you for the actions of this maniac?"

"Pizarro is not an ordinary man and he has little or no patience for incompetence. I can assure you I will be judged harshly for losing his nephew and a chance at finding the Indians' source of gold. For my failure, the Sincaro will be extinct or enslaved by this time next year," he sighed. "I had the arrogance to believe I could do this another way; I am but a fool."

Loud laughter once again sprang up from the beach area. As both officers turned and walked toward their men, another round of raucous howling came from the lagoon. Upon entering the small clearing they saw Suarez hold something in the air as the other soldiers hooted loudly, several even patting each other on their backs. As they looked closer at the strange object the soldier was tossing into the air, they saw it resembled a small monkey. Then Padilla realized it was the same creature he had spied looking at him from the bush only moments before. The captain could clearly see the small animal and its remarkable resemblance to their chattering companions that lived in the trees. In his diary he had listed many different varieties of monkey and other strange animal life, but this was unlike anything he had ever witnessed before in his many travels. On this expedition he had become quite knowledgeable about the far-ranging species that inhabited this new continent, thus the animal that Suarez held in his hands so casually was something he knew to be very special.

"Captain, we have a captive; this little clown tried to steal my satchel with the last of our bread," Rondo Cordoba, the quartermaster, said while gesturing toward the small creature Suarez was toying with.

Padilla and Torrez joined the men to take a look at the creature up close. It was a monkey, or what a monkey would look like without so much as a hair on its body. The facial features were close to that of a man, except for the lips. They framed many sharp teeth and were thick, the upper lip much larger than the bottom one, and the ears were but small holes in the sides of its head. The tail was slick as a taskmaster's whip and it swung back and forth quickly. Padilla surmised that the animal was agitated at being thrown into the air by Suarez. He saw small protrusions of skin like a spiny sail that flared outward down its back every time it was tossed upward.

"Stop tormenting that creature, you ignorant fool!" Torrez commanded loudly.

Suarez stopped, looked angrily for a moment at his captain and then at Torrez, and, without removing his eyes from the two men, arrogantly tossed the small animal into the air again. He caught it and then concentrated his stare on the captain in a silent challenge. Padilla drew his sword and pointed it at the larger man's throat, pressing the blade enough that blood was soon collecting on its steel surface. His eyes were locked on Suarez's and a ghost of a smile touched his lips. He would enjoy sliding his sharp blade into the throat of the very reason for their current predicament, no matter if they needed all the men they could get at that moment.

"As you can see, you fatherless child, our captain is of ill humor today," Torrez said, smiling, as he watched Padilla and a seemingly unshaken Suarez.

Suarez ignored the sword and the neck wound, still holding the animal tightly. He quickly changed his grip to hold the creature by its throat. It made choking sounds; its tail was now jittering in small movements that were more of a spasm than a swing.

Padilla pressed the blade farther into the man's neck, and the arrogance that had been there a moment earlier was replaced by a worried frown, as Suarez just then noticed there was no laughter from the men around him. He saw there was only expressions of anticipation for his seemingly imminent death.

All this time, the animal's eyes never left those of Padilla. It was if the small creature knew it was the subject of the standoff and was awaiting the captain's next move. While the sword remained· in place, Suarez slowly lowered the creature to the white sand that made up the small beach and the monkeylike animal scurried not toward the jungle or the water, but behind the captain. The beast jumped up· and down and spat at Suarez, and jabbered as if cursing the large soldier. As Suarez straightened up, Padilla did not withdraw but pushed the gleaming sword forward, bringing a more satisfying flow of blood to the blade, where it rolled slowly down the shiny surface and dripped onto the few feet of pure white sand.

"We may need this fool, Captain," Ivan Torrez said loudly so all could hear. "We may still have him up on charges upon our return, but we need his strength to fight, or to flee from this place, and, God willing, he may even redeem himself at some point in this nightmare." He placed his hand on the captain's arm as he gave Suarez a withering look.

Without dropping his gaze, Padilla slowly lowered the sword and just as slowly wiped the blood from its tip onto the red sleeve of the big man. Then he slowly slid the weapon back into the ornate scabbard at his side.

The hairless monkey was still holding onto the captain's leg and hissing at Suarez. Padilla reached down and, using both hands, gently picked up the animal and looked it over. It was breathing through its small nostrils and open mouth, but it also had what looked like the gills of a fish right where the small neck joined the head, three rows of soft skin arranged along its jawline, flaring and then closing as they, too, sought life-sustaining air. There were finlike features along its forearms and a small spiny dorsal fin, again like that of a fish, on its back, traveling the length of its spine.

"This is the most amazing animal I have ever seen in all

of our travels," Padilla said softly, as the large black eyes of the creature blinked, not with eyelids like his own, but with a set of clear membranes.

"I think it looks like my mother-in-law," Torrez joked as he slapped the captain on the back, in an attempt to lighten the darkened mood.

The men laughed; Padilla smiled also, even as he chanced a wary eye toward Suarez.

"Captain, look!" one of the men shouted.

Padilla lowered the small creature and looked at the spot his men were pointing toward in the calm waters of the lagoon, where another of the monkeylike species stood holding a struggling fish in both its clawed hands. The first animal scurried up to the newcomer, waddling bowlegged on its paddlelike feet, and started jabbering loudly. The second creature looked across and then tossed the fish in an underhanded throw toward the group of Spaniards; it landed on the sand and flopped around, then lay still. Small claw marks were evident on the smooth skin of the large catfish.

As the soldiers watched in amazement, another and then another of the animals tentatively stood up and waddled from the water, to toss more flopping fish onto the small shoreline. The men nervously laughed.

"Maybe it's an offering?" Rondo ventured to no one in particular.

"Gather the fish, men, we will not waste this gift brought by our new friends," Padilla ordered. "Collect them all so we can also feed the men who are guarding the perimeter."

As the men moved forward to collect the offered bounty, they failed to notice as large bubbles appeared in the middle of the lagoon to slowly circle under the sunlight, then vanish after a moment. Nor did they hear the sudden silence that filled the trees around them as the birds grew momentarily still in their high nests and roosts, but they did see the small creatures glance at one another as they chattered back and forth and headed with apparent deliberation back toward the water. The first one, the one Padilla had saved from the murderous

Suarez, was looking back as it retreated from the newcomers to its beautiful world. To the men who were watching the strange exodus, it seemed as if this animal was saddened at leaving.

Padilla turned away from the lagoon and was amazed at the horde of fish that had accumulated on the sand; he counted over ten species of varying types. But just one particularly caught his eye, and he bent over to examine it. He called Torrez over to see this wonder. The fish had huge scales and very strange fins on its lower belly, and a thick and powerful-looking tail. These most unusual fins looked as if they had small feetlike appendages on the very tips. The mouth was huge and filled with lethal-looking teeth; the jaw jutted far forward unlike that of any fish he had ever seen, almost like a barracuda's, only far more pronounced. As the two officers examined the strange fish, which was lying on its side, its eye seemed to roll and look at them and, as it did, its mouth snapped open and closed. They quickly straightened up and looked at the men, who were starting to build fires for cooking and to guard against the coming night. Padilla once again bent down toward the large fish. He thought he saw something on its blackened, coarse scales; he reached down and lightly rubbed them. The fish moved momentarily and then lay still. Padilla held his fingers close to his face and rubbed them together, as small gold flakes gently fell to the tips of his worn boots.

PADILLA LAY UNDER one of the many ancient and beautiful trees that permeated the area, their massive roots projecting from the earth like a giant's arms ripping through the fabric of a blouse. He held his booted feet close to their small fire, to dry the thick leather as best he could. His diary was in his hands and he had just finished recording the observations of this eventful day. His last entry written before he closed the small book declared that the battle with the Sincaro was due to his own negligence.

He had considered not recording evidence of gold found

lodged in the scales of the fish. But he had never omitted anything from his observations and would not start now. Pizarro would be amazed to read about a source of gold that was so abundant it was actually brought to the surface on the backs of fish. The captain shook his head at the thought as he placed the diary back into his tunic.

Torrez lay beside Padilla, playing with one of the strange monkeylike animals.

"What do you make of them, my captain?" the lieutenant asked, holding out a small piece of bacon for the visitor who sat on his chest, its tail swinging back and forth like that of a happy puppy. Its little claws finally stabbed the small piece of meat and popped it into its mouth. Smiling and jabbering softly at the man, its mouth worked frantically, along with the small gills.

"I think they are an offshoot or very close relative of the monkey, just one that happens to live in the water, surely not a design that God had intended," said Padilla, then he laughed. "But who knows the mind of God, but God himself?" He watched Torrez and the animal for a moment. "What is truly amazing is the fact that you can see their small gills moving like that of a fish, but then you notice that the rise and fall of its breathing is light, almost as if it is taking air through both systems. It must be difficult for them to live out of the water for such long periods of time."

"We need such devices, my captain, for breathing on-board those stinking vessels of ours."

"Yes, if our friend Rondo over there gets a belly full of beans and pork fat, the whole ship is in danger of choking to death or exploding like a musket," Padilla joked.

The two men were silent a moment as they listened to the comforting sound of the men as the soldiers spoke among themselves, talking of things other than death and this accursed mission. Then Padilla placed his diary in his belt pouch and looked over at his friend.

"When we entered the water in the outer valley, the stone monoliths, what did you think of them?"

"I was hoping that subject would not have arisen after the sun went down, if at all," Torrez said as he gently laid the small creature upon the ground and watched a moment as it scurried away. "As for what I thought at the time? They scared me." He glanced over at Padilla and he could make out the captain's eyes on him. "You know me, I fear no man or, for that matter, anything I have come across before. But those carvings gave me chills as I looked upon them, even as I ridiculed our men for the same reason."

"The watchers of this valley, gods of the lagoon, that's what I called them in my diary. They were very old carvings, I suspect even older than some of the Incan dwellings we found in Peru."

"The age isn't what concerned me, my captain, it was the forms themselves. I would hate to run into one of those while bathing, I'll tell you."

Padilla laughed loudly and was about to comment when a shrill, piercing scream ripped through the night around them. The small creatures who had been playing in the sand screeched at the noise and shot off for the water, making little splashes as they dove for the safety of the lagoon. Padilla and Torrez were up in a second, Ivan with his sword drawn.

"What is it?" Padilla called to his men as they entered the circle of light cast by the fire. The soldiers were angry, yelling as they pointed forward toward the small shoreline.

One man stood apart from the others, holding the limp and obviously lifeless body of one of the little creatures. He clutched it by its broken neck and it dangled, almost formless, in the firelight.

"You bloody bastard!" one of his men yelled. "Why did you have to do that?"

The soldier who was standing and facing everyone was none other than Suarez. The huge man stood his ground and stared back at the others, almost daring them to make a move toward him. He wore no armor and his scarlet shirt glimmered in the firelight as if with blood.

"What is happening here?" Padilla asked, knowing all too well the answer to his question.

One of the soldiers stepped forward, a boy of only twenty, pointing out to where the big man stood.

"That bastard did that for no other reason than a lust for killing."

"He bit me, and I will kill anything I wish, man or animal," Suarez said, still looking at the group rather than at his superior officer, shaking the lifeless body of the harmless creature.

"The man is mad, my captain; we must put him down as we would a dog with the foaming sickness," Torrez hissed, stepping closer to Suarez and forgetting his earlier words of restraint. His sword was pointing straight at the big man's chest.

"He bit you by accident; you're the one that pulled the bread away and allowed his teeth to strike your fingers instead," another man said as the others shouted agreement.

"Suarez, you have caused enough trouble and it ends here, now, tonight," Padilla stated flatly and without emotion. He reached over and made his lieutenant lower his sword. "This will be my responsibility; you will stand down, my friend."

"You must not go into armed combat, my captain; we cannot risk losing you. I will do it."

Suarez tossed the dead creature onto the sand, backed up three paces to the water's edge, and slowly drew his sword.

"I will make quick work of anyone that comes for me," he said, slicing the blade through the air.

The rest of the soldiers placed hands on swords or pistols, demonstrating their willingness to dispatch Suarez. They would make sure he brought them no more ill will.

"Stand down, all you men," Padilla said as he advanced, drawing his own thin blade, not removing his eyes from Suarez. "This is your captain's duty."

Suddenly, small explosions of water erupted from the lagoon as dozens of the small creatures burst through to the surface, some clearing the water by two and three feet. They hurriedly swam to the far side of the lagoon, and before the men knew what they were looking at, the fast and agile animals were all scrambling up trees and large bushes on the opposite shore. They jabbered back toward the water they had just exited and then grew suddenly quiet. That was when the men noticed the animal sounds in the deep night had ceased, as if the entire jungle had grown mute while the two Spaniards faced each other.

Suarez had backed farther into the water as he waited for the advance of Padilla. But he had turned at the small creatures' noisy flight from the lagoon.

"Rondo, take five men and follow the shoreline and see what you can see. Something has frightened them," Torrez ordered.

Rondo pointed to five men. They broke free from the group and started to slowly walk down the slim shoreline, buckling their armor and drawing their swords as they did so. Rondo cocked his two pistols and then placed himself at the head of the small band of Spaniards. They walked cautiously, and then they disappeared around some bushes at the turn in the lagoon.

Padilla was as calm as the night around them as he advanced on Suarez. He slowly brought his sword up toward the other man's barrel chest. Suarez smiled and moved deeper into the water while moving his own sword in a slow, deliberate arc, parting the lagoon's surface with a swish of the blade. When he saw how much anger etched the face of Padilla, he backed deeper into the dark water.

The remaining men in camp froze when they heard the large man shout out in terror as he was grabbed from beneath the water. His legs were jerked out from under him so hard that in one moment he was screaming, and in the next he had vanished. Suarez surfaced briefly, splashing and in shock, the whites of his eyes showing brightly, then he was quickly pulled into the lagoon before he could utter a second cry of pain or terror at what was happening. He completely disappeared below the rolling surface. Nothing but bubbles and two quick slashes of his shining sword marked his trail to death's door.

"What in the name of God was that?" Torrez yelled as he ran to the water's edge.

Suddenly the gaping soldiers saw new bubbles and a sharp V-shaped wake along the surface of the water as something else traveled fast toward the far side of the lagoon—toward the spot that Torrez had sent Rondo and the five others. The sounds of splashing and then screams of terror split the quiet night, and then two loud reports followed as Rondo fired his pistols. Then among the screams of men and the dying echo of the gunshots they all heard a sound they would take with them to their graves. The roar was like a deep echo of the worst imaginable enraged demon from their nightmares. The horrid sound reverberated and sent chills down their spine.

The screams of the six Spaniards ended as suddenly as they had begun, and in an instant the night became still once again.

Torrez appeared at the stunned Padilla's side, pressing his armor into his hands. The captain sheathed his sword and slipped the heavy iron onto his back and chest. Then they looked again toward the spot where the men had disappeared just moments before. A dark figure of a man emerged through the bushes and stumbled forward, obviously wounded. Two soldiers ran to him and brought him into the bright circle cast by the firelight. There were deep gouges in the man's face and arms, as if he had been mauled by a tiger. The punctures in his armor were deep and ragged; his left eye was missing. He cried out, claiming for all to hear that the Devil had risen from the water.

Padilla ran over and knelt next to his soldier. He grimaced, as the young man's wounds were some of the worst he had ever seen. The rest of the men turned back toward the lagoon and watched fearfully. The jungle was again quiet around them. The captain heard the man cough out the same words as before, only the ending was different: "The Devil has risen from the water, and he has come for his offering." Then the wounded soldier's remaining eye was devoid of life, as his pain ended and darkness covered him.

Padilla didn't hesitate in ordering his men to form up. The sentries had entered the campsite with swords drawn and flintlocks aimed. They had lost seven men in as many minutes to something in the lagoon that he cared never to see or hear again. He would leave this place, retreat, and never-more venture into the jungle. They would return to Pizarro and tell him they were cowards and that he could punish them however he deemed fit; Padilla would gladly suffer anything not to be sent here again.

"We march west tonight, and we stop only when we are under the light of the Lord's sun once again," he announced.

The Devil can have his home, Padilla thought, and he prayed that no other man would ever find this place, for hu-mans were not meant to be here. He would give the map he had made of the valley to Father Corinth and warn him that this was truly the playground of demons.

With the night sentries on the point, Padilla ordered his soldiers forward. But just as they nervously took their first step, the night exploded around them. This time, the murder-ous animal came at them not from the water, but from the bush. It must have followed the tracks of the soldier who had escaped it. The darkness around the screaming men was rent with the powerful and enraged cry of the beast at it attacked. Padilla felt the warmth of something striking his face and then the coppery taste of blood filled his mouth.

"Captain, into the water while there is time. Fall back, men, into the water and swim for it!" Torrez shouted as he pushed the shocked Padilla into the cool lagoon. "We can gain the trail on the other side."

Padilla was still trying to peer into the blackness as he was pulled away by Torrez. That was when the beast stepped closer to one of the open fire pits and swiped its strangely formed hand at one of the men. The soldier was silent as the claws raked down his face and tore through his chest armor. As the Spaniards watched in horror, the animal was struck from behind with a sword, and then a shot rang out from a pistol. The beast did not slow down, even though Padilla saw the ball strike the animal in the upper chest, slinging scales and red meat into the air. The monster screamed a cry of outrage and quickly reached out to grab and disable the hand that wielded the sword. The animal easily lofted the man over its head and then threw him bodily against one of the large trees as if he weighed no more than a piece of firewood.

Another Spaniard made a break for the trail they had used to enter the valley, and that was when Padilla saw the real speed of the creature. It easily headed off the soldier and attacked from the front, throwing its massive weight against the man and driving him to the ground.

"Look at the size of this devil," Padilla mumbled while Torrez pushed him into deeper water. "It is a man!"

Padilla snapped out of his shock as the cool water closed over his head. He reached for the buckled straps that held his armor in place, and quickly shrugged out of it. The heavy iron was sent to the bottom as Padilla pushed his way to the surface. As his head broke free of the water, he saw Torrez ahead of him swimming for all he was worth for the far side of the lagoon. He started after his lieutenant while the screaming of his remaining men continued on shore.

Padilla began to lose the strength in his arms after ten minutes of swimming blindly across the lagoon. His ears were now filled with his own struggles and the roar of water ahead of him emanating from the waterfall. His arms were flailing and his knee-high boots had filled with water. He was finding it very difficult to keep the momentum needed to propel him forward. As his head dipped below the surface in his fatigue, he started to swallow more and more of the strangely cool and sweet water. He felt himself go under. He thought he heard shouts as he began to give up his struggle and let the pleasant water embrace him.

It was comforting because now he wouldn't have to face

Pizarro or any of his men that survived, and he could accompany those that hadn't on their final journey toward forgiveness for what they had wrought on the innocent Sincaro. Captain Padilla even managed a smile as his lungs took in his last breath of not air but water. Suddenly he felt hands grabbing at him from above. Even his beard was pulled on as he was lifted up out of the water. His eyes rolled as he tried to catch one single blessed breath but found his lungs were full.

"Captain, Captain," Torrez shouted.

Padilla felt ground beneath him as he was forcibly rolled over, his back hit as if it were an anvil. He felt his spine pop as he was pushed on heavily. Torrez had dragged him to shore and was trying desperately to expel the water from his lungs.

"Breathe, my captain, don't you leave me here in this black place!"

Padilla vomited the now-warm water from his stomach and lungs, and the pain hit him in earnest when he tried to replace the liquid with precious air. He felt his body spasm as his lungs slowly brought in the needed oxygen. A loud moan escaped his shivering lips, then he slowly brought in another breath.

Padilla rolled over and tried to sit up but failed miserably. Other hands quickly grabbed for him and he was lifted to his feet. He looked over and saw that the two soldiers were Juan Navarro, a cook's assistant, and Javier Ramón, a blacksmith. They were only feet from the waterfall. Padilla looked up and saw where the water cascaded from somewhere high above. He coughed, trying to clear his throat of the remaining water he had ingested. Torrez stood on the edge of the small shore, staring out across the lagoon.

"The screaming of our men has stopped," he said without turning as Padilla approached. Together, they gazed at the dwindling fires of their destroyed camp flickering in the darkness across the lagoon.

After a moment, Torrez took his captain by his shoulders and turned him away from the distant scene of destruction.

As they walked toward the wall of rock that ascended straight up from the lagoon and bordered the waterfall, Torrez knew they were being watched.

"Look," he softly spoke, not wanting to attract the attention of the other men.

Padilla studied the spot Torrez had indicated. Another statue, here carved into the wall, stared down upon them. It resembled the same beast that had just attacked them, and resembled the two images that guarded the tributary. It had been hidden from their vantage point across the lagoon. This one was larger and it stood alone. How had they missed seeing it during the daylight hours? Padilla didn't know.

They both turned as they heard a loud splash in the water. The noise had come from their destroyed campsite. Both men could see the ripples and the large wake that was streaking toward their side of the lagoon.

"Captain, Lieutenant, there is a cave rising above the waterline under the falls," Navarro said as he approached. "You won't believe it—there are stairs."

Torrez turned to face the sheer cliff in front of them, which held only the carved figure of the animal that was now their god of judgment. Then he looked down the shoreline at the distant jungle. Surely whatever this creature was that was coming after them, it would surface long before they could reach the trees. He looked around frantically and then pushed Navarro forward.

"Take us to this cave, soldier," he shouted, as he pulled Padilla after him.

The three men joined Ramón the blacksmith, who was waving for them to hurry. He had caught sight of the underwater demon as it sped to their side of the lagoon. As they came upon the waterfall the roar drowned out all talk. In vain, Torrez studied the point where the water struck the lagoon. Then he saw it. The cave was just a darker outline against the cliff face, but it was there. It rose about ten feet above the water and then disappeared into the depths. He saw no other choice. He dove headfirst into the water; the others, including Padilla, followed. They had to dive deeply to avoid the crushing rush of the falls, the vortex of which pushed them even farther into the depths as they fought to reach and enter the dark and foreboding cave. As they disappeared from sight, the creature changed its underwater course and swam toward the whitewater of the falls.

TWO MONTHS LATER, a lone survivor was saved from the river. At first, the Spaniards who had discovered him thought him to be an Indian, but soon realized the man had been part of Captain Padilla's expedition. The men had struggled to carry the survivor back into Peru but knew they would never make it. Word was sent to Father Corinth; knowing this, the survivor had miraculously clung to life. The man was dying from exposure and a strange sickness the men in camp had never before encountered. His only possession was a book they had mistakenly taken for a Bible, which the survivor held tightly to his injured chest. Every time they tried to relieve him of the book the man would arise like a tiger to protect it. They even tried to pry his fingers from it when he had passed out, but that had proven just as futile.

When Father Corinth arrived at the small outpost with a rank of Pizarro's personal guard, the man was still alive, only he waited for the priest on his deathbed. For hours the lone survivor of the expedition spoke softly with Corinth. The priest listened, never interrupting, while he examined the soldier's wounds and nursed him through the strange sickness. As the man spoke, gasping in inner pain and getting weaker with each word he managed to hiss out through clenched teeth, he reached into his tunic and withdrew two small objects. One was a large golden nugget. The other was a strange green mineral, a chalklike substance imbedded in stone. It was strangely warm to the touch. The soldier pulled Corinth close to him, close enough that the priest could feel his high temperature rising from his face. A dire warning was conveyed by the dying man, barely audible and with fetid breath. Father Corinth wore a handsome cross that was plated with gold not only for beauty but to give its cheap metal base more strength. It was of a sort the church frowned upon as being arrogant, but it was a ceremonial gift his late mother had given to him on the day he took his vows. It was very beautifully engraved and far too large, and she had spent every ounce of her meager savings to present him with it. Corinth took the cross from around his neck and removed the bottom portion. The inside of the pendant was hollow, and he easily slid the small mineral samples into it. He put the end back on the cross and placed it around his neck.

It was long after sunup when Father Corinth finally emerged from the small hut, and with him he carried the book.

"How is he, Father?" one of the soldiers asked. "Is there any news of our friends, is Captain Padilla still alive?"

"The soldier is dead. His name was Ivan Torrez."

"Lieutenant Torrez? We know this man; he looked nothing like him," another soldier said. Many of the soldierly escort had gathered to hear the priest.

"The plague will change a man's features so you would not even recognize your own brother."

The men stepped away in fear. That one word was enough to weaken their knees and make the brave conquerors cringe; they had no idea, but this was another fatal disease entirely.

"What of the expedition, Father? Did he give a location of their whereabouts?"

"Captain Padilla and his men will stay where they are. Get your men ready to break camp, and bury Lieutenant Torrez deep. Honor him; he was a brave man," he said as he bowed his head and crossed himself. The Padilla diary, which contained the unholy route the doomed expedition had charted, was clutched tightly to his chest.

He slowly moved away from the stunned men. The priest knew he would have to either destroy the diary and the map that would again fire the greed of man to follow Padilla's direction, or bury them so deep no one could ever find them. The diary was the only proof of what wonders the captain had found under the falls of that lost lagoon but, because of men like Francisco Pizarro, the contents must never see the light of day. For only death could come to those that ventured into that dark lagoon, and Father Corinth would take it upon himself to make sure the pope sided with his decision.

A FEW MONTHS before the death of Francisco Pizarro, the general ordered one last expedition sent out to try to trace the route of Captain Padilla's ill-fated journey. The Spaniards found only helmets, rusted armor, rotted clothing, and broken swords on a path that stretched for thirty miles along the Amazon, which was clear evidence of a running battle with an enemy that had since disappeared into the jungle. The trail leading to the deep tributary that led to that dark and beautiful lagoon was never found. As for the men of Padilla's brave band, the search party never found a trace of them or the gold they had sought. Pizarro, in what little time remained to him, would continue to lust for El Dorado. But in the end, another generation of explorers and adventurers would have to do the searching.

Rumors of the lost expedition of Captain Padilla would filter down through the years and even a few old artifacts turned up from time to time as the jungle begrudgingly gave up her digested secrets. Whatever lived in that forgotten lagoon would wait patiently for men to come into its realm once again.

MONTANA TERRITORY
JUNE 1876

Captain Myles Keogh was at the head of troops C, I, and L as they made for the river. Captain Yates had gone with troops E and F to support his assault on the village at a point called Deep Coulee. God only knew the situation with Reno and his companies, and Captain Benteen was still off reconnoitering to the south. He figured Benteen would miss the engagement altogether.

Keogh's orders had been simple: cross the river and attack the northern end of the village. A hundred yards from the edge of the riverbank, they quickly discovered to their horror that what they thought was the end of the enormous Indian encampment was actually its middle. The burly Irish captain called a halt to the charge just as a hundred hostiles came over the top of the riverbank to mix with the already confused column. Amid the initial assault he turned and spurred his large mount back in the direction of the low-slung hills, followed by all three companies. He had failed to see that, downriver, another band of Cheyenne led by the warrior Lame White Man had already swarmed across Medicine Tail Coulee and rushed forward unseen. Keogh belatedly saw that the hostiles had anticipated his retreat route east and cut it off.

As he gave the command to turn south, his companies were hit suddenly from the side of a hill that had hidden another group of Cheyenne. Keogh pulled violently on his reins, but not before six of his troopers in the lead had continued headlong into the advancing ranks of hostiles. The attacking Indians drove his men and their mounts to the ground in a frenzied attack that quickly hid their slaughter in a rising dust cloud. The captain immediately signaled for his three companies to turn to the north, hoping to squeeze his units in between the attacking groups, but immediately saw that there was no clear path away from the Cheyenne assault. To continue going forward would only guarantee being picked off piecemeal, so in the madness of the moment and dictated by their predicament, he ordered his men to dismount—a command of last resort for a cavalry unit, because it would take away the only advantage they had, the quickness of horse. But Keogh had no choice. He remembered a successful dismounted defense at Gettysburg thirteen years before under General Buford; they would hold until relief could come.

As the remains of companies I, L, and C dismounted, arrows and bullets began to find their deadly mark. Keogh pulled his army Colt revolver and started issuing orders to fort up behind whatever they could find. Horses were shot as men threw themselves behind their bulk for protection. Keogh sat tall and purposely in the saddle and fired deliberately at the swarming horde of warriors. He hoped he could inspire his men to gather the courage they would need this dark day. The hostiles were now attacking en masse, no tactic involved other than strike and fall back. Every time they came forward the Indians would leave at least ten of his men either dead or dying.

"Captain, shouldn't we try and reach the general?" his aide called out.

"One spot's as good as the other today; we'll all be eating supper at the same table tonight," he said loudly in his Irish brogue as he fired two quick shots and then jumped from his horse.

Keogh had no hope for relief as he saw farther down the hill that Captain Yates and his men were also in headlong flight. At that point the captain hadn't seen Custer among them; the dust had started to obscure his view. The captain fired his last round at a warrior who could not have been more than thirteen, sending him back three feet when the bullet struck his chest.

While he opened his cartridge pouch to retrieve his last detachable cylinder, a Cheyenne dog soldier, attempting to count coup on him, lunged with a long, red, striped staff. He easily dodged the feathered tip and grabbed for the coup stick, dropping his pistol at the same moment. He pulled the Indian close to him by yanking on the pole and started hitting him with his gauntleted right fist. As he brought up his hand to strike another blow, a bullet struck the warrior in the back of his head. Keogh tossed away the coup stick and then noticed that it had been a nineteen-year-old private that had come to his aide. The captain had just dipped his head in thanks when an arrow pierced the young trooper in the neck and the boy fell. At the same moment, a bullet creased Keogh's forehead through his straw hat and almost knocked him down. The hat flew from his head and was caught in the dust storm being thrown up by the circling Indians.

Captain Keogh shook his head to try to clear his vision, not realizing blood from his head wound had clouded his right eye. He shook his head again as he tried to find his horse, Comanche. The big roan, disciplined as always, stood at the center of the three companies, his reins hanging free. Keogh started walking, struggling to gather his thoughts. Where were they, anyway . . . the Big . . . no, the Little Bighorn? Yes, that was it, the Little Bighorn River. He kept the name running through his mind, concentrating hard on those words as he fought to stay conscious, and then he finally reached his horse.

Instead of reaching for Comanche's reins, he started untying the saddlebags. He reached inside and pulled out a long chain from a steel box. He could barely see and tried in vain to wipe the blood from his eye. He felt the chain through his thick gloves and was satisfied at the touch of the Saint Christopher; next to that were his prized papal medals, and then he finally felt the cross. It was the largest of the four objects, a full seven inches long. He slid the chain around his neck and ran his fingers along the cross once again. He hoped the sight of the holy cross and the two medals would keep the hostiles from mutilating his remains. His breath was coming rapidly now and he felt as if he were starting to lose his battle with staying conscious. Comanche jerked and screamed as a bullet went through Keogh's McClellan saddle and struck the animal across its back. The movement spun the captain around, and that was when things seemed to slow to a crawl as if he were only dreaming this disaster.

Down below his engagement and behind a solid wall of swirling dust, a warrior named Crazy Horse and several hundred Sioux were ending a fight that would haunt the U.S. Army for a hundred years and send the great Indian nations into a bleak future.

Before Keogh struck the ground he saw the guidon for his own company falling just as he was. The letter *I* emblazoned in red struck the grass and lay there. The captain hit the ground as two arrows found the trampled yellow grass next to his head, tossing soil onto his face as he lay blinking against the sun. He didn't even react when a third arrow struck him in his side. He clutched the cross to his chest and prayed and waited.

For ten miles around companies C, I, and L, 265 men of the United States Army's most elite fighting unit, the Seventh Cavalry, met their fate with bullet, lance, and arrow. On a hill overlooking the spot where a foolish man with long yellow hair and a buckskin jacket struck the ground, his swallowtail blue and red flag soon following, Captain Myles Keogh held onto his cross and died. And with his death, he took with him a secret from hundreds of years in the past— lost with the rest of the Seventh in the Valley of the Little Bighorn.

PART ONE
THE FOLLOWERS

Some things that have been created by the mind and hand of God have been placed in the most inaccessible places on our world for a reason. Do not search them out, for one day they may be unleashed upon the world of men, and the minimal and horrible mistakes of our Lord God will become the inheritors of the earth.

—Father Emanuel D'Amato,
Archbishop of Madrid, 1875

1

THE woman paced in the small, cluttered office, pausing for a brief moment to look at the old man sitting in the swivel chair behind an ancient mahogany desk. He was dressed in a chambray work shirt and wore carpenter's overalls. The thick, horned-rimmed glasses would slide down his nose and he would absentmindedly push them back up to their proper place. He handled the old letter, a set of orders actually, carefully and with the necessary respect one had to show documents of that age. The woman wiped away the sweat on her brow and then without thinking about it pulled her blond hair back and slipped a thick rubber band around it, forming a ponytail. She then turned to look out of the five-hundred-year-old leaded glass window, which gave a blurry, skewed look to the world outside.

San Jerónimo el Real was one of the oldest Catholic churches in Spain and was currently closed for a much-needed engineering renovation. The beautiful Gothic building dated back to 1503 and had already seen many restorations, but this time it was work that would allow the building to stay on its original foundations for another five hundred years. The hammering and sound of jackhammers echoed in the ancient edifice, while outside in the streets many of Madrid's older population passed by and crossed themselves in reverence of the church.

"My dear professor, this letter," the man lightly brushed

his right index finger across the dried ink, "could be a clever forgery, have you even considered that?"

The woman turned away from the window to face the archbishop of Madrid. The old man carefully laid the letter down and gently tapped the two pages together, carefully aligning them on his desk blotter. The woman noted the delicate way he handled the pages and knew he believed them to be authentic. She stepped to a chair, opened her small case, and removed a laptop. She typed in a quick command and then laid the computer on the archbishop's desk, carefully avoiding the old text she brought for him to examine.

"The signature on the letter has been identified as that of Father Enrico Fernaldi, clerk of the Vatican Archives. The handwriting was verified by the Vatican Archives, and what you see is a copy of that verification taken from the texts of not less than twenty-seven other documents of that time, including the two-page authorization letter you just examined from 1873."

Archbishop Lozano Santiago, the seventy-two-year-old curator of this and twenty-one other Vatican properties, smiled and looked up from the computer screen that held the image of the very same signature that was on the Vatican letter sitting before him.

"I compliment you on the trap you have so easily sprung on me, Professor Zachary, very clever."

Dr. Helen Zachary, chairperson of the Zoology Department of Stanford University, smiled also. "I mean you no disrespect, Your Eminence," she responded, knowing his blessing would depend upon that very point of proof. As a guardian of one of the most protected Vatican secrets in the world, this man would prove to be formidable.

"Just because the letter and the orders contained in it seem to be authentic, doesn't mean it holds truth in its words," he said as he lightly closed the lid to her laptop. "After all, the Holy Church has been known from time to time to use subterfuge in the handling of state secrets, a small conceit for something as taboo as the information you are seeking.

"The artifacts that are clearly described and mentioned in the order were sent away from the Vatican in 1875, after one of the civilian clerks was arrested by the Swiss Guard for trying to smuggle them out of the archive subbasement in November of the previous year, 1874. As it says in that letter to Pope Pius IX himself, and I quote, 'The necessity of hiding the articles is a must; their presence will only cause corruption in good and decent men.' That is why the mission to hide the artifacts was trusted only to knights of the Vatican, the papal medalists, and why, according to that letter you just read, Pope Pius IX ordered the diary to be sent here to Madrid and hidden away in this very church. The map was to be sent as far away as it could be sent and still be in the trusted hands of a knight of the Holy Order. That place was the United States, but the knight it was entrusted to met an unfortunate end and the map was lost forever."

The archbishop slid his large chair back and stood without much difficulty. For a man that was used to grandeur in all things, he seemed well suited to a working man's clothes.

"You don't strike me as a fanatical treasure hunter." He crossed from behind his desk to the front, where he carefully picked up the two-page Vatican letter. "I was sure the area of zoology tended toward the acquisition of knowledge on a more . . . nonavaricious level."

"I assure you I'm not a treasure hunter. My field is the study of animal life, not hunting down the Padilla legend."

The archbishop regarded the letter once again and then held it out to Zachary. The mere mention of the lost expedition of Captain Padilla, a story handed down by word of mouth from Spaniard to Spaniard and which was fraught with tales of gold and mystery, the legendary El Dorado, was almost enough for him to stop talking immediately.

"You are to be congratulated at the very least for your persistence in digging up such a rare find as a Vatican document as important as this."

Helen took the age-yellowed pages from his hand.

"These were," she hesitated a moment, "lent to me by a friend in the States who collects very old things."

"Indeed," he said. "I would be interested to know how many more secret documents this friend has that belong to the Church. Maybe Interpol would be curious as well."

Helen wanted to steer away from her source of the letter; she didn't need that headache. And the mere thought of Interpol's tracking down her source was almost laughable.

"So you agree it is an authentic order?" she asked.

"Even if it were I would never divulge any information about the Padilla diary or the map, my dear professor. Even if said knowledge was in my possession, I would never allow—I mean, the Church would never allow such recklessness to once again stain its history, and surely not for treasure seekers such as you or whoever is backing you." He turned his back on her. "If I were to guess, you have a partner in this endeavor, yes?"

Helen looked at her feet a moment and then closed her eyes. She held the thin and precious pages gently in both hands.

"I do have a silent partner that will back me for *my* reasons for going, and that reason is not for gold or glory, but for a far greater find."

The archbishop turned and stared hard at the thirty-six-year-old woman. She was tanned and striking, her green eyes ablaze with passion.

"Perhaps it is time you tell me the reason you want to see the diary." He held up a finger when Helen's smile returned. "This is not an admission that I have the cursed thing, or that it is even in the possession of the Holy Church."

"Believe me, Your Eminence, I would never have had to bother you if the quest for the Padilla map had been successful, but I'm afraid it's truly lost."

He frowned. "You are positive?"

"Yes," she said sadly as she moved toward a far corner of the small office, "I'm afraid it's gone forever."

"A shame, indeed, but as you know, the legend says that

Padilla had managed to secure samples from the richest gold mine in history; are they lost also?"

"I have no interest in that part of the legend. Only the fact that Father Escobar Corinth had the map and samples placed into two separate containers of which no description has ever been discovered."

"For good reason perhaps, for even your Vatican letter says that to open these containers would bring a curse upon anyone who defied the Vatican locks."

Helen reached the far corner of the room and carefully picked up an aluminum container. She hefted it and placed it on the desk, narrowly avoiding the laptop there.

"I didn't think the Catholic Church gave credence to such ridiculous superstition."

"It is just a story that is told. We don't believe in curses, officially anyway. Even Satan has taken a backseat, a mere lowercase evil in today's teachings."

"So, is it a tale that is remembered through mere legend, or one that you read in a diary by a long-dead conquistador of Spain?" she asked while matching his smile with her own.

He wagged a finger at her. "You are fishing again, Professor, but this fish is not so easy to hook."

She turned and unsnapped the four clasps on the aluminum box. An audible pop was heard as the airtight container became unsealed.

"*You* are indeed a difficult fish to hook, Your Grace," she said, nodding at the aluminum carrying case, "possibly as hard as this fish would be to catch." She opened the box and stepped away so the archbishop could see its contents.

He immediately froze and found taking a breath had become a chore. He couldn't get enough air into his lungs for that simple reflexive action. His eyes widened and he quickly crossed himself. Around him the noises from the ongoing foundation renovation continued, but it went unheard by the archbishop.

"Our Lord Jesus Christ," he mumbled as old church doctrine came flooding back to him.

Helen Zachary didn't smile or speak. Having had to show the contents of the container was a last-ditch effort to get the archbishop's assistance. Not only that, but much more important, *his trust*. After all, she was only asking him to disobey a papal command in order to help her.

"As I said, the treasures I seek have nothing to do with gold or the riches of man. It's knowledge I seek. I need your help. The rumor of strange and exotic animal life described in the diary may be connected to this object."

"This . . . this, fossil, how old is it?"

Helen looked at the skeletal remains of the hand. They had been carefully packed in a soft foam cutout. The four fingers were long, at least seventeen inches from palm to tip. The thumb was half that length, and the bone was thick and very powerful looking. Three of the digits had very lethal-looking clawed tips. The other claws were obviously absent due to its extreme age. Patches of petrified flesh were visible.

"I'm afraid it barely qualifies as a fossil, Your Grace. We have estimated its age at only seven hundred years, give *or* take a decade, placing it in the time frame of the Padilla expedition."

"Is this possible?" he asked. "No, no, this cannot be."

Helen slowly and carefully placed the lid back on the aluminum container and snapped the clasps closed. Then she pressed a small button on the container's lid once, twice, three times, expelling the air that had entered the protective box and thus any contaminant that may have been allowed in. When she was finished she placed the container back onto the floor and turned back to the archbishop.

"The legend of the Padilla expedition and the rumors surrounding its demise may have been no mere legend, or just a story to scare schoolchildren at night. This is the treasure we are seeking. Can you imagine what we may discover at that site if we can find the route? If you have read the diary, is such a strange and wonderful creature as this described by Padilla?"

Archbishop Santiago slowly made his way to his chair. His

emotions were in a vortex, for he had always prided himself as being a progressive entity in his church. Never one to shy away from real facts of science, he was one of the few that knew the real truth of this world can only strengthen one's faith in there being a God and his son Jesus Christ. But this was something he had *never* counted on, possible proof that man had sprung from something other than God's image. He removed his glasses and tossed them onto his desk. The words he had read many times over the years that sent chills down his spine—were they words that painted a picture of actual creatures and not just the ravings of overzealous imaginations? The legend of Padilla was told by millions of people the world over, and each telling told of the wondrous sights and all described the horrible beast that guarded a magical valley.

"I need to examine that diary. I'm begging you," Helen said as she sat down in a chair. She placed her arms on her knees as she leaned forward. "I know one of your many passions is learning about our past; you even have a doctorate in world history from the University of Venice. So you must see that this fossil is possible proof we didn't develop alone, that we had relatives that grew alongside of us."

Santiago sat in his chair motionless. He rubbed his eyes, at the back of which had suddenly sprouted a headache.

"Was it sent to San Jerónimo el Real for safekeeping in 1875?" she asked point blank, while closing her eyes as if in prayer.

He swallowed and cleared his throat.

Helen looked up and into the man's brown eyes. Her own were now wide and expectant.

"I will not allow the diary to leave church property. You may make two copies of the pages you seek; they may give enough descriptive information of landmarks to allow you to find the area you wish to find. The rest of the diary is not for your eyes, even if it can help you. There's a reason that information is buried in this church. And since the map and gold samples are irrevocably lost to the world, it would seem I have little choice but to help you. I will not be a roadblock to knowledge." He noticed her expression. "You are shocked? At first I was also, but then I thought this is not faith shattering, it only proves that God is still mysterious and his ways unknowable. But that does not mean that knowledge cannot be a dangerous thing."

Helen closed her eyes again and clasped her hands together, not really listening to Santiago's warning. But she refrained from verbally expressing any joy when she saw the archbishop's expression of consternation as he rose from his chair.

She stood also, shaking with the excitement at knowing her search for the diary of Captain Hernando Padilla had come to an end. The artifact she had shown the archbishop had the effect she had prayed for.

"I'm afraid you may have stumbled upon something God has seen fit to hide in an inaccessible place for a reason, and, from what I saw in that case, Professor, you would be wise beyond your young years to leave this alone."

"If I may ask, why are you willing to assist me?"

He turned toward her again, his face a scowl. "I have read the diary, from cover to cover, many times." He saw her expression. "Does it surprise you that I would naturally be curious as to the old legends? But it is not only mere curiosity that guides me, but the fact that there are other things in that jungle besides your mysterious animal I must know about firsthand. You will be *my* messenger, because certain decisions will have to be made about this mysterious world you are going to, and you will assist me in acquiring the information I need to make those decisions. That is the deal, and for that reason alone is why I will help you."

She started to respond but the archbishop had already opened the thick oaken door and was gone.

THE PRECIADOS HOTEL Madrid had luxurious nineteenth-century room decor and twenty-first-century avant-garde public areas. At ten o'clock in the evening, those public areas were crowded with tourists and businesspeople enjoying a warm summer night.

In her room for the past hour after returning from her appointment with Archbishop Santiago, Helen Zachary sat on the edge of the large bed, deep in thought. She looked over at her suitcase that was packed and ready to go. Only moments before, she had moved up her flight to New York and was now booked to leave at three in the morning. Inside her carefully packed suitcase, tucked between some innocuous pages of her notebook, were photocopies of the two pages she had been permitted to see of the diary of Captain Hernando Padilla. She had actually started to shake when the old diary had been placed in her hands by the archbishop. The book had felt warm to her touch. It was as if the weight of the days described within its pages fell directly onto her shoulders. Without reading the tale that was written by a once strong hand, Helen knew the journal told details of wonder and horror. When she opened the diary, the archbishop had removed it easily from her grasp to turn to the agreed-upon pages that described the route one needed to take to find the lagoon and falls that were hidden in a small valley. He didn't trust her enough to allow her to even accidentally read anything other than those two pages.

As she sat there and calculated how long it would be before she could start organizing the million and one things she would have to coordinate to launch the expedition, a knock sounded at her door. She was startled out of her thoughts.

"Yes?" she called.

There was no answer through the thick door. Helen stepped up and asked again as she leaned close to use the peephole. "Yes?"

"It is Madrid, Dr. Zachary, not Tehran," a voice answered through the door. "It is quite safe to open your door here."

She swallowed when she finally recognized the voice. She moved quickly to undo the chain and unlock the door. Standing there, dressed casually, was a tall man in a black suit, white shirt, and scarlet-colored tie. His blond hair was combed straight back and he was smiling.

"Dr. St. Claire, how in the world did you know what hotel I was in?" She opened the door wider to allow him in.

"Professor, your expense account and credit cards have been issued by our mutual friend in Bogotá. Believe me when I say it wasn't at all difficult to locate you." He stepped easily into the room and immediately noticed the suitcase.

"You caught me off guard. I didn't even have time to call you with the wonderful news."

"So your mission to Madrid has been fruitful?" he asked with undisguised excitement.

"Yes, the archbishop relented and allowed me to copy the route from the diary."

"I must know, Helen, what was it like, grasping the diary, something that has been so elusive to us?"

"Oh, Henri, it was indescribable, it was like holding on to history itself."

The tall man smiled and grasped her hands. "I knew it would be. Tell me, did you have to show him the fossil?"

Helen Zachary momentarily closed her eyes and then smiled and opened them. "Yes, he was shocked, but he also knew something of marine life. You were right about that; how did you know?"

"Always know what it is that will move those to your side of the game board." He let go of her hands and looked in a deliberate manner around the room. "Why, it looks as if you are packed; according to my information, you aren't due to leave here until tomorrow."

"Yes, I thought I would get an earlier flight back home as soon as possible. I don't want to waste any time at all in getting things started. If we hurry we can miss the rainy season in Brazil," she lied.

He turned and fixed her with his blue eyes. He smiled broadly, showing his teeth, but Helen saw that the smile never reached his eyes.

"Good news, then; you can return to the States with me. Banco de Juarez International Economica has a private jet refueling even as we speak. We can fly straight to California without the need for a layover in New York."

Helen was taken aback for a moment, then she quickly

recovered and tried to look pleased. "That's wonderful, the sooner the better. Do you think there will be any problems with the initial financing for the expedition, now that we know where we are going?"

"Not at all considering what we are after. Joaquin Delacruz Mendez and his banking concern have never once denied me financing on a project." He looked pointedly at her suitcase. "Helen, are you forgetting something?"

She turned away and removed her coat from the closet. "I don't believe so."

"The copies, you silly goose; may I see them?"

She took a deep breath and started to recite the lines she had memorized just in case she was asked this very question before she returned to home soil.

"I know I'm just being paranoid, but to be on the safe side I sent the copies to myself by registered mail along with the fossil, Henri. I didn't want any Customs problems with either the copies or the artifact." She walked over to her suitcase, in which she had carefully placed the notebook.

"Prudent, but didn't I explain before you left that Customs in New York would have been taken care of?" His left eyebrow rose with the question.

"It completely slipped my mind." She lifted her suitcase and then cringed inwardly when Henri took it for her.

"Well, too late to worry about that now; by the time I return from Bogotá the copies will have arrived, and then we can examine them together and chart our route." He moved to the door and opened it, her suitcase firmly in hand. He allowed her to exit the room, then closed the door and followed. His eyes never left the back of Helen Zachary's head as they walked down the richly appointed hallway. He sensed deceit in her but held his tongue.

"What an adventure we have ahead of us, Henri," she said as she felt his eyes on her back.

"Yes, yes we do, my dear professor, a grand adventure," said the man known to Helen as Henri St. Claire. His real name was Colonel Henri Farbeaux and he maintained his false smile as he carried her bag behind her. An international thief of antiquities, Colonel Farbeaux was wanted by the police agencies and governments of many nations around the world. And they all knew the man could be a cold-blooded adversary. But for the moment he was content to be known as just Helen Zachary's silent partner.

PALO ALTO, CALIFORNIA
THREE WEEKS LATER

HELEN'S offices on the Stanford University campus were dark save for the small sanctuary she called home when she wasn't in the field. The rooms could barely be called an office at all. The outer classroom was taken up with equipment and seating for her students, along with numerous exhibits from her time outside of the university. Her personal space was cluttered with a small lab table, and by maps of every conceivable size that were pinned to every inch of wall space. They all showed regions in South America that were affectionately known as the edge of the world to her many students. A few of them had handwritten legends stating *Here there be Dragons*, as a joke aimed at her cryptozoology leanings. Henri St. Claire stood looking over Helen's shoulder at the map laid out on her desk, showing the route she had painstakingly planned.

"So we will enter the basin from the Brazilian side and not follow Padílla's original route? I would think that you would follow the Spaniard's trail precisely to make sure nothing is bypassed."

"Normally I would, but his original trek was through the Andes and many hundreds of miles of rainforest that we can now avoid by going through Brazil rather than Peru. The mixture of jungle and forest is so thick that even space-based photography is unable to penetrate it, and I really don't relish the thought of boating through that, do you?" She pointed to several color images taken from the U.S. Geological Survey photos. "We know the tributary is there, we have the proof now. Entering the valley and the lagoon from the east is possible; just because we can't see it, doesn't mean its not there. Besides, getting permission from the Peruvian government to cross their territory has proven in the past to be impossible. Now, as long as we are straightforward, Brazil offers up assistance freely, with only the proviso that their government is represented on the expedition to make sure nothing untoward takes place."

"That is also a concern not only of mine, but also of our financial backer, Mr. Mendez. We take security very seriously, Helen; after all, he is not exactly using just his own funds for this venture, but the Banco de Juarez also. Strangers should not be allowed to come."

"Unavoidable, I'm afraid." She made a show of examining the handwritten route as laid down by Hernando Padilla. "Brazil has had an inordinate amount of antiquities leaving their country. They insist on having a Customs official in attendance on the expedition and, believe me, they will tolerate no change in their policy." She laid the magnifying glass down and looked Henri in the eye.

He smiled. "Then that is the way it shall be. So that brings the number of team members to forty-six students, professors, and guides."

Farbeaux looked down once again at the copies of the diary pages that he had methodically examined for himself upon his return from Colombia. He agreed the route Helen proposed was indeed the best one, according to the description laid down by the Spanish captain.

"Very well, Professor Zachary, I approve of the route you have chosen and will relay that approval to Mr. Mendez upon my return to Bogotá for the final payment of the expeditionary funding. Helen, you have done marvelously. All the research, the trail going cold time after time, but your tenacity and your beliefs finally paid off."

"Thank you. If I didn't have the free hand you gave me it wouldn't have been so smooth." She handed him a glass of champagne. "To a new, or should I say, an old life form we hope to bring to the light of day," she toasted.

"To history," he countered, "and lost things," hoisting his glass.

He sat the glass down, carefully avoiding touching the new maps that Helen had worked so hard on. He rolled up the copy she had made so he could deliver it to Bogotá and their financier.

"So I will see you next in five weeks in Los Angeles."

"Helen, this is one boat ride I wouldn't miss for the world," he said as he tapped the rolled-up map against her shoulder.

HELEN WATCHED AS Henri climbed into his rented car and drove away. She laughed softly as she turned and walked back into her small office. She sat at the small lab table she used as a desk and looked down at the map they had just studied together. She used her right index finger to lightly trace the flow of the Amazon River she had depicted. Then she used both hands to wad up the copy of the map and toss it into the waste can in the corner. She did the same with the copy of the Padilla diary pages. It had taken her a full three days to plan the misleading route she had given to St. Claire, and another two days of actually drawing it and creating the falsified diary pages. But she knew it had been worth it, as the good Professor St. Claire had taken to heart her grand forgery and fake route.

After she had tossed the forgery into the trash, Helen poured herself another glass of champagne and walked with it to one of her filing cabinets that crowded the office. She sat the glass on top, unlocked the second drawer, and removed a folded chart and a small file folder. She took the chart, the file, and her glass to her table and sat down. She unfolded the real map and then removed from the file the copies she had actually made of the diaries.

Helen smiled and took a sip from her glass. Then she took

her cell phone from her pocket and started pushing numbers she had memorized. She had never actually programmed them into her phone, for security reasons.

"This is Robert."

"Is everything ready in San Pedro?" Helen sipped from her glass again.

"We're loading the largest of the equipment now, deck space will be kinda tight, but we'll manage; we should be finished in a few hours."

"How about the replacement grad student, the one you found at Berkeley, did she show up?"

There was only a moment's hesitation, then her assistant Robby answered, "Yes, ma'am, she arrived an hour ago and is already situated. I think you'll be more than satisfied with her. She's one of the brightest in her field; she knows animals."

"Good. Look, I'll be down in about three hours, I'm flying into LAX. My attorney should be arriving there about the same time my flight is landing, so please make sure he's shown to the ship's company office and tell him I'll be there soon, okay?"

"You got it, Doc. So how did your final meeting with the money man go?"

"It went better than expected. He gave us the second check and left for Bogotá to pick up the third part of our financing. It's just too bad we didn't need that part. But it will keep him away and out of our hair until we sail. Have our new benefactors arrived yet?"

"Yeah, they're here, all six of them, that Dr. Kennedy guy and five others. What do you want us to do with all of Henri St. Claire's geological stuff, the magnetometers and other mining equipment?"

She took a large swallow of champagne and smiled as it went down. "Leave it on the dock with a note saying, 'Liar, liar, pants on fire.'"

"You got it, Doc, see you in a few."

Helen closed her cell phone and stopped smiling. She hated screwing over someone like Henri St. Claire, but he never should have misrepresented himself as someone who was in this for the sole reason of discovering one of the mysteries of the ages. He was in this for greed, his own and that of the gangster who called himself a banker.

"There would be no hunting for the mythical El Dorado on this trip, Dr. St. Claire. Where we're going, you cannot follow," she said to herself as she placed the real map and Padilla pages in her briefcase, stood, and made her way out into the evening.

THE WHITE HOUSE, WEST WING

The national security advisor sat behind his desk facing his computer monitor that was presently split into four separate pictures. In the far left corner was General Stanton Alford, commanding general of the United States Army Corps of Engineers. On the right top was Rear Admiral Elliott Pierce, U.S. Naval Intelligence; directly below him was the frowning countenance of General Warren Peterson, U.S. Army Intelligence; and to the left of him, U.S. Air Force Intelligence chief General Stan Killkerhan. They were there to discuss a file the CIA, and before them the OSS, the Office of Strategic Services, had kept under wraps since the days before World War II. The gathered intelligence officers weren't taking the new development well.

"If the Joint Chiefs or the president even get an inkling of what we've done it *will* be all our asses in a sling, and it all starts with you, Mr. Ambrose. The last I heard, the president wasn't too fond of his generals around here. I believe the title of the book we opened to the world these past few days is called *treason*. Not only have we supplied an outlawed material to a foreign nation, but now we are stealing actual weapons for use on the soil of a friendly country. This whole plan is spiraling out of control," General Peterson said as he glared into the camera on his end at the Pentagon.

"We have no choice but to send the weapon and team

down to South America as a precaution. What if the old site *is* rediscovered? The prewar material could only be traced back to us if a link is found from the old incursion, something that leads to the storage facility where the material was stored. But other than that, the only way it can be linked to us is if one of you loses his nerve. Gentlemen, if that professor brings that area of Brazil out into the light of day, the whole damned mess becomes public," the national security advisor said angrily.

"I agree," said Stanton Alford. "After all, we may not even have a site that has to be destroyed. I don't believe this Professor Zachary will ever find it. Hell, we don't even know where it is. We only have the material, not the location where it was found. The Corps of Engineers was the only department to document the 1942 incursion, and that report was buried in National Archives files. And since the old material is in Iraq and no longer in this country, it's untraceable back to us unless this one engineer report from the war years is discovered in the National Archives files, and we'll have that file tagged and monitored."

"What about Zachary's source? We're not even sure how she got her information."

Alford was tiring of the debate. "The only other mention of the mine is in rumor and innuendo and a possible diary that's over five centuries old. My department had control of the army samples for seventy years. It was never turned over to the regulatory commission nor was it ever classified as a weapon by the old War Department. So, I say we err on the side of caution and send our team in with the expedition. As I said, that crazy woman probably won't find a damned thing. She's using five-hundred-year-old data from a conquistador, for Christ's sake! It's like finding one needle in five thousand haystacks. She could have only come across the description of the location in the National Archives' database. The diary theory is ridiculous."

"And if the site is found? You say the answer is to possibly eliminate the entire Zachary expedition with your fail-safe alternative, with a nuke and some SEALs? It's fucking murder!" General Peterson exclaimed angrily.

"My men won't let it get that far. I've worked with this particular strike team before and they're very good. No American citizens will be harmed. I can guarantee that," Rear Admiral Pierce said confidently. "Besides, what if this mine *is* still in existence, we could never allow a third-world nation to have access to Pandora's box, now can we? We set the tactical weapon inside the mine and bring it down. Problem solved."

"There are too goddamn many variables, Elliott, sneaking a team in there right under the noses of the Joint Chiefs and the president. I'm not even going to mention how Brazil would react to an intrusion like that. And this tactical weapon you're sending? I don't want to think about what security procedures have been violated for that little bit of skullduggery. This is fucking madness and I didn't sign on to kill American citizens!"

"General Peterson, it's already been decided. We unanimously agreed, you included, that the location of the Padilla site cannot become public knowledge, ever. As for the material—if it's discovered in Iraq, only by a long shot can it be traced back here to our doorstep, because it was neither refined nor mined here. The only way for it to come to light is if some reference is found to it. Yes, this lady professor in her maddening zeal to find the Padilla site discovered one link, but it was a fluke. The only other reference to the area is in the old Padilla legends that the scientific community scoffs at and doesn't take at all seriously. The location of the site and what exactly was mined and brought out of there are buried deep in the memories of the survivors of the initial incursion in the forties, if any are even alive today. Now, *you* went along with the deployment of the material the same as we did, and the aggression was stopped."

"As I said, we've gotten in over our heads here, we need—"

"You'll have your position in the government after the next election, just as I will. The mission is a 'go.' And that particular weapon you are so concerned about, if it is to be used at all, was entered into the naval inventory as inactive and destroyed, so no one will miss it. Anyway, I doubt very much anyone has to be eliminated. Now, that's all, just go about your business, and let Rear Admiral Pierce and myself handle the fine print. Good day, gentlemen."

Ambrose didn't wait for another concern to be voiced that would lead to splintering; it was always best to commit right away so there would be no going back.

The thin-framed national security advisor turned away from his desk and shook his head as he again picked up the morning intelligence report on the border activity between Iran and Iraq. He smiled as he saw the sentence in italics: *As of 0345 this morning eastern daylight time, satellite imagery has verified the total withdrawal of all Iranian combat divisions from the adjoining border with Iraq.*

As he tossed the morning briefing on his desk, he walked over to the coat rack and put on his suit jacket in preparation for the president's morning intel brief. He couldn't help but wonder in the end what price one would pay for peace. He picked up his phone and placed a call.

"Yes," the tired voice said.

"Congratulations on your mission to Iran. How's your jet lag?"

"I'm too tired to think about it, but we did leave the damned Iranians something to ponder. Iraq may not have the bomb to stop them from invading, but they now have something just as terrifying. Now, what about this expedition you briefed me on, this Professor Zachary?"

"We have it covered; there will be no amazing discoveries coming out of that area of the world. And if anyone else here goes digging into the same files the last person did, we'll be alerted; it's been red-flagged and we'll be able to trace it to the computer terminal that's being used. Sometimes it's very advantageous to be partners with the intel chiefs."

"Good. Is there anything else before we brief the president and the press corps on our diplomatic triumph?"

"No, everything is going well. I will be speaking to our partners in Brazil soon, to finalize our fail-safe positions as far as this expedition is concerned, if our SEAL friend fails to do what was ordered."

"I know it is distasteful at times to deal with people such as this, but the end will justify the means. Let's just close up the mine connection for good and move on with the real business at hand."

"I agree. Enjoy all the accolades for your harrowing diplomacy from our current man in office. If he only knew how he was helping us in the election! Anyway, this latest diplomatic coup should put you right over the top in the polls. Peace in our time, right?" He thought he was being smart, quoting Neville Chamberlain.

"I sometimes wonder if it was all worth it. As they say, you can't put the genie back in the bottle."

As the national security advisor hung up the phone he placed the morning report back in the red-bordered file and then he frowned. He knew that the sale of their souls to the Devil was the price all six conspirators had just paid for "peace in our time."

SAN PEDRO, CALIFORNIA

After Robby Hanson closed the cell phone he looked around and, when he saw no one watching him, he turned to the overhang of the second deck and waved the girl over. She smiled and came out of the shadows.

"What did she say?" the twenty-year-old asked.

"She's clueless; as long as she's finally going on her dream cruise down the Amazon, Professor Zachary doesn't care who's on this trip. Besides it's not like we're lying about your being a grad student from Berkeley, is it?"

The girl smiled and leaned forward to kiss Robby on the lips. "I just had to go. How could I miss the trip of a life-time?"

"Yeah, but how much trouble am I going to get into? Remember it was me who helped you ditch your protection. Your father's going to freakin' flip his gourd." Robby shook his head, kissed the girl again, then turned her away from him.

"Go to your cabin and start getting acquainted with your fellow travelers, and stay out of sight until you check your equipment. And by the way, Kelly, your name is Cox. Leanne Cox. God, I'm dead," he mumbled.

She batted her eyes. Grabbing her brand-new seabag, she started for the hatchway leading belowdecks. Then she stopped and turned. "Don't tell me my secret fiancé is afraid of my father?"

Robby smiled and started making check marks on his manifest. "Why would I be afraid of one of the most powerful men in the world, surely not I, Ms. Cox?"

FARBEAUX DECIDED TO drive to Los Angeles from Palo Alto. Taking Highway 1 relaxed him and allowed his mind to absorb the mission and think. He had placed Helen Zachary's map inside a cylindrical container and placed it in the trunk. As he whistled he removed from his jacket pocket a Spanish cross once owned by Father Corinth. The last time Pizarro's priest had seen the cross was in 1534. The warmth of it radiated out into his hand as he looked at it. How clever of Corinth to have placed both ore samples together in this most ingenious way. The large cross had inadvertently fallen to Farbeaux over a year earlier when it had been offered as payment by a former employer for services rendered. It had gone through a few changes while handed down through the Corinth family. Jewels had been added, and a thin plating of gold. The surprise he found inside its hidden compartment was an amazing stroke of luck.

Farbeaux knew the riches to be found in that near-forgotten lagoon were now close to being in his possession, partly thanks to this very cross and the secrets it had revealed to him. A five-hundred-year-old myth, an old legend that refused to die, would soon become a reality that was worth more than all the lost treasures ever torn from the earth.

SAN PEDRO, CALIFORNIA
FOUR HOURS LATER

After her arrival at the harbor, Helen was making a final check of the crated equipment strapped down across the deck of the *Pacific Voyager*. She only hoped that they would have enough room on the river tug *Incan Wanderer* and the river barge *Juanita* when they transferred the equipment in Colombia. Kennedy and his team had three more crates than she had allowed them. On her clipboard she made a check mark by each space that indicated the weight of his crates. She frowned when she added it all up.

"Robby, where's Dr. Kennedy?" she asked her brightest graduate student.

He tossed a coiled rope to one of young girls who populated Helen's expedition and pointed toward the stern of the *Pacific Voyager.*

She bit her lip and handed him the clipboard with the manifest on it. "Give this to the captain," she said, as she turned toward the stern. "Tell him we are over by three hundred pounds, but still within his load capacity."

"You got it, Doc." He watched her for a moment, wondering if maybe he should accompany her to see Kennedy and his men. But he decided that if anyone could handle these guys, it was Dr. Zachary. His eyes next sought out Kelly. She was on deck, checking her camera equipment. The thick-rimmed glasses and dyed hair didn't hide her beauty, but they did go a long way toward hiding her identity. He figured everyone on the ship would find it difficult to recognize her.

Helen approached Kennedy and his associates, who were huddled near one of the ships large stern cleats. They were deep into conversation when Kennedy looked up and saw her walking toward them. He nodded and his men turned and walked away, but not before Helen noticed one of them partially raise his hand toward his forehead. Kennedy's eyes locked on the man in question and he quickly lowered his hand and moved off. She wondered what that was all about.

"Professor Zachary, we about ready to shove off?" Kennedy asked as he straightened and walked over to meet her.

"I have a meeting to attend, but we should be able to depart in about twenty minutes." She zipped up her dark blue coat. "Doctor, according to the manifest, you have three crates that were not accounted for nor inspected, and the weight of those three crates placed us over our limit. It makes me wonder if you were trying to get these items past me."

Kennedy, a man of about twenty-six with short cropped blond hair, laughed. "My pharmaceutical company sent us two computers and a fluoride analyzer at the last minute. Nothing earth shattering, quite boring stuff really."

"Then you wouldn't mind if I inspect them?"

"Not at all, I'll have them opened for you. I don't think it should delay us more than two hours. It's a royal pain but they're packed quite well because of their sensitive components. But we don't want to break any rules. Mr. Lang, will you unstrap the analyzer and her component computers and break down the crates for the—"

"That won't be necessary, Doctor," Helen said, irritated by the possible delay. She was nervous and didn't trust Henri St. Claire at all. It felt as if he might drive onto the dock at any moment and catch them before they could make their way out to sea. "Your pharmaceutical company picked up the remaining portion of the bill for this trip, but please don't assume that gives you the right to circumvent my authority." She turned and strode away.

"I would never think of it," he said to her retreating form. "We value this opportunity to examine the fauna of this new and unexplored area of the basin for the chance at—" He trailed off, giving up his rehearsed speech when she didn't slow down. His eyes remained on Helen as she started down the gangplank toward the ship's offices.

HELEN ENTERED THE office and removed her coat while her eyes adjusted to the brightness of the interior. She finally saw the man sitting in the corner with one of his long legs crossed over the other.

"I honestly thought you were going to keep me waiting all night long in this smelly place," he said as he stood.

"I imagine you've been in worse places." She greeted him with a hug.

"As a matter of record, my dear, your father and I shipped out of this very harbor a million years ago bound for that paradise we know as Korea." He released her and looked her over. "You, young lady, look exhausted."

"Goes with the territory." She patted him on the chest and then sat on the edge of a desk that occupied the center of the office.

"So, you finally got the grant you always wanted for this mysterious field trip. Are you excited?"

"I will be if we ever get out of here," she answered as she looked at her father's oldest friend and family attorney. She was sorry for having to lie to him about where the money came from. She managed to force the guilty thought from her mind. "I've got a secret mission for you, Stan."

"Ooh, sounds mysterious," he said jokingly.

"You don't know the half of it," she said, thinking, *If he only knew.* "You're the only one I can trust to do what I ask, and not ask a bunch of silly questions."

"At my age, I've learned to only ask pertinent questions, never silly ones. What do you want me to do?"

Helen stood and walked to the door. She bent down and retrieved the aluminum case that contained the fossil. She held out the case to the attorney.

"If for some reason I don't make it back by September first, or call you by that date on the satellite phone, I need you to take this sample to Las Vegas and give it to a friend."

Stan took the case and looked at his friend's daughter. "You're kidding, right?"

Helen reached into her pocket and placed an envelope on the top of the container.

"The address is in here, along with my friend's name. There's also a brief on the expedition. My friend has the resources to know how to track me, so for security reasons and your safety, I didn't leave him directions on how to find me. Stanley, will you do this for me?"

He didn't say anything at first, as he made his way to the desk and placed the container on it. Then, "What have you gotten yourself into, Helen? Just where in the hell are you going and why do you need to leave me with such a cryptic list of instructions?"

She smiled and once again patted him on the left lapel. "You worry too much; it's just a competitive type thing, the race for the prize."

"And what prize is that?"

"A big one, Stanley." She rose on her toes and kissed him on the cheek. "It's dangerous only because the place is so remote. I have fifty people coming with me, so I'm not in this alone. Will you do this for me?"

He was about to respond when the ship's horn sounded and drowned out his answer. He grimaced. When the horn stopped blaring there was a quick rapping at the office door and Kimberly Denning, a third-year student, poked her head through.

"Captain said he has to get this tide or you can forget about sailing until morning," Kimberly said, then vanished.

Helen grabbed her coat and put it on. "Wish me luck?" she asked Stan.

"I do. I just wish I knew what it was you were up to."

She smiled and turned for the door, raising her hand in good-bye. "All I'll tell you is that, when I get back, no one will look at the world the same way again."

The door opened and Helen was gone. Stan took the white business envelope from the top of the container as he made his way to the window. Helen turned when she reached the top of the gangplank and waved at him, and he held the envelope up and waved back. Her students were lining the rails and waving at family who were in the parking lot. To Helen's right, standing away from her and her students, was a group of men who were watching from the railing. They weren't waving, just leaning against the steel gunwale as the ship's crew cast off her thick rope lines. Stan watched as the ship drifted away from the pier with her horn sounding. There was an explosion at her stern when the engines began turning her screws and the *Pacific Voyager* started making for the open sea.

Stan turned from the window and looked down at the envelope he held in his hand. He squinted and moved to stand by the desk lamp. Helen's womanly scrawl was written across the white paper in flowing lines. Stan looked up through the window at the receding lights of the blue-painted *Pacific Voyager* and then back at the name and address on the envelope. He read it aloud to himself: "Dr. Niles Compton, c/o the Gold City Pawnshop, 2120 Desert Palm Avenue, Las Vegas, Nevada.

"A pawnshop?" he said wonderingly.

He placed the envelope in his overcoat and looked out the window again, now taking in the few family members and friends of Helen's students as they started their cars and moved out of the small parking lot. Then Stan, for no reason that he knew of, got goose bumps down his arms as the vehicles departed. He didn't believe in premonitions or any of the other strange sciences that occupied the newspapers these days, yet had a distinct feeling that he would indeed deliver this envelope to that pawnshop in Las Vegas. And that the families that had watched their loved ones sail into the night would never again see them alive.

Stan picked up the aluminum container and made for the door. He allowed himself one last look out into the harbor, but the ship's running lights had vanished into the dark Pacific waters.

PART TWO
THE DIVINE WIND

Man has gone to the brink many times in his short history. We must therefore thank God there has always been a human being who could look beyond nationality, color, and religion to examine the truth of what he saw around him, and cried, Enough!

—from the memoirs of Garrison Lee,
retired United States senator from Maine and
former director of the Event Group

3

ARMY Second Lieutenant Sarah McIntire held the porous lava rock in her hand for all to see. Then she winked at Vincent Fallon, professor of Asian Studies from UC–Riverside, and gave a quick nod of her head.

"So this area of the cave *had* been excavated before?" he asked.

Lieutenant Commander Carl Everett stood and watched the reaction of the others. He was on detached service from the U.S. Navy, serving in his sixth year in the highly secretive Department 5656, known to a very distinct few in the United States government as the Event Group. The tightly controlled Group was established officially during the Teddy Roosevelt era with historical arms that reached all the way back to Abraham Lincoln.

Carl watched Sarah McIntire closely. She was the only other member of the Group on station. They had infiltrated the university dig three weeks earlier and he was hoping this mission was a wild-goose chase. But according to Sarah, who was a damned good geologist, it seemed very likely that the research that had been done by Dr. Fallon was accurate. Meaning they might have a biological disaster on their hands, and that meant the mission to infiltrate the archeological dig might have just risen in the danger level by a hundred percent.

Sarah tossed the flame-scorched rock to the floor of the giant cave and briefly glanced at Carl. She knew he was far better than just adequate to provide security for the unsuspecting students and professors on this dig, but it didn't stop her from wishing Major Jack Collins, the head of Event Group security, was here also. The ancient lava-formed caves were dark and powerfully evocative of a past conflict that had been brutal in its cost in human misery.

"There's not only detonation marks on the stone and surrounding lava rock formations, but the density of the back wall shows its loose fall. In layman's terms, Professor, that wall had once been open to this side of the cave and has since been hastily sealed." She adjusted one of the floodlights to show the rock fall she had just examined. "I suspect our Mr. Seito is correct, that there is another chamber behind the rock fall, just as he said there would be."

Carl looked at the old man sitting on a large rock. He had his eyes closed and was slowly rocking back and forth. The interpreter they had been using was standing next to him, silent, as he watched the analysis of the cave progress. The old man mumbled something and then the Japanese linguistics student from the University of Kyoto smiled and translated it.

"Mr. Seito says that his memory has failed in many areas, but it will never shed what had occurred during his last days on this island."

Carl half-bowed toward the old man who had reluctantly explained in detail the last terrifying days on Okinawa. He had told them with complete clarity that he was one of the men who had sealed this very cave in 1945. That he had joyously destroyed that which Professor Fallon was desperately seeking. The old Japanese soldier had closed his eyes when he recounted how he had assisted in the ritual suicide of the island's commander, Tarazawa.

"I must remind you, Professor Fallon, if the find is actually there, it must be immediately secured by my government," said Mr. Asaki, an official from the government of Okinawa, as he carefully eased his way over the loose stone. He stopped before the professor, removed his glasses, and cleaned them with a white handkerchief.

Carl kept quiet as the professor nodded and responded, "We're all well aware of your orders, Mr. Asaki, and we will be glad to turn over any substance find along with the vessel itself as soon as we verify it was actually a part of Kublai Khan's battle fleet, and not until then; that was our deal with Tokyo."

Asaki didn't comment but did bow quickly, and then he waved for his man at the cave's opening to allow the woman scientist into the excavation.

Sarah smiled and started to move away from the group to continue her inspection. She couldn't resist saying, as she patted the naval officer on the shoulder on her way by, "Oh, boy, Ms. Personality is coming in, Carl. I think she has the *hots* for you."

Carl didn't respond, but Sarah could see him shudder at the mention of the woman they both disliked. The navy man watched as the two women passed each other and nodded their heads out of courtesy; their greeting was chilly at best. The woman was Dr. Andréa Kowalski. She had been recruited by Dr. Fallon and held credentials from the Centers for Disease Control in Atlanta. Unlike Sarah and him, she was here legitimately and not undercover. She was of average size, and that was the last place you could use the word "average" when describing this woman; she was a knockout. Her red hair was done up in a ponytail and she wore her extreme-environment suit unzipped and tied at the waist. Her one flaw as far as he could see was the small fact that the woman was a total bitch.

"I find your friend extremely rude," Andréa remarked to Carl as she joined the group of people at the mouth of the excavation.

"She has a fondness for you, too," Carl said, looking away and winking at the old Japanese soldier.

"I know *she* is a geologist and is needed on this venture, but what is it *you* do again, Mr.—"

"Knock it off, Andréa, you know he's in charge of logistics. Remember, he's the one that got all that fancy lab equipment here in one piece," Professor Fallon called out. "Now I suggest you go and set up; Sarah says we can be through the wall in the next hour if we're lucky."

After giving Carl one more questioning glance, Andréa turned away and started setting up her equipment.

"Wonderful analyst you found there, Doc; she has the personality of a vampire bat." Carl smiled and bowed at Seito, whose toothless grin seemed to indicate he understood the insult directed at the viral specialist.

As the old man sat his mind drifted back in time to those awful last days on Okinawa—the original discovery of what they now sought, and the horrible consequences that once could have changed the course of a war that had ended seventy years ago. Seito shuddered at the memory and, as he looked around the cavernous enclosure, he couldn't help but see and feel those days once again . . .

OKINAWA, JAPAN
MAY 14, 1945

The American F4F Hellcats from no less than five fast attack carriers had been bombing the Ryukyu chain of islands since mid-March. For the past several weeks, the sorties had gained in intensity as the Americans prepared for the invasion of the last stepping-stone before their final thrust at the throat of the Japanese Empire.

Admiral Jinko Tarazawa, once a trusted advisor to Admiral Isoroku Yamamoto, had been in disgrace for two years for his failure to stem the tide of American resistance in the Pacific at the war's turning point, known to the Americans as the Battle of Midway. He had been blamed for this along with his commander, Chuichi Nagumo, and as a result was now in command of the island's defense instead of fighting and dying for his beloved navy. A hero of the empire only three years before for his coleadership in planning the greatest naval attack since Lord Nelson ruled the seas, he now found himself a long way from Hawaii and Pearl Harbor. His dishonor was great. To be relegated to building bunkers instead of commanding one of the last battle groups remaining to the Imperial Japanese Navy was humiliation nearly beyond endurance.

As the admiral stood with his arms behind his back, looking out to sea, he was approached by his intelligence officer and handed a message. He read it quickly and gave it back to the Imperial Marine captain. The message burrowed deep into his mind, lodging there and bringing on a new wave of despair. The estimate from the naval attaché based in Spain had reported to Tokyo that the Americans were mounting the largest invasion force one nation had ever assembled. More than one thousand ships of war would soon be pointing their guns and sending their young men to the shores of this island. Tarazawa quickly nodded for the young marine to return to his duties, then closed his eyes and prayed for the safety of the emperor, for he knew this was to be the last blow before the Americans invaded Japan itself.

As rumbling from the excavating of caves shook the volcanic island, he saw several Hellcat fighter aircraft fly low over the island, bringing quick eruptions of antiaircraft fire from their hidden batteries.

Tarazawa was interrupted by another marine, this one a fresh-faced lieutenant who was running up waving his hands, forgetting even to bow to his commander.

"Sir, I have a report from the naval engineers on the north side of the island."

"What is it? I cannot go rushing off from here every time they have a small cave-in!" he said. "Just tell them to clear it and start moving the medical supplies and civilians in as soon as possible; we are very short of time."

Tarazawa was surprised when the young man stood there, disobeying his order.

"I beg for your indulgence, Admiral."

"What is it?" he asked.

"The northernmost cave, sir, the army and naval engineers have found something you must see."

Tarazawa's curiosity was piqued by the boy's eagerness. "What is it they have found that has you in such a state, Lieutenant Seito?"

The nineteen-year-old finally removed his blue cap and stepped agitatedly from one foot to the other. "When we blasted through the cave's far wall we broke into another chamber, a chamber that had been sealed up for many, many years, Admiral."

"This is good, is it not? That means they won't have to expand on that particular cave as much as they had originally thought."

"Sir, they discovered—I mean they found a ship inside. A very old ship," the boy said excitedly.

"Unless the ship you speak of is a new aircraft carrier with attack planes onboard, I don't see how this would interest me, young man," Tarazawa said with a frown.

The boy momentarily looked deflated and brightened when he remembered a detail. "Sir, Colonel Yashita says it is our salvation, at least that is the information he has received from a few Chinese laborers he used to examine the vessel!"

The admiral just stared at the boy and shook his head, not understanding anything except that foolish army colonel was not following his orders to expedite the expansion of the caves. And now he is pulling his prisoner labor force from their duties? Tarazawa quickly decided he would visit the cave and have a talk with that particular soldier. This disrespect of his orders would end if he had to execute an officer as an example to the rest. He might be old and disgraced but he was still a warrior of the Bushido code.

AN HOUR LATER, Admiral Tarazawa entered the front of the cave. He could see immediately that the natural feature was created by large lava flows that had once reached to the sea. It took twenty more minutes of finding his way in the semidarkness and avoiding the collisions with more than two hundred Chinese and Korean laborers clearing debris from the interior before he saw light at the rear of the monstrous cave.

There, yellowish lights played on the outline of a very old ship's hull. The admiral could see army personnel carefully crawling all over its ancient decks. They had even gone as far as erecting wooden scaffolding, even though lumber was getting scarce and thus critical. Tarazawa stopped in his tracks, fuming.

"How long has work been stopped at this site?" he asked in a very low and controlled tone of voice while grinding his teeth together.

Lieutenant Seito again removed his hat before speaking.

"Thirteen hours, sir."

Tarazawa closed his eyes and lowered his head. Then he forced himself to calm down as he breathed deeply. He reopened his eyes to the bright spectacle before him and walked slowly toward the short man who, unaware of his presence, was busy shouting orders from a large stage of lava rock.

"What is the meaning of this?" the admiral asked loudly so he could be heard above the portable generators.

Colonel Yashita had been a veteran of many campaigns in China before being ordered to Okinawa. He had had to suffer many indignities from higher-ranking officers who thought him to be an arrogant pig, but he would tolerate no interference from a disgraced admiral. He merely responded with a smirk.

"I asked you a question, Colonel!" Tarazawa said as he stepped onto the lowest scaffold below the rock that Yashita was standing upon. The workmen ceased their labors and listened.

"If you must know, Admiral, I am endeavoring to save our empire and our beloved emperor; and you, at the moment, are delaying this great task!"

"Explain yourself! I have thousands of men working until they collapse to make the defenses ready and you are here, instead of building a hospital as ordered. You are needlessly delaying construction because you are in a fit of delusion! You are not going to be fighting defenseless Chinese in the coming weeks, Colonel, but battle-hardened American marines and soldiers who actually shoot back!"

"Very well, I will indulge the admiral." Yashita calmly ordered his men back to work. "Have you seen this type of vessel before? You have vast experience; you should recognize her design. I did after only a moment." He rocked back on his heels while he bragged. "I have an advanced degree in history and engineering from London Polytechnic," he said, .reminding Tarazawa of his rich heritage.

Tarazawa glared at the colonel, then quickly scanned what could be seen of the deteriorating ship. The gunwales were deep and her deck was sloped to the extreme. The stern of the vessel was high, topped with wooden railing; there was no mast as it, along with the sail, had long since succumbed to age. He knew what the vessel was and where it came from, he just couldn't fathom why it was here on Okinawa. Nor how it came to be entrapped in a cave that couldn't have seen the ocean for centuries at the very least.

"It is a Chinese junk, of course. You have stopped work on one of our important underground hospitals for this?"

Yashita turned away as if he hadn't heard the question. He paused to adjust the black-sheathed samurai sword on his belt. "This ship, according to my Chinese laborers, two of whom used to teach on the mainland, once belonged to an enemy of Japan, a seemingly invincible foe such as the Americans appear to be. But like the Chinese, they will suffer when they try to land their marines on our soil."

"Quit speaking in riddles, Colonel, and explain why you are disobeying my orders!" Tarazawa said as he stepped menacingly closer to Yashita.

"This vessel was part of an invasion of our homeland over seven hundred and thirty years ago, Admiral." He looked significantly at Tarazawa, his brown hat firmly angled on his shaved head, its single silver star blinking brightly in the lights. "Yes, I can see you understand now," he said as Tarazawa added up the years and then appeared perplexed. "The year you are searching for is 1274 and the name you have misplaced in your aged mind is Kublai Khan."

Tarazawa quickly reacted. "Impossible! The invasion fleet sank or was driven off in a storm hundreds of miles north of Okinawa. This vessel cannot belong to the grand Chinese fleet of the Khan; again, you waste our time!"

"I and my Chinese historians would have to disagree, Admiral. This ship, according to dates we have uncovered, was a part of the fleet that was destroyed by the Divine Wind."

"*The Divine Wind*," Tarazawa mouthed the words.

"Yes, Admiral. The Kamikaze, the Divine Wind of the gods, the very same wind that reached out to destroy the invasion of Kublai Khan in 1274. And now, the discovery of this ship, which was separated from the main fleet by a storm over seven centuries ago, will be the answer to millions of prayers. Only this will be a divine wind of our making that will carry with it the death of every American in our home waters. This war will be ours!" Yashita shouted loudly and then started laughing.

FOUR HOURS LATER, after the second shift of laborers left the new excavation, Tarazawa sat inside the ancient junk's cargo hold. Lieutenant Seito and one of the Chinese workers sat with him. An oil lamp sitting between them cast an eerie glow on the faces of the three men. They had been that way for the last three hours after examining the strange porcelain jars that the workmen had found inside the vessel. The jars were three feet high and there were over thirty-two of them. All were sealed permanently closed at the mouth by clay, porcelain glass, and beeswax, effectively making them airtight. The nature of their contents had been elusive to the Chinese for the first half of the day after Yashita had brought the containers into the hold. Their only clues to the jars' contents were the dried and crumbling clay markers around the neck of every jar, explaining the use of the material. Tarazawa and the others didn't know the exact name for the strange weapon that Kublai Khan had intended to use on their ancestors, but they quickly learned it was lethal.

As one of the seals was cracked open, the Chinese laborer had failed to see that some of the powder had adhered to the cork sealant. The elderly Chinaman blinked his eyes and felt the powder soak into the pores of his skin. He immediately convulsed once, then again more violently. He coughed, a deep fluidic sound that forced burst membranes to spew forth an avalanche of blood and mucous. His eyes bulged and the pupils rolled back to show the whites that were quickly filling with blood.

The admiral and Seito backed away in horror as the man started to come apart from the inside. Tarazawa watched in terrified fascination as the infected man fell to the hardened and rotted wood decking, coughed out another glob of blood, and then finally lay still in death.

"What have we uncovered?" the admiral asked aloud as he and Seito moved quickly to the makeshift ladder leading to the upper deck. They climbed as quickly as possible to safety.

Lieutenant Seito, his young face scrunched up in horror at what they had just witnessed on the old petrified vessel, hung his head. Then he looked up with hope in his young eyes. Seito was one of the Imperial Navy's brightest. He had been drafted into the service just last year. He, like many in his class, was also a realist and knew no matter what the fanatical right wingers in the government said, Japan had lost the war. He only hoped there were still people around in his homeland after the shooting stopped. He was one whom those fools called defeatist, one who wished for an immediate cessation of hostilities no matter what the price might be, even to the point of the emperor having to abdicate and admit his false divinity.

"Surely this horrible plague, this substance, shouldn't be

potent after seven centuries? Well?" Tarazawa questioned the eldest of the Chinese who had only moments earlier escaped the fate of his countryman inside.

"As it is in a powder form, the Khan must have planned to disperse this substance on the winds if his invasion met with disaster."

Above them, on the makeshift scaffolds extending from the deck that they sat on, they heard the return of Colonel Yashita and his men. Then the thud of block and tackle as it struck the scaffolding and strongest parts of the ancient deck.

"He's come to take the cargo from the hold of the vessel," Seito said, removing his cap and wiping the sweat from his brow. "Are you going to allow this?"

Tarazawa stood and picked up the lantern. "Colonel Yashita's intention is the salvation of the war, and is dishonorable for the single fact he would only prolong this conflict for his own selfish reasons, and would possibly kill many hundreds of thousands of Americans, bringing on a retaliatory response that could possibly end the Japanese civilization. This must not be allowed to happen."

"What are you saying, sir?"

Tarazawa didn't answer. He just looked from the Chinese laborers to the lieutenant and then lowered the wick in the lantern until it dimmed and then died, casting them and the Japanese Empire into darkness.

OKINAWA, JAPAN
PRESENT DAY

As the last of the rocks were moved away by Japanese contractors hired on the island, Professor Fallon called a halt. He asked the islanders and most of the Cal Riverside students to leave the cave for safety reasons. After hearing the story as told by the old soldier Seito the week before, the professor wasn't taking any chances. The documents he had uncovered in Beijing twenty years ago with the aid of the Chinese government, during one of their more friendly and nonenlightened periods, had told him that beyond that wall could be found not only a great archaeological find with the Chinese junk, but also one of the most dangerous substances known to man.

Of the six people left to remove the last of the lava rock and stone, Sarah was out in front. A trained geologist, she would watch for instability in the rock fall when the opening was cleared. She was joined by Dr. Kowalski, who bore with her a device they called a "sniffer." It would measure and analyze the air particles, and immediately alert her if any of the substance had become airborne after Tarazawa had sealed the excavation in '45. Both women were now dressed in airtight chemical suits. Carl Everett wondered if their animosity was coming through their small speaker systems as they removed the last stone.

"Stand clear, Ms. McIntire, if you please. I must be able to get a solid reading," Andréa Kowalski said.

Sarah was about to respond when she heard Carl clear his throat from about ten feet away. She instead backed away as ordered.

Andréa handled the microphone-shaped probe expertly as she eased it cautiously through the door-size opening, careful not to touch the stone itself. Once it was inside the opening, she placed a thin panel of steel over the hole and then thumbed a switch on the sniffer's small control panel. Inside the darkness of the cave, the microphone-shaped device came apart with a small pop. The heavy springs inside engaged and sent two hundred small darts in all directions. Each dart was tungsten tipped and the small shaft was made of lypcochlorinide, which upon impact sent a burst of moisture into the air, activating any minute amounts of any substance that may be embedded in the lava rock. The tungsten heads were miniature radio units that would relay any findings to the device's control panel. Of the two hundred darts, some found rock, others sand, and still others tumbled into the blackness. Andréa slowly brought up the particle gauge and read the virtual readout. The device was so sensitive it immediately broke down all the airborne elements in the old excavation.

The others watching Andréa's progress could see the woman in her yellow chemical suit slowly relax her shoulders as the small darts sent back their vital information on the air quality in the cave. But none of them realized just *how* tense she had become.

Carl finally took a breath, not even knowing he had been holding it. He relaxed when he saw her remove the small steel plate from the hole.

Andréa removed a small round object from her belt, leaned into the opening, and tossed the small device as far as she could. The round object was a one-time-use portable analysis pod. Once thrown, it would separate into five different sections and its components would read the interior air of the confined space. It was so accurate that it picked up the traces of cordite and TNT that had been used in 1945, over sixty years before.

Andréa removed her hood. "All clear; only one strange reading I can't figure out," she said. "But it's nontoxic."

"What is it?" Professor Fallon asked, with concern.

"Trace amounts of blood."

The others started to remove their own protective equipment.

"Don't do that, please; just because there is nothing in the air doesn't mean we won't disturb trace amounts when we enter. The petrie darts only cover about ten percent of the cave; that leaves ninety percent capable of carrying something that could kill you all," Andréa said blandly as she placed her own hood back in place.

As she turned and entered the cave, Professor Fallon and Carl and two other members of the dig team hefted the portable lighting they would use in the initial phase of the recovery. Sarah was the first to follow the CDC specialist into the opening. She switched on her flashlight once she was inside. At first, all she caught in the light was floating dust and the back of Andréa, who was waving another metal probe that was connected to her readout, this time making sure their footsteps weren't bringing death with every movement they made. Then Sarah's light caught the geometric shape of wooden scaffolding standing out through the dust swirls. Out of the darkness rose a black ship. Still legible on its side was what looked like a faded dragon carved into the dark wood. It ran the entire length of the ship and its tail wrapped around the stern. As she played her light around it, she could see that the bottom half of the vessel had deteriorated badly. The rotted planks that made up its hull were starting to collapse, causing the top deck to sag into the interior of the vessel.

"Director Compton would have loved to have seen this."

Sarah jumped at the sound of Carl's voice. "Jesus, don't do that," she admonished. "You scared the hell out of me." *But he was right*, she thought, Niles Compton, the director of the Event Group, lived for discovery like this, and he also would have loved to get it into one of the Group's vaults for further study. Sarah shook off the thought of Niles and brought her focus back to where it should have been; after all, they were here to make sure the old legends about this ship weren't true. That was the whole reason for her and Carl's infiltration of this college dig in the first place.

"We may have a dangerous situation here," Andréa said from the lowermost scaffolds.

"Danger?" Fallon asked as he looked at the ship, still giddy at proving his research right and vindicating Seito's elaborate tall tale of an ancient vessel buried in a cave.

"The junk is collapsing in on itself. If that upper deck gives way, it will crush whatever cargo this vessel was once carrying, and if your theory and old Seito's memory are correct, we could contaminate all of Okinawa."

"Before we find out, doctors, I suggest you bring the old man in here and ask him a few more questions," Carl said after he gained the top of the scaffold that looked down onto the main deck of the Chinese junk.

"He isn't authorized, Mr. Everett," Fallon said as he carefully eased his way to where Carl was standing.

"What have you got up there, Carl?" Sarah asked from below.

"The reason why Dr. Kowalski's equipment was picking up trace amounts of dried blood," Carl replied as the professor joined him.

"Good God, what in the hell is this?" Fallon exclaimed when he saw what Carl was looking at.

"Are you going to keep us in suspense up there or are you going to act like professionals?" Andréa said from the lower level.

"I think our old Lieutenant Seito needs to tell us why there are three skeletons in Japanese Army uniforms up here," Carl said flatly.

THEY WERE ALL amazed an hour later when the old man, along with his interpreter, both now dressed in yellow chemical suits, bowed deeply at the waist at the remains of the three skeletons on the upper scaffold.

"Who is it?" Carl asked the old soldier.

The old man straightened with the aid of the interpreter. They could hear him breathing deeply of his oxygen, almost hyperventilating. Then he began to speak in his native Japanese.

"He said," his interpreter translated, "that it is his great shame that this is Colonel Yashita and two of his army soldiers. Murdered, shot in the back by himself and Admiral Tarazawa."

"He wanted to excavate the cargo, didn't he?" Carl asked. "Yashita wanted to use it if it was still viable."

The old man understood the question without need for the interpreter and nodded. Then he said something too low for the others to hear.

"Mr. Seito says it was a traitorous act on his and the admiral's part, but that he would do it again. There had been enough death. They resealed the cave and in their report attributed the unfortunate loss of the colonel and his men to a cave-in."

The group was silent. Carl just nodded his head at the old man and Sarah patted Seito on the back.

"Where is Dr. Kowalski?" Fallon asked suddenly.

Carl looked around; Andréa was nowhere to be seen. Then he heard the sound at the same time the others did. There was noise coming from inside the ancient cargo hold.

"Goddammit!" Carl exclaimed as he quickly stepped down onto the uppermost deck. His foot immediately crashed through the rotted wood as if he had stepped on a glass floor. As he gently tried to pull his booted foot free he saw the others rushing up the old wooden scaffolding. He held up his arm quickly. "Stay back! This damned thing is coming apart, I'll—"

That was as far as Carl got, as his weight was enough to crack the rest of that section of deck. He felt weightlessness at first and then his stomach lurched up into his chest as he started to fall. There was a momentary darkness, then a bright flash of light. He felt something soft break his fall. He heard a loud grunt and then an expletive that sounded like French. Then he felt himself, and whatever it had been that broke his fall, strike the bottom of the hold.

"You clumsy oaf, you could have broken my equipment," Andréa said from beneath him. "Or me! Now get off," she ordered as she pushed at him.

As they both stood up, she silently held her light on something. The sight of it made her freeze instantly. She gestured for him not to move, by holding out her hand. Carl raised his light and in its beam he was amazed to see at least thirty large containers, yellowed with age and standing three feet in height, leaning against one another, still bound with the remains of old rotted restraining ropes used to keep them in place over seven hundred years before. The jars all had a red dragon, dimmed with age, painted on their sides.

"I'll be damned," Carl murmured under his breath.

"If whatever is in there is still viable, we all may be damned," Andréa said as she stared at thirty-two containers of a mystery weapon Chinese legend said was the Breath of the Dragon.

TWO HOURS LATER, after the dig team had assisted Andréa in setting up her equipment outside of the junk's hull, they waited anxiously for her to confirm their worst fears. The grad students and Professor Fallon knew if the cargo was still an active powdered agent, they wouldn't have a snowball's chance in hell of examining the ancient junk.

Carl finally put all the puzzle pieces together. The previous year, a seven-hundred-year-old Chinese laboratory had been unearthed during an archeological dig outside Beijing. When it was discovered by an Event Group infiltration unit that students of Beijing University had found trace evidence of a biological facility that was hundreds of years ahead of its time, the news had shaken the virologists at the Event Group badly. Trace amounts of chemical agents had been discovered inside the remains of kilns. Rudimentary microscopes made up of eight or nine different lenses of glass, providing the magnification needed to study the spread of disease, were also unearthed at a nearby, separate excavation that was also tagged by the Group. Those two elements side by side painted a historical picture that would shake modern science to its foundations if word was let out. Then it was discovered in old marching orders uncovered by the Computer Sciences Department at the Event Group that a powdered compound had been intended to be released into the air over seven centuries earlier by Kublai Khan's invading force. The findings were passed up the chain of command until the president gave reluctant permission for the Fallon dig to include Carl and Sarah for reasons of national security, after they found out that Dr. Fallon had discovered the site through an alternate means while researching survivor records in Shanghai that told of a mysterious shipwreck on the island of Okinawa.

Still in her chemical suit, Andréa set up a small worktable

inside the cargo hold of the Chinese vessel. Carl strung some makeshift lighting inside and stood by as the doctor made her analysis. Carl was the only member of the dig team she allowed inside, and only then because he was already there. Thus far she had carefully used a special drill to penetrate the beeswax and porcelain. Without extracting the drill she carefully slid a rubber collar down the drill bit and made it secure to the outer wax sealant, then withdrew the drill bit from the container and rubber gasket. As she freed the tool she quickly capped the rubber gasket with a rubber stopper, then she took a deep breath and sat back. From the supplies she had assembled on her small table, she pulled out a small vile of a clear chemical and shook it up until it turned amber in color. She then placed the very tip of the probe into it.

"If you're a religious man, Mr. Everett, now's the time to pray whatever this stuff is has deteriorated over the centuries and has become inert; if not, I'm afraid there's one hell of a cleanup ahead of us."

Carl didn't respond; he had been silent throughout the entire procedure. Ever since he had fallen through the rotted decking of the junk, he had been keeping his eyes open and thinking a few things over. He had studied Dr. Kowalski's dossier that Niles Compton had forwarded from the Group in Nevada, and it had said nothing about the good doctor's speaking French. The information didn't seem critical, but the dossiers were made up by the National Security Agency and they left nothing out. Still, he would be on the alert now for other slips.

As Andréa slowly pulled the small rubber cork from the gasket, she quickly plugged it again with the telescopic probe, then began cautiously to inch it into the porcelain container. Carl could hear her short, controlled breaths as she held her arm steady. She inserted the probe into the container until she met resistance and then she let go and shook her hands as if they had fallen asleep.

"Whatever is in there has hardened over the years. That's

good news; it means it may not be a powder any longer and easier to move if it proves active."

"Makes me all giddy inside to know that, Doctor," Carl said, keeping his eyes on Andréa and the container.

Andréa frowned behind her faceplate and then retrieved her portable analyzer from the table. She took two small electrical leads that protruded from the steel probe she had placed in the porcelain container and attached them to her laptop computer. Next, she took the 1/8-inch clear rubber tube on the probe and also inserted that into the side of her analyzer. Then she took a deep breath of her oxygen and started tapping commands on the keyboard. Suddenly the analyzer beeped three times in rapid succession. The indicator in the upper right corner of the analyzer flashed red.

"Well, that doesn't look or sound too good," Carl said.

Andréa didn't respond. She laid the analyzer down slowly, leaving the probe in the container, and carefully stood. She backed away slowly and keyed her radio on the yellow sleeve of her chemical suit.

"Well, what is it?" Carl asked as Andréa backed away from the container.

"Professor Fallon? I don't fully understand how the Chinese did it seven hundred years before they were supposed to be able to, but they managed to—"

"Dr. Kowalski, Mr. Everett, would you be so kind as to join us up on the scaffold please," ordered a familiar voice. "I don't wish to be unpleasant to your colleagues."

Andréa looked at Carl.

"May I assume you have a weapon on you, Mr. Everett?" Andréa whispered as she reached into a small satchel attached to her side and brought out a Beretta nine-millimeter automatic pistol.

Under his faceplate Carl raised his eyebrows. "Is that standard CDC issue, Doctor?" he mouthed as he reached into his satchel and brought out a Colt .45 automatic.

"Is that Asaki, the nerd from the Okinawa government, talking?" Andréa asked quietly.

"Yes, and I don't think I care for his tone," Carl replied as he steeled himself for confrontation.

"Mr. Everett, if you are armed, please toss your weapon out onto the upper deck before you appear, or I'm afraid our friends here will do something distasteful," Asaki warned.

Carl gestured for Andréa to slide her pistol into her chemical suit. Without hesitation she quickly released the Velcro, unzipped her suit, and plunged her Beretta inside; it was almost as if she had anticipated Carl's order.

"We can remove the protective suits for now, there's no trace of any airborne particles," Carl said loudly.

He removed his hood and faceplate, tossed his .45 through the opening he had made when he fell through the deck, and then turned back toward Andréa.

"So, what agency are you with, Doctor? NSA, CIA, or is it someone else?" he whispered.

"Please come out on deck, so we may finish our business," Asaki ordered. "Any untoward antics and we will begin harming your friends, starting with the students."

Carl took a deep breath and waited for Andréa.

As she passed him, she removed her faceplate and hood, then shook out her red hair. She stopped long enough to retrieve her glasses from the small table. Then she turned and faced Carl as she put them on.

"In answer to your question, Mr. Everett, I guess you could say you know my husband, or ex-husband to be more accurate. You see, Mr. Everett, I also know you are no field security man contracted for the university at Riverside, but actually the number two man in the security department for what is known in very private circles as the Event Group," she whispered. "My name is Danielle Serrate, formerly Mrs. Henri Farbeaux. Now I'm afraid we must do as they say before we get one of those innocent kids killed."

Carl couldn't move for a moment. He expected something, but not the former wife of the Group's number one enemy. Now he knew why she cursed in French when she was caught off guard. Colonel Henri Farbeaux had been a thorn in the side of his organization for the better part of fifteen years. Farbeaux was far better at gleaning the historical record than most nations gave him credit for. Although ruthless in his pursuit of antiquities and technology, not necessarily in that order, he was a man who rivaled Group director Niles Compton in the IQ department, which was why he was so dangerous and had a death warrant out for him by at least five countries.

"No wonder you were such a bitch," he mumbled to himself as they started up.

CARL IMMEDIATELY TOOK in the situation and knew from a military, or defensive, standpoint, he was going to be like a one-legged man in an ass-kicking contest. With the way the bad guys were deployed in and around the cave, he could see he was hamstrung. Asaki had a crew of his own men and had organized six different areas in which he was holding the field team inside the cave. Carl knew Asaki had to have additional men, either in the larger cave or outside, more than likely both. Sarah and Professor Fallon, along with the old soldier Seito, were standing next to the Okinawa field representative, which Asaki obviously wasn't or, worse, he was pulling double duty as a thug *and* bureaucrat; moreover, standing next to him, holding his very own Colt .45, was the old man's interpreter.

"Please step aside and let Dr. Kowalski join us, Mr. Everett, we have much to do and a very short time to do it," Asaki admonished while waiving a small pistol of his own.

Carl allowed the newly disclosed Danielle Farbeaux, or as she said, Serrate, to step up from behind him. He still wasn't sure she wasn't a part of what was happening here.

"Very good; as you can see, things are not as they seem. Your situation has turned from one of discovery to that of cooperation. Do this and I assure you no one will be harmed," Asaki said loudly enough for all in the cave to hear, his voice carrying easily in the small enclosure.

"You . . . are a . . . dishonor," said Seito in halting English.

Asaki ignored the old man and gestured for Danielle to come forward.

"Now, what sort of biological agent are we dealing with, Doctor?"

"I haven't completed my analysis yet."

"I think you are lying, but have no fear, Doctor, we have people for that; we will remove the weapon first and then—"

Andréa cut him off. "If you make one mistake, you could doom yourselves to a horrible death," she hissed as she stepped directly on the remains and tattered uniform of the World War II army colonel. Her foot had come down on the colonel's samurai sword. "Just why are you doing this?"

"The man you are so casually standing on is my grandfather. My real name is Yashita," said the man they knew as Asaki.

Carl now understood at least part of what was happening. *Who would have figured?*

The government man adjusted the aim of his pistol and pointed at Seito, "He was murdered by this man and the cowardly, disgraced Admiral Tarazawa because they didn't have the fortitude to save the war as my grandfather had wished to do with this gift from the gods. But today, old wounds will be healed and I will kill two birds with one single stone."

Seito, the old warhorse and feisty to the end, spat at Yashita. Sarah, seeing the rage cross Yashita's features, stepped in front of the old soldier without thinking. Then a strange calmness came over the government representative's face and he smiled as he wiped the old man's spittle from his cheek and neck.

"As I said, by the end of today my sense of justice will be satisfied."

"What will someone like you do with a biological agent? Sell it to the highest bidder?" Carl asked, his hands still up.

"Nothing so mundane, I assure you. You Americans always think it's the money. Money, money, money," he said with a snarl. "The war never ended for many of us, Mr. Everett. Like my grandfather before me, I am a patriot and still very much active in the war with your country, as are many from all over the world." He stepped forward and motioned below as ten men dressed in green chemical suits started up the scaffolding. They all carried large zippered bags. "After we have the weapon analyzed, it will be dispersed worldwide. Every element in our cause against the West will receive one canister. Who would have thought the great and mighty Kublai Khan would come to the aid of our struggle? This will be used to avenge the rape of my country and the senseless slaughter of hundreds of thousands," he said as he watched Carl take a menacing step forward.

"Please, continue to advance, Mr. Everett, and we can begin this right now if you wish," Yashita said as he aimed his gun at Sarah.

Yashita's men pushed by Carl and Danielle, knocking them together, a move that forced Carl to grab her to keep her from tumbling off the scaffold. As he righted her, he found himself standing on the old samurai sword.

Yashita shouted in Japanese and his men below herded the students to the outer cave. Then he climbed the last scaffold, placed the protective hood over his head, and easily lowered his body into the hold to see the containers for himself.

The interpreter and three of Asaki's men herded Sarah, Fallon, and the old man toward Carl and Danielle.

"You two all right?" Carl asked.

"I've never felt so damned helpless in my life," Sarah said angrily.

"This is a little different than your clean classrooms in Nevada, isn't it, Second Lieutenant McIntire?" Danielle asked.

Sarah didn't respond to Danielle's sarcasm; she instead raised her eyebrows as she looked at Carl.

"Our Dr. Kowalski, as it turns out, is Danielle Serrate, the former Mrs. Henri Farbeaux."

Sarah allowed her shock to show as she momentarily dropped her arms, eliciting a loud rebuke from their captors. She quickly raised them again. Then she laughed.

"No wonder she's such a bitch," she said, echoing Carl's earlier comment.

TWENTY MINUTES LATER, the armed men allowed them to lower their arms and ordered them to sit on the creaking wooden scaffolding. Carl was careful to place his ass right over the colonel's old sword, as uncomfortable as it was.

"You work for the French Antiquities Commission?" Sarah asked.

"Yes, my being here has not been authorized. I learned that my former husband had started learning all he could about dangerous biohazards; he had an extensive file on the Kublai Khan invasion, which mentioned this vessel in several passages, so I thought he might show up here."

"You went through all that trouble to track down your ex? Were you in that much of a reconciliatory mood?" Sarah asked.

"My mood was a bit darker, little Sarah; I was going to kill him," Danielle answered coldly.

"He used to work for your department. What would your director say about that?" Carl asked her.

Danielle slowly turned toward Carl and smiled grimly. "I *am* the director of my department."

Sarah and Carl exchanged looks.

"Who *are* you people? Is anyone who they said they were, when they signed on?" Fallon asked angrily.

Poor Fallon, Sarah thought. What could she tell him, that she worked for the most secret organization in the American government? That all she did is collect data from history and analyze it, catalog it, and learn from it to make sure her country didn't make the same mistakes twice? A job that required her to infiltrate field digs from universities, and hire into private companies to gain information about anything and everything? That she was there to protect the American people and sometimes the world from themselves, because what they didn't know is that their government agency knows most everything from the truth of religion to that of UFOs?

"Professor Fallon, all we can say is that we are here to help," Sarah answered.

"I'm sure that will comfort him," Yashita said as he climbed back up from the inside of the ancient hold. He removed his protective hood. "One thing you should know, all of you: there are no more heroes left in your part of the world, only robots that do the bidding of Washington and other dying entities just like it."

"I think there may be one or two left in the West," Danielle said smiling.

As if on cue, screaming started from the outer cave. Yashita looked confused and ordered his three men to investigate. As they started down the scaffolding, Danielle unzipped her protective suit, pulled her Beretta, and quickly fired, but missed Yashita as he jumped from the topmost scaffolds to the bottom one, landing hard and rolling. As he tried to stand, a tremendous explosion rocked the cavern, knocking everyone over. The chemical-suited men began exiting the hold of the ship on the ladders they had installed for their descent, and pulled handguns from their satchels. The interpreter started shouting orders and then the men turned their weapons on their captives.

"Oh, shit," Carl yelled. He struck out with a rubber-booted foot, hitting the closest man and knocking him from his feet. He quickly grabbed for the man's weapon, a small-caliber Colt, and fired into the facemask of another of Yashita's men. As he did so he saw several others suddenly flop to the scaffold, as something unseen and unheard took them down. Their added weight hitting rotten wood was too much for the structure. It cracked and folded in on itself. Just before it did Carl saw several holes stitch across one of Yashita's men as he fell backward into the cargo hold. Then that was it—they were all falling.

There were shouts coming from all areas of the cave. Carl was lying in the hull, stunned, with Danielle on top, fighting to get a hundred pounds of rotted wood off them. He could hear Sarah from somewhere shouting that Yashita was over to the left. Suddenly Carl felt himself lifted and shoved over. He felt hands reaching under him and then whoever was assisting him disappeared into the dust and smoke. Then he heard Sarah shouting again.

As the scaffold started coming down, she had grabbed for the interpreter's weapon. It had fired and Sarah felt a searing pain crease her shoulder. The man had then fired point-blank at Seito. She yelled again in warning, and saw the old soldier jump to the right, pushing debris from the scaffolding out of his way as he did. Sarah started to pull herself out of the mess of rotted wood, when she saw Yashita above her, firing at someone in the cave below. She wondered if the students had somehow gotten free and started this nightmare. Suddenly she felt herself lifted, by none other than Yashita. He was bleeding from the mouth and shaking her.

"Who are you people?" he screamed.

Below them, Carl finally pulled Danielle to her feet, took the Beretta from her firm grasp, and then tried to step free of the debris that covered the cave floor. As two men took aim at him, he knew he couldn't get the pistol up in time, but even before he could try to shoot, a line of tracers struck the men and they went down. That was when Carl noticed someone dressed in black Nomex and wearing a nylon hood and gas mask step out from a rock outcropping. He was about to shout when he heard other, louder screams of outrage coming from behind them. The man in black ran forward; Carl and Danielle quickly followed.

"I want out of here! You will allow me to pass or this woman's death will be on you, not I," Yashita shouted again. His pistol was pointed right at Sarah's temple. She had a scowl on her face as if she were far more angry than scared.

The man in black acted as though he hadn't heard; he slowly inched forward, his Ingram submachine gun not wavering a millimeter. Carl reached out and tried to stop the black-garbed commandos but the man easily shrugged his hand away. From behind the black goggles and a night-vision scope placed over the gas mask, the man's eyes were trained directly at Yashita. Carl knew that if the commando fired, Yashita could have a knee-jerk reaction and kill Sarah anyway.

Suddenly there was a loud shout in Japanese and a figure jumped out of the darkness. The bright and shiny edge of a blade made a streak in the darkness, and Yashita's pistol hand fell away from Sarah's head. Sarah was sprayed with blood as she pulled free of her captor's other arm. Then all movement stopped as all eyes fixed upon Seito. He held the samurai sword high. Blood was coursing down his chest, staining the yellow plastic of his chemical suit. With a scream of outrage, he brought the sword down and into Yashita, severing him from the neck to the center of his chest. The old man watched his enemy collapse. He continued to stand there quietly, sword unmoving, his brown eyes focused on the dead man before him. Then he slowly allowed the sword to fall from his arthritic grasp as he crumpled onto his right side.

The man in black ran forward with his weapon still trained on Yashita's head. When he saw no movement, he quickly went to Sarah and, with one powerful arm, lifted her to her feet. Carl and Danielle ran toward the fallen Seito. Carl immediately saw the bullethole in the old man's chest and exhaled in exasperation. He then lowered himself and raised Seito's head. Danielle sadly took the old man's hand into her own.

THERE WERE SEVEN commandos all together. Six of them had herded the students and Fallon into a protective bunch at the cave's opening; all were in good shape, from what Carl could see.

"Had to go and play soldier again, huh?" he asked the dying Seito.

"The . . . man . . . had no . . . honor."

Carl nodded.

Seito smiled as he looked at the man in black Nomex. The old man started to say something in English but failed.

Instead he croaked out a few sentences quickly in Japanese, the words slurring as he finished, and then his eyes closed and he was gone.

"I wonder what he said," Carl asked, brushing some gray hair out of the old man's eyes.

"He said he had heard what Yashita said about there being no heroes left," Danielle translated.

The man in black removed his night-vision gear, gas mask, and hood in one movement. Jack Collins, the director of security for the highly secretive Event Group and Carl's boss, looked down at Seito.

Danielle frowned. "He said that Yashita was wrong; where there are good men, there will always be heroes."

4

ALTOGETHER there were sixteen Japanese Red Army faction members dead, including their cell leader, Tagugi Yashita, the most wanted man in Japan. The embarrassment of the Japanese government of having a known and wanted terrorist so deeply ensconced in the Okinawa civil authority would be something debated for many years to come. But Yashita had indeed used his family influence to place himself as deeply undercover as he could, biding his time while directing the assaults on Japan's officialdom from the safety of his governmental position, even receiving notices of gains against the JRA movement. His activities would scar the government for many years.

The Japanese Army Special Forces unit that had planned and carried out the assault on the cave complex had allowed Major Jack Collins access to the operation only because Jack had had a hand in training their officers in the fine art of covert assault years before. The information Jack had given them was also a deciding factor in allowing him to come along, with the Japanese military believing fully that he was still a part of the Fifth Special Forces out of Fort Bragg. But little did they know he had been on detached service to Department 5656 for the past year and a half.

The Japanese assault element was now working closely with the home island's chemical warfare department for the safe handling and removal of the powdered agent. Altogether, 865 pounds of the unknown powder was present in the hold of the old junk.

Sarah McIntire walked up to Jack and didn't say anything; she simply grabbed his wrist for a brief moment and squeezed. Collins winked at her.

"How in the hell did you know what was happening here?" Carl asked, walking up to Jack as soon as he had made sure Fallon and his graduate students were safe and secure outside.

Collins safed his Ingram and eased it onto his shoulder; the whole time he never took his eyes off Sarah. Then he finally looked around and found the person he wanted to speak to, Danielle Serrate.

"Since it had been a woman who called Director Compton on his private line at Group two days ago, and we know it hadn't been Sarah, because we couldn't get through to you or Mr. Everett on your radios—if you check to see, I suspect they have been tampered with—and since we can eliminate Dr. Fallon's students because they don't even know we exist, may we assume it was you, Miss . . ."

Carl shook his head. "Jack, this is Danielle Serrate, the head of the Commission des Antiquités of the government of France."

Danielle stepped forward, her chemical suit was unzipped and the upper half tied at her waist. Carl saw that she had a few large scratches on her arms, but other than that she had come through the hostilities with little damage.

"The United States government is indebted to you. But if I may ask, why call us? French commandos would have been more than happy to jump into the fray," Jack asked.

She clicked the safety back on her Beretta and then placed the pistol in her satchel. "My government does not know about this operation. I was on a personal leave of absence."

"Okay, now can we have your real name?"

"Jack, her married name is Farbeaux," Carl said in a low tone.

"I no longer associate myself with my ex-husband, Mr. Everett. I believe I informed you of that earlier."

"Well, the plot thickens," Jack said, turning from Danielle to Carl. "That would explain how she came by Director Compton's private phone line." Jack turned back to the Frenchwoman. "Ms. Serrate, may I offer you our hospitality and a chance to explain yourself?"

"I am afraid I cannot allow you to take me to the Japanese authorities, as that would leave too much explaining to do to my government."

"No problem; we have a ride coming that'll take us to a secure location. I think we can leave the Japanese government out of this one."

"This is not the sort of hospitality I would expect after aiding you in saving all of these lives."

"That's what I'm curious about, ma'am—just why would the ex-wife of an antagonist contact us instead of using her own national resources? Commander Everett, assist our savior outside. I believe our ride is here," Jack said, as the sound of a helicopter could be heard outside of the cave.

THE GRAY MH-60 Seahawk flew low to avoid becoming an unknown blip on any airborne radar. The navy chopper skimmed only a few feet above the masts of Japanese fishing vessels. Jack Collins, Sarah McIntire, and Carl Everett, still in their covert guise, sat calmly without talking. Their cover as naval special weapons people was still intact, a story sanctioned by Niles Compton and the president of the United States. Danielle had seen dossiers on all three from her husband's files recovered in the raid on his Los Angeles home. She knew Sarah to be a new second lieutenant in the U.S.

Army, the new head of the Geology Department. Sarah had been an integral part in another mysterious operation in the American desert last year. The same with Jack Collins; it was rumored in the dark places where governments meet that it was the major who had actually headed the bizarre mission that had confronted a UFO. Danielle had only heard rumors, only bits and pieces about the Event from intelligence speculation.

The person that interested her most was Lieutenant Commander Carl Everett, a former SEAL. Currently it was surmised by French intelligence that he was the number two man in the Group's security department, under Collins. The man was a brute. But he intrigued her nonetheless. Maybe it was his immediate dislike for her, she didn't know, but she would learn as much about him as she could. He wore his emotions on the outside and thus could be very helpful to her in the future.

As she thought this over, the Seahawk started climbing at a high rate of speed. Danielle adjusted her earphones and leaned over in her seat toward Major Collins.

"Am I to assume I am to be taken to a small CIA trawler off the coast and *asked* some questions, to a little ship of torture perhaps?" she asked, raising her right brow.

Carl snorted and turned away, shaking his head. Sarah just absently scratched her nose. Jack Collins leaned forward and in all seriousness pointed out the side window. "No ma'am, no torture, no CIA, and definitely not a small ship," he said, his blue eyes never leaving hers.

Danielle turned to where the major was indicating and was stunned for the first time in many years. She tried not to show it as she looked upon the largest object she had ever seen in her life that wasn't anchored to the ground. The Nimitz-class aircraft carrier was making at least thirty-plus knots. Her massive bow tossed the green seas high into the air as she cut through the Pacific 130 miles off the coast of Okinawa.

The Seahawk crew chief lowered his microphone so he could speak to the others on board the naval version of the Blackhawk.

"Ma'am, please sit back for landing, and welcome to the USS *George Washington*."

THE CAPTAIN'S QUARTERS aboard *Big George*, as the men fondly called their ship, were spacious and very well appointed for a United States naval vessel. The skipper had excused himself and allowed the members of the Event Group to utilize the largest and most secure cabin on the ship to debrief the foreign national. The captain of *Big George* didn't believe they were any sort of naval special weapons people. He could smell CIA.

As the mess stewards brought in coffee and a small tray of sandwiches, Jack took the time to remove his Nomex assault gear. He would have to thank SEAL Team Six, which was aboard, for the loan. Sarah poured everyone coffee and sat heavily in one of the overstuffed chairs that lined the conference table. Her arm had been tended to by the ships surgeon and the painkillers they had given her were dragging her down.

There was a rap on the cabin door and navy lieutenant JG Jason Ryan stepped in. He smiled at everyone and walked up to Jack, who was wiping his hands on a face towel. He shook Jack's hand.

"Glad to see you made it in one piece, Major," Ryan said as he turned to shake the hands of Carl and Sarah.

"Are you getting reacquainted with old friends?" Jack asked, as he sat down and pulled his cup of coffee toward him. "Ms. Serrate, this is Jason Ryan; he used to fly off these carrier things the navy plays with. He works for me and the Group now."

Danielle took a sip of her coffee and nodded toward Ryan, who took a chair next to Sarah and winked at her.

"By the way, Jack, the captain has cleared Ms. Serrate here for a flight leaving within the hour aboard a C-2A

Greyhound heading for Narita International in Tokyo. Director Compton has arranged a first-class flight out of there for our guest to Paris." Jason looked over to the redheaded Serrate. "The director wished to pass on his personal thanks for the warning you gave us that Mr. Yashita wasn't who he seemed to be."

"Can you explain how you knew this?" Jack asked.

"I came across Yashita's name in my ex-husband's file on this site. It said that he was a man of unscrupulous nature, and was known to the Okinawans as Mr. Asaki. So, when we were introduced to that gentleman on the island, it wasn't a stretch to put two and two together and that is why I called your director. Now, am I to be released?" she asked, looking from Ryan to Jack.

"As far as we know, you're not wanted by Interpol, the FBI, or any other foreign intel service; in other words, Ms. Serrate, we can't link you to any of your husband's transgressions," Jack said.

"To make it crystal clear, we can't arrest you for being married to an asshole and murderer," Carl added, looking directly at Danielle, waiting for a reaction.

Jack cleared his throat. He was watching the subdued anger rise on the Frenchwoman's face. "The million-dollar question, Ms. Serrate, is why you were there in the first place."

Danielle placed her cup of coffee down on the table. "Several months ago I became aware of my ex-husband's interest in the rumors of this site on Okinawa. In this and several other locations across the world where there were bizarre rumors of lost ships, cities; anywhere there could be found the legends of ancient alchemists—advanced science, if you will. Why? I do not know, as my husb . . . ex-husband's schemes are his own. But he has become an embarrassment to my government, my department, and to me. As his current interest seems to be beyond his normal pursuits, I believe he may be mixed up with foul elements that may be of concern to both your government *and* mine."

"So, tell us what you've got," Jack said, knowing that a hidden tape recorder was running, taking down everything the Frenchwoman was saying.

"I thought he would have been here in pursuit of that vessel. We came across a safe house in Mexico and another in Los Angeles, where we uncovered several research items on the possibility of an ancient weapon of mass destruction that was buried with that ancient junk," she said as she took a sip of her coffee. "It was my hope he would show himself here so I could cancel his bogus affiliation with my government. And I wished to do this in front of his most ardent enemies, as proof of my department's commitment at cooperation."

"You and he were married for how long?" Carl asked, standing and walking over to the silver coffee service and pouring another cup. He then walked over and refilled Danielle's.

"I married him when I was eighteen."

"Please continue, Ms. Serrate," Jack said.

"My husband has been quite . . ." She stumbled for the right word to use. "He's been rogue for some time and is up to some very disconcerting research, for a reason that I cannot yet fathom. He even had a complete scientific investigative report commissioned on an obscure legend about a Spanish expedition in Brazil that supposedly took place over five hundred years ago, a very expensive research project."

"Do you have anything else he may be working on?" Sarah asked her.

"All I have is that he has found a new financier and has been dealing with an American professor on a project. I was hoping it was Professor Fallon and the Okinawan site. Now I fear I am at a dead end."

Jack looked at his watch. "I'm afraid we're out of time. Mr. Ryan, would you escort Ms. Serrate to the flight deck, please, and get her outfitted?" He faced the director of the French variation, albeit a far weaker version, of his very own organization. "May I assume we can count on cooperation with your agency instead of harmful competition in the future?"

Danielle stood and pushed her chair in. "That is not up to me, or you, I'm afraid. Times are dangerous and people aren't very trusting in these very violent days. But I will promise you this: where I can, I will forward as much information as possible if it affects your government where Colonel Farbeaux is concerned. I will start there."

"You do that," Carl said, as he held her eyes. "But we won't hold our breath."

"Before you go, can you let us in now on just what it was that was in those containers?" Jack asked. He looked at her sharply.

Danielle returned the stare. Obviously this man was good at his job. He knew she was aware of what they had been dealing with all along.

"The most virulent form of anthrax that has ever been produced, enough to kill most of a continent if unleashed."

"I think you could have informed us earlier," Carl said angrily as he glared at the Frenchwoman.

Danielle returned the hateful look and then turned away to follow Ryan out of the cabin. Carl watched her go without further comment, pushing his full cup of coffee away from him in disgust.

"I told you she liked you," Sarah half-joked.

THE ZACHARY EXPEDITION
BASE CAMP, BLACK WATER TRIBUTARY

"HAVE you seen the professor?" Robby shouted.

Kennedy looked past Robby and saw that two of his men were missing. The animal's assault had caught them in the middle of changing positions inside the mazelike tunnels and shafts.

"No, the last time I saw her she was . . . she was injured—that's all I know, kid. I just hope my two men are with her," he said loudly above the din of rushing water. He moved his flashlight from Robby to the shaft they had dove into at the last moment before the creature had brought the tunnel's ceiling down upon the survivors. A split second afterward he had heard automatic weapon fire coming from the other side of the rock fall.

Robby, Kelly, and three others had come from somewhere down the opposite direction where another small group had run to.

"Kid, is there a way out back there?" Kennedy asked, his flashlight revealing the scratches and filth that covered Robby's face.

"Yeah, but it leads right back into another tunnel, and you know what's waiting for us out there, right?" He looked at the man for a moment, noticing for the first time the deep gouges that crisscrossed his black wetsuit. A few were ringed with Kennedy's blood. "Hey, you know what's there, right?" he repeated. "You guys did something to piss it off, didn't you? Just who in the hell are you guys? Because of you, we're dead!" the boy screamed.

"Not unless it can be in two places at once," Kennedy answered. "It's not in the lagoon, because I'm pretty sure that big bastard is in here with us somewhere."

Robby was about to say something to the effect that he suspected there was more than one of the beasts, when they heard the primal roar of the animal. The sound was seeping through the rock slide the beast had created in its attempt to kill Kennedy and his people. The hoarse cry was bone chilling.

"Let's get the hell out of here, it could be anywhere. It must know this shaft as well as it knows that damned lagoon." Robby turned and waved the two women and one man forward. "Come on, guys, we'll go with Dr. Kennedy, he has a plan," he lied. Then as he counted heads he saw he was one short. "Where's Kelly?" he shouted.

"Who's Kelly?" one of the girls asked as she whimpered in pain from a possible broken arm.

"I mean Leanne, Leanne Cox!" Robby remembered her alias.

"We lost her somewhere back there," the girl answered. "She was angry because she wanted to go back and find Helen. She went back, I think." The frightened girl kept looking from Rob to her rear, terrified something was back in the darkness waiting to spring.

"Oh God, no," he said as he turned and fixed the man in the wetsuit with a withering glare. "Look, Kennedy, get us out of here any way you can; I have to find that girl!"

Kennedy didn't like having any extra baggage, but what could he do? Shoot them? No, they needed one another if they were to escape this valley. As Robby pushed angrily by, Kennedy saw that the other surviving girl was breaking out in a rash. He could tell she was feverish as she brushed against him. *God*, he thought, *another one?* The girl wore a faraway look as she reached out for Robby. Her once blue eyes were half covered in semitransparent pus. Kennedy closed his eyes to shut out the sight. This girl, Casey, he thought her name was, would mark the seventh member of the expedition to come down with the poisoning. For all he knew, they all had it. He knew he did; it had started this morning with vomiting, just as the others' had. As the three survivors from the lagoon pressed ahead of him, Kennedy pulled back the charging handle on his MP-5 machine gun and followed, stepping ahead and taking the lead.

HALF THE EXPEDITION, including three of his men, had been caught on the shore at the base camp. He had assigned the men to watch the sick kids that had started coming down with what looked like a bad rash. It was soon followed by fever and the shakes. Diarrhea and severe vomiting was a stage that most of the sick had stabilized at when the professor announced it was time to leave. He realized his responsibility for the people in his party after they had fielded ridicule from not only himself, but Robby also. He was reminded that they were up against not only the animals of this godforsaken valley, but also an invisible disease that struck anyone who had ventured to the lower levels of the ancient mine.

The camp was hit before they could get off a call to the mine teams inside the endless catacombs of shafts where they were gathering the last of the specimens Helen had arranged to take back with them. Then, not ten minutes after the slaughter onshore, the animal, or animals, had struck them in the mine. It had attacked the party as a whole and then hunted each splintered group down one at a time. Upon separation of the larger group, they were taken down piecemeal. Now, as far as Kennedy was concerned, this was the last group. It was a terrible assumption, but one that had to be made. He was on his own and he had collateral baggage he knew couldn't make it out of here alive. He had to move, and move as fast as possible, because he had the distinct feeling that the creatures who watched over this place weren't just killing them for being there. They were being tracked and hunted for breaching some kind of ancient rule. And he figured the hunters would be merciless in their pursuit to make sure no one left the valley.

IT WAS CLOSE to two hours later that they saw daylight ahead. All four of them froze, almost afraid to hope that it was real. None of them had expected to ever see sunlight again.

"Okay, we can't go running out of here attracting attention to ourselves. Kid, what about the barge and ship—did either one run aground?"

"No, the ship went down like a rock. The barge stayed afloat for about an hour, but it eventually went down, too," Robby whispered. "A few things came to the surface and we gathered what we could and beached them near the base camp on shore, but then . . . then the creature hit us. Most didn't stand a chance. The sick were caught right in their beds and killed quickly. Some ran to the water where something else attacked them, a larger animal, long necked. I don't know what happened to them after the screaming started. I tried to radio the professor and you, but there was no answer."

Kennedy watched the kid. He had been impressed with Robby since the expedition had started; it was a shame he couldn't allow him to live.

"We didn't know what to do since you went into the mine two days ago, so we traveled north along the lagoon until we saw that." Robby pointed at the opening. They could see the small waterfall that covered the prehistoric cave's mouth and hid it to nature's perfection. A thousand times smaller than the large falls that disguised the main entrance to the mine, this fall was easy to miss.

"Listen, you saw what was in the mine, right? I don't have to spell it out for you?"

"I saw enough to make sure you and whoever you work for will stay behind bars for a long fucking time." Robby spat out the words as if they tasted sour. Then he realized he had shot his mouth off to the wrong sort of man.

Kennedy reached into his wetsuit and pulled out his old dog tags. On the chain was a strange-looking key. It was thick, then thin, then thick again. It was about six inches long and one inch wide, and almost round as it corkscrewed to a bulbous end. He held it up to examine it and made sure it wasn't damaged.

"Listen, one of our containers had a yellow rubber casing around it. It was about three feet long and two feet wide. Was that one of the crates you and your people salvaged from the ship? It was sitting on deck and should have come free once the boat went under."

Robby thought a moment, his eyes never leaving the strange key. "Yeah, I think that was one that we pulled ashore—what is that?" he asked. The key made him forget his sudden anger at Kennedy.

"Look, vacation's over; it's time to cut our losses and try and head out of here following that old trail your professor found a few days ago."

The girl behind Robby stepped forward. Her voice cracked and she looked around nervously. "That container you were asking about?"

Kennedy eyed the scared girl. "Yeah?"

"I don't know how, but I swear it was in the main chamber, by the falls. I only noticed when—"

Kennedy grabbed the girl by her thin arms and lightly shook her.

"The box is in the mine? Are you sure?"

Robby reached down and pried Kennedy's hands off the girl's arms. He then stepped between her and the man who now had a crazed expression on his face.

"That's enough, what the hell's wrong with you?"

"Get them out the best you can, kid. I have to get to that container."

"What about everyone else?" Robby asked, trying to keep his voice low so the others couldn't hear. His thoughts kept returning to Kelly and how helpless he felt, trapped in here.

"Look, kid, there is no one else. I saw that animal close-up and I don't think it had a merciful bone in its huge-ass body. Maybe the smaller one, but not that big-ass mother-fucker."

"How in the hell could it outthink us like that?" Robby moaned.

"I saw its eyes. They were like nothing I've ever seen before," Kennedy said as he pulled the half-empty magazine from his automatic weapon and inserted another. "It's smarter than us, kid; this is its turf and we're the visiting team. According to Zachary, its kind has been knocking around this world for one hell of a long time, a lot longer than us, at least seventy million years longer." He gripped the key in his right hand, wrapping its chain painfully tight around and around his wrist.

"It didn't strike us until you went into the mine; even then it still allowed gold to be taken out for examination. What happened to change things?"

Kennedy knew exactly what happened but wasn't going to be the one to volunteer the information. What remained of Zachary's team had not been in the main chamber, so what was there would remain a secret. They should never have brought out samples. He alone was responsible for that. He had basically killed all of those kids who became ill—and his own men, as well, in the usual attacks that followed; not only that, he had jeopardized his mission and his employers were not very understanding of failure.

Casey, the young girl with the sickness, suddenly screamed. Robby and Kennedy jumped. She was pointing at a shadow that had passed in front of the sunlit falls outside. The two men looked but saw nothing. Kennedy kept his weapon pointed in that direction nonetheless. He was about to lower it when a sudden, piercing scream almost made him pull the trigger. Robby reacted and pushed the barrel of the machine gun downward as one of the small animals ran down the damp shaft from the lagoon outside.

"No, its one of the Grunions," he said and he caught the small creature as it leaped into his arms. The professor had jokingly named them for the small fish that come onto Southern California beaches at times, using their small legs.

"Goddamned thing, why do they have to scream like that?" Kennedy asked, shaking his head.

Robby rubbed the scaly little animal between the eyes and calmed it. "I don't know, haven't exactly figured that out yet," he said, as a sad look crossed his features. Kelly had fallen in love with these strange creatures and had many theories as to their evolution. God, he prayed she had somehow escaped this massacre.

Suddenly the mine wall behind Casey split and crashed in. The roar of the large creature numbed their minds as it struck Casey and then the man and the girl with the broken arm. The man that was dressed the same as Kennedy, in a black wetsuit, was slammed hard into the rock wall as the small creature sprang from Robby's arms. Kennedy fired at the beast but his rounds only struck wall as he was thrown backward by the impact of the falling rock. He tried to move his legs but they were under at least a ton of rock. He lifted the MP-5 and fired again, knowing the dust obscured his target to the point that he couldn't be sure if he hit anything. The screams of the second woman were cut short suddenly, as if her volume control had been shut down.

"Get the hell out of here, kid," Kennedy yelled to Robby, who had jumped free of the rocks into the safety of the mine shaft. "Go find another way out!"

Robby turned and didn't hesitate as he sprinted down the small river of water that covered the shaft floor. As he sped into the dark he felt the small creature close on his heels, the small claws splashing through the water. He rounded a bend and the light was suddenly cut off as he entered the shaft that never saw outside illumination. He would have reached for one of the ancient torches that lined the old tunnel but he was terrified it would draw the other, vicious animal his way if he lit one.

The tunnel was suddenly lit up by a long burst of automatic gunfire. That was quickly followed by screams. It was Dr. Kennedy. He yelled and then screamed again as the sound of rocks being pushed aside came to Robby's ears. Then Kennedy fell silent and Robby didn't wait to hear any more. He turned and ran, the small creature now leading the way. Then he started crying and felt he would never stop.

As he rounded a bend that put him into the far reaches of the mine the Spaniards had called El Dorado, he heard the triumphal roar of the wild animal as the protector of the valley once again proclaimed his superiority against the intruder.

The second expedition to the hidden valley of the lagoon had come to the same end as the first.

The creature roared once again as the darkness engulfed Robby, wrapping around him like a blanket, and sent him on a headlong flight away from the God of the River.

Calm filled the beautiful valley as birds sang their songs

and the small hairless creatures waited for their God to grow still once again.

MADRID, SPAIN

The archbishop yawned as he slid the strap of his coveralls up over his shoulder, trying to do so without spilling his tea. It was still predawn, so he reached out and turned on the interior floodlights that had been arrayed around the church for the workmen to see by in the darkened cathedral. As his eyes adjusted to the bright light, he saw the ugly skeletal scaffolding that had been erected, and shook his head. His eyes traveled to the frescoed ceiling where art restorers had been working to repair the magnificent frescoes using the godawful-looking scaffolds to do so. He sipped his tea and then noticed something out of the morning norm. He lowered the cup and squinted through his thick glasses. A man was sitting in one of the front pews looking toward the dais. He had his arms outstretched, resting casually on the backrest of the long wooden pew.

"Santos?" the archbishop called out, thinking it was the renovations interior foreman.

The figure didn't move.

Archbishop Santiago was about to call out again when a hand fell on his shoulder. He was startled enough to spill his tea. As he turned he saw a large man with a shadow of a goatee standing behind him.

"Please," the man gestured toward the seated man at the front of the cathedral, "he has a few questions for Your Eminence." The words were spoken in the New World Spanish accent that Santiago immediately placed as South American.

Hesitantly the archbishop followed the large man toward the front of the church. As he approached he could see that the figure in the peak was dressed in a black suit and sat with his right leg crossed over his left. The seated man was looking at the magnificent figure of the sculpted Christ the church had received as a gift from the Vatican Archives twenty years before. Santiago sensed danger in this man.

"This is a marvelous piece. Isn't it by Fanuchi?" the man asked as he continued to look up at the Christ as depicted upon the cross.

"A modest work of Michelangelo's," Santiago said. He sat down, as his rather large escort had suggested with a gesture of his equally large hand.

"Amazing, a Michelangelo piece that has never been cataloged," the man said as he turned to face the archbishop. He was smiling. "You must have friends in high places, Your Grace."

"It's but a modest piece," Santiago responded. "Are you here to steal it?" he asked, placing his tea cup on the seat beside him.

The man laughed and removed his arms from the back of the wooden pew. "As magnificent as the work is, alas, no, I am here on an entirely different matter."

The archbishop now saw three more men had stepped into the light from the surrounding blackness of the early morning.

"And that is?"

"Your visitor of a couple of months ago, a Professor Helen Zachary, she's the reason I have come to visit you at this magnificent cathedral. I need for you to share with me the information you so readily imparted to her."

Santiago could see that the man, if he were to stand, would be tall. His blond hair was well combed. He watched as the man absentmindedly brushed some lint from his pants.

"I am afraid I fail to see your interest in a private meeting I had with Ms. Zachary."

The man smiled and leaned closer to the archbishop, once again placing his right arm on the back of the pew as he whispered, "The diary, Your Eminence, she copied two pages from the diary of Captain Padilla. Unfortunately, my former partner was also very accomplished at forgery and falsified the copies she gave to me. Now the woman has further betrayed me and gone off to adventureland without me."

"I will tell you the same thing I told Ms. Zachary, Señor—?"

"Farbeaux, Henri Farbeaux. And please, do not bother saying you did not acquiesce to her request, that would be wasting valuable time, both mine, and by the look of your renovation, yours also. Time is a quantity neither my benefactor nor I have in abundance. So please, answer carefully and be precise. Are you willing to assist my men and myself in acquiring the diary of Captain Padilla? As I said, answer carefully," he warned as his smile faded.

Santiago looked from Farbeaux toward the men, who calmly watched the proceedings. There was no doubt in his mind he was in trouble; his only hope was that he could stall them long enough until the workmen came in.

"I have seen that look a hundred times, Your Grace. You see, it's in the way the jaw sets and the eyes don't blink. You are thinking to delay in answering until help arrives. But I assure you this will have been all a memory by the time that happens. Either a memory or a news story, you choose."

Santiago heard one of the large men knock something over. When he turned toward the sound he saw that a fifty-five-gallon drum of paint thinner now lay open on its side. The clear liquid was emptying onto the floor, which had been lined with white painter's tarps.

"San Jerónimo el Real," Farbeaux said as he looked the archbishop directly in the eyes. "A most famous and beautiful structure. It would be a shame to lose such a wonderful church to such a tragic accident as fire. But things like that happen during a major renovation. Careless and senseless things." The blond man stood and buttoned his suit coat. "I personally would hate to see this tragic event come to pass, but if these walls do not contain the information I seek, that would be most upsetting, and I become rather accident prone when I'm upset. Now, the diary, if you please. That woman already has a month's head start on me."

Santiago was horrified at what was happening around him. The smell of the paint thinner had reached his nostrils.

From the expression on the face leering over him, he knew beyond any doubt this man would carry out his threat. If it was just his old leathery life he would defy this man, but the church? He could not risk it.

"Your Eminence, time is a factor here, for both you and me. I truly hate threatening something as magnificent as this cathedral, but I will burn it to the ground without hesitation. I need that diary!"

"Please, I have the diary, you may take it, but do not harm the church."

Farbeaux ordered his men to right the drum of paint thinner and recap it. He instructed them to clean up what had spilled. The archbishop would never know that Farbeaux would never have given the order to burn the five-hundred-year-old church. That would have been sacrilegious to him. Farbeaux wasn't put in the world to destroy such beauty; he was born to own it. Fortunately, the archbishop would stay quiet about the theft of the Vatican secret because he loved his church so much; the mere threat of burning it to the ground would keep him silent. There would be no need for violence, even if Farbeaux's benefactor had given him orders to the contrary. He regretted even the threat of violence as he assisted the old man to his feet, but knew that was the way of the world. And the prize he was seeking was far too valuable. He was willing to do anything to attain it.

He smiled at the old man and watched as the men he had been assigned did as they were told. He knew they had been given orders to assist in eliminating all who knew about the map, but he would make sure the archbishop avoided any *accidents*.

FARBEAUX LOOKED AROUND the empty cathedral to make sure he was the last man to leave. He had assured the archbishop no harm would come to the exquisite building, and, after all, he was a man of his word.

He followed the other men to three vans and they made their way to the airport. As the last vehicle exited the gravel drive, a man in a rented sedan stepped from the driver's side of his car and watched to make sure the team was not going to return. His pencil-thin mustache had small beads of sweat lined above and below it. The man removed the set of polarized sunglasses he was wearing. He adjusted his light green sport coat and walked past the now idle work trucks and equipment. He made his way easily to the rear of the mammoth church and found a back entrance that was covered only in a thick sheet of plastic. As the dark-skinned man eased the plastic away from the door frame, he placed his hand just inside the sport coat and then stepped into the cooling shadows of the small alcove that led into the back of the church. When he saw there was no one present, he stepped gracefully around several piles of books that had been removed from the shelves of the small alcove, and moved up to a door that read OFFICE. He leaned close and listened for movement. He heard only the soft hum of an air conditioner. He reached out and lightly turned the brass doorknob and eased it open. He saw movement and immediately brought out a nine-millimeter pistol with a long black silencer attached.

The rotund man dressed in work overalls didn't hear the door open as he was busy picking up books from the floor around a large desk. The man at the door noticed that the big man seemed to be crying. The gunman turned away and looked behind him to make sure his entrance into the office area had gone unnoticed. When he turned back the man in the office had straightened up and was just standing there; he was looking right at the doorway where the gunman stood. The man opened the door all the way. Archbishop Santiago placed the books he was holding on the desk, then slowly crossed himself as he saw the object the man was holding.

The tall, thin assassin knew exactly who was standing before him and it angered him that this task had fallen to him, a man raised in the Catholic faith. The Frenchman had failed to carry out his explicit orders calling for a death that looked accidental. Now, because there was a severe shortage of time, that could no longer be accomplished.

"I was given the promise that nothing shall befall my cathedral," Santiago said as he reached into his coverall and felt for the crucifix there.

"And nothing shall befall your church, Your Excellency," the man said coldly in Spanish as he raised the silenced pistol.

6

EVENT GROUP CENTER
NELLIS AFB, NEVADA

ONE mile below the sands of Nellis Air Force Base, the department managers of the Event Group sat around the conference table of sublevel seven. The debriefing had gone mostly without comment from the department heads, as only Niles Compton, the Group's director, asked any questions. The conversation had centered mostly on the assistance they had received from the Frenchwoman and whether this may have possibly been an attempt by her to thaw relations between the United States National Archives and their French counterpart, the Commission des Antiquités, which had been strained for many years under a corrupted director and his aide, Colonel Henri Farbeaux. The French government knew nothing of the Event Group and Department 5656, as they thought the Group was just a section of the National Archives. For reasons he could never figure out, Niles suspected Colonel Henri Farbeaux had shared their existence with his ex-wife alone. He knew the reasons were selfish ones, but still the answer to why Farbeaux didn't tell the French government about the Group was beyond him.

"So, the person who called me on my private line was the new director. And she's Farbeaux's ex-wife?" Niles Compton asked. "Looks like you two owe her your lives," he said to Lieutenant Commander Everett and Second Lieutenant McIntire.

Carl and Sarah just nodded without comment.

"And she stated that she was hunting down Farbeaux to kill him?" he asked Jack Collins.

" 'Eliminate' was her word," Jack answered.

"I guess that's what you can call irreconcilable differences," Niles said without much humor.

The others around the table thought Niles was straining to make this meeting light, but the attempt failed when they looked into his worried eyes.

"The anthrax, have we generated a report yet on how it was manufactured by the Chinese seven hundred years before it was possible?" asked Virginia Pollock, deputy director and head of Nuclear Sciences.

"There's nothing official as yet from the Japanese government. Sarah did have a chance to speak with Danielle Serrate some before we left the island."

"Did she impart a theory?" Niles asked, turning and looking at the new second lieutenant.

"Well, it's a rough theory, but she thinks they used human blood, possibly intentionally infected with the anthrax antibodies carried by cattle. Really amazing for the time to have known the extreme nature of the infectious disease they were dealing with. Anyway, our Ms. Farbeaux, or Serrate if you prefer, thinks the ancient Chinese developed a way of synthesizing the anthrax organism in the animal blood and incubating it with human material inside clay ovens. Recent discoveries of alchemist's dwellings, actually very rudimentary laboratories if you will, have been recently uncovered just outside of Beijing. The buried site was complete with eight- and twelve-lens microscopes, amazing technology for the time. The Chinese took no chances on the spread of the anthrax so the whole laboratory system was destroyed, buried forever, or so they thought. Once the incubation cycle was tested, again we assume on human guinea pigs, they mixed the dried blood with nothing more than rice starch, thus rendering the anthrax in powder form as a weapons-grade airborne bacterial substance, very ingenious for the time. God only knows how many people died in its manufacture. The

Japanese can thank the heavens for the storm that sent that ship off course and the rest of Kublai Khan's invasion fleet to the bottom of the sea."

"And the former Mrs. Farbeaux thought her ex was going after the anthrax?" Niles asked.

"According to her, yes, he was. It seems our friend has expanded his interest to include weapons-grade material instead of just antiquities," Jack said. "She stated that was just one of several sites he had investigated. But since they had an eyewitness that said the Chinese junk was in reality buried inside a lava flow chamber on Okinawa, she took a leave of absence in the hope he would be there, that being the most viable site to date."

"Okay, I'll turn Ms. Serrate's interview tape over to the president and he in turn can ask the FBI and our *friends* at Homeland Security to keep an eye out for our French friend."

Niles looked around the table at his department heads. "All right, remember we have a briefing tomorrow at ten on the joint field trip to Iraq by the University of Tennessee and Cal Poly–Pomona. So I need names of Group personnel being assigned from the departments that are applicable." He looked at his notes, "That's you, Bonnie," he said, indicating Professor Bonnie Margate of the Anthropology Department. "And you, Kyle," he glanced at Kyle Doherty of the History Department. "Jack, I need a minimum of four security men on this trip. There's no need for a cover for them as it's Iraq—we'll just give them credentials from the State Department and National Archives; they'll be there to assist the Iraqi government at the site, okay?"

Jack nodded his agreement.

"You two." Niles pointed toward Sarah and Carl at the end of the long conference table. "If Jack agrees, stand down for a week. You did an excellent job out there. More than likely saved some lives. Be sure you get a good once-over in medical to make sure you didn't bring some of that Kublai Khan face powder back with you. Thank you, that's all I have."

The assembled group in the conference room moved for the door as the meeting broke up.

"Jack, you have a minute?" Niles asked.

Jack placed his case and notes back on the table. His uniform's silver oak leaves glittered in the light as he pulled out his chair and sat. "Sure," he answered.

"This development with Farbeaux is worrisome. Why would he switch interests when all he ever did was to go after antiquities? It's not making a whole lot of sense."

"I can't figure it myself. I did some rough estimating on the plane ride home. The anthrax, even if only thirty percent of it had been viable after so many years, it would have been worth five hundred million dollars on the open market."

"God almighty, Jack, would he have had any takers at that price?" Niles asked, astonished.

"That sum would have eliminated any low-budget fringe elements that pass themselves off as terrorists, but the new influx of Middle Eastern money has filled the wallets of JRA leadership and a few others, so they can afford it. Also, don't forget Osama bin Laden and his boys, so yeah, there are those willing to pay big money for crap like that. If we had had more time on this operation we could have passed this information on to the FBI through another channel and they could have set up some kind of sting and netted a whole bunch of bad guys," he said with regret.

"What in God's name is Farbeaux up to?" Niles asked, not wanting to comment on the lost opportunity.

Jack just sat there and shook his head. "You can bet your retirement pay it's not good, Niles."

BOGOTÁ, COLOMBIA

Farbeaux was feeling the jet lag. He sat and listened to the tirade of Joaquin Delacruz Mendez, chairman of the board, Banco de Juarez International Economica, as Mendez paced in front of him. The spacious boardroom was empty save for the two men.

"What's done is done, my friend, screaming will not return the professor to us. She has five, almost six weeks on us but, regardless of that, if we move quickly we can reach the area in a quarter of that time. It's a very good thing we did not go down and chase after her with the documents we had in hand; we would have gone the long way around through Brazil instead of the direct route through Colombia to the north. I can't believe she went right under our noses, through your own country."

Mendez didn't respond to the slight insult of having Professor Zachary and all her team and equipment take a route that had brought them through his own nation, but he did force himself to calm down. His temper had climbed in the years that followed the collapse of the larger and most organized of the Colombian drug cartels. Cartels in which he had garnered an immense financial empire by handling the money end of their drug transactions. While those he served were tracked down and killed one at a time or thrown into prison, he had stayed safely behind the scenes, actually assisting in a few captures and ambushes on the government's behalf, for his self-benefit.

"What about your equipment?"

"I took the liberty a week ago of ordering replacements from the States when I found out the good professor double-crossed us. We can be ready to travel in three days. With the equipment that was left on the dock in San Pedro with her little note attached, we should be fine. I guarantee, an hour after we arrive on site, whatever Zachary has found will be in our possession."

"You are very confident for a man that was so easily fooled by this woman," Mendez said with a mocking smile that made his thick mustache look comical.

Farbeaux was tempted to tell him just how ridiculous he looked, and then thought better of it. As he looked around the richly appointed conference room at the antiquities he had personally collected for Mendez, he was reminded of just how ruthless this man could be.

"My estimation is that she could not have arrived on site any sooner than eleven days ago. Her interest lay in areas outside of the El Dorado aspect. So she will be making time-consuming exploration in areas outside of the mine, looking for her amphibious legend."

"You're sure of that?" Mendez asked as he thought of the riches that the legend of El Dorado described—the very gold mine that had supplied the great Incan and Mayan empires of the gold they had used for thousands of years.

"My friend, I have never let you down. All your treasures here and in your home are there thanks to me. Because you trusted me to get them for you, so trust me on this."

"In the past year I have been pleased with your work and the many objects of beauty and wonder you have recovered for our mutual benefit. I will stake my entire fortune for a chance at El Dorado. And then I will gladly trade that for the mineral, if it is truly there. That is where the real El Dorado lay."

Farbeaux thought about Mendez and his last statement. Yes, he was positive there was gold in that small valley and, according to Padilla's description of the mine, it had to be the legendary El Dorado. But unlike himself, gold didn't interest Mendez any longer. The Colombian was after something far darker and less shiny than gold. As the Americans say, Mendez was after the gift that keeps on giving. And it had nothing to do with diamonds or gold.

"You are right, my friend, there has never been anything like this, all of this," Farbeaux said as he gestured at the priceless antiques of the Incan and Mayan civilizations, "is nothing compared to what awaits us."

Mendez paced to the large window looking down on Bogotá, placed his hands behind his back, and rocked in thought.

"Very well, I approve of your expedition," he said without turning.

"Excellent, I will get started right away," Farbeaux responded.

"There is one thing more. I will be accompanying you."

The Frenchman was taken aback for a moment, but showed nothing. Then he smiled. "Either here or there, does it matter where you receive what's coming to you? Of course, you are most welcome."

As Farbeaux left, Mendez turned and watched the large double doors close in his wake. Then he went to the long table and pushed a button on the console in front of his large chair.

"Yes?" a voice answered.

"This is Mendez; I have approved the operation in South America," he said.

"What is it you wish me to do?" the voice asked.

"I want wire taps on this Professor Zachary's phone at Stanford, and I want her office watched. I am curious to know if her absence has caused curiosity from the outside."

"Yes, I can do that."

"Anything else?" Mendez asked.

"*Sí, jefe*, it seems your French partner has recently made another large purchase of equipment not associated with the articles he told you about, which included ultrasound and other equipment stolen from a shipment belonging to Hanford National Laboratory. This fact and his failure to cover his tracks in Madrid make me believe he has his own agenda. Why this particular shipment should come from that field is suspicious, yes?"

"Enough so that we must keep a closer eye on our friend," Mendez answered thoughtfully as he broke the connection with Los Angeles.

7

THE GOLD CITY PAWNSHOP
LAS VEGAS, NEVADA
SEPTEMBER 5TH

FAMILY law attorney Stan Stopher sat in his rented Chevy and made sure the address was correct. He glanced at the envelope and the name, and they matched with what was on the old neon sign out in front of the building. Stan opened the car door and stepped into the Las Vegas heat that hit him as if someone had just opened the door of a blast furnace. He walked back to the trunk, retrieved the aluminum box, then hesitated. This act of delivering the case was tantamount to admitting that he would possibly never see her again. He knew she was in trouble, but for the life of him couldn't figure out why she was sending the fossil to a pawnshop.

He closed the trunk, walked up to the door, and pushed down on the old thumb plate. The door easily opened. He didn't notice that the cameras placed in the doorway and three more across the street followed his every move. He felt the blessed air-conditioning strike him in his face, instantly cooling his sweaty brow. He set the case down and removed his sunglasses as his eyes adjusted to the brightly lit shop, then retrieved the case and followed a cramped aisle toward the back of the shop. Two young girls were going through the used CD collection, but other than them, the pawnshop was empty of customers. A large black man was seated behind the counter, reading a newspaper, both of his muscular arms resting on the glass. At least, to an untrained eye, he was reading. Stan was an observant man and he saw the black man's gaze take in his thin frame. Then the man closed the paper and looked up at him overtly. His left hand stayed on the glass countertop but his right disappeared.

"Hi, there," the black man said. "What have you got? I hope it's not vinyl LPs; can't get rid of 'em anymore," he said, indicating the aluminum case.

Stan placed the shiny box on the counter and smiled. "No, I would never sell my collection of phonograph records."

"Oh, then how can I help you?" the clerk asked. His right hand was still not in view.

"Well," Stan reached into his shirt pocket and brought out the envelope and his business card, "a close friend of mine asked me to deliver this," he said, tapping the container and handing the black man the card.

The clerk looked more closely at the bright aluminum box and then stepped on a small red button on the floor by his foot.

"I see, Mr.—" he looked at the business card, "Stopher. Let's start with who your friend is and then we'll move on to what's in the case."

At that moment another man stepped out from behind a curtain at the back of the counter and without looking, only whistling, walked around to a rack of sunglasses. He started using a pricing gun left-handedly to mark the price of the glasses.

"Well, the container belongs to a very dear friend whose name is Professor Helen Zachary. She is director of Zoology at Stanford University, and what is in the box is for the recipient only."

"And that is?"

Without looking at the envelope he said the name he had memorized, "Dr. Niles Compton. Does the good doctor own this establishment?" Stan asked.

"He owns the building, we just lease. I can deliver this, as long as it's not a bomb," the clerk said and smiled. The man pricing sunglasses didn't. The fingers of his right hand were lightly tickling a Beretta automatic pistol lodged just inside the front of his shirt.

"No, nothing as exciting as a bomb, I'm afraid."

"Well, we can get it to him. Can I help you with anything? Maybe add to your collection of LPs?"

"No, thank you, your prices are kind of steep, I noticed." Then he became deadly serious. "Look, I need to know where this case is going. This is a very dear friend of mine and I'm worried beyond measure."

"Sir, if you were instructed to deliver this package to Dr. Compton, you can bet action will be taken to help. I'm sure someone will be in touch as soon as possible."

The attorney wasn't satisfied, but put his faith in the fact that Helen must have known what she was doing.

Staff Sergeant Will Mendenhall watched as the old man left the shop. He looked at the card and then over to Lance Corporal Tommy Nance, United States Marine Corps.

"We better get this X-rayed," said Mendenhall, standing from his stool, where he had been in easy reach of the .45 automatic holstered behind the display case. As he grabbed for the aluminum box, he heard the click of an M-16 being placed on safety from behind the curtain. "Watch the store, Corporal, and try to get those two girls to buy something."

Corporal Nance straightened his collar and walked over to the girls, his broad smile gleaming.

"Hi, there," he said as suavely as he could.

The tallest one turned around and smiled, revealing a mouth full of braces. She couldn't have been more than fourteen years old. Nance's interest deflated. He kept busy ticketing for the next twenty minutes, listening to the two underage girls giggle and flirt with him. *Sometimes gate duty truly sucked.*

THE BACK ROOM at the Gold City Pawnshop was no different in appearance than a hundred others within the Las Vegas City limits. Stored there were items just tagged as collateral and others that had been pulled off the shelf for not selling. It was the door in the back that led to the office that hid the wizard behind the curtain.

Staff Sergeant Will Mendenhall was sitting and looking at the aluminum case and shaking his head. He had just finished speaking with Lieutenant Commander Carl Everett, who had ordered the attorney followed. A two-man team was currently tailing Stanley Stopher to wherever he was staying. Just in case they needed him for any reason. When Mendenhall had explained what the X-ray had turned up, security protocol went into immediate effect. The case and envelope addressed to Director Compton was sitting on the watch commander's desk.

Mendenhall heard the elevator arrive from the lower level, and the false-fronted wall slide aside. He turned and stood when he saw it was not only Carl who had arrived, but Major Collins also.

"So, we have a skeletal hand in a box?" Jack asked.

"Yes, sir, wasn't expecting that," Mendenhall said with a smile.

"And our tail is still in contact with our attorney friend?"

"Yes, sir, they just checked in. It seems Mr. Stopher is heading for McCarran airport. You want them to follow along?"

Jack pursed his lips and thought. "I'll have the USC field team pulled off duty and tail him long enough to make sure he's who he says he is."

Jack looked the container over and then read the heading on the envelope. He then pulled the computer monitor around to face him and Carl. The X-ray image was still up and he examined it. "Nothing but the aluminum case, bone, and foam, with a hard rubber gasket lining the lid and soft neoprene for atmosphere evacuation. The computer is one hundred percent on this?"

"Yes, sir."

"Still, how is it that someone can walk right in off the street and know that this is a gate to the Group?" Carl asked.

"Simple, if he didn't know it was a gate and was instructed to deliver the item to this address by a former Group member," Mendenhall ventured.

Both Jack and Carl stopped talking and stared at the sergeant.

"Or maybe not," Mendenhall said, looking embarrassed for interrupting the two officers.

Jack looked from Mendenhall and then back to Carl, who slapped the sergeant on the shoulder.

"Look, Will, anytime that you see your commanding officers overlooking the obvious, feel free to make them look and feel like idiots," Carl said.

"Yes, sir."

"Well, let's play postman and deliver the mail," Jack said as he pocketed the envelope and lifted the container.

EVENT GROUP CENTER
NELLIS AFB, NEVADA

Two hours after they had delivered the strange box and envelope to Director Compton, Jack was with Sarah on the first vault level. He was supervising the installation of the new eye-scan security system that was to be patched into the Cray supercomputer, Europa, which would allow the new system to be fully operational in each of the eleven thousand vaults on the three levels of artifact storage. Sarah McIntire was in charge of the actual installation, due to her experience with the surrounding granite walls, as it wouldn't do to have a cave-in on the vault level. This particular level was one of the first excavated in 1944 when the caves underneath Nellis were expanded for the new home of the Event Group, as ordered by then president Roosevelt.

Jack tested the last system installed on this level by placing his right eye to the rubber-lined glass lens. The smoke-colored glass panel to the right printed out his name and rank and parent service. Then Europa, which replaced the sexy-voiced computer system of the old Cray, told Jack that he was cleared for Vault 2777 just as the fifteen-foot stainless-steel door opened with a hiss.

"Goddammit!" Jack said aloud when the familiar sexy female voice cleared him to enter. The last time he had worked with Europa, the electronic voice had been programmed with a new male auditory system, clean, functional, and definitely not sexy. Someone had gone back and intentionally synthesized the old female voice that sounded uncannily like Marilyn Monroe's.

"What is it?" Sarah asked as she stepped up with a clipboard after checking the wall and ceiling strata for the thousandth time.

"I'm going to ream Pete Golding's ass in the computer center. Someone changed the auditory program on Europa back to that female voice."

"There was a rumor that someone was going to do it. No one liked the male voice. It sounded too much like—" Sarah caught herself before she said it and bit her lower lip. "You want to get something to eat?"

"Sounded too much like what?" Jack asked, narrowing his eyes.

Sarah smiled as she pretended to write something on her clipboard.

"Lieutenant, while you're writing, you may as well place yourself on my shit list if you don't answer my question."

"All right, everyone thought it sounded like *you*. It was just too damned creepy."

"Like me? It didn't sound like me . . . who said it sounded like me? . . . it wasn't me at all," he protested.

Mendenhall joined them. "Last sensor is in on this level, Major," he said as he flipped a screwdriver into the air and caught it.

"Sergeant, did the Cray auditory system sound like me?"

Mendenhall stopped suddenly in his tracks. "You know, I didn't peel the plastic protectant off the monitor screen. I'll be right back and then—"

"You're not going anywhere; answer my question."

"It was weird, Major, I'm not kidding. It felt like Big Brother . . . and . . . well . . . it was just . . . strange," he said as he looked down at his boots.

"I told you."

Jack was about to say something when Alice Hamilton's voice came out of the speaker built into the vault's door frame: "Will Major Collins please report to the main conference room, please, Major Collins to the conference room."

"Hey, wasn't that Alice?" Sarah asked brightly.

Jack didn't respond at first. He looked at Sarah and then Mendenhall.

"We're not through with this voice imprint thing. I want to know who was in on it."

"You want us to rat on our comrades? The sergeant here said you would try and track down those involved . . ." She stopped when she saw Jack smile. "What?"

"Lieutenant, you just told him who was involved," Mendenhall said with his chin on his chest.

"And tell Commander Everett I'll be speaking to him also," Jack said as he turned and walked away.

Sarah flinched and closed her eyes, and the sergeant grimaced.

"Shit," both Mendenhall and Sarah said at the same time.

ALICE HAMILTON, THE semiretired administrative head of the Event Group, greeted Jack at the door just as she had when he had first arrived over a year ago. She was beaming and looking quite a bit younger than her eighty-one years. She was wearing her hair in her customary bun and holding her ever-present file to her chest. Jack walked up and hugged her.

"Alice, I forgot how your smile brightens this place up," he said, placing her at arm's length to look her over. "What the hell's going on? Did you find a fountain of youth out there?"

"Oh, knock it off," she said, embarrassed.

"How is the senator, getting along all right?"

"He's a bear, constantly pacing back and forth in his

study. I suppose Niles has told you he calls the poor man every other day, asking what's going on."

Jack had only worked with the former director of the Group on one mission prior to the president's retiring him, but in that short amount of time the former OSS operative and senator from Maine had made an indelible mark upon Jack's life. The man was, to put it frankly, brilliant.

"Niles said he looks forward to bouncing things off the senator; I'm sure he's no bother. So, what brings you here?" he asked.

Alice frowned and looked around the reception area. Niles had not yet exited his office across the way to begin the meeting, so she thought to take a brief moment and fill Jack in.

"Jack, we have a serious situation down in South America. A former member of the Group has gone and gotten herself . . . well, lost. She hasn't been heard from as she missed her call-in time to her associate three days ago."

"Go on," Jack said as he walked with her.

"Well, this professor was asked to leave by the senator fifteen years ago. She became obsessed with something she came across and couldn't let it go. It drove her close to insanity, she even went as far as to 'borrow' certain files from the Group, from the senator's private files as it turned out, and she accessed other areas, we're not sure which, but they had to have been serious intrusions for Garrison to act as harshly as he did. It was Niles who brought all of this to the attention of the senator back then; basically he was the one responsible for the Group's firing her."

Jack stopped and looked at Alice. His brows rose as he waited for the punch line.

"She was Director Compton's fiancée, Jack. They had been engaged for two years. I'm afraid Niles is real close to this situation, but we can't dismiss his participation in this, because the good professor may have stumbled onto something she has searched for a very long time. You have the power to say no to Niles for security reasons *if* he wants to go after her; just hear him out before you decide."

At that moment Niles Compton walked from his office with his new assistant following close behind. He saw Jack and Alice and nodded as he continued on to the large conference room. His assistant rolled her eyes as she fought to keep up. Jack gestured for Alice to proceed, and he followed her into the room.

FIVE MEMBERS OF the upper echelon of the Event Group were present in the room, and one person Jack didn't know. They all took their seats when Niles cleared his throat. The director picked up a remote control and punched in a button. A wide-screen television slowly slid down behind him.

Consult Group number one consisted of Jack, as head of the department's security; Niles, as director; and Alice, because she knew most of the 298,000 files and vault contents by heart and could access her amazing memory at a moment's notice. Then there was Virginia Pollock, the deputy director of Department 5656; Pete Golding, of the Computer Sciences Department; and, for a reason the others weren't privy to, Heidi Rodriguez, of the Zoology Department.

"I excused Mathew Gates from this meeting as it really didn't concern languages, at least not yet. I did ask Heidi here to join us, because for the past two hours she's been quite busy assisting me with some research and can speak for the scientific end of things." Niles gestured to the dark-haired diminutive woman of about forty, who smiled and nodded to the others.

Niles pushed a button on the remote and a three-dimensional image appeared on the screen behind him. The visual was assisted by a small multicolored plate that acted as a 3-D lens. It produced a clear and precise picture that would have been the envy of Hollywood.

"Good God, what is that?" Pete asked.

"It's a fossil that former Group member Helen Zachary's ex-husband sent back from Peru fifteen years ago, when he had been a construction consultant for the Peruvian government. They were dredging and widening three tributaries of the Amazon River, for added space for commerce along the river," Niles said. On the screen behind him, a full-color image of the fossil slowly turned 360 degrees.

Virginia Pollock cleared her throat.

"Yes, Virginia?" Niles asked.

"We're not going to start this again, are we? I mean—"

"I know what you mean. For those of you that don't know, Helen Zachary was terminated from the Group for her fanaticism about this fossil," he said, frowning in the direction of Virginia. "Things have changed. Helen came into possession of new information about the Padilla expedition," he said, looking around the room.

"You can learn about the legend of that expedition from the folders in front of you; due to the hurried nature of the situation, we will not cover the historical aspects of this at this meeting. We must move on," Alice said.

"Helen used the files she stole from the Group's first complex in Virginia, where our old data and equipment are stored. She deduced from those files where the diary of Padilla was possibly hidden in the Vatican Archives in 1874. It seems one of the files contained an old OSS report of an Army Corps of Engineers study of the region in the Amazon basin and its history from the late thirties to 1940. She used that information to track down one or two known sources that depict the exact route of the Spanish expedition. In short, she may have found the valley and the very lagoon detailed in the legend, as taken from the diary."

"Did she leave you the route, Dr. Compton?" Jack asked.

Niles smiled and removed his glasses. "Helen is a very complex woman, Jack. She trusted no one in her search for the origins of the fossil." He rubbed the bridge of his nose and then continued. "The Padilla legend has many parts; the diary and lost maps were only a couple of the stories to come out of that time. As Helen reported to us a few years ago, she discovered that the Vatican put the clamps on the diary, a supposed map Padilla had made in case the diary was lost, and two samples of something, probably gold, which the survivor *may* have carried out."

"So, if she had made these discoveries in the old files, why didn't the Group move on her request?" Jack asked.

"Because in the end, even with all of her data, it was all just circumstantial, no hard evidence at all. In the end, the Padilla legend is just that, a legend, a story handed down, about which not one single fact has come to official light."

"Fifteen years ago, the Group was split as to the authenticity of the legend, even though our top anthropologist was adamant that she was dealing with fact, not just a myth. Her department was able to finally verify that Padilla did actually exist and that he was regarded as one of Pizarro's best officers. The files that were stolen also detailed the rescue of a group of doctors from Princeton and the University of Chicago from Brazil in 1942. I don't know what she could have learned from them. The team of OSS men was led by our own Senator Garrison Lee."

"As I said, it's all just a fanciful legend," Virginia said as she pushed the file away from her. "What have we learned about this fossil?" she asked.

"I'll let Heidi answer your question. Please make it quick, Doctor."

"Well," Heidi Rodriguez said as she stood and walked to the screen. "I'll try and abbreviate my conclusions, although this specimen hardly calls for an abbreviated anything. To begin with, the age of the fossil is between four hundred and eighty and five hundred and eighty years old," she said, "an accuracy measurement of plus or minus one hundred years."

"What?" Virginia asked as she stared at the image on the screen.

"Yes, our methods of dating fossils are much improved since Helen Zachary was here. But then she suspected its age anyway, because of the legend." Heidi picked up a pointer. "Now, if you will look here you can see dried and hardened tissue, more than likely cartilage of some sort along the third knuckle of each digit, even the thumb. It appears to have been scaled tissue that stretched from digit to digit and between the index finger and thumb."

"What are you saying?" Pete asked as he took a break from chewing on his pencil.

"I'm saying that the creature this hand belonged to had webbed fingers. And that, ladies and gentlemen, is fact and not legend," Heidi said, looking at Virginia.

"Helen is missing. She left for South America five weeks ago and hasn't returned, hasn't checked in." Niles held up the letter Helen had left him. "She stated in this letter that the diary was in the possession of the Archdiocese of Madrid. She also stated she had received help from a man," he looked at his notes, "a Mr. Henri St. Claire, a French money man. We indexed that name with our files, and lo and behold, the name of an old friend came up as using that particular alias once before, Colonel Henri Farbeaux."

Silence at first greeted Niles's revelation. Of all the people in the world to have turned up, none of them expected that.

"It seems Dr. Zachary has fallen in with a bad crowd," Jack said finally.

"Yes, it would seem," Niles answered. "I have a call in to our supposed new friend in France, and Ms. Serrate has agreed to pay us a visit here in the States in case she can be of assistance. I don't like the fact that his name has surfaced twice in just a matter of a few weeks. And now with Helen's disappearance, I fear she may have stumbled onto something outside of her expertise." He gave the letter to Alice. "Bring everyone up to speed on what Helen had to say."

"I'll read just the pertinent information," she said, opening the letter.

"Read it in its entirety; leave nothing out," Niles said as he sat heavily into his chair.

Alice scrutinized him a moment, then read

Dearest Niles—
I know this must be a great shock to you, but you are the only person in the world I can turn to. Hold on

*to your hat, I've found the route of Padilla! I have the
exact location of the valley and am on my way this
very day. Imagine, after all these years, the valley
everyone told me did not exist, in my sights at last! I
wish you were coming along, but I know it would be
difficult for you for many reasons. I know I hurt you
deeply, but I must ask something of you, dearest Niles.
I'm afraid I have made some enemies in my quest for
my Captain Padilla outside of the senator and yourself. It seems people may, just may I say, be coming
after me. One of my earlier backers, a Mr. Henri St.
Claire, could come after the diary or discover the
trail of the papal medalists that led me to the archbishop. If you receive this letter, that means I have
found trouble. I cannot give you details of my route to
the site in case they track this letter to whom I left it
with, but you may begin with the archbishop of
Madrid. You should have no trouble from there in locating me (hopefully). The other items the legend says
came out with the Padilla diary are lost forever, I
tracked them through foreign-born papal medalists
involved in hiding them with papal authorization in
1874, and know for a fact that one of the items no
longer exists as it was lost forever. The other is still
buried at the Vatican Archives, having never left. But
thanks to those old dusty files the senator had, and
which I'm afraid I stole, I found the last and best
piece, the diary itself, hidden in Spain.*

*I think of you every day, Niles. Please forgive me
after all these years.*

Love always,
Helen

Everyone in the room looked from one to the other. None
of them looked at Niles and he seemed grateful for that
small mercy. He unknotted his tie and stood.

Virginia cleared her throat as she always did when she

had a point to make. "She seems to give away a lot of information for someone to track."

"No. We have the files in the Group's old facility in Arlington, so no one but us can get to them," said Niles.

"If Farbeaux is involved, that makes this . . . this situation delicate, to say the least. Obviously, according to his history, he would be after—" She opened the file and flipped through the pages until she found the one she wanted. She raised her glasses to her eyes and read, "The El Dorado of the Americas. Now if that is just a legend or not, it makes no difference. Between Farbeaux's making a play for whatever is there and those missing kids, I feel we must go. If we can, that is," Virginia said as she closed the file and looked at Niles expectantly.

"Jack?" Niles asked, holding his breath because he knew the auspices of the security department could veto the Event declaration for safety reasons. Niles knew he could override every voice in the room except Jack's; his was the only one Niles could not because of losses of Event personnel in the past. Jack's department was their only fail-safe to keep losses at a minimum.

"I agree, but regardless of the need you feel to hurry, we have many problems to overcome, the least of which is finding out just where in the hell it is we are going."

"I'm not as worried about that as much as what we'll find once our people get down there," Pete said as he stood.

There was a knock at the double conference room doors, and Niles's new assistant walked over to answer it. She stepped aside and a private first corporal in the red-trimmed coveralls of the Communication and Signals Department entered.

"I figured the first place to start is to get a team to Madrid to speak with the archbishop, for obvious reasons," Niles said. "PFC Hanley here was to make an appointment for us."

Instead of announcing anything to the gathered department heads, the private went straight to Niles and handed him a slip of flimsy, then departed the room. Niles scanned it and then looked around the table.

"Well, who's to go to Spain?" Virginia asked.

Compton handed the yellow paper to Alice and then removed his thick glasses.

"It looks like we have to do this the hard way," Alice said, as she lowered her own glasses, which dangled from a long gold chain. "It seems Archbishop Santiago was murdered yesterday afternoon."

The news was greeted with silence and dismayed looks.

It was Alice who broke it.

"This does not fit Mr. Farbeaux's profile at all. He's not a cold-blooded killer, he only takes life as a necessary function in saving his own skin, and the archbishop would have posed no threat to him."

"I think we may have to reevaluate certain realities here. Something is out there that is driving people to extremes, so let's start with blank paper and not go in with any preconceived notions," Jack said, looking from face to face.

"We'll have to start here, in our own files. The answer is there, Helen Zachary found it, and so will we. I'll break down everyone's duties and get back to you. As of," Niles looked at his watch, "0945, I am declaring an Event. I'll speak with the president. Excused," he finished.

PART THREE

THE SEARCHERS

The warning of Captain Padilla as described in his journal is that the Eden he has discovered, like the Eden of old, is still forbidden to be entered by God-fearing men, and to do so will bring the swiftest of punishments.

—Father Escobar Corinth,
Catholic representative to the Pizarro expedition,
in a letter to Pope Pius IX

8

BLACK WATER TRIBUTARY

ROBBY was alone. All he knew was that he was near the point of collapse. The heat in the lower levels of the mine was close to unbearable. Exhausted, he let his own weight work for him as he slid down the damp wall. His worn-out body came to rest on the rudimentary thousand-year-old wooden tracks that coursed through the ancient shafts like a million miles of twisting and undulating snake.

The tunnels had gone quiet as a tomb in the last forty hours as he fought his way through the darkness only to find he wasn't climbing but descending deeper into the great mine. The cascading water that had been engineered a millennium ago by unseen and mysterious hands flowed through the shafts beside the old transport track and wooden ore carts. Robby had taken the time to examine these strange canals and found that they had been carved out of the sheer rock flooring of the immense structure. He surmised that the canals were used to transport much heavier or larger loads to the lowest depths of the shafts. But that was the riddle. Why send gold to two different areas for processing? He had discovered rocks inside one of the old ore cars; they were speckled with large streaks of gold. These cars were on tracks that led from down below and went on toward the higher levels. He had tried to follow these upward but the tracks most times eventually traversed through small openings into shafts that were close, and he was afraid he would get caught in one. Try as he might, he would eventually lose the track and then before he knew it, he was heading down again. Disoriented and confused, he had decided to quit fighting it and follow the canals down.

As he tried to slow his breathing a noise caught his attention. He tried to penetrate the darkness to see what was around him. Then he heard it again. It sounded like whispering. Then suddenly a light flared from down below the next bend. His heart started pounding in his chest. He could now see the reflection of a large orange flame as it bounced off the water of the canal.

He steeled himself. "Hey!"

He heard two sharp yelps, as if his voice had caught someone totally unaware. Robby closed his eyes in thanks nonetheless when the flame around the bend started to advance toward him.

"Who's there?" he called out.

"Robby, is that you?"

"Oh God, Kelly?" he called and fought to gain his feet.

The next thing Robby knew, he was being embraced by the most welcome vision he had ever seen.

Kelly kissed him all over his face and hugged him until he had to pull away for air.

"You're alive, I can't believe it!" she cried as she pushed him away and looked him over. The girl holding the torch was Deidre Woodford, Professor Zachary's office assistant, who couldn't help but smile at the reunion.

"The others, how many are with you?"

"We have about twelve in our group," Kelly said as she nervously looked around her. "Come on, we have to get back. We can only be out for twenty minutes at a time."

"What . . . what are you talking about?" he asked as he was pulled along.

"It will take too long to explain, Robby, but just to let you know, we're the houseguests of the owners of El Dorado."

He was pulled along until they reached a great carved-out chamber and, as they entered the light of several torches, Robby gaped at the spectacle before him.

"Something, isn't it?" Kelly asked as she led him around a large grotto of clear, clean water that filled the center of the huge, once natural cave.

"Look at that!" Robby was gazing up at more than a thousand life-size statues of the beast they had seen and been attacked by. They lined the walls as if they had been arranged to have their stony gaze watch the interior of the enclosure. Situated between each statue was a small opening and in some of these openings firelight flickered. He was looking at over five hundred living quarters that had at one time housed the slaves that worked this mine.

"Come on, we have to get inside before the creature comes back. It's almost lunchtime," Kelly said as she looked at her watch. "Every twelve hours like clockwork. And that big bastard is never late."

"What in the hell are you talking about?" Robby asked as he was led into one of the enclosures. He saw that very old animal skins, along with a strangely woven cloth, covered the mouths of these strange dormlike rooms.

"The thing that attacked us out on the beach?"

"Yeah?"

"It thought we were trying to escape the valley and these mines," Kelly said. She lit another torch. And in that light she could see he wasn't following her. "Robby, that creature is our jailer. It's been trained to keep us right here. To keep us close to our work and to stop any attempt at leaving the mine." She reached down to retrieve something, and thrust it into his right hand. "Here, you must be starving."

He saw that she had given him cooked fish. He crammed it into his mouth, just now realizing how long it had been since he had eaten. The white meat tasted as good as anything he had ever dined on before in the best restaurants. When he finished, he leaned over and kissed Kelly.

ROBBY COULDN'T MAKE out the reasoning behind what she was saying. The dots that were supposed to be connected swirled before his eyes. Then in the torchlight he saw the cave paintings of long ago, rendered by a very primitive culture, possibly the Sincaro Indians. Their whole story was there for him to read and finally get a mental grasp of. As Kelly held the torch out for him to follow, he saw a long and brutal history of slavery and mass murder as depicted by a long-dead hand.

That was when a warning call sounded from outside in the grotto. "It's coming!"

.Kelly quickly placed the torch on the floor and stepped on it until it was extinguished. Then she took Robby's hand and pulled him back to the mouth of the small cave. Kelly held her index finger to her lips as he started to ask a question. She gestured out toward the semidarkness of the giant cave.

Then he saw it. The creature was standing right at the water's edge, watching the people inside their small enclosures. The beast grunted three, four, five times. It was enormous. The long arms, muscled and sinewed, hung leisurely at its side, then the waters of the grotto erupted with sound and splashing water as the small amphibious monkeys broke the surface of the large underground lake. Robby watched as they struggled to the rock shoreline and saw that each had its own burden to carry ashore; each had one, two, or three struggling fish in its clawed hands. One by one the monkeys tossed a flopping handful toward the humans who cowered inside, watching. Then the amphibians splashed back into the strange grotto and vanished. The giant beast looked around and then slowly stepped back until it was covered in water and disappeared.

"If I make it out of here alive, I've got the making of one hell of a thesis," Kelly said with a grin. Then she saw the confused look on her fiancé's face.

"Don't you understand? It's lunchtime for the slaves. And our guard and his trained staff just brought the food."

He couldn't say anything as his mind raced. These prehistoric creatures had been trained to watch and keep human slaves? But why?

"I can see the questions racing around that Stanford-type brain of yours, so let someone from Cal–Berkeley and real higher education explain it to you. It didn't take that long to figure out. Why would the ancient slave masters of the Sincaro go through the difficulty of training the wildlife here to act as prison guards when they could have just as easily watched over their slaves themselves? The answer is simple. They didn't want to die as their slaves did by the thousands. I'll bet my eventual master's degree that not only were the Sincaro driven to near extinction, but five or six other large tribes throughout El Dorado's history were murdered till not a one survived in this place."

"For what? Gold?" Robby asked incredulously.

Kelly lowered her head, then took Robby by the hand and pulled him out into the enormous cave. Then she turned and called for the gathered survivors to douse their torches. As they did, little by little the cave went dark.

"I don't get—"

"Watch," Kelly said as she turned toward the walls.

As Robby's eyes adjusted to the blackness around him, he saw first the many statues of the creatures start to give off a dim glow. Next, the very walls around them became alive with a green luminescence that grew in intensity. Then, as his jaw fell open in amazement, he discerned long streaks of ore coursing through the rock strata. They glowed as if they had an inner fire.

"No, Robby, they didn't die mining gold, they died digging *that* out of the earth. And why should the slave owners risk their own lives guarding what could be done by the highly evolved amphibians of this lagoon?"

The giant cave was now awash in the soft glow emanating from the carved stone and the streaks of strange ore that shot through the stone like rivers of green fire. Then Robby suddenly understood. Everything fell into place and he realized what he was looking at. With a shudder, he knew what their fate would be at the same time Kelly voiced it.

"If we don't escape the hospitality of our guards soon, I would say we'll all die a very long and agonizing death."

EVENT GROUP CENTER
NELLIS AFB, NEVADA

The twenty-eight department heads had been notified that an Event had been called, and so the Group went into action. At Department 5656, when an official Event is called, it means that something bordering on an important history-altering situation has occurred, one that could affect the lives of people in the present, an event that may have to be passed on to the president, or something that was beyond mere investigation by a group field team.

Pete Golding, in Computer Sciences, was in charge of doing the investigative work in several areas, including the timeline of the Events. Both the Padilla episode and the incursion in 1942 now fell into that category. He had the assistance of Assistant Director Virginia Pollock. The computer section would be running three shifts in an effort to uncover all the facts they could on the legend of the Padilla expedition, and most important, on the cryptic lead Helen had given in her letter regarding the papal medalists and the lost map. Niles had decided to take a silent part in Pete's investigation, working on his own.

Communications would also be diverted to the computer center because they would be using the Group's KH-11 satellite, code-named Boris and Natasha, to sweep the Amazon Basin from Brazil to the Peruvian Andes. They immediately started with the elimination of anything west of the mountains, for obvious reasons. The technicians, the best recruited specialists from the most advanced corporations in the United States, would be taking high-resolution images of the rain forest and jungles in the basin, and maybe with a little luck they would uncover something that would shorten the search for the tributary that led to the lost valley as described in the legend. But for now, the only descriptions were fictionalized accounts by very obscure and long-dead Italian authors who had claimed to have seen the journal or map—scenarios very unlikely, as the accounts varied wildly in their reporting and descriptions.

The three departments covering religion would be hard at work trying to uncover all they could from the Vatican Archives. The Cray computer system, Europa, would be set loose on the Vatican's formidable cataloging and supposedly secure IBM Red Ice system. The Europa was a system that Cray had built for only four federal agencies, the FBI, the CIA, the NSA, and covertly, as a favor to former director of Event Group Garrison Lee, Department 5656. The Cray was able to break in, or go through, the backdoor security of any system in the world, including the supposedly impenetrable Red Ice mainframe. Pete Golding called what Europa did "sweet talking." The three religion-based departments would try to sweet talk their way into the Vatican system and find out all they could on the diary, the map, and the reputed gold samples that had always been a rumored part of the story. It was a task that would be more than just a little daunting, being as the Holy Roman Church was the most experienced body in the world for burying secrets.

Heidi Rodriguez and her Zoology Department was joined by the Paleolithic Studies, Archaeology, and Oceanography divisions, to find out all they could on the species of animals that may have existed in the past that were no longer viable, or extinct. Heidi had already committed heresy in her three departments by requesting the assistance of a department no one spoke about in the sciences divisions. The strange group was located on the deepest level of the department, level thirty-one. Some said they were buried so deep by Director Compton just so they couldn't contaminate the labs of the *real* sciences. But Niles knew, more than anyone, the importance of this department and insisted it had value.

Niles had started the Cryptozoology Department three years ago as a fallback contingent to the extinct animal sciences group and nobody, absolutely nobody other than the director and Heidi, took them seriously. Their desire to find out about the Loch Ness monster, Bigfoot, and werewolves, among other laughable studies, was a running joke in the science levels above them. The department was chaired by a crazy old zoology professor named Charles Hindershot Ellenshaw III.

The three departments had met for exactly fifteen minutes before an argument broke out between members of the Crypto Department and Paleontology. Will Mendenhall had the complex security duty for the day and tried, along with Heidi Rodriguez, to bring the team back together. But Mendenhall found himself staring at the head of the Crypto Department, entranced by the long, wild, white hair of the man. Finally he was nudged by Heidi.

"Now what is this about?" Mendenhall asked, his eyes still on Ellenshaw.

Everyone started talking at once. Wild gestures and pointing fingers were jabbed by the people surrounding Sergeant Mendenhall.

"One at a time, *please*!"

"We don't have to stay here and be insulted every two minutes by these people; we're just as valuable to this facility as they are," a young woman with thick glasses said, staring a hole through Professor Keating.

"Just because your science is getting national recognition because of television, doesn't make you a viable scientific resource."

"Dr. Ellenshaw's theory, that a species of vertebrate separated from outside influences and has its own ecosystem, is a viable one!"

"B movie stuff!" Keating shot back.

Mendenhall shook his head. *This is going to be a long day*, he thought.

NILES WAS SITTING in the Europa direct contact center. The system was networked throughout the complex, but it was here that a person could interface with the Cray system on a one-on-one basis. According to Pete Golding, interacting with the system directly helped both the technician and the Cray, because it was a binary learning platform that could think light-years ahead of its questioner and actually *feel* the line of interrogation to reason out a solution on its own.

The director wanted to work alone, separate from the others, for reasons of a personal nature. He had tried earlier to distance himself from Helen's possible plight and allow his people to work without micromanaging them. He wished to continue his own duties, of which there were plenty, but he had soon found that he kept coming back to Helen, her face, how she had looked in the morning those many years ago. He figured being by himself would help him concentrate, especially while conversing with nothing as sentimental as a bunch of new-generation silicon bubble chips.

His first line of questioning was simple. He would start at investigating the lead Helen had given them in the letter regarding papal medalists.

"What have we got so far?" Niles asked as he leaned back in his chair.

From the accounts taken from public records and clandestine facilities, the total sum of papal medalists alive in the year AD 1875, were six hundred seventy-one, said the female auditory system of Europa.

"And that is with the elimination of Spain and Italy as home to these medalists?"

Yes.

Niles was slow to proceed. He knew he was shooting from the hip; after all, all they had to go on were written accounts of rumors that had started as far back as 1534. He surmised along with Pete that since the diary had been delivered to Spain by Father Corinth himself, they could safely eliminate that nation as one of the hiding places for the map or the reputed ore samples. And obviously, since Helen said that these papal medalists were all foreign born, they could also subtract Italy, the home of the Vatican. Now it was simple, that left only the rest of the world as their haystack.

"Access Vatican Network," Niles said.

Access has already been gained by the Computer Sciences Department, P. Golding authorization.

So Pete had already started sifting through the archives. Niles knew he should leave Pete to it, since he knew his way around not only Europa but all the security that had to be in place in the Vatican, which was there to keep someone from doing exactly what they were doing.

"Is there any correlation between San Jerónimo el Real, in Madrid, Spain, in 1874, and papal medalists?" Niles asked, as he was interested in verifying the fact that one of these knights did indeed deliver the diary to Spain, and to a knight there for the diary's safekeeping.

Formulating.

Niles was thinking of eliminating coincidence from his obvious guesswork.

Catholic cleric Father Sergio de Batavia, papal medalist, 1861, for actions while serving with the Battalion of St. Patrick's during the time of his service in Ireland, when he was asked to join the Papal Guard in 1862 as a reward for services at Castelfidardo, Ancona. He was awarded the Pro Petri Sede and Ordine di San Gregorio medals of Saints Peter and Gregory, for bravery. At the time his service to Pope Pius IX was ended, he was given leadership of San Jerónimo el Real in Madrid, Spain.

"I wonder what the odds had been that it was he who was given the diary for safekeeping," Niles said as he thought aloud.

Is the question directed at Europa for answering? the female voice asked.

Niles let out a small laugh. "Not unless you can calculate the odds."

Formulating.

Niles lowered his glasses and stared at the large liquid crystal display. It went dark for a moment, sending the entire room into blackness. He couldn't believe that Europa was going to figure the odds.

The number of papal medal recipients who received orders to Spain in the year AD 1861, according to Vatican archives, was four. The calculated odds are three to one.

"Pretty good, low enough to place a bet on," Niles said. "Question. How many recipients of the papal order were from the Battalion of St. Patrick's?"

Six received the order of Pro Petri Sede, two the order of Ordine di San Gregorio, and two received both honors.

Niles quickly reread the letter from Helen and made sure of the facts she had mentioned about the trail's leading to the map would be found through research of the medaled knights of the papacy. He refolded the letter and looked back at the screen. Helen had given him a starting point for trying to find something that she had claimed was unrecoverable, but it was the only real lead they had as to her whereabouts.

The last words spoken by Europa were still there, written on the large screen. Niles unzipped his clean suit and let in some air.

He pursed his lips as he thought. The odds were in favor of the map and diary having gone to highly placed men who Pope Pius IX had trusted, which would most likely have entailed the pope's having met them in person. So, papal medalists seemed the appropriate road to search, and that was how Helen had tracked at least the diary, and supposedly the map also. And since they would never have access to the diary, thanks to Farbeaux, they would have to follow the same trail as Helen had. The legend stated that the diary was separated from the gold samples and map by sending them in different directions—the diary to Spain, the map to the New World, and the samples to the Vatican Archives under lock and key. The diary and map had been despatched their separate ways in 1874. He removed his glasses and bit on the ear piece.

"Question," he said. "How many papal medalists were still alive on North and South American continents in 1874?"

Formulating.

Niles knew it was a long shot, but hoped anyway.

According to public records, seventy-five medalists were in the United States, sixteen in Canada, twenty-one in Mexico, and one in Brazil.

"Question. How many served with the Battalion of St. Patrick's and received both papal medals?"

Formulating.

Niles placed his glasses back on and looked at the screen.

Four recipients of both papal medals were also veterans of the Battalion of St. Patrick, Europa answered. *One recipient in Canada, one in Mexico, one in Brazil, and one in the United States.*

Niles sat up. It couldn't be that easy. "Question. How many of the four were stationed at the Vatican in 1874?"

Formulating.

Niles waited.

No recipients at the Vatican in AD 1874.

Niles felt deflated, but then decided to take a shot in the dark. "Question. Number of the four alive in 1874?"

Formulating, Europa said as the screen flashed again.

Niles started to stand, feeling his side investigation was going nowhere.

According to Royal Canadian death records, the general census of citizens of Mexico, the official census of Brazil, and the state and territorial records of the United States, one member was still alive in 1874, Europa answered.

Niles looked at the printed answer on the screen with renewed hope. "Question. What was the last name of recipient?"

Formulating.

Niles knew for a fact it had to be a priest, probably in the very same order of St. Patrick's as the Spanish father's where the diary was sent. As he watched, he could hear through the glass in front of him Europa's robotic systems pulling programs at a fantastic rate. Normally he loved to watch the Cray system in action, but right now it would only make him more anxious.

All records of identity of medalist erased from former

system hard drive 11/18/1993. No further account remains in center files.

"What? You mean the old Cray system file was erased?" Niles asked as he leaped to his feet in anger.

Affirmative. All records of case file beyond census data for 1874 of Vatican papal medalists has been dropped from the Nellis file system.

"Authorized user of last data query on current subject matter?" Niles asked but already knew the answer.

Professor Helen M. Zachary, 11/18/1993, clearance—

"Goddammit! You left us a dead end!" he said gritting his teeth.

Europa has failed to adequately understand question and/or statement. Please restate.

Niles didn't respond to the confused Europa; he stormed out of the clean room knowing they may have lost their one clear chance of finding Helen's team.

ALICE SAT AND listened to the phone conversation between Niles and Senator Garrison Lee.

"The only thing I remember about some of those old files Dr. Zachary made off with is what I personally put into one of them in 1942. At the time of the theft I couldn't figure out, other than the obvious fact it was about Brazil, why she would have been interested; the file was just the After Action Report about the recovery of some scientists from the States. The rest were army and Corps of Engineers field reports from some sort of South American field operation that held no interest for the OSS or, later, the Event Group. Our part was to pull them out, nothing more; we weren't anywhere near the Amazon when the rescue occurred."

"If you weren't anywhere near the Amazon during the rescue, how could Helen have come up with anything that helped her in those files? The papal medalist leads, I can see her eliminating as a way to trace her actions, but this OSS file of yours, I don't get it," Niles said, leaning toward the speaker box on his desk. He was hoping beyond reason that Lee, having been one of "Wild Bill" Donovan's best OSS agents during the war, could come up with something to help.

"I haven't a clue, Niles; maybe she discovered something in the army paperwork that was forwarded with the file, I just don't know. And now that we're positive the file was erased from our former Cray archives along with any medalist's clues, you may never find out. But then again, although she knew she had covered her tracks, she knows you'll be able to uncover her tracks. But how, is the question."

"Perhaps the men you rescued in 1942 said something to you after you pulled them out, that could shed some light on this, Garrison," Alice suggested.

"Sorry, old girl, but army and navy intelligence kept those boys pretty much hushed up about their activities down there. There is one thing, though; we were supposed to be pulling out far more people than we ended up rescuing. And even as we made our way out of that hellhole, the men we rescued weren't much good; they were in shock and two of them were close to death from exposure. The only reason they were found is because they left their radio on and the army triangulated their position. That was when the military asked for help from the OSS contingent in South America to assist in recovering their team. That's all I have for you, Niles, with the exception of one item."

"And that is," Niles asked. ·

"This trouble in South America, with the file on that particular subject of papal knights being deleted from our files—where would you go to get something that is that old? Remember, the original file was transcribed from what to what?" .

"Paper files to electronic," Niles said, knowing the answer to the senator's riddle immediately. The Event Group's original facility, built by then president Woodrow Wilson, was now a storage facility for all its paper files originated before 1943. They had all been entered into the original Cray system back in 1963. And that system was housed in Arlington, Virginia, at a place hidden far beneath the National Cemetery.

"There's your lead, my boy. There is no way Helen could have gotten into that facility, and she knew you could. She was smart enough to know where the paper files were stored in a closed-loop computer system. She knew that and the fact that you would have access to them when you hit the dead end here on Europa. You remember where the facility is, I take it?" the senator asked facetiously.

Of course Niles knew, and had to smile at the old subterfuge. Imagine, having the original Event Group housed in an underground facility not unlike the current complex. Woodrow Wilson had authorized the first complex built in 1916 and had placed it where no one would ever suspect.

"Yes, sir, I remember."

"Good, just be careful of the ghosts. And remember the first thing I taught you about the Group, Niles? We are what?"

"Alone and not trusting of anyone, and assume everyone is three steps ahead of us. I remember."

"Bingo. But there is one man you confide in, you know who?"

"Jack," he answered with a small smile.

"Right, tell him everything. Give him every detail, because I don't like the way this smells ever since you told me about our French friend."

"I will, and thank you."

"Sorry I couldn't be of more help, Mr. Director," Garrison said on the other end of the phone.

"Well, I guess all we can do is keep looking with Boris and Natasha, and hope the satellite comes up with something. In the meantime I'll get over to Complex One and see if I can find a certain file. Thanks, Garrison."

"Anytime, Niles; by the way, tell that old woman to bring home some real milk and not that soy crap," he said as he hung up.

9

BOGOTÁ, COLOMBIA

THE Banco de Juarez building was a glass and steel monstrosity, very out of place in one of the poorest neighborhoods in all of Bogotá. It stood towering over the shanties as if it were a dark tower from the pages of a dark fairy tale.

Henri Farbeaux stood looking out of the plate glass window on the thirty-second floor, which afforded a panoramic view of the city below. They were far above the filth and poverty that permeated the city.

"So, are we prepared?"

Farbeaux turned to see Joaquin Delacruz Mendez standing in his doorway. The chubby banker was dressed ridiculously in a tan suit with jungle pockets in the front. The clothes were impeccably pressed and Mendez wore a brand-new pair of work boots. With great effort, Farbeaux kept himself from smiling. He, himself, was dressed in Levi's and a long-sleeved denim shirt. His black boots were broken in and waterproof.

"Yes, we are ready. The supplies have been received and are being loaded as we speak. Our helicopter is awaiting us on the roof."

"Excellent, and what of the boat?" he asked.

"We have chartered the *Rio Madonna*, a worthy ship that has plied those waters for twenty years. Her captain is a man who knows how to keep silent about certain aspects of our journey. His family has worked the river for generations," Farbeaux said as he turned away from the window and retrieved his Windbreaker. He didn't mention how much it was costing Mendez for the captain's silence.

"The weapons and my security staff, they are all ready?"

"All in place," Farbeaux answered.

"Very good."

"Shall we go, then," Farbeaux said.

"Yes, please go on, I will meet you upstairs. I must take my Dramamine for the flight down to Peru," Mendez said, the lie flowing easily from his lips.

Farbeaux bowed, catching the lie. He knew his employer never took Dramamine, as the man lived most of his life in one aircraft or the other.

Mendez watched the Frenchman leave and then he picked up the phone.

"Yes, *señor*?"

"Has there been any activity at Stanford?" he asked.

"No, *jefe*, we are monitoring every minute of the day. The phone rings but no one has answered, and no one other than the janitorial service has entered the professor's office."

"If there is in the future, use your own judgment as to the danger they pose, and adjust your reaction accordingly. I do not want interference in any way once we are on the river, is that understood?"

"Yes, *señor*, it is understood."

"Good," he said and hung up, and then rubbed his hands. Just thinking about El Dorado and its being *him* that discovers its hidden whereabouts—after all those centuries of men having looked for it, from Alaska to Argentina—was mind-boggling. The drug lords of the past would never have thought such wealth was possible. And that, coupled with the new information that the Frenchman had in his possession about a possible source of new energy in the same mine, was too much to dream for. No, no one could have the vision he had. He was the only man who always had the imagination to dream of higher things. Higher things that demanded he have the most advanced security force and black operations team in private. employ in all of South America, not to mention most of the world. Yes, he thought, the adventure he had always craved was now upon him and the mysteries of Padilla would soon be his.

EVENT GROUP CENTER
NELLIS AFB, NEVADA

"That's where we are right now. Since I'm the only one not assigned to any research, I'll take Mr. Ryan and head for Virginia to see what we can uncover in the old files. And Everett, I have a job for you also. You are to meet our former Mrs. Farbeaux in San Jose and escort her to Stanford. Once in Palo Alto, you'll gain access into Professor Zachary's office and see what you can uncover; she may have left some clue there."

Carl wanted to protest about being the one to escort Danielle, but held his tongue.

"Yes, sir," he answered instead.

A knock sounded on the conference room door, and a blue-clad lance corporal walked in and gave Niles a note. He unfolded and read it, and then gave the note to Alice.

"More potatoes have been added to the stew," Niles said, looking around the table. "We ran the security footage recovered from the San Pedro shipping company responsible for getting Helen and her team into place. We now know her starting point was Colombia; from there all we can assume is that she went south toward either Brazil or Peru. But we have uncovered something else. It seems she may have had a second source of financing from someone we must assume has accompanied her on her trip."

"Second source?" Jack asked.

"According to the ship's manifest taken from a copy that was filed at their offices, the articles loaded onboard included several that did not belong to Helen and her team, but were in fact signed for by someone not on the original team roster and do not show up in any university records. This man, his name is Kennedy—he and five others were issued two cabins onboard *Pacific Voyager*."

"Helen, what did you get yourself into?" Alice murmured, shaking her head.

AN HOUR LATER, Niles had their lunch brought into the conference room, where they made detailed plans on who and what equipment would be needed for an expedition if the Event Group found the route of Padilla.

"Before we get into what Boris and Natasha has or has not come up with on her latest pass, and before Carl has to leave," Niles said as he looked at his watch, "I want to discuss river transport. I want a secure vessel if at all possible, not a local river traveler. I want something that can be in place in a day, if and when we go. Jack, Commander Everett, any ideas?"

"Best if you ask the swabby," Jack said, looking at Carl.

Carl stopped toying with his plate of potato salad and looked up. "As a matter of fact, I may have just the man that can supply us with something along those lines," he said as he thought. "He's somewhat eccentric, but he's one hell of a designer. Built assault craft for the navy; he was in on the hydrofoil development until it was canceled by the Defense Department. I think the navy hid him away in Louisiana someplace, developing experimental river craft. But mostly they stashed him there to keep him out of trouble."

"As soon as you complete your assignment in Palo Alto, detour on the way home and find out. Anything you can add about this man?" Niles asked as he wrote in his notepad.

"Well, I know he may need a push because, as I said, he's a little strange. But he can be ordered. He's still a master chief petty officer in the navy. They haven't found anyone with enough guts to go down and retire him yet, so he's still building boats. Maybe you can tug on some official strings and get his cooperation," Carl said.

"Good enough, I'll do just that. Leave his name with Ellen outside," Niles responded. "You'd better be off to meet our French lady friend."

"Yes, sir," Carl said as he nodded to those around the table and touched Jack on the shoulder.

As Carl left, Niles absentmindedly pushed the plate with his ham sandwich on it away from him as he pulled the latest satellite imagery toward him.

"Okay, Pete, what in the hell is Boris and Natasha telling us?"

"Well, the KH-11 is on the very range of its ability to see into Peru and Brazil on its current track," Pete answered from his office in the Comp Center. "We would have to re-task it to get to the areas we need to look at. But Europa has uncovered some covert stuff from NSA that was taken two weeks before Professor's Zachary's departure from Los Angeles, and that film has just confirmed what we already know. As you see," he used a pointer, tapping the monitor's screen, "the suspected area is mostly unexplored rain forest, and has tree canopies so thick that we can't see anything. Radar imagery," he pointed to a grouping of pictures, "picks up just what we would expect, thousands of miles of winding river, tributaries, and lagoons, not to mention hundreds of waterfalls. You could throw a dart at the images and have just as much luck as to which patch is our target site."

Niles shook his head. He wanted to shove the hard copies of the pictures away and off the far end of the table in frustration, but caught himself. Boris and Natasha was not the answer. He stood up and stretched, and then his eyes caught the still frame of the security video on one of the large screens. He froze. His eyes roamed over the grainy image. Then he moved quickly to his console at the conference table and started tapping keys. The others watched him for a moment as the black-and-white frames started to project in reverse. Then he stopped tapping as the picture caught the twin images of two people to the far right of Helen Zachary and Kennedy. Niles tapped a few more commands and then pushed the button on the intercom. "Pete, are you getting the image on the screen on monitor one-seventeen?"

"Let's see here, yeah, I see it, the dock security footage?"

"Yes, can you have the computer blow that frame up and

enhance it? Order the shots to come in tight on those two kids by the ship's rail to the right."

"Yeah, Europa can probably clean up the footage," Pete answered through the speakers around the room.

As they watched, the camera footage went dark and then cleared and the two people became larger. The quality was now much better.

"Again, Pete, tighter, concentrate on the girl, the right image," Niles ordered as he stepped closer to the large monitor.

The picture on the screen fragmented again and then came together line by line until the smiling face of a young woman covered most of the screen.

Without turning to the others sitting at the conference table, Niles said, "You're all excused with the exception of Major Collins."

Questions were mumbled, but they all left their lunch and gathered their notes and walked out of the conference room. Even Alice left, though she knew the director well enough to know that Niles had spotted something that had caught him off guard and stunned him.

Jack stood up and walked to where Niles was standing.

"Major, we have a whole new priority here."

"What is it?"

"The girl, her name wasn't on the manifest, at least not her real name," he said as he stepped up to the monitor for a closer look. "If that's who I think it is, this Event has taken on a whole new, nightmarish perspective."

10

CARL immediately recognized Danielle Serrate. Her red hair was up but her features, despite her having a little more makeup on, had the same model beauty as before. She saw Carl and for some reason he felt gratified that she had recognized him. He was dressed simply in slacks and a short-sleeved blue shirt. He stepped up to her and took her suitcase from her hand.

"Ms. Serrate, you're looking . . . a bit cleaner."

"You have a singular wit about you, Commander," she said as she gave him the once-over.

"I'm like that, singular and witty," he said as he started for the door. "If you don't mind, ma'am, we have a busy day ahead of us."

"May I ask our destination?" she asked, catching up with the much taller officer.

"You may ask," he said as he flagged down marine corporal Sanchez, who would be accompanying them to Stanford. Carl lifted the trunk lid and laid her case inside, then paused. "Is there anything you would like to retrieve from your luggage?" he asked with his hand still on the trunk.

She smiled and opened the rear door of the rented Chevrolet. "No, I have everything I could possibly need," she said significantly as she entered the car.

Carl slammed the trunk and walked to the other side of the car and climbed in. Her answer meant that she wasn't armed. He wouldn't push the point of the illegality of her having a weapon even if it were still hidden in her suitcase; after all, he wouldn't like it if someone took his toys away if he visited France.

"Again, I'll ask you our destination." She looked at Carl over her sunglasses.

He tapped Corporal Sanchez on the back of his shoulder, signaling him to drive.

"Stanford University," he said curtly. "And I want you to know, I was 'volunteered' for this assignment."

"I look forward to spending time with you also, Commander."

Carl could see her mocking smile in the reflection of the window.

EVENT GROUP CENTER
NELLIS AFB, NEVADA

Professor Charles Hindershot Ellenshaw III was deep in thought. He had been staring at the same CT scan for the last twenty minutes. He had compared the latest shots to that of the sample of material in the electron microscope. He couldn't figure it out. The film was cloudy around the third finger of the fossil, as if the film had a flaw in it. But it was the same on the first set of scans they had done. If he didn't know any better, he would have thought someone was playing a joke on him.

"Heidi, would you look at this please?" he asked, handing over the film.

Heidi Rodriguez took the X-ray and reviewed it. "Looks like bad film; is this a shot of the claw's third digit?"

"Yes, it is, but the same thing happened on the first CT scan, look," he said as he held out the second set of film. "And if you would take a look at this also," he said, pointing to a monitor that was connected to the electron microscope.

Heidi looked from the film to the monitor. "All I see is bone, Professor. Are you seeing something different?" she asked, looking closer.

"Right here, that spec, that isn't bone," he said, using a pencil to point out a black object that couldn't be seen with the naked eye.

"Dirt, or sand perhaps," she said.

"It's right in the area where the CT scan didn't take. It's as if the entire area was wiped clean."

"Interference?" she asked.

"I don't know, probably just coincidence. It does look like an outside contaminant, sand probably. It must have been placed there postmortem. But let's get some more film on it. If the blur continues to be in the same area, it may indicate a malfunction in the scanner itself, either that or our ancient friend here has been playing around with a radioactive isotope."

He glanced up but saw Heidi wasn't smiling at his small joke. Instead she was looking at the monitor with renewed interest.

"This is no flaw in the film or the machine," Heidi said as she looked closer at the image. "And you're right, Professor, the only thing that could cause this effect is . . ." she paused, "radioactivity."

STANFORD, UNIVERSITY
PALO ALTO, CALIFORNIA

An hour and a half after he picked his burden up in San Jose, Carl waited while a janitor let him and Danielle into the classroom that had been left vacant for the summer by the departure of Helen Zachary and almost a quarter of her students. The university's security department, after examining Carl's falsified identification, hadn't hesitated to cooperate. Oh, the FBI ID card was real enough, but the bureau had no idea that the Event Group had been authorized to issue them to nonbureau personnel by the president of the United States.

"Nothing more eerie than a classroom with no students in it," Danielle said as she looked around at the empty lab tables and displays.

"Especially one with a bunch of animal skeletons," Carl said, half smiling. "Here's the professor's private office." He tried the knob and found it locked.

Danielle stepped forward and eased Carl out of the way. She produced a small device; spreading its thin, wirelike probes, she easily slid it into the door's lock and jiggled. There was a click. Danielle turned the knob and the door opened.

"Standard issue?" he asked.

"Every woman should have one," she said as she stepped into the office and turned on the light.

Carl felt as though control of their small investigation had suddenly changed leadership.

Several filing cabinets had been left standing open. Danielle looked closely at one of the locks and called Carl over.

"What do you think of this?" she asked.

He could see small gouges in the chromed steel of the lock around the mechanism's opening. "It's been picked," he said. "Someone has cleaned this place out."

"I agree. Whatever your professor had here is now in the possession of another," she stated as she perused the maps on the wall. "Her interests in South America are clear nonetheless," she said as she traced a finger along the Amazon.

Carl opened his cell phone to call Niles but its indicator showed the signal strength was very low. He closed the phone, picked up the receiver of the office's desk phone, and listened for the dial tone. On a hunch, he punched the number nine and a new tone told him he had an outside line. Then he placed a cup-size instrument over the earpiece of the phone. Danielle recognized it as a programmed descrambler.

"Can't get a signal in here, so I have to be careful what I say. This won't be a secure line, at least on our end." It had taken Everett a few seconds to close his cell phone, enough time to allow a bad guy to track his usage number if the signal was bugged.

"You Americans, always so paranoid," Danielle said as she lifted a champagne flute and looked at it curiously.

IN THE PARKING area outside of the sciences building, four men sat in a panel van. The vehicle was full of state-of-the-art monitoring equipment purchased through a dummy corporation. The fine print on the invoices could easily have been traced back to the Banco de Juarez, if anyone had been interested. Each man monitored an area of the office that had either been bugged or tapped into.

"I have an outside line open on the office phone," one of the men said in Spanish.

"Contact Captain Rosolo," another of the men said.

The side door slid open suddenly, illuminating the interior and shocking the communications men. They scrambled to stand in the presence of their commander.

"Keep your places. What is it you are monitoring?" the captain asked as he sat himself in front of a computer and started typing commands. "I take it you are wired into the classroom security cameras?"

The four men were unsettled that Rosolo had been that close to them, and their nervousness showed. The captain had a reputation for unforgiving ruthlessness.

"There are two people in the classroom office. One is a large man and the other a woman," the supervisor said nervously. "We tagged the man's cell phone, but he failed to get a signal out so he has utilized the office landline. But once he's clear of the building, we'll be able to track his cell's movements and him also."

The computer monitor connected with the camera feed to the professor's area inside the building. Unfortunately it showed only the classroom, not the office. Rosolo typed in another command and the video rewound until the two people were clearly seen. He didn't recognize the man, but the woman was another story.

"Patch in the gentleman's conversation," he ordered.

Carl was speaking with Jack and Virginia.

"The place is cleaned out," Carl said.

Then instead of a voice on the other end, a series of clicks, beeps, and static filled the air around the speaker in the van.

"The other end of his conversation is scrambled," Rosolo announced, as he picked up a set of headphones and listened more closely.

"Uh-huh, yeah, we can do that. Have you contacted the Department of the Navy? I'll need some force behind me in New Orleans; as I said before, the master chief is definitely one bottle short of a six-pack," Carl said.

More beeps and screeches.

"Have you informed the director?" Carl asked.

Scrambled response.

"He's already left for Virginia?"

The noises once again.

Now, Rosolo could tell by a muffled sound that the man who was talking placed his hand over the mouthpiece of the telephone. The captain still could clearly understand what was being said to the woman in the office.

"They think they have an outside shot at recovering the map of Padilla. The director will be landing there in about three hours," was the mumbled comment. Then Carl returned to his telephone conversation. "Yes, sir, I'll contact you from New Orleans."

Rosolo laid down the headphones as the connection was terminated. He looked at the frozen picture of the woman on the computer screen. Then he made a decision.

"Contact B team and have them ready the aircraft with an open flight plan ready to move at a moment's notice," he said without looking at his men. "Tell them we will leave within thirty minutes. We now have this man's cell phone tapped and flagged and what he knows, we know. He is not going after the map, so he and this woman are not going to be our target at this time. We'll wait and see what they uncover in Virginia. Inform our team at San Jose International to stand by for immediate departure when and if they discover anything worthwhile."

The four communications men went to work as Rosolo assigned a file name to the picture of the woman on the monitor. He quickly brought up a secured e-mail address, keyboarded the picture to it as an attachment, and hit send. Then he picked up a satellite phone and punched in a number, as he slid the side door open and stepped out.

"Señor Mendez," he said when the phone three thousand miles away was answered.

"Yes, Captain."

"I have sent you some information that is a concern for security reasons. Check your computer when it is possible to do so. Alone."

"Yes, I will do that," Mendez said.

"It seems our friend's ex-wife is on official business in Helen Zachary's office; she is with a man who has just conversed with someone using a scrambled and encrypted phone on a secure line. Therefore, we must assume this is not to our benefit."

"I agree; is there anything else?" Mendez asked.

"Yes, a very serious development. Whoever these people are, they may have stumbled upon a means to find the whereabouts of the Padilla map."

"We cannot allow that map to fall into the hands of those that could harm our quest. I assume you are in the process of handling this disturbing matter?"

"The order has been given. It may take time, but if they locate the map, we'll be there soon after." Rosolo hung up and tossed the phone back inside the van to one of the technicians. Then he walked to the entrance to the sciences building and waited.

It was only five minutes before he heard footsteps and talking through the double doors. He straightened his tie and opened the right side door quickly.

"Oh, excuse me," he said as he bumped into the woman and then moved out of her way.

Danielle smiled politely and she and Carl stepped through the doorway. As they did so Rosolo, still appearing to fuss with his own garments, adeptly placed a tracer bug on the woman's suit jacket. As he held the door open for a moment, he turned and watched Danielle and the large man leave the building. When he was sure they were out of sight, he returned to the large van.

Captain Rosolo, chief of security for clandestine operations for the Banco de Juarez International Economica, would make sure there was no interference from anyone, now that Señor Mendez was on his way to Padilla's golden site.

The trail to that same destination would end for these two people in New Orleans, if they proved to be more resourceful there.

ARLINGTON NATIONAL CEMETERY
ARLINGTON, VIRGINIA

Director Niles Compton was still shaken and Lieutenant JG Jason Ryan could barely refrain from teasing him. The director had unceremoniously lost his cookies somewhere over Kentucky on their flight into Andrews Air Force Base. The air force enlisted men acting as their ground crew wouldn't be too happy cleaning that mess up. But Niles had wanted to get here as fast as possible, and Ryan had just fortuitously two days before finished his transition from the navy's Super Tomcat to the air force's F-16 B, two-seat trainer, which they had used to get to Virginia. Niles hadn't been happy with the choice of aircraft but reluctantly borrowed one anyway from the Nellis AFB inventory. Every few minutes while they were aloft the director would glance at Ryan and try to catch him in the act of snickering. He knew he was going to have a talk with the lieutenant about the barrel roll as they descended from altitude. Their drive to Arlington was chilly at best.

As Ryan pulled the green government car up to the guard shack at the National Cemetery he rolled down his window, allowing the hot and muggy summer air into the air-conditioned interior. He flashed his naval ID; and Niles, his

National Archives card, which indicated he was the equivalent of a four-star general. The guard waved them through. Instead of taking the main road that led to the cemetery's parking area, Ryan followed the directions Niles indicated and instead drove directly to the old mansion. As they approached the house on the hill, Niles was thrilled to see it once again, not only because of its historical significance, but because he knew this was the very first Event Group Complex, housing the very first discoveries from the early, heady days of the Group's formation by Teddy Roosevelt through the administration of Woodrow Wilson.

The nineteenth-century mansion seems out of place amid the more than 250,000 military grave sites that stretch out around it. Yet, when construction began in 1802, the estate had been intended as a living memorial to George Washington. It had been built by the first president's adopted grandson, George Washington Parke Custis, and eventually became the home of one of the most beloved men in American history, Robert E. Lee, and his wife, Mary Anna Custis. They had lived at the house until 1861, when the Civil War broke out. During the succeeding occupation of Arlington, several bases were constructed on the 1,100-acre site, including what would later become Fort Meyer. The property was eventually confiscated for the official reason of back taxes, but many influential people saw it as a punishment for Robert E. Lee for his participation in the rebellion. It became a cemetery in 1864.

As they went past the many-columned facade of the mansion, they followed the drive around to the back of the property. They saw several National Parks guards eyeing them. They drove directly to the maintenance shed adjacent to the back of the grounds, entering its open double doors. Once they were inside, the doors closed automatically and several dim lights came to life around them. Ryan reached to open his seat belt but was stopped by Niles, whose hand eased over and grabbed his arm as a hidden speaker gave an order.

"Please remain in your vehicle, Lieutenant Ryan."

Ryan grinned and looked around the dimly lit shed. He could see no one. "I take it we're in for more Event Group spooky crap?" he asked Niles.

Niles just shrugged and let go of Ryan's arm.

Suddenly Ryan felt his stomach lurch as the dirt floor of the maintenance shed began to descend into the ground. He couldn't help but become a little queasy as he watched the sides of on unlit giant elevator shaft quickly lower the car into the Virginia hillside.

"Don't like it, do you, Mr. Ryan? It's a lot harder when you don't know it's coming and some wise guy starts messing with you. Stomach a little upset?"

"Okay, I'm sorry for the barrel roll. I won't do it again. I get your point."

Niles smiled in the darkness surrounding them.

The elevator finally came to rest 1,700 feet below ground. As the lights of level one came into view, Ryan could see two men in Event Group coveralls awaiting the car. Then the two security men came forward to open their doors, inviting Niles and Ryan to step into the very first Event Group compound, which had been built in 1916.

"Welcome to the depository, sir."

"Thank you, gentlemen. This is Lieutenant Junior Grade Ryan; he's one of your security department officers."

Ryan nodded his head and glanced around the first level. The cement walls were clean and white in the overhead fluorescents and looked as if they were well maintained.

A lance corporal came forth and wrote the names of the visitors onto a clipboard. "Where will you be going today, Director Compton?"

"Archives. I take it the old Cray is up and working?"

"Yes, sir, Mr. Golding keeps to a rather strict maintenance schedule."

"Good, good."

"Will you be going to level seventeen today?"

"No, we'll not be touring today, just research," Niles answered, even though he would have loved to show Ryan some of the first discoveries of the Event Group. Not the Ark of the Great Flood, which had been moved to the Nellis facility, or the other large finds like that, but the smaller ones such as the body—replete with armor—of Genghis Khan, or the mummified corpse of Cochise, the Apache leader thought to have been secretly hidden away by his people. Just the samples of the original plague from the Dark Ages would be enough to scare the bejesus out of poor Ryan. But that would have to wait for now, as they were desperately short of time.

"Very well, this way, sir," the lance corporal said.

Niles and Ryan fell into step behind the two security men. They walked down a corridor beyond which the secrets of worlds past surrounded them.

UNITED STATES NAVAL SHIPYARD
(DECOMMISSIONED)
NEW ORLEANS, LOUISIANA

As Carl drove among the old docks, he could see his country's naval history as it was scrapped: cruisers, tin cans, and frigates were being dismantled and sold for recycling. There was nothing sadder to a naval man than seeing these magnificent ships meeting such an inglorious end.

Upon arriving in New Orleans, they saw a city that was still rebounding from the hurricane of '05. The people had returned in record numbers to rebuild to try and make the Big Easy the city it once was. The U.S. Navy had helped out by positioning ships earmarked for the scrapyard here, their part in easing the rampant unemployment of the damaged city.

As Carl counted down the numbers painted on the sides of the buildings, he saw that most of them were now rundown and dilapidated. They had gone unrepaired while the U.S. Navy decommissioned the entire dock area. The navy was now in the process of turning over the acreage to the money-strapped city.

"There it is," Danielle said, as she pointed out the large building coming up on their right.

Carl eased their rental car into a space that was crowded with old ship parts and skeletons of boats of all kinds. Some were navy, whereas others were nondescript and nothing more than junk. They could hear the barely audible thump of heavy metal music coming from inside the building in which they had been searching.

"What an awful place for your navy to put a man. Did you say he was once a master chief in your SEAL unit?" she asked.

Carl walked up to a large steel door and slammed his fist against it several times, making a loud banging that they could hear echo inside. "Still is a master chief and the meanest son of a bitch I've ever met in my life," he said turning back toward Danielle. "He was a SEAL before it was glamorous to be one. He was in on the Son Tay raid in '70 before I was even born."

"That was where your Special Forces tried to free your prisoners of war?"

He was impressed with her knowledge. "That's right," he said, banging again on the steel door, but keeping his eyes on the woman.

"I did my thesis on colonialism and the French involvement in Southeast Asia, particularly Vietnam. You look surprised."

"I admit, I may have underestimated you."

"Score one for the enemy," she said, her own eyes locked on his.

Carl stepped back from the large metal door and looked around.

"Go away, this is government property, dickwad," said a voice from the other side of the door.

"That's Master Chief Jenks all right, not a good word to say to anyone," Carl said as he stepped back up to the door. "Watch that mouth, Chief. You're addressing a United States naval officer!"

"I don't give a flying fuck if it's John Paul Fucking Jones, get the hell out of here. This is my project and I let in who I want."

Danielle placed her hand over her mouth, hiding her smile.

"Told you, Father Flanagan he's not," Carl said jokingly, then turned back to the closed door. "All right then, Chief, how about there's a lady out here who needs to use the head; she's been on a plane for three and a half hours."

"Lady? She good lookin'?"

Carl turned to look at Danielle. "Gorgeous," he said as he quickly turned away from her.

There was silence on the other end for about two minutes, and then they heard the hum of an electric motor and the music inside came blaring out of the opening door. "Welcome to the Jungle," a song by Guns N' Roses, drove Carl back a step.

The music was lowered. After their eyes adjusted they saw they were looking at a giant tarp that had been hung from the old rafters. It covered most of the interior of the building from view. A man in dirty overalls approached them, down a set of stairs. He was wiping his greasy hands on a red rag.

"Who the hell are you and where's this woman?" At that moment the man caught sight of Danielle. "Fuck me three ways from Sunday, you were right, she's a looker."

"The navy never managed to tame that filthy mouth of yours, huh?" Carl said.

The master chief looked him over, and then the light of recognition lit the older man's eyes like a lantern.

"I'll be dipped in whale shit. Toad?"

Carl turned red at the mention of his nickname, but grabbed the master chief just the same and hugged him.

"Commander Toad to you, you slimy bastard," he said.

The two men hugged and patted each other on the back as Danielle watched. Then Jenks pushed the younger man away suddenly.

"Hey, you didn't turn gay on me, did you, boy? Could have sworn you grabbed my ass there," he said as he smiled at Carl, then at Danielle.

"No I didn't, and that's not very PC of you. Chief Jenks." He gestured toward his companion. "This is Danielle, she's—" he hesitated for a split second, "she's a friend of mine."

Jenks looked her over, his eyes lingering on her chest a moment longer than necessary. He continued smiling but didn't offer his hand.

"As I said, she's a looker all right," he stated flatly. He looked accusingly at Carl. "She's also a *spook*, I can smell it. You should watch the company you hang out with, Toad," he said as he slapped Carl on the arm and walked away.

Carl frowned at Danielle. "He has a nose for people," he whispered, and then called toward Jenks, who had gone back to wiping his hands on a greasy rag. "She's not a spy, Chief, she's in the same line of work as me."

Jenks stopped but didn't turn. "And that is?"

"Let's just say I'm still in the navy and we're the good guys and leave it at that, okay?"

Jenks finally met his eyes again. "Okay, Toad, you're a good guy. Now what the fuck do you want?"

"We came to see your project," Carl said.

"You're not getting it, so go away. Hell, it's not even finished and probably won't be before the navy shit cans the project and *me*."

"I may be able to help you there, Jenksy, now; just let us see the damned thing."

Jenks put his left hand on his hip, then removed his dirty white saucer cap and ran a still-filthy right hand through his crew-cut gray hair. Then he reached into his overall pocket and withdrew a stub of a cigar. Carl smiled, as these were signs that told him the man was relaxing.

"All right, but you're not getting her. I've still got major logistical concerns here; she won't be ready for river trials for . . . hell, maybe never." Jenks started for the giant tarpaulin covering three-quarters of the building. "Unless you have a check on you for about five and half million bucks."

Carl began to follow Jenks. Danielle came up close to his side. "How cute, your nickname was Toad?"

"Yeah, and I don't want to talk about it," he said as he stepped around a large empty crate. It was stenciled with a bright red logo that had several lines painted on it, depicting a bright light. It read LASER DEVICE, HANDLE WITH CARE.

"Come on, why did they give you that name?" she asked, smiling and ignoring Carl's curious glance at the empty crate.

"Because the stupid bastard used to jump six feet in the air every time ordnance went off around him in training, that's why," Jenks said as he started to pull the tarp aside. Then he stopped and looked at Danielle. "But he was still the best damned SEAL I ever trained and, as I hear it from people, he's the best there ever was, so as you can see, he worked out that little problem with loud noises he had when he was a kid." He pulled hard on the tarp. "Ain't that right, Toad?"

Carl smiled embarrassedly as the tarp was pulled away. His smile faded as he looked up and saw for the first time the master chief's project.

"Goodness," was all Danielle could utter.

"Damn," Carl mumbled as they stepped into the mad scientist's naval workshop of wonders to take in a gleaming jewel hidden away in a city that had come violently close to being deleted from the American landscape.

The vessel looked like something taken straight out of a science-fiction movie. The nose was enclosed and comprised mostly of glass except for the framing. It was shaped like a boat in the bow but that was where the resemblance ended. Except for the tri-hull shape of its body, the vessel looked more like a sleek submarine. It was over 130 feet long and was sectioned in twenty-two-foot compartments. Some areas were open on the top at the midway point, as an upper deck with seating around the gunwales. It had a high observation tower amidships that rose forty feet into the air, which included the ship's radar and antenna domes above the crow's nest. The vessel was gleaming white. Toward the stern, *USS Teacher* was in blue cursive and punctuated by a large illustration of a woman's eye, with the brow perfectly and beautifully arched over it. Large portholes, six-foot rectangles of thick glass, ran along the length of each section, both above the waterline and below. At the bottom of each section were four small protrusions that looked like the water jets of a speedboat.

Carl climbed a scaffold so he could see inside the glass nose and make out some of the command bridge. There were large chairs for the command pilot and a seat for a copilot. The interior of the bridge was dark save for a few glowing instrument lights.

"She's beautiful, Jenks," Carl said, admiring the composite graphite hull.

The master chief smiled and then looked hard at Danielle.

"She is that," she said quickly as Jenks grunted satisfaction with her late response. "But why did you name her *Teacher*?" she asked.

"I don't know, because she's built to teach, I guess . . . plus it was an old Jethro Tull song I liked, you know, I thought it was cool," he said, lowering his head, waiting for them to laugh at his mention of the old rock group.

"She's a river craft? She's long and looks too big to navigate tight waterways," Carl said as he came down from the metal scaffolding.

Jenks tapped the composite hull. "Let me tell you something, Toad, this baby only draws six and a half feet of water. She rides high but is capable of taking on ten thousand pounds of water ballast. She has a whole section in the middle there that lowers deeper into the water by telescoping her hull by fifteen feet for observation purposes. She has an enclosed two-man submersible and an observation diving bell.

In her stern housing, she has fifteen different unmanned, radio-controlled probes for underwater research. She has cabin space for fifty-one people. Her galley is better equipped than any vessel in the navy. She's totally sealed and air-conditioned. Her electronics suite is state-of-the-art, and she has three labs on board and room for one more if we clear out some storage lockers. She has a glass-enclosed live well that holds five thousand gallons of water and is fully oxygenated. The sections can be separately maneuvered by independent water jets to match the tight turns involved in river operation, thanks to the expanding rubber gaskets between the sections; and the water jets are controlled by computers so accurate she can bring her bow all the way around and kiss her own ass. She can be dismantled and flown anywhere in the world and be in the water ready for action within twenty-four hours. Each section is light enough to be carried by a Blackhawk or Seahawk helicopter."

"This is the most amazing thing I've ever seen," Carl exclaimed.

"Took ten years of my life, and now the navy's trying to shortchange me," grumbled Jenks as he ran his hand lovingly along *Teacher*'s side.

"This is an amazing science platform," Danielle said.

"Yeah, but I doubt if she ever has a chance to see the water," the master chief said glumly.

Carl walked straight up to him and smiled. "Chief, we need to borrow her and you, too."

"Look, Toad, she needs about another two tons of electronics. Hell, she needs her whole navigation and mapping system. So unless you can write me a check for about five and a half million dollars and get the Department of the Navy and the president of the United States to give her to you, you're up shit's creek without a paddle, boy. Besides, I'm done kowtowing to those bastards anyway. You can't have her."

"Well, Chief, I only go up the creeks I'm told to sail, so however much and what it is that you need, I'll have it here within the day, and the people you need to assist you in installing it," Carl said as he brought out his cell phone.

The master chief looked at Carl and then at Danielle, who smiled and nodded her head, letting him know Carl was serious.

"Put the damned phone away," he said. "I'm not the whore you seem to think I am, Toad. The answer is no!"

Carl stopped dialing. "Where we're going, we'll need one *hell* of a boat. This is your chance to get this baby into action and prove what she can do. They stuck you down here to keep you out of the way, Chief, so that means they don't think you have anything to offer the navy anymore."

"You think you can play me like a fiddle? Well, my boy, you have another fuckin' think comin'. I would just as soon burn this thing as to—"

"There are college kids down there, Chief. They haven't been heard from in weeks. We need you. And we need *Teacher*." Danielle held Jenks's glare with her own softer version. Then his features relaxed and his eyes traveled down to her chest once again, like a magnet drawn to steel.

"Kids, huh?"

"A few of them the same age as your granddaughter."

Jenks addressed Carl. "Low blow, Toad." He angrily tossed the stub of cigar away. "Well, you gonna make that call or not? I need a lot of shit to complete this tub!"

Carl made the call.

Danielle looked *Teacher* over again and hoped the vessel was everything the master chief said she was. They would need every possible advantage for where they were going.

As for Carl, he was more practical. He just hoped the gleaming white experimental boat would float.

EVENT GROUP COMPLEX NUMBER ONE
ARLINGTON, VIRGINIA

Niles stood looking at the old computer center used by the Event Group. The complex contained custom-made filing cabinets and shelving that stored a million or more accounts of historical, mythic, or legendary events—everything from the location of Atlantis to the incredible stories of yetis, the mythical beast of the Himalayas, to the suspected ancient power sources discovered by Egypt three thousand years before.

"Some computer center you have here, Mr. Director. A little bit behind the times, aren't we?" Ryan asked as he ran a hand along one of the old filing cabinets.

"The information covered in these files, Lieutenant Ryan, is the whole of our ancient and modern world. Facts and stories, even rumors are stored here. The combined knowledge of the ancient world started this facility."

"And you expect us to find something here, sir?" Ryan said as he brushed some dust off his hands.

"Actually, we have the Librarian. One of the first Crays ever installed in a government facility," Niles said as he made his way over to a small cubicle. "At first it was one of those card-wielding Univac machines that we updated from time to time, but we eventually upgraded in 1980 to a system that was called, naturally enough, the Librarian."

Niles used a key to open the door to the cubicle that sat in the middle of the gymnasium-size storage area. The room was dark and dank and had a musty smell that made Ryan wiggle his nose.

"Smells like the old Librarian may have kicked the proverbial bucket, sir."

Niles ignored the comment and flipped on the overhead lights, illuminating the small computer station whose speakers were mounted on both sides of the large desk. There was only one chair and Niles sat in it. Ryan looked around and decided to just cross his arms and wait.

"The auditory system was installed two years ago by Pete and me to make research easier for historians of the group. I'm afraid this voice isn't as feminine as what we have with Europa, but it's kind of quaint."

Ryan watched as Niles adjusted a microphone in front of

him and pushed a small button, activating a small but adequate monitor pop-up on the right side of the desk.

"Let's just hope what Professor Zachary erased on Europa back home is still in here."

"Hello, Librarian," Niles said into the microphone.

The monitor came to life as the speakers did.

Good afternoon, Dr. Compton, or would you like to be addressed as Director Compton now? the male voice asked, referring to his promotion since the last time they'd spoken.

To Ryan it sounded disturbingly like the voice of HAL from *2001: A Space Odyssey*, the same computer that went nuts and killed everyone.

"Dr. Compton is fine. Librarian, can you access my last log-on to your sister system, Europa in Nevada?"

Yes, Dr. Compton, I can; I enjoy interfacing with Europa.

"I imagine you do," Ryan mumbled.

THE PENTAGON

Rear Admiral Elliott Pierce was studying an intelligence brief, on the continuing withdrawal of Iranian armor divisions from the border with Iraq, when a knock sounded at his door. He summoned the person in and was given a note.

"This just came in from Signal, sir."

Pierce took the note from the young signalman and excused him. As he read the communication, his face fell. He immediately picked up the phone and called a number at the White House. The president's national security advisor picked up on the first ring.

"Ambrose," the voice said.

"We have a problem," Pierce said softly, for no other reason than he felt deceitful.

"What?"

"The Red Flag we placed on the National Archives file that Professor Zachary used, which is cross-referenced with our database, has just been activated."

"Jesus Christ, by whom?"

"It says terminal 5656, but there is no terminal 5656, according to our intelligence records."

"So, maybe it's a glitch," the national security advisor said in an annoyed tone.

"I don't believe that much in coincidence, do you?" Pierce asked smugly.

"Well, what can you do?"

"My signals team was able to track the terminal's location; you won't believe it."

"We don't have time for this. Where is it?"

"Arlington National Cemetery—the mansion's maintenance facility, of all places."

"Goddammit, what in the hell is going on here?"

"I don't know, but we'd better get someone over there or this could get rather sticky."

"Do you have access to outside nonmilitary people for this?"

"Yes, and they're right down the road. They can be onsite in twenty minutes with equipment that could trace this phantom computer terminal. Are you going to say anything to *him* about this?"

"Hell no, just take care of it, he's got enough on his mind already. He has a meeting with the president about an appearance at a fund-raiser for his campaign tonight. Just eliminate this problem any way you can, understand?"

"This is getting to be too costly. We're going to hang for this if we're caught."

"Then the object here is—what? Not to get caught. And don't inform the others about this development, they're getting cold feet enough as it is. Eliminate whoever is snooping into that file."

The director of Naval Intelligence hung up the phone and removed a small black book from his desk drawer. Whoever had accessed that unlisted computer terminal wouldn't live long enough to benefit from it.

EVENT GROUP COMPLEX NUMBER ONE
ARLINGTON, VIRGINIA.

"Okay, Librarian, is your interface complete with Nellis complex?"

Yes, Dr. Compton, Europa is online.

"Good, Europa, identify last three queries, Compton, Niles, Director Department 5656."

Yes, Dr. Compton, formulating, the female voice answered. *Last three queries made by Director Compton to Europa at Nellis complex were: Question number one, Number of the four papal medalists still alive on North and South American continents in 1874; question number two, What was name of recipient? And question number three, What, you mean the information was erased from the old Cray system?*

"Okay, Europa, thank you. Librarian, have you located said files?"

Yes, Dr. Compton, the HAL-like voice answered.

"Answer to first query, how many papal medal recipients were still alive on North and South American continents in 1874?" Niles asked as his palms started to sweat.

Searching, Librarian answered as the small screen flashed to Niles's right.

Niles shifted impatiently, hoping this hadn't been a wild-goose chase.

According to Royal Canadian death records, the general census of citizens of Mexico, the official census of Brazil, and the state and territorial records of the United States, one member was still alive in 1874, Librarian answered.

Niles read the duplicate printed answer on the screen with renewed hope; it was the same answer that Europa had given back at Nellis, so the file might just be intact after its initial transcription into the new system. "Question. What was the last name of recipient?"

Searching, Dr. Compton, Librarian answered.

"I guess this is it, huh?" Ryan asked. He, too, felt nervous and leaned closer to the monitor.

"It could be life or death for a lot of people lost down there in the Amazon," Niles said as he bit his lower lip, waiting for the much slower computer than Europa to disgorge the wanted information. Suddenly the voice activated and the monitor flashed to life with a green glow.

Name of remaining recipient; Keogh, Myles Walter; occupation, United States Army; born: 1840, County Carlow, Ireland; recipient of earlier-described papal honors and veteran of the Battalion of St. Patrick's for armed service to the Vatican.

The name that Librarian had said was familiar; Niles was sure he had heard it before. So was Ryan. "Hey, that name, it sounds—" blurted the lieutenant.

"Question," Niles said, cutting off Ryan as he slowly sat back in his chair. In a low voice, almost as if he was afraid to ask the question, "Date and place of death?"

Searching.

Niles stared at the liquid crystal screen and waited, Ryan planted only inches from his shoulder.

Death occurred at present-day Crow Agency, Montana, United States, June 25, 1876.

Niles felt his heart start to sink. "Question. What was the unit Keogh served with, and the historical name of the location of death?"

Searching, Librarian said in its flat and insane-sounding voice.

As the answer came on screen, Niles lowered the volume of the speakers as history came flooding back in on him, burying all hopes of finding the map if it had been with Myles Keogh when he died. The map was indeed, as Helen had said in her letter, lost forever.

"Jesus Christ, we're fucked," Jason Ryan muttered as he looked at the screen.

Printed out on the monitor was Librarian's answer to his last two inquiries.

Place of death: Valley of the Little Bighorn, Montana, U.S. Territory. Captain Myles Keogh served with operational line unit, Company I, Seventh United States Cavalry.

EVENT GROUP CENTER
NELLIS AFB, NEVADA

Niles was linked by conference call from the center in Arlington, three thousand miles away, as the team at Nellis gathered for his briefing on what he and Ryan had just learned from Librarian. Jack and Virginia were at the conference table, along with Pete Golding. Alice sat in her regular seat beside Niles's empty chair.

"Okay, Pete, Virginia, did you get a chance to check my facts from this morning?" Niles asked.

"Yes," Virginia said as she picked up her notes. "Without looking at your research as you requested, we started our own track on the papal medalists, and came up with the exact same information when it dead-ended on the date of Helen's theft."

"May I ask what it is you are talking about?" Jack asked.

"I'm sorry, Jack. Let me get you up to speed. The Padilla diary, as we all know, has been stolen from the archdiocese in Madrid. We have a pretty good idea who took it, but the map seemed a dead end until we linked it to a Spanish priest who, in 1874, has been a papal medalist and a veteran of St. Patrick's Battalion. I won't go into it all here, but suffice it to say in Professor Zachary's letter to me, this was the way to uncover the facts of the map's whereabouts. We linked it to other veterans at that time with whom the Vatican had direct contact, men who could be trusted, and, to make a long story short, we believe we have traced the map to our own country. But just where and to who it was sent has become a major problem," Niles related mechanically over the speakerphone.

The director took the next ten minutes to explain the bad news about the map. The four people around the conference table shook their heads, knowing the odds of the map's being their salvation was now a moot point.

"I started making phone calls from here and I managed to contact descendants of Keogh, who currently live in New York State. Nobody has or ever heard of such a map. Whatever he had taken with him to the Little Bighorn were not among his personal articles returned to his family. His body was disinterred from the battlefield and moved to New York, and was buried with nothing other than his papal medals and uniform," Niles said. "The medals were returned because they were still on his person at the time after the battle by General Alfred Terry's column. He was also known to have had a large cross at the time that the regiment left Fort Abraham Lincoln in the Dakota Territory. This fact is mentioned in several memoirs, not only by other officers, but even in an account of Libby Custer's, the general's widow. She had personally given Keogh a package that was forwarded to him from New York by courier before the ill-fated campaign began. She even said it was a large, gaudy-looking thing that belonged on a wall and not around a man's neck."

"What do you think, Niles? Is that cross something the Vatican may have entrusted to Keogh," asked Virginia.

"I do."

"And records of items recovered at the Little Bighorn or Indian accounts of pillaged material at the site has never made mention of a large cross?" Jack asked.

"I asked Alice to get into the National Parks Service database. Alice, you have anything?" Niles asked.

"We are currently waiting on the most current archeological listings that were conducted by the National Parks Service. They have been unearthing so much since the big brush fire in the 1980s. They just conducted the last field hunt only five weeks ago, and have not published their findings yet," Alice said, taking a breath. "But the odds are good that some warrior may have taken the cross, since that item was very familiar to them, unlike the papal medals the captain was known to have worn."

"I see. Let me know when you get the information on the dig," Niles said. "Now, I want all historical divisions, and I mean everyone, combing through what we have on the Little Bighorn in case we uncover something about the missing map. Just in case it's found and is still in Montana, I want you, Jack, to head there right now. Take someone who knows something about the Battle of the Little Bighorn because I'm afraid I have the American History Department split in two helping Latin American Studies. Besides, we have to get stepping ahead of this thing or those kids down there may die."

"Yes, sir."

"And I have the perfect person to accompany you, Jack," Alice interjected. "She's quite an expert on the Battle of the Little Bighorn. It was her thesis topic."

JACK LOOKED AT his watch and saw it was only moments before the geology class let out for the afternoon. He peeked into the classroom window. He anticipated the instructor's wrath when she learned he had already gone into her room to pack some field gear for her, to hurry the process along. Unknowing of this, Sarah McIntire was enthusiastically explaining something with the use of a virtual diagram that was holographically projected onto a small podium at the front of the room. As she spoke, the three-dimensional diagram of an underground chamber rotated in colors of green, blue, and red. Jack stepped into the room, and gestured for Sarah to continue when she frowned at his intrusion. The fifty-two students, mostly military personnel, turned to look at him. Not just a few eyes lingered on the man who was quickly becoming a legend at the Group.

"Now as I said before, don't be fooled just because a room in a tomb has no apparent exits. Ancient designers usually had emergency egress points that only they knew about. Most didn't favor being trapped before their job was done."

Sarah pointed to a seemingly solid wall on the hologram that was outlined in blue. "The key to these escape routes are usually found in some sort of ornamentation, such as this found in KV-63."

Jack knew that KV-63 stood for Kings Valley 63, a tomb uncovered more than sixty years before in Egypt's Valley of the Kings, not far from where Howard Carter had made his discovery of King Tutankhamen fabulous tomb.

"As you see," the hologram magically enlarged to show an ornate wall symbol that had at one time been a torch holder—several were placed strategically around the chamber, "this was discovered purely by accident."

The laser close-up became enhanced even more and, as it did, the ornate holder in the shape of a jackal's head twisted. The facing popped free of the wall.

"Surprise, surprise," Sarah exclaimed, "The cover was concealing a fulcrum release switch, which operated a gravity feed doorway."

As the students watched in awe, the laser hologram depicted a lever inside the wall being pulled down, which in turn activated a sand pour that went into a large container buried in the wall. As it grew heavy with sand (five tons of it, Sarah explained), the hidden escape door inside the closed tomb started to rise. Once it was up, a green laser stairway was presented that led up and out of the tomb.

"So you see, never think that the ancients were dumb enough to box themselves into a corner; they always had an emergency way out of a tight jam. This technology was not only discovered in ancient Egypt but also in many other places around the world, in Peru, Central America, and even China."

A soft chime sounded and Sarah looked up. "Okay, that's it for today. I'll see you next week and, don't forget, I want some more examples of the amazing fulcrum release points found in other areas, not just tombs. I want the modern-day equivalent."

There were a few moans but most of the students left the class knowing more than they had coming in. Every member of the Event Group had to take advanced collegiate courses in order to stay in the Group, and most heartily volunteered to attend them, in any case.

Jack nodded to the students who smiled and said hello as they exited the classroom.

"There's a rumor you're hard on homework," he said.

Sarah gathered up her notes and turned off the hologram. "Not as hard as I would like. But they do have their regular duties here; can't usurp all their time."

"Well, Teach, I have a duty for you. Your bags are packed, let's go."

"Where we going, Major Collins?" she mocked him just a bit.

"To play cowboys and Indians, Lieutenant." Jack picked up her briefcase and then took her by the elbow.

"Huh?"

"We're going to Montana. Someone seems to think you know something about the Little Bighorn."

"Okay." Sarah stopped and looked at him with her eyes narrowed. "Wait a minute, just who packed my stuff?"

Jack winked and led her out of the room.

ARLINGTON NATIONAL CEMETERY
ARLINGTON, VIRGINIA

As Niles and Ryan sat in the green sedan on their ride back to the surface, the young lieutenant could see the director was deep in thought. The camouflaged dirt floor above them parted to allow the massive lift to complete its journey to the surface, where they were met by a lance corporal. He waved and then disappeared into a small maintenance cubicle that doubled as the security office. Ryan started the car as the large double doors parted and bright afternoon sunshine once again filled the interior. He backed the car out and onto the gravel drive at the back of the mansion. With a last wave at the marine guard, he put the car into drive and headed toward the front of the grounds. As he passed two men in light Windbreakers, Ryan had the queer feeling they were being watched. He lifted his hand and adjusted the rearview mirror in time to see the two men turn and raise their own hands, only theirs weren't full of car mirror. Ryan immediately saw the submachine guns. He pushed Director Compton down hard to the left by grabbing his suit coat, and leaned down across him. Just as they both hit the seat, bullets smashed through the rear window and into the interior of the vehicle. Ryan felt flying glass as he blindly slammed his foot down on the accelerator and shot off the road into the cemetery proper. Niles had the good sense to keep down.

"How many?" he asked without attempting to rise.

"Three," Ryan said loudly over the noise of more rounds striking the metal skin of the car. As he lifted his head to see where to steer toward, he saw a dark green Dodge pickup truck with two men in the front and one standing in the back. It slid sideways in an attempt to head them off. Ryan threw the wheel to the left and turned the car around, narrowly avoiding a large tree. He tried to head back the way they had come. He was starting to wonder where the Parks Service men were when he saw one of them sprawled on the grass not ten feet from his spinning front wheels. "Five!" he called, correcting his earlier statement to Niles.

More bullets pinged and thumped into the moving car, and the passenger-side window blew inward as a larger calibered weapon opened up from the back of the pursuing truck.

"Goddammit, this ain't going to last long if we don't get some help!" Ryan shouted as he slid down again in his seat. As he did so, he crushed the accelerator down to the floor, again narrowly missing some of the outer white crosses that marked the resting place of fallen soldiers and statesmen. Reaching under the seat, he brought up the only weapon they had, an old Colt .45 he had brought along simply because Jack's regulation was that no security man left on a field assignment unarmed. So he chose a weapon he had first qualified with in the navy, the venerable Colt.

"Hang on, sir!" he cried as he swung the car into a complete 180-degree turn. He used his right hand to steer and with the left he pointed the .45 automatic out of the window and started pulling the trigger as fast as he could at the oncoming truck. Several of the large rounds hit the truck's windshield and one or two found their mark, striking the man standing in the pickup's bed. The bullets struck their attacker so hard he went flying out of the back; Ryan was amazed to see him bouncing like a rubber ball until his body struck one of the white crosses and came to an abrupt stop with blood misting the air around the memorial, staining the white marker crimson.

"Hah! Got one," Ryan cheered in momentary triumph.

Niles sat up to see. "Look out!" he shouted as he saw the first two men. They were both standing in the road, shocked that the car was speeding right for them once again.

Ryan pulled the wheel to the right just in time as the two men again opened fire. Several bullets hit the windshield and spider-webbed the safety glass. One of the bullets grazed by his head, only inches from his skull.

Niles reached out and pulled the gun out of Ryan's hand, swinging the weapon out of his broken passenger window. He was cursing up a storm, already angered by the futility of his computer search and, on top of that, at the indignity of being shot at in this hallowed place.

"Son of a bitch!" he screamed as he fired off the last four rounds in the Colt's clip.

Ryan quickly glanced out the side window and was amazed to see one man grab his face and careen into the other, sending his fire off target. Then an amazing thing happened. Ryan didn't see the tree and they slammed into it. It was a rear-right-side quarter-panel graze, but enough to stop the car. At the same time, the dark green pickup truck found the road and came screeching toward them. Ryan figured in a split second that was it, as he turned the ignition and there was nothing but the clicking of the solenoid. The car was as dead as they soon would be. As he thought this, the truck suddenly swerved, as loud popping noises sounded from a distance away. The truck's front window blew inward. The man in the passenger seat grabbed his chest just as his face disintegrated in a hail of large-calibered bullets. The driver of the truck slammed on his brakes and turned the big vehicle around, stopping only to retrieve the one man who was standing and carrying his partner. The driver waited only long enough for the man to throw his buddy into the back and climb in, and then sped away toward the front gate.

Ryan closed his eyes as the silence grew around him. He heard the ticking of the cooling engine and the heavy breathing of Niles, but that was all. He looked around and took stock of the damage. He shook the director until Niles looked at him with a blank stare.

"You okay, sir?" Ryan asked, himself a bowl of jelly.

"How does Jack do it? I mean, that's the first time I have ever been shot at," Niles said as he slowly laid the gun on the glass-covered seat.

"I'm sure he hates it as much as us, sir."

As they watched, several Arlington guards and the Group's undercover marines made their way to the car. Ryan opened the car door; it creaked loudly and fell to the grass. In the next second, the black hand of the lance corporal who had moments earlier seen them off was helping him out of the car, and then the director.

"Ballsy bastards, weren't they?" he said.

"Yeah," Ryan said. "They must have wanted us stopped from leaving here pretty bad."

The lance corporal checked Niles for injuries. "A few more minutes, you might have taken up permanent residence here."

Niles remained blank faced. How in the hell could someone send a team into a covert site, and how in the hell did they know he was there?

"We've got to get back, Corporal. Get us some transport, please," Niles ordered, "before the Parks Service starts asking questions about us."

"Yes, sir," the corporal said as he sprinted off back toward the maintenance shed.

"Mr. Ryan, someone knows what's up here in Washington."

"Yeah, and I would sure like to know who it is. I could have that F-16 trainer armed with no trouble . . ."

"I admire your sentiments, but we have to get back to the Group, ASAP!"

THREE HOURS LATER, Ryan and Niles were in the F-16 somewhere over Nebraska when they received a scrambled transmission from the Group's information center. The director was surprised to hear Jack's voice on the other end of the call.

"Major, I thought you were heading out to Montana."

"Copy that, Doctor. We delayed in the hope of tracking down the identity of the man Lieutenant Ryan shot in Arlington."

"And?" Niles asked from twenty-eight thousand feet.

"Niles, the body was gone by the time our security arrived up top. Someone beat us to it."

"Who in the hell are we butting heads with? Major, we'll talk again when we arrive; hang tight until I arrive, then we'll figure out how to proceed."

"Roger. By the way, Mr. Ryan tells me you may have saved both of you with some good shooting."

"I was scared to death!" Niles said quietly into the face mask.

"All battles are fought by scared men who would much rather be somewhere else, Mr. Director. And pass along to Ryan, well done."

Ryan smiled under his mask. *Praise from Caesar.*

EVENT GROUP COMPLEX
NELLIS AFB, NEVADA
FOUR HOURS LATER

Niles had showered and was sitting in the conference room with Alice, Jack, Pete Golding, and Virginia Pollock; Lieutenant Commander Everett was on the speakerphone from

New Orleans. The director filled them in on the details of his trip and the murderous attempt on his life in the cemetery. After they were all updated, there was a knock on the door. An army signals officer entered and gave Niles a sheet of paper. Niles read it and then reached for the remote. He punched a button and a ten-by-six-foot liquid crystal screen slid down from the ceiling at the head of the conference table. He then pushed another button and the numbers 5156 appeared on the screen. Then suddenly a face appeared, blurred and then refocused and stabilized, A woman smiled into the camera and she stepped aside and allowed an elderly man to step into view.

"Director Compton?" the man asked. "I can't see you; we have all of our monitors in use at this time. There is quite a bit of excitement going on here at the moment," the gray-haired man said as he turned and hushed everyone behind him.

"I can hear and see you, Nathan," Niles assured the excited professor as he looked around the table and spoke in hushed tones to the others. "Dr. Allan Nathan, expert on American history, has combined his department with Anthropological Studies to see what can be found out about the Little Bighorn archaeological projects."

"Good, good. We have just received the pictures from the National Parks Service on items they recovered on their most recent dig." Nathan disappeared from the screen for a moment, but his voice could still be heard. "I am forwarding the pictures to you now."

As they watched, over 150 small images of items filled the entire liquid crystal screen. Some were easily recognizable, such as arrowheads, a rusted navy Colt pistol with the wooden handgrips missing, a boot that had deteriorated to the point that it had no leather upper any longer. Buttons with "U.S." embossed on them, belt buckles with the same, and, most disturbing of all, bones. Finger bones, a pelvic bone, and what was easily recognized as a large femur.

The room was quiet as they looked at the images.

"The Parks Service had a real good dig this time out, as heavy rains removed even more topsoil than the fires had a few years back. Now what's so exciting here, Mr. Director, is the fact that for the first time they concentrated heavily on area 2139." As the professor spoke, the images of the artifacts disappeared from the screen and a Parks Service rendering of the battlefield took their place. On the illustrator, at a spot just north of Last Stand Hill, where Custer and his companies had met their grisly fate, was a yellow circle. Inside the circle was a legend with the letters C, I, and L. "This is where Captain Myles Keogh made his stand with the remnants of the three troops, or companies. We have found quite a few artifacts besides the brass and copper shell casings, which indicated, by the way, that the three companies had put up one hell of a defense; the Parks Service discovered thirty-seven military-issued and nonmilitary items in this group that they believed had been carried to the Little Bighorn by Seventh Cavalry troopers."

Niles stood and walked closer to the screen. Jack Collins remained seated, and was writing down the details of what the history department was saying. He had never studied the battle in 1876 the way he should have, only tactically at West Point, never thinking of, or trying to imagine, what it must have been like to have fought and died there.

"According to eyewitnesses, mainly a few Northern Cheyenne and Sioux, Keogh and his men fought bravely, with the captain standing firmly in the center of his dismounted troopers. Some say the image of him like that was the mistaken reason why Custer has always been depicted that way, but the Native Americans swear it was Keogh and not Yellow Hair that was directing the hardest fight."

"Professor, please, we can go over the Seventh's exploits at a more convenient time," Niles said impatiently.

"Yes, of course, I was just trying to set the stage somewhat for you." Now the photos of the total recovered artifacts replaced the map of the battlefield. "These items were recovered inside the areas defended by Keogh's three companies."

As he said this, the computer images began to drop away, until only thirty-seven artifacts remained. "We have several items here that could have possibly contained the map: two army-issue saddlebags, ten leather pouches, most for tobacco storage, and three bottles. We do have several Christian crosses, but the most interesting item is this box here."

A yellow circle centered itself on a metal box that appeared rusted shut and heavily dented. As they watched, the item rotated 160 degrees to show the back, below the old hinges. In the center they could barely make out three letters. The first letter was totally wiped out due to rust, so all they could clearly see was "W.K."

Nathan continued. "So the initials were a blank, then *W* and *K*. Do you see what I mean? This may be the best lead we have, as it just might have belonged to either Myles Walter Keogh or a sergeant by the name of John William Killkernan, a sergeant attached to L Company. The odds are fifty-fifty."

"Have you contacted the Parks Service and asked if the metal box contains anything?" Niles asked, trying to hold down his excitement.

"That's the bad news, I'm afraid. They say they haven't examined the items as of yet, beyond the initial cleaning and photo stage. They are currently displayed at the battlefield as is, before any forensic work is performed. We requested access but it was denied by the University of Montana, as it was their dig, and the Parks Service gave us lip service about shared responsibility."

"Thank you, Professor Nathan. Pass along to your people that you may have saved our butts on this one, and continue your research. I'll get someone out there. Can you spare someone to accompany?" Niles asked.

There was silence at the other end of the speaker. Then Nathan came back on. "Yes, I can spare *me*. My team has their chores to do and I'm only in the way."

"Good, I'll set you up with security and another volunteer that knows something about the Little Bighorn. Again, thanks, Professor. Be ready to leave within the hour."

Niles walked a little more briskly back to his chair than when he had left it. He took a deep breath and looked at Jack.

"Major, I think it's time you get to Montana."

"I'll take Mendenhall and Jason Ryan along so I don't have to talk too much to Professor Nathan."

"Take Mendenhall, but I would appreciate it if you leave Mr. Ryan here. I need him to do something and I need you to plan it before you leave here."

"Okay. Alice, you said you had a candidate that knows something of the Little Big Horn?"

"Yes, Director, a certain Second Lieutenant McIntire," Alice said, looking at Jack.

"Good, gather your things and alert Mendenhall and the lieutenant. You'll have transport in thirty minutes at the base. And take care of Nathan, will you, because he's not really a field man."

Jack nodded and started for the door.

"Jack?" Niles said as he hesitated with the phone halfway to his ear.

"Yes?"

"You and Ryan come right back after you've alerted McIntire and Mendenhall as to your travel plans. Mr. Ryan will also be traveling, but a little farther south. And while you're at the battlefield, be careful, we don't know who else is after the map. If Farbeaux is in it, things could turn ugly real quick, and we don't need to lose more soldiers at the Little Big Horn."

"You have something for Ryan I need to know about?" Jack asked.

"I want him to liaise with a rescue element in Panama. I don't know how yet, but we need something in place down there."

"Good idea. We have to come up with a way to feed them real-time intel on what's happening, if we can get down there."

"Jack?" Carl had said nothing until this very moment, on speakerphone from New Orleans.

"Yeah?"

"Watch your ass, buddy. There are bad guys out there looking to stop you hard. The way they went after Niles and Ryan says they mean business."

"I'll do just that, and you and Ms. Serrate stay put and watch yourselves; they may be onto you, as well. Did you start getting the equipment we've started sending out from our stores?"

"Yes, sir, the master chief is like a hog in mud; he's working now with our techs, getting the first of our gifts installed."

"Very good, Commander Everett, see you as soon as we get back from Montana."

Jack winked at Alice and left the conference room, feeling pretty sure that the Little Bighorn could not claim any more U.S. soldiers.

TEN MINUTES LATER, Niles had fully explained to Jack his and the president's plan for Jason Ryan. Jack had concurred and he left quickly, going into Signals to request the equipment needed for Niles's South American safety valve, leaving Ryan standing in front of the director's desk. The plan was contingent upon Ryan and his team's meeting up with an experimental platform that might or might not be used. It was all they had, and using it would be a long shot, but Niles still wanted something, anything, set up in case Jack and his team ran into trouble down there.

"I have a job for you, Lieutenant."

"Yes, sir."

"I've seen your training record. Jack's been running you ragged, hasn't he?"

"Yes, sir, he's a real hard—"

"I see you're up-to-date on your jump training, is that accurate?"

Ryan looked at Niles and became a tad off balance. He had indeed finished his jump training, but had quickly found out, after his ejection over the Pacific last year in a naval mishap, that he hadn't taken to parachutes all that much.

"Accurate . . . I . . . uh, yes sir, the record is accurate."

"Good, high-level jumps?"

Ryan closed his eyes and remembered Jack and Carl's laughter as he did his three required high-altitude jumps over the Nevada desert. He also remembered screaming for almost two miles through the air before he realized it would do no good.

"Yes, Dr. Compton, high-altitude rating."

Niles smiled at Ryan's fidgeting. He then slid over a large yellow envelope containing the lieutenant's travel orders that instructed him to report to Fort Bragg, North Carolina, to the officially nonexistent Delta force operational team complex there.

"With the apparatus you'll be flying in, you have to have high-altitude jump training for emergency reasons."

Ryan read his orders and then looked at Niles. He started to say something and then stopped, and then decided to ask the question anyway. "I'm not going to help on the Amazon River thing?"

"No, Mr. Ryan, you're helping on the Black Operations . . . thing."

TWENTY MINUTES LATER, Alice stuck her head in through his office door.

"The president is on the red phone."

Niles nodded and Alice disappeared. He hesitated before touching the phone on the right corner of his desk. The report was in front of him on the physical comparison check Europa had completed on the girl in the picture taken in San Pedro, and the news had confirmed their worst fears. And now he would have to tell a worried father about his missing daughter. He wished he could have told him before, but that was when they were only guessing as to her identity. Now they were sure. Ninety-six percent accuracy was as sure as the supercomputer could be. And that meant Kelly was indeed in the Amazon with Helen. He steeled himself and picked up the phone's red receiver.

"Mr. President. I have several updates for you. But first I

have to ask you a few questions, if you don't mind, and request that you prepare your computer to receive an e-mail attachment."

"Fine, Niles, ask and e-mail away. I only have more shmoozing to do for our esteemed secretary of state. It never ends."

"Mr. President, your oldest daughter is in Washington on summer break?"

"Kelly? No, she's out at Berkeley for the summer. As a matter of fact, she's in deep with me. She went and ditched her protection team to see some boy out there. She called and said not to worry; we traced the call and it was from a pay phone in Los Angeles. It's a secret around here, but I have about three hundred agents of the secret service and FBI trying to track her down before the press gets ahold of it. Why do you ask about her?"

Niles e-mailed the still frame through to the president. "Is this your daughter, sir?"

The president looked closely at the enhanced image. "Goddammit, where is she?"

"That photograph was taken on the very same ship that Professor Zachary sailed on a month ago."

A shocked silence, then, "I'll get the secretary of state down to Brazil and see if we can have their cooperation to send some troops into that area. In the meantime, Niles, get your people moving!"

The connection was terminated and Niles replaced the receiver on his phone. He ran his fingers across his bald scalp.

"This job never gets any easier," he mumbled.

Niles opened his computer's monitor to a large map of South America. His hand reached up and touched the jagged course of the Amazon River; the clear plastic of the touch screen felt cool to his fingertips. As he crossed the open flow of the giant river, his fingers traced red lines that were reactive to his light pressure. Then he saw that wherever he ran his finger, the tracking line followed, and he realized just how much the computer graphic looked like blood.

He removed his hand quickly and looked at the spots his outstretched fingers had been. The flow of red was not only the color of blood, but it was also in the shape of four long claw marks.

SAN JOSE, CALIFORNIA

The man sat in the forward compartment of the Learjet. He listened to a single headphone jack and smiled as he caught only the intelligible side Everett's conversation. But it was enough. Captain Juan Rosolo, former commander of the Internal Security Division of the Colombian government and inside man for the Cali drug cartel, had the destination for his special squad of men. He made sure the team he was sending to Montana understood in no uncertain terms what the price of failure would be. The quest for the map would end tonight even at the cost of all their lives, either by this Major Collins's hand, or by his own.

FIFTY MILES SOUTH OF BILLINGS, MONTANA
THREE HOURS LATER

"Where are you, Jack?" Niles asked into the scrambled security phone.

"Right now we're about five miles out of the battlefield on US 212; we landed at Logan airport in Billings about six forty. Why, what's up?" Jack asked, looking over at Mendenhall, who was driving. Sarah and Dr. Allan Nathan were in the back debating the merits of General Sheridan's ruthless three-pronged attack method used for the campaign against the hostiles in 1876.

"Jack, I'm getting ready to call the president. We have received some disturbing news about a couple of the passengers onboard the *Pacific Voyager*. They are Department of Defense employees, Jack, that's all I'll say on this line. Now more than ever, watch your behinds out there; you're a long way from help."

"Warning received and appreciated, Niles, thanks."

The connection was terminated and Jack closed his cell phone. No one spoke for a moment as Mendenhall turned off the highway at the battlefield exit. Jack reached out and turned up the air conditioner, then closed his eyes in thought.

"Look at this, Major," Mendenhall said, indicating a far-away sight outside of his window. The passengers in the backseat were also quiet as they, too, had caught the same image against the darkening eastern sky.

An eerie silence filled the rental car as they followed the asphalt track. A sense of history wasn't the term Jack would use; it was something else. He felt this way very rarely but he did recognize it. He gazed at the monuments sitting atop a small rise in the land, with the tallest in the center catching the late afternoon sun, and the whiteness of the grave markers gleamed. He had a feeling of loss, or more to the point, a feeling of being near a happening, a moment in time that transcends mere history.

The Little Bighorn Battlefield was a place that will be forever remembered. At Last Stand Hill, a man named Custer once stood and fell with over 265 of his men. It was also a place where countless indigenous peoples had fought and died for their right to exist.

Sarah and Nathan knew beyond any doubt it had to be one of the most haunted spots in the world. A small shudder traveled down Sarah's spine as their car traveled over a steel cattle guard that spanned the flowing Little Bighorn River.

"I always heard from people that this place was creepy; now I know what they meant," Sarah said as she watched the monuments fade over the rise.

"I don't know if soldiers were ever meant to be here, for any reason, Major," Mendenhall said, looking out of the window.

Jack didn't comment, only because he thought the sergeant was right—soldiers weren't meant to be here, then and maybe even now.

As they drove up the winding road, several cars passed them. As they entered the gate, they could see more than twenty Native Americans place picket signs into the backs of pickup trucks and vans, as they made ready to leave. A few even waved as Jack's car drove past them.

As they went through the gate and toward the visitor's center, they failed to notice the two large SUVs waiting about a mile away, well off the dirt road and outer RV camping area.

JACK, MENDENHALL, SARAH, and Dr. Nathan walked down the path after parking in the lot next to the visitor's center. It was now close to seven thirty and the area was deserted with the exception of a green pickup truck that had a National Parks Service emblem on its door.

Jack tried the door to the battlefield museum first and found it locked. He leaned close and peered through the glass but could see the building was empty. Construction materials were strewn about, as the visitor's center and museum were readying for a much-needed expansion. But the workers had all left for the day hours before.

"Hi there, sorry, the museum closes at six on weekdays," said a man walking down the path toward them. He wore a Smokey the Bear hat and a tan uniform.

Jack stepped forward and held out his hand. "I'm Jack Collins; I believe you were contacted earlier by my boss in Washington," he said. He noticed immediately that the man was armed.

"You the army, Major?" the ranger asked, shaking his hand.

"That's me."

"We expected you before closing time, Major; my partners out front are locking up the gates right now, and the others are around on Reno Hill making sure no one gets locked in."

"Well, we have to see the exhibits. It's very important," Jack said, releasing the taller man's hand.

"National security, I heard your boss. What department did you say you worked with again?"

"The Smithsonian Institute, and Ms. McIntire and Dr. Nathan here represent the National Archives," Jack answered, the small deceit rolling easily from his tongue.

"Well, my boss in D.C. said to let you in, so I guess we'll let you in," said the ranger. "But I must ask that none of you handle anything in the museum. You're to look only, that clear?" he asked, looking beyond Jack at Sarah, Mendenhall, and Nathan.

They all nodded.

"Good, then welcome to the Little Bighorn. I'm Park Ranger McBride, and you're in for a treat if you've never been here before," he said proudly as he pulled a large ring of keys from his pocket.

McBride opened the door that guarded the past of Custer, his men, and the American Indians who had pulled off the biggest upset in the history of the American West, and they followed the ranger inside.

ANOTHER RANGER WAS at the front gate saying goodbye and joking with a group of Northern Cheyenne protesters who were a part of the revitalized American Indian Movement (AIM), men the park ranger had come to know by name, as many were there every day in rotating fashion, just like clockwork, to let the public know their discontent on the current state of Indian affairs in Washington, which as always was nearly nonexistent and what little was there was very poor. The ranger laughed with them; he had grown very close with a few. About five of the AIM discontents were members of their separate tribal council police departments and wore their badges inside their coats. As the ranger started to swing the gate closed, he stopped when he saw two large Mercury SUVs coming down the paved road, nearly missing two of the Cheyenne as they drove past, drawing angry glares and a few curses. The ranger stopped with the gate partially opened and went out to greet the park-goers. He held up his hand as the first vehicle pulled up to the gate.

"Sorry, folks, we open again at eight in the morning," he said as he stepped up to the passenger window.

The window rolled down and the ranger was face to face with a man with a thick mustache. The ranger saw the silenced pistol as it was raised and aimed at approximately his right cheek. The rear door of the SUV swung open and he was quickly pulled inside. The ranger was knocked unconscious and stripped down to his underwear. A man of approximately the same size and weight quickly dressed in the ridiculous ranger uniform and then stepped from the SUV. He walked over and pulled open the gate, and the two vehicles entered the park, and then the man closed and secured the main gate with the keys that were still hanging from the lock. Then the imposter walked over to the ranger's truck and followed the first two vehicles as they went toward the visitor's center.

THE STRANGE SCENE at the front gate had not gone unnoticed. Fifteen Cheyenne Indians no more than three hundred yards away knew the park was closed to visitors at night. And they also knew that a place they held as sacred was filling up with white men once again, and that was bad news.

AS THE FOUR visitors entered the exhibition hall, McBride turned on the fluorescent lighting and the museum came alive around them. There were magnificent representations of all the tribes that had taken part in the battle. Also mannequins dressed in uniforms of the Seventh Cavalry were there, and others were garbed authentically as Plains Indians. Behind glass enclosures were artifacts that had been recovered from the many sources they had eventually come to after June 25, 1876. There were horse bridles, several rusted and broken Springfield rifles, and Colt pistols. Bullets and balls of every caliber were on display, along with very old powder horns for old flintlocks used by some of the tribes. Broken lance points and arrowheads were well protected behind glass. There were reproductions of the

Regimental flag, the blue and red swallowtail flag sporting Custer's personal choice of two crossed sabers. Jack perused these items and then turned to McBride.

"The artifacts we're interested in are the recent finds from the dig that was just concluded."

"Ah, I see, those are removed every day to the storeroom so work can be continued on them until noon every day; that was the price we had to pay to keep them on display. They're right back through here." He gestured to a door at the back of the museum.

"This is a going concern here; I didn't expect all this, to tell you the truth," Sarah said admiringly.

McBride stopped with keys in hand as he turned toward Sarah.

"We found out a long time ago that there is something that has lodged in the cumulative American psyche about the battle here, be it Indian or other cultures. It's hard to put a finger on because there have been so many far more devastating defeats on this continent for the American military," he said as he inserted the key into the lock and opened the door. "But for some reason the Little Bighorn haunts this country, maybe not because it was the last stand for Custer and his men, but maybe because, as it turned out, it was the last stand for the men and women he fought against. The tribes here may have won this battle, but it doomed them as a free-roaming people, thus in truth, destroying them. My personal belief is that Americans have always pulled for the underdog, and this place reminds them of what we did to these great people. Besides, all the men, no matter what side they fought on, in this place at least, had to have been the bravest there were at the time. You feel them here. You can even see them here when you're alone."

Sarah knew what the ranger was talking about. She knew they all did, from the moment they laid eyes on the fenced monuments on Last Stand Hill. This place was alive and they all felt it.

McBride turned on the overhead lights as he escorted the

quartet into a room that had examination tables from one end to the other. The artifacts they had come to see were in varying positions on the tables, left as they were when the lab was closed for the day. Jack and the others took all this in with a feeling of awe.

"There you are, the latest field finds. Some amazing stuff, to be sure," McBride said.

Jack's eyes went immediately to the time-worn and -eaten saddlebag. The bottom was nearly rotted completely through as it lay under a circular magnifier-lamp. He walked over and snapped on the light, which lit up the lens, and then he pulled out a chair and sat.

"Hey, I said you're not supposed to touch anything!" McBride called out.

"Easy, chief, we're not here to harm anything," Mendenhall said as he grabbed the larger man's arm, restraining him. With his free hand he reached out and deftly removed the ranger's nine-millimeter handgun.

"What the hell is this?" McBride protested.

"I believe you were told there were national security issues involved," Mendenhall said.

"Really, we're not going to harm anything," Sarah chimed in, in an attempt to calm the ranger.

"Oh my," was all Dr. Nathan could muster, staring at the pistol that Mendenhall had removed from McBride's holster.

Jack was meanwhile engaged in looking through the magnifying glass. "Has anything been found in this saddlebag?" He looked across at the ranger, who was still in Mendenhall's arms.

"No, it hasn't even been examined yet."

Jack nodded and took a deep breath. He leaned over and examined the old leather pouch again. Taking a large pair of tweezers, he carefully lifted a small corner of the leather flap. It tore away and Jack cursed.

"You'll destroy it!" the ranger said angrily.

Nathan stepped forward and removed the tweezers from Jack's fingers.

"I think we can probably x-ray that, Major. That should show us the contents pretty clearly." Professor Nathan gently carried the saddlebag to the lab's X-ray area that was behind a screen.

"Just like a bull in a china shop," Sarah mumbled as she leaned over the table to examine the old steel box that had been recovered along with the saddlebag.

Jack shrugged his shoulders at Sarah's halfhearted reproach.

It took Nathan all of five minutes to get the shots of the saddlebag done. He reported, "The only items left in the saddlebags were more than likely organic in nature, perhaps field rations the Indians didn't find. Nothing even remotely resembling a cross, I'm afraid. There was no metal left on the leather at all; even the leather rivets had rusted away."

"Damn." Jack turned and looked at Sarah.

She was turning the metal box over and Jack saw it was the same box as they had seen in the pictures back at the complex. The initials *W.K.* were on the back in between the rusted hinges.

"Open it," Jack ordered.

"I'm not opening this; I can't do it without destroying it," she protested.

"So why don't you put it down?" McBride asked, fuming over the destruction these people could be causing to the valuable finds he was in charge of protecting.

"You know we're looking for a cross," said Sarah. "Why won't you help us?"

"Because my job description says nothing about assisting thieves and vandals, whoever you are," he said to Sarah's back. Then he turned halfway around and faced Mendenhall, who twirled the ranger's automatic on his right index finger and then quickly placed it back in McBride's holster.

"There, a gesture of trust and goodwill, Ranger. If she destroys the box looking for the cross, you can shoot me," Mendenhall said, looking over at Jack, who nodded his head.

McBride looked away for a moment in thought. Then he

looked back at Will Mendenhall and actually brought his right hand up halfway to his holster. Then he dipped his head and relaxed.

"Dammit!" Sarah said. He'd called her bluff. She put the box down.

Jack shook his head and pursed his lips. "Well, that's that. They were the only items linked to Keogh."

McBride cleared his throat. "Don't ask me why I'm telling you this," he said as he stepped toward the examination table nearest him. Mendenhall looked questioningly at the major, who shrugged his shoulders. "But those aren't the only items Captain Keogh had on him at the time of his death." He reached out and pulled a black cloth away from a lone Christian cross that had been placed on the table for examination.

Sarah's heart raced when she saw what had been right in front of them. It was a large cross measuring seven inches by four in width. It didn't resemble any of the crosses they had seen in the original ISO photos at the Event Group meeting.

"That wasn't in the report and pictures we received," Jack said.

"Well, it wasn't cataloged until this afternoon."

"What makes you think it was Keogh's?" Sarah asked.

"Since its discovery, it's been cleaned and examined by experts." McBride addressed Jack. "And his name is on it, in small letters on the crossbar of the cross itself. And our historians also know its Keogh's because there are several accounts of his having one just like it delivered to him before he left the fort."

Jack's eyes lingered on McBride a moment as he remembered the Libby Custer account Niles had mentioned. He knew the man had to be telling the truth because he was not only a park ranger, he also was a tour guide and one that had to be very knowledgeable about the battle and all its strange aspects.

Jack walked over and looked at the cross more closely. He picked it up and turned it over; sure enough, engraved in small script on the back of the cross member was the name: *Myles Keogh, for Papal Service.*

"I'll be damned," he said.

Sarah went up on her toes to see it. Then her eyes widened and she gently removed the rust-spotted cross from Jack's fingers. *Why didn't the Parks Service experts see this?* she wondered as she stared at its base.

"The pope and his archives people were sly ones." She gestured for the others to come over as she felt the goose bumps rise on her arms. She slowly twisted the bottom of the cross, and they all heard it crack in her fingers. McBride grimaced, thinking she had broken it. Then they heard a small pop as if a cork had been pulled free of a bottle.

"Would you like to have the honors, Ranger McBride?" Sarah asked while holding out the cross.

He shook his head quickly. He wanted nothing to do with the new discovery by whoever this woman was.

Sarah looked at Jack.

"You go ahead, Sherlock, it's your show," he responded.

Sarah gently tapped the top of the cross as the others slowly leaned inward. Nathan had his mouth open as if that would help whatever was inside come free. She tapped again and nothing happened. She tapped once more and *again* nothing. She tapped it harder against the stainless-steel table and, as they all watched, the edge of a piece of yellowed paper could be seen. Sarah swallowed and laid the cross down. She reached for a pair of tweezers and a pair of surgical gloves. She then picked up the cross and used the tweezers to gently pull on the corner of the exposed paper. It slid out as easily as if it were placed inside only yesterday. She lay down the tweezers and cross and carefully unfolded the paper. The paper cracked along the fold lines but Sarah pushed on. Particles of very old fiber floated around the map. They all breathed a collective sigh of relief when it was fully open.

The map was eleven by seven inches. Its cursive lettering and artwork were meticulous. Sarah took a deep breath and let out a small whoop, startling the others and making Nathan duck as if a ghost had taken a swing at him.

"Sorry," she said.

"What is it?" McBride asked.

"Just a five-hundred-year-old map that was written by a very brave man," she answered exuberantly.

As they examined it, they could see it was very detailed and showed the route to the valley and the giant lagoon clearly. They even had to smile when they saw that the area was marked with a small *X*. Then they all noticed one thing at the bottom, near the spot marking the lagoon, written more boldly than the other calligraphy: a warning Padilla had penned so that anyone could read it. Unfortunately all but the ranger understood the simple Spanish immediately.

Aguas Negros Satanicos.

"What does it say?" McBride asked as the sound of a helicopter slowly started to penetrate the wooden structure.

Sarah looked at him and then the others. "Roughly translated, 'The Black Waters of Satan,' " she answered a split second before bullets smashed through the door, slamming into her and Ranger McBride.

JACK AND MENDENHALL drew their sidearms and hit the tiled floor before the echoes of the attack had faded. Jack crawled over to Sarah, who was unmoving on the ground where she had fallen; she had tried in vain to cover the park ranger. When he saw blood spreading out in an ever-widening pool around the two prone bodies, his own racing blood froze in his veins.

Mendenhall fired three quick shots, two hitting drywall on either side of the door and one through the door itself, after rolling away from Sarah and McBride. The sergeant couldn't believe his eyes when he saw Professor Nathan standing upright as bullets slammed into the walls and fixtures; the man was slowly walking toward the rear of the examining room as if nothing out of the ordinary was happening. Apparently the sudden explosion of violence had unhinged the professor's thought processes and he thought just leaving would make it all stop. Mendenhall saw what had caused it. Dripping from Nathan's chin was blood and brain matter. "Get down, Professor, for Christ's sake!" he shouted as he fired twice more through the closed door.

"Sarah, Sarah!" Jack called loudly over the gunfire.

His heart lurched when she turned over and rolled under the lab table where Jack was lying. "God, are you all right?"

"Yeah, one barely clipped my shoulder. Not much of a wound but it stings like hell. Ranger McBride's had it though, caught one in the head."

"Goddammit!" Jack said. Then he looked up and saw the feet of Nathan as he slowly walked toward the rear door. "Nathan, get your ass down!" he said loudly.

"He's in shock, Major!" Mendenhall called out.

More automatic fire erupted and chunks of drywall started flying around them. Even more of the rounds were striking the examining tables.

Nathan continued for the steel back door. Mendenhall quickly popped up and returned fire. Six shots left his Beretta and slammed into the drywall separating the examining room from the museum as he tried to cover the oblivious professor. Then all hell erupted through the false ceiling as more rounds penetrated through the roof of the building. A heavy-caliber weapon had just opened fire from the unseen helicopter.

Jack rolled until his body struck McBride's. He felt the ranger's still-warm blood as it soaked through his shirt and Windbreaker. He quickly rolled the man over and unsnapped his gun from its holster. It was a Beretta like his own. He checked McBride's belt, opened one of the leather pouches, and pulled out two extra clips of nine-millimeter ammunition. He slid the weapon and clips over to Sarah, who immediately checked the gun's chamber and removed the safety. Without rising, Jack reached up and started feeling around the tabletop until his fingers found what they were searching for: Padilla's map. He quickly stuffed it into his pocket, ripping the map almost in two as he did so, and then rolled again. He grabbed Nathan by the foot and pulled his leg out from underneath him, then grabbed his belt and tugged until the professor fell onto his back.

"Now you stay down, dammit, Nathan!" Jack hissed as he kicked the steel door twice with his foot. "That's a steel door and it's locked; what's the matter with you?"

More fire entered through the front door and struck the expensive equipment lining the walls.

"Will, get on your cell phone and see if you can get ahold of the county sheriff, we can't stay in here," Jack said as he fired his Beretta five times into the steel lock of the door. He was satisfied when the chrome disintegrated under the nine-millimeter onslaught.

With a shaking hand, Nathan reached up and wiped some of the gore from his cheek and jaw. "I . . . I . . . wasn't thinking, Major, I just . . ."

Jack ignored Nathan's shocked rambling as he kicked at the door again; this time it swung open, letting in fresh air. Whoever their assailants were, they must have heard the door open, because Jack heard running footsteps heading out and away from the inside of the museum. Jack first waved Sarah out the door and then quickly stood and picked up Professor Nathan and shoved him through. He looked at Mendenhall, who tossed his cell phone aside after a stray round had ricocheted off a table and smashed it, almost taking off his hand. He then fired his last five shots through the steel door. On the way out, he ejected the spent clip and inserted his only backup.

The fresh air revived Jack as they ran away from the visitor's center toward the parking area. If it weren't for Sarah they would have run right into several men running straight at them from the gravel parking lot: Jack pushed Nathan to the grass when he saw Sarah fall flat into a defensive position. Laser sights reached out for them in the dusk as Jack fired from his own immediately prone position. One round caught the first man in line and Mendenhall shot the second, using two rounds. Sarah turned onto her back toward the visitor's center and fired three quick shots at five men running from there. To Jack's amazement, two men fell, one grabbing his leg and the other falling to the gravel surrounding the building and then not moving at all.

"Did you reach anyone before your phone died, Will?" Jack asked.

"No signal; I'm afraid we're in deep shit here, Major," Mendenhall shouted over the din.

Jack fired five more times in the direction of their pursuers. He dropped one and, from what he could see in the gathering gloom, there were still five more, minus the one he had just shot, that came out of the visitor's center, and at least three remaining from the parking area group. Jack fired twice more and Mendenhall once, as the evening grew darker. At Jack's command they turned as one and sprinted away, Jack taking the aged professor by the arm and helping as best he could. Out of the dusk, more automatic fire started up, and they could feel as well as see the tracer rounds thumping into the grass around them. Then they heard the helicopter as it swung in from somewhere beyond a far hill. It made a run at Jack, and he saw tracer rounds striking the dirt and gravel around him. The black helicopter swooped by and disappeared over a small rise.

"Sarah, head for the slope and that iron fence. Hurry, we have to get to some kind of cover," Jack called out as he turned quickly and fired at the shadowy shapes chasing them. This time he didn't see anyone fall, but Mendenhall, who had fired at the same time as Jack, brought down another of the pursuing men.

Sarah was out of breath by the time she made the outer fence that encircled Last Stand Hill. As she opened the unlocked gate, she turned around and saw Jack coming with the professor in tow. She could make out Mendenhall bringing up the rear. Sarah crouched by the open gate and fired six times into the darkness, making the pursuers hesitate momentarily. The gunmen stooped over, lowering their silhouette.

Mendenhall took advantage of Sarah's cover and sprinted the last thirty yards to the open cemetery. He followed Jack and Nathan, and ducked behind the first marker he came to. Then he popped up and fired five times into the gloom and heard a satisfying yelp as one of his nine-millimeter slugs found the mark.

"Out!" he shouted as he ejected the spent clip.

Sarah tossed him one of the spare Beretta clips and Mendenhall slammed it home. Jack ejected his own empty clip and inserted his last one. They were each down to their final rounds of ammunition. The helicopter came over the rise and Jack finally identified it as a Bell ARH, the newest attack chopper on the market. Whoever these guys were, they were well funded. The ARH was equipped, Jack knew, with a FLIR, a forward-looking infrared targeting system. That meant that no matter how dark it was, they could be hunted down and killed. The black bird again swooped in and fired, narrowly missing Sarah and the professor as rounds chipped away the stone monuments around them. He could feel the wind as the pilot arrogantly flew low enough to stir the dried grass into a storm cloud.

"Take cover and pick your targets; maybe all this noise will bring the rest of the park rangers running," he said as he quickly fired two rounds.

Collins was answered by a steady stream of automatic fire that tore into the headstone he was hiding behind. When it had settled, he turned to see where Sarah was and wasn't surprised at all when he saw she had moved and taken up station right behind him. The stone marker that covered her and also marked a bodiless grave read BOSTON CUSTER, then below that, CIVILIAN and finally on the bottom, FELL HERE, JUNE 25, 1876. As he watched, three rounds struck it and took off the top of the stone. Sarah popped right up and fired. Behind them was the tall monument placed there in honor of all the men that fell; the green grass around it suddenly erupted as a long stream of bullets tore it up. Jack cursed and stood upright, and fired five times into the dark.

He hit two men as they fell screaming. He ducked back just in time as the marker he was behind disintegrated and he rolled away to another, feeling his back and chest pelted by stone. The roar of the Bell ARH's turbine announced its presence as it passed low overhead.

"Goddammit!" he shouted in futility.

Mendenhall yelped as a round ricocheted off a marker and slivers of stone struck him across the forehead. "Damn!" he echoed.

Jack peered around for Nathan, who was crawling quickly to hide behind the largest of the monuments, where bullets had struck the grass just a moment before. Then he turned his attention to the assault that was coming from the front. He saw five men, darting in a zigzag, move toward the cemetery. He rested his back against the marker and closed his eyes. He was trying to think how to give Sarah and Nathan time to get out, when suddenly there were shouts and whoops as heavy fire erupted from behind them, from the far side of the cemetery. Then several blasts that sounded like shotguns boomed to the right of the attackers. Two men fell in agony as buckshot tore into them. Jack managed to stand and fire his own weapon into the running men; he brought down one and thought he wounded another. As he watched in confusion, the ARH attack chopper came in and then suddenly turned away, flying quickly to the south.

"Who in the hell's out there?" Mendenhall hollered.

Other, much louder whoops rent the night, as now there was shotgun fire opening up on the left. Whoever had come to their rescue had the attackers in crossfire hell. Several pops from handguns sounded and then they heard the sound of a bullhorn.

"This is the U.S. Parks Service, lay your weapons down!"

The attackers didn't listen; they opened fire in the direction of the amplified voice. Jack took the opportunity to sight in on the muzzle flashes and downed one more of the men. And then that was it, he was out of ammunition. Suddenly, screams again made Jack's blood run cold as more shotguns opened up on the remaining men. Then, as abruptly as their rescue had begun, it was over. There was an eerie silence one hears after a firefight that goes against all reason. Suddenly the field was alight as floodlamps were turned on in the cemetery. Several trucks came barreling up and then the bullhorn sounded again.

"In the cemetery, lay your weapons down and place your hands in the air."

Jack tossed his Beretta to the ground and stood. "Don't shoot! Major Jack Collins, United States Army, on government business to the battlefield!"

"Yeah, well, we'll see about that," a voice said without the aid of the bullhorn.

Jack, Mendenhall, and Sarah stood. Nathan wasn't about to stand up just yet; he found the large stone monument and its surrounding fence comforting. As they watched, they saw a large man in a tan shirt and green pants step into the light. He was followed by two more park rangers and, to Jack's surprise, about fifteen Native Americans.

"I'll be damned," was all Jack could say.

The Indians were all carrying shotguns and they followed the rangers inside the cemetery. Additional men were checking on the attackers, who were all down in the grass, either dead or very near so.

The three watched as they were slowly surrounded by the men who had saved their collective asses. Jack had to smile at the deputized protesters, he couldn't help it.

"May I ask what's so funny?" the large ranger asked Jack as he frisked him.

Jack looked at the nodding Native Americans, who were miles ahead of the clueless park ranger, as they alone understood the humor Jack found in the situation; it was one of them who finally pointed it out. Holding a shotgun crooked in the elbow of one arm, the man stepped forward. A black cowboy hat obscured the Cheyenne policeman's two long braids.

"He's smiling at the irony, Ranger Thompson, 'cause the

last time we had an American army officer surrounded on this spot, we weren't in the mood to bail his ass out of the fire."

"I'm glad you were on my side this time," Jack said as he held his hand out to the AIM protester.

The man took Jack's hand and shook. "Maybe you're just lucky you didn't identify yourself before the shooting stopped," the man said, smiling.

That simple gesture and comment ended the second battle of the Little Bighorn.

TWO HOURS LATER, Jack, Mendenhall, Sarah, and Professor Nathan were handcuffed and sitting in a large room facing the county sheriff and an agent from the FBI's Montana field office in Billings.

The four had said little other than to thank the Native Americans who had bailed them out of a tight jam. The FBI agent paced in front of them, stopping now and then to peer at one or the other of them. They smiled and returned the look, frustrating the man to no end. He was in the process of looking at Nathan because the older man had averted his eyes when stared down, possibly a chink in their armor. The fed was about to pull the professor out of the room and question Nathan alone when the phone rang and the bored-looking county sheriff picked it up.

"Interrogation," he said. "It's for you." He held the phone out to the FBI agent.

"Special Agent Phillips," he said into the mouthpiece. "Yes, that's right, we have two National Parks rangers dead and I . . . well, yes, but you listen here, Mr. Compton, I don't know who you think you . . . yes? My director?" he said as he swallowed. "Yes, sir; no, sir . . . I understand . . . yes, sir, national security, but . . . but . . . yes, sir, immediately," he said as he handed the phone back to the sheriff without looking at anything other than his highly polished shoes. Then he adjusted his tie, which hadn't needed straightening, and turned to the sheriff. "Cut 'em loose," he said.

"What . . . on whose authority?" the sheriff sputtered in protest.

"On the authority of the director of the FBI, and above him, the president of the United States. Do you need any more names?" the agent responded angrily. "Now take those cuffs off."

Jack looked at Sarah and Mendenhall and raised his brows.

"May I borrow your phone, Sheriff?" he asked.

The bemused county sheriff slid the phone over to Jack. "Probably long distance," he mumbled.

Jack hurriedly punched in numbers and then waited as he was connected to the Group's secured phone line. After a series of beeps and static it was answered.

"Compton," the voice said.

"It's Collins. This line isn't secure."

"Confirmed, phone line is not secure. Now, are you all right? Sarah, Will, Nathan?"

"Yes, we're fine. Niles, we have the item in our possession," he said as he turned away from the sheriff.

"Thank God!"

"Listen, the people that hit us, the sheriff's office and the FBI have identified them as Colombian nationals. Did you tell anyone else we would be here in Montana?"

"Commander Everett, remember? He was in on our conference from his location in New Orleans," Niles stated flatly, suddenly knowing where Jack was heading.

"Did Everett use a land line?"

"Yes, his cell had no signal. His end of the conversation was in the clear."

"They must have had a tap, what we call a SATAG on the phone. That means they may have tracked him to New Orleans and, through our conference call, tracked us to Montana. Where's Carl now?"

"Making ready the expedition's transportation in New Orleans," Niles answered.

"Call him and tell him to use only his secure cell and to

watch for visitors. I'll send him more security; he may have more company headed his way when the powers that be find out they failed out here."

"You got it, Jack. Get home."

EVENT GROUP COMPLEX
NELLIS AFB, NEVADA

Niles made the necessary calls and the compartmentalized Event Group went into action to prepare hurriedly to get a rescue team down to the Amazon. Departments went through an amazing array of logistics to supply the team with everything they would need for the exploration of Padilla's lost valley and to search for any survivors of Helen Zachary's expedition. The equipment that Everett had ordered could only be partially filled with Event Group stores; the rest had to come from such companies as Raytheon, General Electric, Hanford Laboratories, the Brookings Institution, and Cold Spring Harbor on Long Island. The expedition was officially sanctioned as a rescue operation, but scientific investigation would still be performed.

An Event Group tech team comprised of sixty men and women were already en route by air force transport to Louisiana to assist Master Chief Jenks on finalizing the installation of the equipment and outfitting *Teacher* for river duty. There would be no time for a shakedown cruise.

The Group's Intelligence Department made arrangements to be a privately funded surveying mission to map the Amazon River depths from the Peruvian government, which was a nice cover to get into Brazil, which had steadfastly denied permission for American military personnel to cross into their territory.

Niles and Alice were busy in his office with a team of assistants, coordinating the paper end of things, and that wasn't going well at all.

"The president," Alice said, holding out the red phone.

"Mr. President, thank you for securing the cooperation of the navy, it's much appreciated." Niles watched Alice leave the room.

"I have the FBI report on those photos your people sent over from San Pedro," the president said tersely. "It seems the man named Kennedy, which is his real name by the way, is a U.S. Navy SEAL, and another was identified as an air force captain named Reynolds. The others have yet to be identified."

"Has the navy and air force explained the reasoning behind infiltrating a university-sponsored expedition with a bunch of young people?"

"So far they haven't said anything. They said they have an intense inner investigation going on to find out. And to me right now, that isn't goddamned good enough!"

"You mean to say they don't know what their special operations people are doing?"

"So far they came up with records that show Kennedy and Reynolds were on detached duty out west. I put my bulldog on it. My national security advisor, Ambrose, will get some results."

"Someone is out of control here and there are lives at stake—"

"Dammit, Niles, I know whose lives are at stake!"

"Yes, sir, I apologize. Those kids may be lost or fighting for their lives down there, and I have a team getting ready to go in. I need to know who we can trust!"

"All right Niles, you and I need to keep a perspective here. Even though my own daughter is in danger, I'm afraid my hands are still tied up to a point. I can't risk a shooting war just because my daughter stepped out. Here's something for you to think on: no matter what reason Kennedy and those other men have for being attached to that expedition, doesn't it ease your mind a little that they have at least one SEAL with them?"

Niles was slow to answer, as he didn't feel comfortable

with the military involvement, no matter if there were special operations people giving Helen and her kids a better chance at survival or not. So he decided to answer truthfully.

"It would make me feel better if in fact they hadn't been off the air for over a week now."

"I'll keep pushing Ambrose on my end; a hard task, since he knows nothing of the Group's existence."

"I understand."

"Now, your Lieutenant Ryan has been cleared for Fort Bragg. The Proteus team will be waiting on him, along with his Delta squad. Remember, Niles, even though my daughter's life may be at stake, I have only okayed the Proteus backup mission. Again, I stress the fact that I can't allow a military ground incursion, even if we know it to be a rescue mission, into a friendly nation by American troops; it just won't fly. I'm sorry, it's Proteus or nothing."

"Mr. President, I—"

"No," the president cut him off, "we can't have American ground troops on friendly soil without invitation. Too many things can go wrong. If your backup plan works properly, Proteus should give Major Collins a nice edge if it's needed."

"Sir, that damned weapons platform hasn't worked right since testing began; we're running an awful risk with Operation Spoiled Sport as our only backup. What if there is close-in fighting down there? Proteus can't possibly help out in that situation."

"I'm sorry, Niles, it has to do, we have too many black eyes given to us by bad press lately. It's not that I'm sacrificing any of those kids or my own daughter for political reasons, but I can't let American boys die in a rescue attempt that would surely be challenged by Brazilian troops. Tell Major Collins to find our people and get his butt back in one piece, and Niles, please bring my daughter home. I'm sorry Proteus is the only backup at this time, but it can be disguised as civilian whereas fighter aircraft can't."

Niles stared at the screen, knowing full well the president was right. The burden of getting those kids out of that green and hostile world was squarely on the shoulders of the Event Group.

WASHINGTON, D.C.

Ambrose drove himself over to Foggy Bottom. The Department of State was clearing for the day, so he had no bothersome eyes watching as he took the stairs three at a time.

He was escorted to the secretary of state's office by two guards. As he entered the office, Ambrose saw the secretary was busy jotting something down on paper. For someone who was only fifty-two, the cabinet member's hair was turning a distinguished shade of gray at the temples. Ambrose had watched earlier in the day as the president praised him on television for his unyielding stance with the crisis that he had thwarted in Iraq. He was definitely the flavor of the month. But as Ambrose set his briefcase down and took a seat, he could see the man who would soon become the next president of the most powerful nation on earth was angry.

"I take it your conversation with the president was enlightening, Mr. Secretary?" Ambrose asked.

The tall man behind the ornate and ostentatious desk finally looked up.

"How in the hell could this happen?"

"How were we supposed to know his daughter was on that ship?"

"That little bitch has been nothing but a royal pain in the ass since the president took office and her presence in Brazil could bring our whole shaky house of cards down around our neck."

Ambrose swallowed as he listened to a man who was world famous for keeping his cool, a man who *planned* the outcome of events, never just hoping for a favorable one.

"They haven't been heard from since—"

"It doesn't matter, you fool, even if the whole expedition is dead, do you think for one goddamned minute the president will let the body of his daughter go unclaimed down in the fucking jungle?" He stood up and tossed the ballpoint pen he had been using at Ambrose, who flinched as it bounced off his shoulder. "Now he tells me he's authorized not one, but two naval task forces to the south. Sailing orders that you should have informed me of!"

"He consulted with the secretary of the navy directly. I didn't know anything until a moment ago. Look, we can steer him away from a recovery effort, just advise against it. I *am* his national security advisor, goddammit, and *you're* his secretary of state."

"That bastard just ordered me, ordered *me* to Brazil. He wants inroads laid so we can either clear the way for a rescue operation by the marines, of all people, or at least get the Brazilian military in there."

Ambrose had been briefed as to what the president was going to say to the secretary, so he wasn't surprised by his orders.

"It's the president doing the requesting, so why don't you just put it as a threat? President Souza won't take too kindly to that. Make the situation hot enough to where there is no action taken at all. What will he do, invade a friendly nation over his wayward daughter who is most likely dead already?"

"Yes, goddammit, you work for the bastard; he loves his daughter no matter how much of a pain in the ass she is!" the secretary yelled as he paced to his large window behind his desk. "And now he knows about the team the intelligence chiefs sent with the Zachary group, who may or may not have eliminated the very team the president wants us to rescue!"

"Then all the better we get this thing to blow up. Cover our tracks where no one can trace our involvement in either Iraq or what was taken out of that damned valley down there. With any luck, Kennedy blew the goddamned thing up and buried everything and everyone forever."

The secretary of state turned toward Ambrose, his eyes afire. "If even a *hint* of this gets out, the election is lost. Remember, I'm still tied to the president's coattails whether I like it or not."

"That doesn't worry me all that much," Ambrose said as he stood.

"Oh, and why is that?"

"If even a hint of what we've done leaks out, we're all going to hang for treason, because the danger you failed to foresee when we took into our confidence the military chiefs of intelligence is that they will indeed cover their tracks, any way they can. And in case you didn't know it, Donald, they do have the assets to get that part done, and we would be the one to be covered up. Good luck in Brazil, Mr. Secretary. I'll do what I can from the White House."

"If they were so good at their jobs, why did we have the fiasco at Arlington?"

"That was contract work; for us, they'll come themselves. You have to look at the military hierarchy. The men we are dealing with are hungry for power, and that power lies in the climbing of the corporate ladder. This plan of yours was to help them in doing just that. They won't be happy if they sense it's too hot," Ambrose said. He opened the door and left.

The secretary of state watched the door close and then sat heavily into his chair. He knew he would virtually have to start a war in South America to confuse the situation and make that godforsaken valley in the Amazon vanish from everyone's radar.

Then it struck him. The president would never rely on just one option. He, like himself, always thought in the same terms as that of a master chessman, thinking five and ten moves ahead. That son of a bitch would have a second option already in the planning stages at least. That meant if his diplomatic queries failed, the president might even have an armed team on the ground or in the air for a rescue operation, hell, maybe even more options. An illegal and underhanded rescue attempt done behind the back of the Brazilian government? The secretary realized he had his out. An operation such as that would constitute an invasion of a friendly country. He had his main asset in the Brazilian Air Force, and he would alert that man that he might be needed.

He picked up the phone and called the front desk to have Ambrose turned around. He had one more instruction to give the advisor. All he needed was to know the location of that goddamned valley. He was sure the Brazilian authorities would welcome a tip that either their airspace or their ground territory was about to be compromised.

And that, he surmised, could get messy, and that mass confusion could be his best ally.

PART FOUR
BLACK WATERS

Man has always feared that which he cannot understand, hasn't conquered, failed to tame, failed to make his own. When man is confronted by the unknown, his greatest fear, and I daresay excitement, takes hold. And the death of innocence is always our answer to that fear in the end.

—Charles Hindershot Ellenshaw III, cryptozoologist

11

AFTER almost seven full years of continuous warfare, the USS *John C. Stennis* had been mysteriously ordered from her home port of San Diego, California, with only half of her complement of warplanes. And those that weren't actually on the roster for flights were stored belowdecks in their hangars. The ship's crew of nearly five thousand–plus were curious as to the strange craft that lay in eleven distinct pieces of ten-foot sections on her flight deck. They knew they would find out soon enough, as another warship had joined them early that morning. The USS *Iwo Jima*, a navy assault ship, was brimming with U.S. Marine Corps helicopters, and the scuttlebutt said those choppers would be removing the strange package from the *Stennis*'s flight deck.

Off in the distance, the Department of the Navy wasn't taking any chances, as another carrier battle group was two hundred miles east of the *Stennis*'s position, to assist in an emergency, since they were shorthanded on attack planes. The USS *Nimitz* was riding shotgun, making the crewmen onboard the giant ship feel somewhat better about their hurried sailing orders.

The Styrofoam-packaged sections were flown from Louisiana to Los Angeles, where they were transferred onto army UH-60 Blackhawks and then flown out to the *Stennis* just 160 miles from South America. This would negate the need for flying over foreign territorial land and sea, as well as the need for asking permission from governments that become overly curious and suspicious. The plan was devised by Niles Compton, using the authority of the president. The mission was classified as a field test by a private company. That company just happened to be the Event Group.

Master Chief Jenks and the support team from the Group were still working on the engines and the electronics suite for *Teacher*. The task was made far more difficult because of the rush out of New Orleans to California and then having to install everything with the boat lying in eleven sections. The master chief had already threatened the lives of almost everyone on his team and some of those of the *Stennis*. Jack had actually and absentmindedly reached for a sidearm he wasn't wearing when Jenks had confronted him about something Jack had no control over. Actually, Jenks was mortified when he found out that Jack Collins was serving as head of the expedition and was essentially the man that saved his boat from the scrap heap. So Carl had seen him do something the master chief had never done before: he apologized to the major.

Carl joined Danielle on the signalman's platform overlooking the flight deck and was grateful for the sea air.

"This is what I miss about sea duty," he said as he stood by her side, "the air, can't find it in the desert."

She smiled and went back to watching the activity below with *Teacher*.

"Hi there," Sarah said as she joined them.

"Well, if it isn't Wild Bill McIntire," Carl teased her.

"Funny," she said as she lightly punched him on the arm.

"Seriously, Jack said you handled yourself at the Little Bighorn like a pro."

"So, Ms. Serrate, has Jack assigned you any duties yet?" Sarah asked as her attention swung to the Frenchwoman.

"Yes, it seems I will be assisting Professor Ellenshaw's Crypto group, *all three of us*," she answered. "And please call me Danielle. We're going to be shipmates, after all." She smiled but her eyes bore into Sarah's.

Sarah didn't respond. In her mind, something wasn't quite

adding up with this woman, and she couldn't put her finger on it. Of course it just might be the fact that the attraction between Carl and Danielle was evident to anyone with eyes. Sarah wondered if she was jealous for her best friend who had died over a year ago. The friend and woman Carl had loved was killed on a mission not unlike the one they were currently undertaking. Now, here, the ex-wife of Colonel Henri Farbeaux, an enemy anyone in the Group would give five years' pay to bag, just conveniently showed up with her offer of help? Sarah wasn't buying what this interloper was selling, even though her director and even Jack seemed to be.

"I understand you'll be heading your own science team," Danielle said.

Sarah nodded, leaning back so she could see around Carl. "Yes, a two-man geology team, but we'll be a part of Virginia's overall sciences attachment."

Danielle was about to comment when the steel hatch opened.

"The major says we're needed in the ward room. Professor Ellenshaw wants to speak to the Group," Mendenhall said as he popped his head out of the hatch. His forehead was still half-covered by a bandage from the stone chips that struck him in the gunfight two days before.

Carl was about to say something, but Sarah held her hand up and stopped him. "We already heard about your little nickname for Ellenshaw's Crypto Department, so don't say it," she said as she anticipated his small joke.

"What, that we're about to be briefed by the 'Creepy-zoologist'?"

Sarah just rolled her eyes.

PROFESSOR CHARLES HINDERSHOT Ellenshaw III gave a briefing on the skeletal hand. But the facts just weren't there to support any conclusions as to the animal's origins or design. He had a lot of speculation and had prepared well for any contingency, but still had no real information to give other than the fact he would consider it a crime to harm such a species if it truly did exist. Jack cut him short as he started to preach about animal rights and how special and unique this creature would have to be to be alive at all in the modern world.

Sarah's briefing was more to the point and actually had a purpose. Gold, if any, would not be touched. The mine, if it existed, would be placed off limits because of the fact that the president had ordered it so. The geology team would follow its orders to the letter. With the assistance of Major Collins and his security team, if the mine did contain any gold deposits as the legend said, it would be treated as property of Brazil.

"Major," Mendenhall said as he entered the ward room. "The *Iwo*'s helicopters are starting to line up and almost ready to start taking on *Teacher*."

The helicopters would airlift the sections of the boat to the small village of Rio Feliz, on the Amazon a hundred miles west of the Peruvian border. That was where the Event Group would start its expedition, saving valuable time by flying through a gap in the Andes and going straight to the source, the confluence of the Rio Negro (the Black Tributary) that fed off the main Amazon River. The route was exactly as Captain Padilla had laid down on the map and also what he had supposedly described in the diary.

The president had supplemented information to both the Peruvian and Brazilian governments on the pretext that they were experimenting with new mapping procedures and software, and that the two governments would be the beneficiary of those experimental new devices and the more accurate underwater maps—a pretext that the team would be doing as routine procedure in any case.

It was an amazing sight to see the Seahawk helicopters, the navy's version of the Blackhawk, lined up in the air off the stern of the *John C. Stennis*. One by one they would approach and hover as Jenks supervised the hookup of the sections of *Teacher*. Eleven Seahawks in all would ferry the sections to the village where the parts would become a whole, and everyone prayed the thing would float. The discovery team was on deck as the last section, the bow, covered in form-fitting plastic, was lifted into the air. Then the last hovering craft came in and, in amazement, they watched as the U.S. Marine Corp's MV-22 Osprey, the stubby-winged, tilt-rotor assault craft, slowly landed on the *Stennis*'s flight deck, its two massive propellers making a humming sound from their perch atop the tip of the short wings. Before they realized it, a second Osprey landed in back of the first.

"I hate these things," Carl yelled into Danielle's ear.

"Why, because it's a radical design?" she asked, holding her bush hat in place through the wind the Ospreys created.

"No, it's because a marine pilot is driving that radical design!"

As they loaded their bags and personal items, Jack turned and looked at the flying bridge. There, the captain of the *Stennis* waved and saluted. Jack returned the gesture. The *Stennis* would stand off while the mission was in progress, in case they ran into trouble.

And so the third expedition was on its way to Hernando Padilla's valley, where a beautiful lagoon was ready to spill her secrets. What this group didn't know was the fact that another faction was already closing in on the legendary dark water.

12

THE AMAZON RIVER,
45 KILOMETERS
EAST
OF THE BLACK WATER TRIBUTARY

THE helicopter had rendezvoused with Mendez, Farbeaux, and the crew of the charter boat *Rio Madonna*. Her captain had maneuvered the large ten-cabin river tug with precision, to receive the chopper's passengers. The first had been Captain Juan Rosolo, a man that Henri Farbeaux despised as an ambush killer of the lowest order, and the men that followed

him onto the deck were probably no better. This development was most unsettling, but it was also one that Farbeaux
had made allowances for.

Rosolo reported immediately to Mendez and the two had
conversed in loud tones, enough so that Farbeaux knew
Rosolo had failed his master in some capacity or other.
Mendez, with all the delicateness of a wrecking ball, had
spewed forth a list of his favorite profanities. Farbeaux was
content to stay at the bow of the boat and keep out of it. He
still heard the approach of Rosolo as the captain came forward after his browbeating by Mendez.

"What is it, watchdog?" Farbeaux said without turning to
face the man.

"Do not call me that name, *señor*. My employer would
like to see you at the stern," Rosolo said with a sneer.

Farbeaux watched the deep waters of the flowing Amazon for a moment longer before he turned and brushed past
Rosolo.

The river pilot, Captain Ernesto Santos, gave a quick
two-fingered salute to the Frenchman as he walked past the
bridge. This captain seemed to know his business. His reputation and self-proclamation of knowing every inch of the
Amazon were known to all onboard. He said he and his family had plied the river for generations.

But when their destination was finally revealed to him
after they had set off, the scraggly bearded captain had
grown quiet and sullen. He had protested in vain that the
Rio Negro had no such inlet at that point of the river, that
the only way in was several hundred kilometers to the
east, and even that was only navigatable during the wet
season. The argument didn't last long when he was presented with his overly large charter fee in cash.

Farbeaux maneuvered to the small fantail, where Mendez
was waiting. Rosolo came up from behind and lightly brushed
by him, obviously returning the gesture for Henri's brushing
him a moment before. Farbeaux ignored Rosolo and sat at the
small table where Mendez was examining some photographs.

"Ah, Henri, our friend here has brought with him from the States some rather disturbing news. As you know, we had Professor Zachary's office monitored. And we had some fish wander into our net." He slid a picture of Danielle toward Farbeaux. The Frenchman merely glanced at the picture, and then he looked at Mendez, who slid another eight-by-ten glossy toward him. "She was accompanied by this man," he said, watching him for a reaction. He wasn't disappointed; Farbeaux reached immediately for the second photo.

"The man in the tunnels," he said under his breath.

"Excuse me?" Mendez said, leaning forward.

Farbeaux stared at the picture for a moment longer and then let it fall to the table. "Last year I ran into this gentleman in an unusual situation in the American desert; I believe his name is Everett."

"Lieutenant Commander Carl Everett, of the U.S. Navy, to be more precise," Rosolo insisted. "I was unable to uncover his current duties or station, but it is a matter of closed naval records that he was once a SEAL, and a highly decorated one," he said, watching the tall Frenchman closely.

"I believe he is on detached service from the military. He works for what is best described as a think tank. The military is where the organization gets all of its security people, and they only surround themselves with the best." He turned his eyes toward Rosolo. "And you, watchdog, if you truly knew anything about the special operations units of the American navy, you would know that a man is never a former SEAL, he *is* a SEAL."

"Regardless of semantics, this is upsetting at the very least, is it not, Henri?" Mendez asked as he brought out more pictures and shoved them toward Farbeaux.

"These were taken at a national park in Montana. Do you recognize any of these people?" Rosolo probed.

Farbeaux looked the four photos over. They were grainy and taken from a distance with a telephoto lens through the glass windows of a vehicle.

"I have never seen these two before," he said. His eyes

lingered on the close-up of Mendenhall. "But this one here," he slid a photo of the black sergeant back toward Mendez, "may work with the SEAL, Everett."

"Then the puzzle fits together. Our friend Señor Rosolo overheard a conversation Everett had with a second party on a secured and scrambled phone, that these people would be in Montana searching for the map of Padilla. To make a long story short, Rosolo attempted to stop them from recovering something that would lead them here and, I am sorry to say, he failed miserably, only managing to kill two federal park employees. And he was still unable to recover or destroy the map." Mendez's eyes looked directly at his assassin.

"They found the map?"

"We must assume they have, and they will undoubtedly act upon it," Mendez said, slapping his hand on the tabletop angrily.

"The organization in question is rather tenacious when it comes to getting at the heart of any matter. I have learned through experience that their resources are astounding and their pockets very deep, even deeper than yours."

"Well, they seem to be everything you admire about them. I came very close to ordering a hit on your ex-wife and their big man in New Orleans. But what sense would there be in closing the gate after your dog has already run away?"

Farbeaux closed his eyes and forced himself to relax. He slowly pulled out a chair from the table and sat down.

"I will state this very clearly to both of you. No one is to ever lay a hand on Danielle. Do I make myself clearly understood?" His blue eyes never flinched. His gaze froze Rosolo, after the killer had quickly risen from his seat to stare at Farbeaux after his not-so-veiled threat to his boss.

"Is that so?" Mendez asked.

Farbeaux leaned back in his chair. "It is I who will end her life, not you, and most certainly not him," he said, nodding toward Rosolo.

"Let us hope it is after this excursion, so you may be allowed to take your time with this troublesome woman, which is a husband's right, yes?" Mendez said, trying to break the tension he had created.

"If I know these people, they may already be on their way here. Of course, your security chief here would know that, if he would have stayed and done the job you pay him for, instead of showing up here in the one place on this planet where he is clearly not needed."

"It will take those people weeks to gather the means to follow us here. They will not be coming anytime soon!" Rosolo argued. "And I go where I am told to go, and I was told to come here."

Farbeaux lightly shook his head. Then he felt the gentle vibration under his feet first, as it traveled all the way up to his arms long before the sound reached his ears. He saw the concerned looks on the faces of the two Colombians. It would have been comical if he himself didn't have so much riding on the line.

"You'd better tell the captain to throttle this boat into a faster speed and get this expedition to our destination, because we are about to have company. A lot of company," Farbeaux said, standing. "And if I were you," he added, looking at Mendez, "I would fire this fool for incompetence, because the people he pronounced so proudly weren't coming anytime soon have just arrived." The Frenchman looked skyward and then easily backed under the bridge decking and out of sight.

Captain Santos, to his credit (or the instincts needed by a smuggler and gunrunner), quickly maneuvered the large boat under the overhanging canopy and expertly sliced the bow into the mud, effectively bringing the boat to a harsh stop and hiding her at the same time from any eyes that could spy them from above.

The quiet river was rocked by the sound of helicopters as they flew high overhead. Through the thick trees that crowded the riverbank, Farbeaux could see cargo of some kind hanging from cables attached to the gray-colored choppers. As he watched, he could see the words UNITED STATES MARINE

CORPS stenciled in darker gray paint on their rotor booms. The eleven helicopters were followed by two strange-looking craft that screeched over the flowing Amazon. The MV-22 Ospreys shook the jungle as they roared past with their famed tilt rotors in the three-quarter position that supplied them with speed greater than that of any helicopter in the world. The Frenchman noticed the fact that they were traveling low to the ground, possibly meaning they had to stay below radar. Indicating the intruders might not have official clearance to be in Brazil.

But nonetheless, the Event Group was indeed here, and Henri Farbeaux helplessly watched their arrival from the shadows.

EVENT CENTER,
NELLIS AFB, NEVADA

Niles and Alice had just received notice of the Group's arrival near the Black River Tributary. The director was talking with the president while Alice listened and took notes. Niles's other assistants were busy in the communications center, monitoring radio traffic for as long as they could before the expedition went in to radio-dark territory. Director Compton was in the process, along with Pete Golding and the computer center and Jet Propulsion Lab in Pasadena, California, to retask Boris and Natasha, and once that was done the satellite would have been moved farther south by a thousand miles to a place directly over the lagoon and valley. After it had been found, they not only hoped for satellite communication with the Amazon team, but also they thought it possible to get a video feed from Jack.

"Niles," the president said, "the intelligence chiefs of the three branches are gathering what information they can find. But no one has a clue as to why Kennedy and his men would have been on that boat. The consensus is that they were working outside the command of the navy and air force, possibly freelance. I made inquiries with the FBI. They say they have verified there was gunfire at the cemetery and that there was damage sustained to some of the monuments, but there were no bodies."

"With your permission, sir, I would like to start working on this and the Kennedy connection myself, if you concur, of course."

"Granted. Someone somewhere thinks they can do as they please around here. Find out who it is. Now, tell me about the progress of the rescue team."

"We now have competent people in the field and moving upriver, Mr. President. I believe we will know more this time tomorrow. Major Collins knows what the priorities are in this situation. I briefed him about your daughter." Niles paused. "Jack will get those kids home. And maybe it will work out for the best that her expedition was tagged by those SEALs, for whatever reason they were there. I can't see them allowing harm to come to innocents."

"Agreed," the president said. "You keep me informed on what's happening out there when you can." He hesitated. "Something far more precious than gold or prehistoric animals is at stake for me here." He cleared his throat. "I have the coordinates where Proteus will be passing by the site. Damn, they have to be inside Brazilian airspace for a long time. I hope they're not tracked as something other than a commercial airline."

"That's a chance we have to take. Proteus is Jack's only backup in case the school bully shows up."

"I just don't think we can protect her over the target area."

"If they run into trouble, Proteus has her fighter escort. They may be able to drive any hostiles off her until she gets out of Brazilian airspace."

The president did not respond for a moment. Then he told Niles, "If I allow a fighter escort inside Brazilian airspace right now, and if they either intentionally or accidentally fire on any attacker, it would be construed as an act of war. The president of Brazil is already giving me one hell of a hard time through the secretary of state."

Niles deflated. Now Proteus was going to be flying into hostile airspace without her needed fighter protection. The mission backup was nothing of the sort. The odds of it working were astronomical, and the odds that they could even get over the right area of jungle even greater.

"We'll talk soon, Niles. Let me know as soon as you hear anything from Major Collins, please."

Niles faced Alice. "Jack has to find Helen and those kids alive."

"You know, Niles?" She looked him straight in the eyes. "I think you should unburden yourself and tell me what has you and the president so frightened."

"How did the senator ever keep anything from you?"

"I'm waiting."

"Helen's graduate students, well, one student in particular . . ." Niles shook his head. "She slipped her Secret Service protection and got on that boat with Helen and the others. She's the president's eldest daughter, Kelly."

CONFLUENCE OF THE BLACK WATER TRIBUTARY AND THE AMAZON RIVER

The stern section was the last one to be lowered into place with the assistance of navy divers sent by the repair ship USS *Cayuga*, of the *Stennis*'s battle group. They detached the cable and the U.S. Marine Corps Seahawk peeled away over the thick canopy of trees and circled, awaiting the order to pick up the ten navy divers.

In the water, Master Chief Jenks, wearing shorts and a T-shirt, placed the last of the joining bolts through the flanges that attached each section to the thick expandable rubber gaskets that gave *Teacher* the flexibility she would need to navigate the tributary. The rubber was so thick, a man alone couldn't bend it, but with *Teacher*'s powerful water jet thrusters, the gaskets between the sections stretched as easily as pulling on a rubber band.

The technicians from the Group's Logistics department, who had been chosen for the first phase of the mission, were busy pumping out brackish water that had accumulated in *Teacher*'s bilges during her assembly. Jenks was assisted by three men from the Engineering department for the initial firing of the two huge diesel engines. The rest of the crew was busy pulling double duty in readying *Teacher* for her journey. Two Seahawks had scouted as far down the Black Water Tributary as they could before they had lost sight of the river as it fell under the thick canopy of trees. One of the pilots had thought he had spied something under the canopy, but upon closer inspection nothing was visible when they passed again over the *Rio Madonna* ten miles back. The marine choppers pushed as far forward as fifty miles before their fuel state dictated that they needed to return to the rendezvous.

Sarah and Jack unstrapped equipment in the research labs while Carl and Danielle assisted Professors Ellenshaw and Nathan as they filled the immense tank that would hopefully hold live specimens. Mendenhall was with the rest of the security team, consisting of Corporal Henry Sanchez, Lance Corporal Shaw, Spec 5 Jackson, army specialist Walter Lebowitz, and army sergeant Larry Ito. They were carefully charging the batteries of the small two-man submersible and filling the *Teacher*'s fuel bunkers with diesel from two five-hundred-gallon rubber bladders a third MV-22 Osprey had settled easily upon the riverbank. The rest of the crew was made up of fifteen lab assistants whose department heads were Virginia Pollock, Dr. Heidi Rodriguez, Dr. Allison Waltrip, head surgeon of the Event Group, and Professor Keating of the Anthropology team. The assistants loaded the supplies of food, water, and other essentials for their journey.

Jenks placed the last expandable bolt and torque-wrenched it down. Then he tossed the tool to the frogman who was standing atop the gracefully rounded stern, just above the boat's emblem that was painted on both sides of the fantail. The beautiful woman's eye, set in green against the white hull, stood out starkly on the green-tinted river. With everything but the firing of the engines complete, the frogman called in the last of the Seahawks to pick up the remaining men that would return to the *Stennis* battle group. A few villagers from Rio Feliz gathered and were quite excited to see helicopters hovering and flying about, a rare sight for many of them. But by far the item to draw the largest group of onlookers was *Teacher* herself. She sat anchored to the shore of the Amazon, her gleaming white hull shining in the bright sun, the tinted widows of her forward pilothouse sparkling. The villagers had never before seen a craft whose upper bow was glass enclosed as *Teacher*'s was. They could see figures moving inside and were amazed by the amount of people that would occupy the boat. Jack had ordered gifts of candy bars and a few medical supplies to be handed out to the village elders as a goodwill gesture for the disturbance the Americans were causing to the small outpost of families.

Jenks watched as the last of the frogmen were lifted away. A single Seahawk would patrol in a circular pattern until *Teacher* was well underway. The master chief climbed a ladder in section five, amidships of the 120-foot craft, and observed a three-man team from the Computer Center hook up the last of the communications gear. He had been impressed by the breadth and quality of everything Toad Everett had brought in. He didn't know who exactly these people were, but you only had to explain to them one time how to do something and after that it was assholes and elbows. He was satisfied amidships as he looked up and saw that the radar array had started its sweeps atop the forty-foot three-span main masts that swept back at a streamlined and aerodynamic angle toward the stern.

"Hell of a design you have here, Chief," said Tommy Stiles, one of Pete Golding's wunderkinds of the Computer Center who had joined the Group two years before, after having been a tech aboard the Aegis missile cruiser USS

Yorktown. Stiles would be serving as *Teacher*'s radar and communications technician. Another man, Charles Ray Jackson, would serve as her sonar and underwater detection tech. He came to the Event Group via the "Silent Service," having served his last year aboard USS *Seawolf*. He nodded his agreement that it was a great boat, at least in appearance.

"Yeah? Well, it just tweaks my fucking ass and gives me goose bumps all over that I could please you two candy asses," Jenks said as he opened the upper aluminum hatch and started down the steps. "Goddamned surface navy and pigboat swabs, what in the hell do you know about anything?" he mumbled with the cigar clamped in his teeth.

Stiles looked over at Jackson, who was winding the excess coaxial cable into a roll for storage. Jackson shrugged. "Just like old times," he said.

"Do all master chiefs have to take a course on how to be the biggest prick in the navy?"

"Nah, they're born that way," Jackson answered.

JENKS STOOD BY the pilot's chair and stared at his lighted and totally digital control console. The joystick on the chair's left arm was a total departure as a way of maneuvering the boat. She was operated by input signal to the main computer, which interpreted what the pilot was ordering and fired the appropriate electrical motors that operated the water jets at the stern of the boat, thus eliminating the need for cables and hydraulics. The system was known worldwide as "Fly by Wire." Jenks glanced at Jack. They were both sweating profusely; the enclosed areas of *Teacher* were sweltering due to the lack of air-conditioning while the main power was offline.

"Well, I guess we'd better see if this fuckin' thing will even start," said Jenks. "Or we'll begin this little trip treating everyone for heatstroke, huh, Major?"

"Would be nice to know if she works, Chief," Jack said blandly.

"Of course she'll work, goddammit! What would an army

major know about it, anyway? What the fuck was I thinking even asking a ground pounder?" Jenks slipped into the pilot's seat. "Are you ready back there?" he asked as soon as he had his headphones in place.

"All set," Mendenhall answered nervously. He had been tagged as the mechanical assistant on this little safari; he and the other members of the security team were doubling as motormen, much to the master chief's chagrin. An engine start-up warning tone sounded over the boat's intercom system from the engineering section in the last compartment of the boat.

"Toad, are you there?" Jenks asked.

"Here," Carl answered through his com system.

"Good. If those engines don't start, bash that big black sergeant in the head with that fire extinguisher; he's the one that hooked up the starter."

"Bash head, got it, Chief," Everett said, grinning at a scowling Mendenhall.

"Okay." Jenks reached over and uncapped a clear plastic cover over a red button that had a computer-generated glowing word: START. "Here we go," he said as he pushed the button and clamped down even harder on his cigar.

Suddenly there was a deep rumble throughout *Teacher* as the twin diesels fired up. The digital gauges and controls were illuminated blue and green, and the tachometer read that the engines were idling at an even one thousand rpms. Red gauges showed the critical areas of the boat's function, such as engine status, fuel, temperature in each section of the boat with hatch status, and ballast. The blue and green noncritical areas, such as battery state, amperage, speed indication, water depth, and river width, flared to life, the main computer generating their ever-changing numbers and gauges. A large display in the center console allowed the pilot to see a virtual computer-generated display of the area directly to the front of the boat; with a flip of the switch, it could change to a split-screen version that showed all sides including the stern, even underwater. Sensors and a sonar device automatically and constantly relayed signals that the computer interpreted, to generate an ever adjusting image of *Teacher*'s surroundings.

"I'll be damned," the master chief said as he slapped the major on the ass. "How 'bout that, the bitch is breathing!" His laughter was infectious; Jack could hear the cheers of dozens of men and women throughout the boat as they all heard and felt the powerful engines come to life.

"See, they love her, too," Jenks exclaimed as he removed his cigar and smiled widely.

Jack winked. "Either that or they're just happy the air-conditioning's on," he said as he pulled the semitransparent sliding door aside and left the cockpit.

Jenks, his smile fading, watched as Jack left. "Eh, what does he know," he mumbled as he flipped a toggle switch on the thick right arm of his command chair. "Stand by in the stern and bow to bring up the anchors," his voice rumbled more forcefully throughout the boat on the speakers embedded in every section.

Carl pushed a button mounted on the wall of the engine room. He could hear the winch engage, which controlled both the bow and stern anchors. Then there was a satisfying click as the winch stopped. He gave Mendenhall and Sanchez a thumbs-up.

CARL MET SARAH and Doctors Nathan and Ellenshaw at the base of the large spiral staircase in the section four lounge that led to the upper and outermost deck of *Teacher*. They went up and Carl opened the large acrylic glass bubble. They climbed out into the heat. A ten-by-ten-foot section in the center of the boat just aft of the radio and radar tower allowed them a view of the river. Three sections to their front, they saw Jack and Virginia climb out on deck and then sit in one of the many weatherproof chairs lining the gunwales.

They felt *Teacher* shudder as Jenks applied power and she slowly backed away from the crumbling riverbank. She backed up until her large stern was well out into the main channel of the Amazon, and then they heard her transmission shift into forward gear and *Teacher* almost leaped out of the water. Her tri-hull rode gracefully, cutting through the greenish water with ease as the large boat started her maiden voyage down the most famous river in the world on her way to a tributary that to the modern world existed only in legend.

TWO HOURS LATER Collins, Everett, and Mendenhall were outside the glass-enclosed cockpit while Sarah sat with Jenks in the copilot's chair, talking about, what else, the chief's boat.

Corporal Sanchez had volunteered to be the expedition's cook, much to Mendenhall's dismay, and he brought them a tray of coffee. He handed two cups through the door to Jenks and Sarah, then left the tray on the centerline table in the navigation department.

"I don't think the master chief likes me," he said, wiping his hands on a towel.

"That man doesn't like anyone except this woman," Carl said as he patted the composite side of the boat.

"Ain't normal," Sanchez called as he walked back through the hatch and back to his cooking.

Jack returned to the large glass table. Padilla's map had been scanned and placed in the main navigational computer. Laid before them in detail were items that had been added to the map by placing known terrain colors and features from U.S. Geological Survey RORSAT photos. The display was "current position" capable, meaning they could see their position the entire way on the computer-generated map. In the next few hours they hoped to have telemetry set up with Jet Propulsion Labs in Pasadena to allow them access to live images from Boris and Natasha.

Carl spun a steel ball embedded in the side frame of the map table and slid forward along the image of the river from their current position. While he sipped his coffee, he studied the area that worried them the most. The Padilla map showed only the winding river; on the more scientific survey maps that had been superimposed over the Spaniard's, there were only trees and jungle. From above, there was no river to speak of, as it had disappeared from view under the rain forest canopy. A computer line marked where the tributary *should* be according to the Padilla map beneath it.

"There are so many variables—width, depth, and other factors—that could stop us right in our tracks," Carl said.

"Well, I guess that's when we'll see if *Teacher* is as magical as the master chief seems to think she is," Jack said.

"I think she'll be," Mendenhall offered. "He's right; she's something, isn't she?"

Both Carl and Jack looked over at the sergeant but didn't comment.

"That doesn't mean that I like him or anything, just that he built a great-lookin' boat," Mendenhall said defensively. "I think I'll go check on the arms locker and scuba gear," he said, feeling like a traitor for praising their pilot. He picked up his coffee and excused himself.

"What's going on in navigation? Any change in course? We still trying for that phantom cutoff onto that Black Water Trib?"

Jack hit the com button and selected Cockpit. "No change in course; according to Padilla, the tributary is hidden, looks like a normal bend. So stay to the right of the center current," Jack said as he released the switch.

As the two men looked at the screen they saw the cutoff. It was marked by a rendering of trees that had grown so thick even in the Spaniard's time that Padilla had made a black *X* through the drawing of the sun. Carl mumbled something.

"What was that?" Jack asked.

"I guess that's where we fall off the edge of the world."

Jack didn't respond; he just nodded.

THREE HOURS LATER, with Carl at the helm, Jenks and half the team were at dinner in the crowded lounge in section four. At only twenty-three and a half feet wide, *Teacher* lacked what would be properly known as elbow room. Sarah, Virginia, and Jack sat as far away from the master chief as they could to avoid any unnecessary charm he might add to their conversation. They were all enjoying their view of the passing river in a most unique way: the bottom port windows were actually underwater, and the green flowing river eased by like a huge aquarium before them.

"Are we prepared in case we run into our French friend?" Virginia asked, forsaking her chance at Sanchez's ham and cheese casserole, instead opting for a cup of coffee and salad.

"It all depends on circumstances, I guess. He's no fool; he'll wait until he feels he has the advantage in numbers, or surprise. I figure he'll wait until we've done most of the work; that's his pattern, from what I've learned."

Sarah listened but didn't comment, so Jack knew there was something on her mind.

"What are you thinking, short stuff?" he asked.

She laid her fork in her plate and sighed. "It's Danielle, her showing up at the dig in Okinawa. If she was so intent on tracking her ex-husband down, why use us? I mean, surely she has other resources at her disposal, so much so that we should have been irrelevant."

"Well, you heard her explanation. She didn't really want to bring in her own people for personal reasons," Virginia said.

"I'm not buying it," Sarah insisted.

Jack gave her a look she knew all too well.

"Knock it off, it's not just that I don't like her, or because her former name was Farbeaux. It's the way her agency has so conveniently become cooperative right now. Besides, so soon after Lisa's death, I think she's a bad influence on Carl."

"Oh, that's it—you don't think Carl's man enough to avoid an entanglement. Or is it that you're jealous for Lisa?" Jack asked.

"Listen, Jack," she said, then caught her mistake a split

second after it was out of her mouth. "I mean Major, leave that crap out of it . . . it's just that maybe Lieutenant Ryan would have been better off working with her, instead of Carl," she said, picking up her fork to indicate she was ending her part in this awkward conversation.

"Where is Jason, anyway? He's usually attached to you and Carl like a pet," Virginia commented.

"I assigned him another project," Jack quickly replied. "And Ryan is the last man you want around a Frenchwoman anyway," he joked, hoping to steer the conversation away from the lieutenant's whereabouts.

"Chief Jenks, Major, come to the bridge please," Carl said over the intercom. "We're coming up on the area where our Spaniard said the Black River starts."

JENKS AND JACK passed Danielle in the companionway that joined the navigation area with the cockpit. She smiled and nodded a greeting. The master chief stopped and tilted his head to admire her from behind, then entered the cockpit to relieve Carl at the controls.

"Had Frenchie keepin' you company, Toad?" Jenks asked as he squeezed into the command chair.

"Nah, all by my lonesome up here," Carl answered.

Jack caught an inflection in his answer and, instead of going into the cockpit, turned and looked around the navigation compartment. He went to the map table. The computer rendering of Padilla's map was up. Jack remembered shutting it down earlier, and surmised that Carl must have turned it on when he took over for Jenks. He ducked his head into the cockpit and saw that the map was also up on the monitor between the two seats. Everett must have used the map table first and then routed the program to the cockpit.

"We have a branch coming up. We have about fifteen feet of water under our keel, so no problem there, yet," Jenks said.

"I was thinking," Jack asked, "what would have made Captain Padilla take this particular tributary route instead of keeping with the main river?"

"What do you mean?" Carl asked from the copilot's seat.

"It makes no sense, there had to have been something his scouts had seen that made Padilla choose this route over the Amazon, a peculiarity in the river perhaps, or a man-made object. I just don't see him arbitrarily leaving the main river."

"I see what you mean and I don't have a clue. If that's the case, others in the five hundred years since would have seen the same thing and ventured down the tributary," Carl said. "So whatever it was that drew him to it—"

"Isn't there anymore," Jack finished for him.

"Well, this is going to be one short-ass trip, boys. Look," Jenks said as he throttled back on the engines.

"What the hell, we must have taken the wrong route," Carl exclaimed.

Up ahead, *Teacher* was dwarfed by sheer rock walls in front of her. A waterfall splashed down and created a beautiful scene in front, but that was it. The tributary ended after only ten miles. Jenks looked down at the sonar picture.

"She's deep. We've gone from fifteen feet under the keel to thirty-five," he reported. He reached down and pinged the bottom with a blast of sound, getting a clearer picture of the bottom landscape when the sound waves bounced back.

"Lot of boulders and shit on the bottom, some pretty large schools of fish, but that's about it. Wait a minute, look at this," he said, tapping at the still shot of the computer-generated sonar picture. He used a cursor and backtracked a little. "That's a weird-shaped rock."

"Damned near looks like a head, doesn't it?" Carl ventured.

Jack leaned in and nodded his agreement. The boulder, if that's what it was, looked as if it were a head, with ears, nose, and everything.

"Ah, sonar plays tricks on you sometimes, just a weird-shaped rock, that's all."

"Chief, those fifteen fancy remote probes you have from TRW, I think its worth one to see what that is, I'm betting it's something," Jack said, still looking at the frozen sonar picture.

"You're betting about five thousand bucks, Major," Jenks responded as he stuck a fresh cigar in his mouth. "I have only five that are programmed and operational; there were priorities in the work assigned the last two days."

Jack just looked at him.

"You're the boss, I'm only a galley slave," Jenks acquiesced. "Toad, on your console, hit the button that says UDWTR Bay 3, will ya? It's time to see if I trained you right the last few hours on the operation of our Snoop Dog."

Carl found the button and pushed it. Somewhere below they heard a short whine coming from somewhere. Then a small console popped up on the thick armrest of Everett's chair. It was equipped with a small joystick. Jenks reached out and switched the main monitor between them to another channel, which was filled with static.

"Now, raise the small plastic cover there," he said.

Carl saw the switch cover by the joystick and raised it. Underneath was a red push button that illuminated when the switch cover was raised.

"Push it, Toad," Jenks ordered.

Carl pushed down until it clicked. They heard a gush of air and saw bubbles rise to the surface ahead of them.

"Hey, hey, watch it, you'll run her into the bank. Swing her around, swing her around!" Jenks called out loudly.

"Shit!" Carl said as he saw on the monitor the little torpedo-shaped probe was heading for shallow water. He took the small joystick and twisted it to the left. The angle on the monitor changed and the compass located in digital form at the bottom of the screen swung from east to north to south.

"Okay, Toad, now you're headed right for us; twist the top of the joystick, that's your speed control. Toad? Slow down, goddammit!"

The picture angled right at *Teacher*, the tri-shaped hull clearly visible, the probe slowed.

"Damn, kid, keep the speed down, will ya? Now, push down on the joystick. That controls your dive on the probe, push down for down, and pull up for—"

"Up?" Carl said smartly.

"I knew they made you an officer for a fuckin' reason, Toad."

Carl turned the probe again until it started heading away and then threw the four-foot-long radio-controlled unit, dubbed "Snoopy," which TRW had developed for the navy, into a spiral headed down, trailing her near-invisible fiber-optic power and control cable behind it.

"You catch on fast, now try not to run it into the mud. We can still recover her and use her again. Major, ask that kid Mendenhall to get to the fantail and make ready to bring the probe aboard, and tell that army fella not to fall overboard, it's heavy."

Jack did so using the intercom.

On the monitor the picture grew darker. A light just under Snoopy's nose came on with the use of an installed rheostat sensor that automatically lit up in darkness. The probe edged deeper with every turn it made, the small fins on the zero buoyancy craft keeping the device in a tight spiral. Jenks looked at the depth and called it out.

"Ten feet to bottom, eight feet, six . . . ease up, Toad," he said, watching the depth gauge and ignoring the picture. The probe slowed.

"Let me tell you, for a dead-end tributary, I'm having one hell of a time keeping this thing trim. Every time I head east, it wants to keep going. There is really one bitch of a current out there," Carl said as he fought the small joystick.

Through the window, Jack could make out some sort of thick vegetation behind the wide waterfall. He then turned his attention to the computer screen.

"Okay, you're at four feet; level her off and come right three degrees. That should put you on top of our rock," the master chief said.

Snoopy banked to the right for a split second and then

quickly righted itself on command from Carl. The light was picking up nothing but murky water and a fish now and then.

"Where in the hell is it?" Jenks asked.

The light picked up a darker outline ahead of Snoopy. Carl eased the probe forward, steering into the strengthening current. Finally the light picked out what looked like large teeth. Then the mouth and nose, large pointed ears, and eyes that stared back at them through the monitor. The head was at least ten feet tall and it looked as if there was even more buried under the mud.

"Chief, can we pipe this through the boat into the science labs?"

"Yeah," Jenks said as he pushed a button labeled BOAT MONITORS. "There, now the whole ship can see Toad's future father-in-law," he said, laughing.

Jack pushed the intercom. "Doctors, look at your monitors. Does anyone have any guesses?"

The probe made a complete turn around the huge head, picking out other small details—the feathers coursing along powerful-looking arms, the breast piece which was made up of a different type of stone from the rest of the body. All around its circumference, only half of the stone was above the mud and silt of the river's bottom; the rest disappeared into murk.

"Can you see if the figure is holding something in its right hand?" asked the voice of Professor Ellenshaw over the speaker mounted next to Jack's head.

Snoopy swung down and traveled a few feet. The probe ran along the rather large belly of the statue and protruded above the mud. The images revealed that it was indeed holding something.

"What do you think?" Carl asked.

"A pitchfork?" Jenks suggested, adjusting the brightness on the monitor.

"No, not that, but close," Jack said as he flipped on the intercom. "Professor, we have a trident in the right hand and a battle-ax in the left, crossed over at the midsection; anything else is under the mud."

"Good, good, gentlemen. You have just proven beyond any doubt that at one time at least, the Inca had passed this way. They thought it important enough to leave some strong medicine here. That is the Incan god Supay, god of death and lord of the underworld. Also the lord of all underground treasures," Ellenshaw said in a mysterious voice.

"I also believe this is Supay," Professor Keating said from one of the labs.

"I concur; the likeness etched in stone in front of us is exactly that, Supay," the voice of Professor Nathan agreed. "God of the underworld."

"Nice," mumbled Jenks.

Jack was listening but at the same time studying the cliff walls above them. There were many large ledges, so it was completely possible for the statue to have broken, or have been knocked free from one of those outcroppings by an earthquake perhaps, or just erosion.

"I think that would have been a guide, or at least reason enough, for Padilla's expedition to sidetrack," Carl said, still looking at the monitor.

"But where in the hell did he go?" Jenks wondered. "Maybe they climbed out of here and over the cliffs and picked up the tributary at another point."

Jack didn't say anything; he continued to look at the walls around *Teacher*. He left the cockpit and returned to the navigation section. There, he brought up other maps, selected the one he wanted, and clicked the mouse on the side of the navigation console. A U.S. Geological Survey map came up and on it Jack located the area where they were, thanks to their global positioning transponder. He traced the small tributary above them, the one that the waterfall was created from, and followed it. It routed right back to the main Amazon, in about a two-mile loop. He electronically sent the map to the console monitor up front and then went back to the cockpit.

"I don't think they climbed any cliffs; the small tributary that is responsible for the falls ahead, the Santos Negrón, is nothing but a hundred-mile-long tributary that's not even that old. It was created by flooding no more than five years ago. I think Padilla stuck to this tributary; it had to have been the only natural one in existence five hundred years ago."

"How did he and his people go forward, underwater?" Carl asked.

"If not underwater, how about underground, or both?" Jack asked.

Carl and Jenks didn't say anything; they looked straight ahead toward the expanse of ancient and man-made falls.

"But what are the odds that these waters would have covered by accident the very route that Padilla took?"

Jack turned to see Danielle Serrate standing behind him, leaning into the hatchway.

"Fluke," Jack said. "The new tributary would run wherever rainfall had created a trough beyond where the Brazilian government had controlled the flooding. Once it reached this point in unsurveyed and unmapped land, they really didn't care what new tributaries were created."

"I wouldn't care to wager the house on that," Danielle said. "Is that the American phrase, bet the house?"

"Yeah, that's what they say, but that's exactly what I think we should do," Carl said as he took a firm hold on Snoopy's joystick and brought its nose up. The view on the monitor changed and the picture became brighter as the probe emerged from the murkiness of the bottom toward the surface. Jack patted Carl on the shoulder. Snoopy sped up east toward the falls that were now starting to rock the probe left to right with the turbulence of the falling water. Carl directed the probe ten feet deeper as it approached. The monitor was filled with white water and bubbles as the impact of the high-falling tributary struck the flat surface below it. Carl adjusted the trim and sent Snoopy ten feet deeper, still believing the impact of the water would be enough to damage the TRW probe. Suddenly Snoopy was into darker but calmer water, where it snagged on an obstruction as an alarm sounded on the console.

"Whoa, cowboy, you rammed something. See if you can back her up some," Jenks said.

"Chief, how close can you get to the falls?" Jack asked.

"I can take her right under if I want; that little water hose of a falls couldn't dent this composite hull."

On the monitor Snoopy had successfully backed away and rose by fifteen feet to the surface.

"What is that stuff?" Danielle asked.

The master chief fired up *Teacher*'s engines and started edging the large boat toward the falling water.

"It's bushes, water plants, and vines, a thick curtain of them," Carl described. "It's a wall of them behind the falls; Snoopy was stopped by them. Goddamn, you may be right, Jack."

"Right about what, c'mon, what's he right about?" Jenks said as *Teacher* slowly drifted toward the turbulence of the water.

"He thinks he knows where and at what point our intrepid Captain Padilla disappeared into history, Chief," Carl said as he brought Snoopy to the surface next to *Teacher*. "And look at the center there, it's been recently penetrated; see where a lot of new growth has occurred? I suspect that weakened area tells us that Professor Zachary has been this way also."

"Ask Mendenhall to bring the probe aboard; she earned her keep," Jenks said.

Jack ordered Snoopy brought aboard.

"Well, I suppose you want me to take *Teacher* through there?" Jenks asked.

"It would probably take us over a day to hack our way through there, maybe get a couple of people hurt seriously with that falling water," Jack said as he leaned in closer to view the falls ahead.

"Wouldn't the vines and plants be more damaged if Professor Zachary had come this way less than three months ago?" Carl asked.

"Bubba, this is South America; the growth rate of plants

down here can be measured in minutes, not days or months," Jenks said.

"Well, let's go then," Danielle urged.

"Unless you don't think the old girl has the wherewithal to punch her way through it, Chief," Carl said without looking at Jenks.

The master chief clamped his jaws down on his cigar. "You officers think you can play me like that? You think you can use that shit you learned at officers' school," he turned around and stared at Jack, "or West Point, in Psyops, to goad me into taking her through there?"

"Not at all," Jack replied quietly.

Jenks looked at his digital controls on the panel in front of him and said nothing. While the others thought he was thinking it over, he was actually figuring the stress tolerances of *Teacher*'s composite hull. He was silent for two full minutes.

"Major, Toad, get some help and lower the sail tower and jackstay; we're riding too damned high to get her through that opening. We're also going to put a lot of weight onto this girl's ass." The master chief saw the expressions of confusion from Jack and Danielle. "We have to take on one hell of a lot of ballast; we have to ride low, dangerously low, to get her through whatever that is up ahead," he explained. "And it's still no fucking guarantee we can do that. We may get through the opening and find a dead end fifty yards into it."

"Or, on a brighter note," Carl said as he squeezed out of the copilot's chair, "we just may fall off the edge of the world."

13

TWO hours had passed since the order was given to lower the radar tower and jackstay. Collins, Mendenhall, and Everett were on the upper deck of section four, bolting down the retractable tower that was now laying along two whole sections, while the rest of the crew was below making ready for a rough ride in case they ran into something other than a tunnel leading to the mysterious east end of the Rio Negro.

Jack had been the first one to notice, but he kept working. It was Mendenhall who cleared his throat.

"I see it, Sergeant," said Jack. "Just stay busy like you don't see them."

"How long have they been there?" Carl asked as he lashed down his last tie to the tower.

"About twenty minutes that I know of; wouldn't have noticed it at all if I hadn't caught the sun gleaming off their glasses."

"With the tower down, so is our radar, so we won't be able to confirm who they are," Carl said, straightening.

"Probably that boat and barge we saw on the river coming in this morning. Can't you feel our friend Farbeaux close by?"

"I sure can," Mendenhall said.

"Come on, let's get this show on the road," Jack said as he headed for the hatch.

"STAND BY," JENKS said into the intercom as he fired up both of the Cummings diesels. "Is our board green, Toad?"

Carl checked the status of all hatches and windows. The companionways in between sections all read green—closed and secured.

"Board is green, Chief."

"Major, pull down that jump seat in the aft bulkhead and strap yourself in; this could get bumpy and I don't need you in my lap at the wrong time," Jenks said as he lit his cigar and started *Teacher* forward toward the falls. "Everyone, strap in at whatever station you're at. You can follow our progress on the nose camera at the bow; it promises to be the must-watch TV show of the year." He laughed loudly as he throttled forward to two knots.

In the sciences compartment, Sarah looked at Virginia and cringed. "That guy makes me a *little* nervous," she said.

"A little?" Virginia asked.

"HERE WE GO," the master chief said as he eased back on the twin throttles and let *Teacher*'s forward momentum carry her into the falling water. Suddenly the boat rocked violently from side to side, just as Snoopy had done two hours earlier. The sound of water striking the hull was deafening, and all the while Jenks had a smile from ear to ear as he edged *Teacher* into the darkness.

Carl reached out and flipped on the exterior running lights as water covered the acrylic windows in the bow. Jack flinched as the first of the water struck; he thought the nose glass would cave in. But the boat slid neatly through the falls. The roar slid down the entire length of *Teacher* as the crew felt every inch of her entry. Then the bushes and vines snagged her and she bounded to a stop. The chief bit down on his cigar and throttled her engines forward. *Teacher* lurched into the water plants and undergrowth, making a screeching sound as her hull came into contact.

"There goes the paint job," Jenks said loudly as he goosed the engines again.

"Low ceiling!" Carl called loudly above the din of water striking the hull.

"Give us another three thousand pounds of ballast," calmly ordered the master chief.

Carl turned on the ballast pumps. Although he couldn't hear them engage, he was satisfied as he saw on the digital readout that the distance between keel and the bottom was decreasing.

"She's down a full three feet, Chief," Carl reported.

Outside their windows the crew could see the greenish waters lapping six or seven inches above the sealed frames.

Jenks applied more power as *Teacher* strained to break free of the undergrowth. Her engines were churning up water as she struggled for momentum. "Going to fifty percent power, hang on!"

Teacher seemed to be stuck in place. As they viewed the situation in their monitors, the crew each willed her either forward or for their pilot to back off.

"Going to seventy-five percent power," Jenks called out and pushed the throttles forward to the three-quarters mark, but still the bushes, roots, and vines clung to the hull like tentacles of an octopus, refusing their advance.

"Engines are overheating," Carl shouted.

"No news is good news. Can that shit, mister, going to redline!" Jenks shoved the dual throttles all the way to their stops.

STRAPPED INTO THEIR seats, Mendenhall and Shaw were standing by in the engine compartment, sweat rolling down their faces. The heat was overpowering the air-conditioning, and the section was slowly becoming unbearable. The diesels were so loud that the two men couldn't converse. Suddenly something popped and a small fire broke out as a gasket failed and diesel fuel sprayed out onto the deck.

"Fire!" Mendenhall shouted but Shaw had his ears covered and couldn't hear him. The sergeant unsnapped his harness and ran for the fire extinguisher. He emptied the extinguisher, momentarily smothering the flames. Mendenhall threw away the empty and grabbed another, as the engines seemed to strain even louder as they went to full power.

Suddenly and very slowly the vines started to separate with loud popping and tearing sounds. Still the master chief kept full power to the engines. Then all at once they were through. Outside the view ports of the cabin, they saw the vines and bushes suddenly slide by as *Teacher* was sling-shot into the giant cave. Her lights picked out rock walls and sides as she sped into the void.

"Engine shutdown!" Jenks cried. "Toad, hit the forward jets, stop this goddamned thing before we slam into a wall!"

Carl engaged the two forward water-jet thrusters and applied full throttle to them both. *Teacher* started to slow. Then before they knew it, the large boat was at a standstill. All was silent except for the forward thrusters. Carl reached out and shut them down. The voyagers found themselves in a giant cave sitting in the middle of a slow-moving underground grotto, with the river leading out to the east.

"So this is the missing east end of the Rio Negro," Jack said as he reached for the intercom. "Okay everyone, we're through. Welcome to Captain Padilla's Black Water Tributary."

BEFORE STARTING DOWN the long corridor of darkness, Jenks inspected the engine room and declared engine number one down. He, Mendenhall, Shaw, and the amazingly and hereto unbeknownst mechanically inclined Professor Charles Hindershot Ellenshaw III, who volunteered his services in their capacity, began to change out the head gasket on number one and replace the fuel line that had split. They would run in the meantime on engine number two, as Jenks didn't think they would be calling for speed anytime soon. He inspected the rest of *Teacher*, and aside from a few rubber window gaskets that had leaked, she had come through the falls just fine. They were under way at five knots ten minutes later, still running low in the water through the blackness that engulfed the boat.

FARBEAUX WAS AMAZED at what he had just witnessed through his glasses. That strange-looking craft actually went through the falls.

"These people never cease to amaze me," he mumbled as he handed the field glasses back to the captain. "And to think our lady friend, Professor Zachary, also found it and made it through—surely we must respect them. Do you agree, *señor?*"

"So, what do you plan to do?" Mendez asked annoyedly.

"I expect we will wait for two hours, and in that time we will prepare to follow them. Captain, get your crew ready and let's cut the profile of the *Rio Madonna* down some so we may attempt to enter the cave; the barge is low in the water so should not pose a problem," Farbeaux said as he walked off the flying bridge.

"*Sí, señor,*" the captain responded, and started shouting orders to his ten-man crew.

Mendez felt better that Farbeaux was taking such complete charge, it gave him the benefit of not having to coordinate the effort but still be critical if need be. He walked back to the fantail and sat down with Rosolo and his team of twelve bodyguards.

Farbeaux walked to the port side of the *Rio Madonna*, stood by the gunwale, and lit a cigarette. He was getting an old familiar feeling that came upon him when things were not under his complete control. He felt there were more elements involved than he had accounted for. As he looked around the jungle surrounding them, he was starting to feel like a small piece of a much larger puzzle, a puzzle that could become very dangerous if he wasn't the one to figure it out first.

EVENT GROUP COMPLEX
NELLIS AFB, NEVADA

There was a knock on Niles's door. He rubbed his eyes and looked over at his nightstand. It was only ten at night and that was when he realized he had fallen asleep in his clothes. He shook his head and reached for his glasses.

"Yes?"

"Sorry to disturb you, Niles, but you'd better see this, Boris and Natasha are now on the job and they caught something," Pete Golding said from outside the door to Niles's quarters.

"It's open, Pete," he called out as he turned on the night-stand table light and put his stocking feet on the carpeted floor. He stood and made it over to his desk, where the day's paperwork still lay undone.

Pete walked in, holding several pictures in his hand. "Your computer up?" he asked.

"Yeah, why?"

"Good, we won't have to use these wet stills, then."

Pete stepped up to Niles's computer. He quickly typed in some commands and his security clearance, then he turned the monitor toward Niles.

"These are only twenty minutes old and were taken on Boris and Natasha's first pass."

Niles looked down at the monitor. It displayed a night shot that the KH-11 satellite had taken over its new position. He could see the river in dark relief, and then he spotted many small, glowing objects. The photo, obviously infrared, showed about fifty warm bodies moving along the river in the only section for thirty miles that had any clear opening through the massive canopy of trees.

"Where are these people?" Niles asked.

"The exact coordinates the major reported from this afternoon. Now, Jack says he suspected they were being trailed by a boat with a barge attached, which has disappeared, by the way, but he doesn't know anything about people on the ground. And look at this," Pete said as he typed in another command on the keyboard.

The picture started to resize itself. White squares appeared upon white squares and they started to swirl. The picture had been enlarged by Natasha until Niles could clearly make out the men walking along the river in the dark.

"Goddammit!"

"Yeah, those are troops; you can even make out most of their equipment," Pete said.

"Just who in the hell are we dealing with?"

"Could be anyone, but my guess would be Peruvian, most likely," Pete ventured as he leaned back away from the picture he had been studying for the last hour.

"For a goddamned secret valley, enough people seem to know about it," Niles said, rubbing a hand over his balding head. "We have to contact Jack."

"We tried. There's nothing since Jack reported they were going into the cave."

Niles slumped into his chair and pushed the daily reports away from him. "Contact Lieutenant Ryan," Niles said as he looked at his watch, "he and his twelve-man team should have arrived in Panama by now. Tell him Operation Conquistador is now on full alert."

"You got it, Niles," Pete said as he gathered up his photos. Then he thought better of it and placed them back on the director's desk, and then left the room.

Niles studied the monitor briefly and then pulled the topmost wet photo off the pile and stared at it. He hoped Jack would be able to make contact if and when they exited the cave. Because if they couldn't at least get a signal up and out to Boris and Natasha, they would be cut off with no chance of help arriving.

As Niles contemplated the images, he knew there was a whole lot of trouble heading their way.

Hell, he thought, *also trouble from a source that was probably already there waiting for them*, just as it had been for the Padilla and Zachary expeditions.

14

TEACHER was cruising in the dark at a revised three knots. Thus far they had been in the cave for three hours and had been amazed at the carvings they had documented that covered the rock walls—depictions of wild men in different hunting poses, Incan gods and warriors, and strange beasts and fish. Thus far they had cataloged three hundred different carvings. The work had been meticulously worked and showed in minute detail what life had been like for those who traveled the ancient tunnel before them.

Carl was at the helm in the cockpit, kept company by Jack who assisted with fathom soundings and as a lookout for rock projections, which had nearly done them in twice. *Teacher* was still riding low in the water with the extra ballast they had taken on, as the roof was only ten feet above them and as low as a mere yard in some spots. Every once in a while they saw bats flutter in and out of the floodlights.

Jenks was in section seven, assisting the science team with the expandable observation module, which would be lowered to allow them a view of their new underwater domain.

The center of the section was taken up by a large boxlike structure made mostly of glass and aluminum framing. There were seats inside this eight-foot-long vessel for six crewmen, and it was fully equipped with small cameras, for both still photos and video. Jenks assisted Danielle, Dr. Nathan, Sarah, Mendenhall, Heidi Rodriguez, and Professor Ellenshaw into the observation module and checked to make

sure the hydraulic pressure was up. Then he removed his cigar from his mouth.

"Okay, I suspect you're going to feel a little queasiness
when you're lowered. The section is telescopic so you won't
actually be out of the boat, just under her some. Ready?"

The six passengers nodded as they turned toward the
sides and the glass that for right now showed nothing other
than the outer composite hull.

Jenks pressed a button on the intercom. "Toad, you're going to feel some drag as we lower the section into the water,
Teacher's computer should compensate after about thirty
seconds, so don't worry about it, got it?"

"You got it, Chief; right now we have about thirty-two
feet under the keel. We'll give you plenty of notice if we run
shallower than twenty-five," Carl said from the cockpit.

"Okay, boys and girls, hold onto your asses," Jenks said
as he raised the switch cover and pressed.

The hum of hydraulics sounded from motors embedded in
the sides of *Teacher* as the section started to telescope. The
passengers grabbed the armrests of the seats and looked up as
they were lowered. The faces of Jenks and the rest of the sciences team became obscured as the rush of passing water was
heard. They turned toward the glass again when the small
boat-shaped platform broke into the river. Mendenhall was
sitting in the frontmost seat and so was nearest the bow-
shaped and aerodynamic front. A mere six inches of acrylic
separated him from the rush of greenish water being split by
the platform. First they were lowered by five feet into the
river; next, another section started sliding from the hull of
Teacher and the platform was telescoped another five feet
into the river. Then floodlights blazed to life and the underwater world was illuminated around them in stark detail.

"My god, this is great," Sarah said.

Above them, a section of soundproof decking slid over
the top of the submerged platform, sealing out light and
noise from *Teacher* and the crew above.

All about them, fish of every freshwater species darted

about, some curious as to the strange creatures staring at them, enough so that they returned the favor.

"Damn, look at this—it's got to be the largest damn catfish I have ever seen. Look at its color," Mendenhall said.

Outside the glass of the pointed bow, an albino catfish, with a wide mouth that was at least large enough to take a man whole, swam by curiously but sped away when it came into the center of one of the floodlights.

"We're invading its home," Danielle remarked as she watched the black walls of the cave slide by her.

"Look at that," Ellenshaw said. "Supay, the god of the Inca underworld."

Outside the acrylic windows, they could see a statue, at least forty feet in length. It lay on its back. *Teacher* easily cleared it and, as she passed over, they could see the slanted, snakelike eyes as it watched the strange craft ease by above it.

"Professor, look!" Danielle said loudly.

"Oh my god! Someone start filming this, please!" Ellenshaw cried as he found himself face to face with a freshwater coelacanth, a fish that was supposed to be extinct more than 60 million years before. More than one saltwater species had been caught off the coast of Africa, but this was the first live specimen Ellenshaw had ever seen, outside of some rare footage of one that was filmed four years before. It was just inches from his face.

"Cameras are running, Professor," Jenks called through the intercom from above.

"This is amazing," he said as he raised his hands to the glass. The huge fish swam easily, its strong finlike appendages able to maneuver it like a swimmer with hands.

"This is not the saltwater species found in the seas, look at her! She must be two hundred pounds, and in freshwater, remarkable!" Ellenshaw exclaimed. "Professor Keating, are you seeing this?" he asked with the aid of the intercom.

"Indeed, I am. This is truly remarkable."

As Sarah joined them at the window, the prehistoric fish suddenly moved with the speed of a snake striking a victim.

It smashed itself into the window, making all inside fall back, either into chairs or onto the deck. It swam away and then attacked the glass again. It repeated the aggressive action three more times as it gathered more speed with every turn. Then the five-foot-long fish apparently finally decided enough was enough and swam off into the murky water.

"Well, that was fucking exciting; not exactly something you would put in your tank at home, is it?" Sarah said as she was helped up by Mendenhall.

"Do we have film of this?" Ellenshaw asked.

The speaker came alive and Jenks answered, "Got it all, damn near thought he was going to punch a hole in that acrylic."

"It was indeed splendidly aggressive, wasn't it," the wild-haired Ellenshaw said excitedly.

"Yeah," Mendenhall said, looking at the professor as if he had lost his mind.

"Okay, folks, that's enough for now, too dangerous while we're under way. Bringing her up," Jenks warned.

The ceiling above them slid back as they resumed their seats. The bottom section telescoped into the first, and that into the main hull. All six crewmembers exited with a feeling they had just returned from another world.

"I hope we can get a specimen while we are here; that would be marvelous," Ellenshaw said as he slapped Mendenhall on the shoulder.

The sergeant just gave him an uneasy smile, then turned to Sarah and rolled his eyes.

LATER, WHILE JENKS was at the helm in the cockpit, *Teacher* suddenly broke free of the cave and into the star-filled night sky. It was so sudden he didn't even realize it until the moon lit up the cockpit. He reached out and slapped Lance Corporal Walter Lebowitz, who had been sleeping and was supposed to be assisting him.

"Wake up, jarhead!" Jenks called out loudly and then lit his cigar.

The lance corporal didn't know where he was for a moment, and the brightness of the moon clearly confused him after the hours inside the pitch black of the cave. He looked around at the jungle and forest that crowded the riverbank in every direction.

"Go wake Lieutenant Commander Everett and Major Collins. Tell 'em we're clear of the cave and have to stop to blow out our ballast tanks and check the boat out. We'll get under way again in—" Jenks looked at the digital chronometer on the command console, "—two hours; got it, Corporal?"

"Yes, Chief."

"Then why aren't you moving, boy?" Jenks growled.

The pilot watched him go and then shut down the exterior lights, throwing the outside world back into darkness with the exception of the lowering moon. The cockpit lights were switched off, and only the green-blue glow of the instrument panels illuminated Jenks. He reached out and throttled back on both engines. He shut them down and then put the auto pilot in hover. The electrically operated jets would keep *Teacher* in the center of the tributary with small adjustments on her thrusters. Only the forward jets would be working full-time to keep the boat from drifting back with the slow current. He then turned the knob that read BALLAST PURGE, and throughout the boat a loud hiss of escaping air woke most everyone. Large bubbles of exploding air and water surrounded *Teacher* as the tanks emptied and the boat's hull rose high into the air after her being half-sunk for the need of having a low profile.

As Jenks relaxed and looked ahead, all he could make out was more darkness as the tributary went under the never-ending canopy of trees once again. He suspected this would be the last location for a while where the major could make contact with anyone back home.

"Hello, may I join you?" a female voice asked.

Jenks turned in his seat to see that scientist-type woman with the great legs, as she moved in and sat down in the copilot's seat.

"Dr. Pollock, isn't it?" Jenks asked as he slid his side window open and tossed the remains of his cigar into the river.

Virginia was in Levi's and a black mock turtleneck shirt. "Yes, how are you, Chief?"

"Me, I'm fine, what can I help you with?" he asked, his eyes roaming over her chest and then quickly back to her eyes. "You come a-slummin', or what?"

"Well, I was up in the galley, waiting for coffee, and I thought I would come up front and see the ogre himself. Judge for myself and see if you're the gruff bastard everyone says you are," she said, raising her left eyebrow as she removed her glasses.

"Well, am I?" he asked.

"I don't know yet. I did hear you yelling at that poor marine from all the way in the galley. *You* seem to think you're mean and tough, but I don't know; I haven't formed an opinion just yet."

He looked the tall woman over even more closely than before, or for what etiquette called for. One eye twitched as he tried to figure out what she was about.

"Would it make a difference if I kicked your ass?" he suddenly blurted.

"Perhaps it would," she answered, "but how about taking a break and buying me a cup of coffee instead. Then we can discuss the side of you no one sees." She stood up and left the cockpit.

Jenks followed her with his eyes and then leaned over to look as she went through the glass hatch and into the navigation compartment. He started to reach for a fresh cigar, then thought better of it and stood and followed. He stopped long enough to look at himself in the large window next to the navigation table as he entered section two, and decided a trip into the head wouldn't be a bad idea. His eyes were bloodshot and his breath smelled as if he had just come off leave in Shanghai. He didn't know it, but Virginia Pollock had a thing for lost causes, and the master chief was definitely one of those.

AT THE BREAK of dawn, with the antenna array up and operating, and the radar dish turning to Jenks's satisfaction, Jack attempted to check in with the Event Group Complex. They had an opening in the tree canopy of only sixty feet or so, and thus he hoped Boris and Natasha had made the move that had been planned. Pete Golding responded as clearly as if he were talking from the riverbank. Jack reported that they had penetrated the falls and had found the tributary just as the map had indicated. Then Pete handed the conversation off to Niles.

"Jack, we should have visual of you in the next hour or so, via Boris and Natasha. When you find yourselves in thick canopy country, we'll use space-based radar to keep track of *Teacher*, using her heat signature," Niles said.

"Okay. We're just now getting under way; nothing earth-shaking to report as of yet."

"Jack, we have two problems. One, the president will not, I repeat, will *not* permit Ryan and the Delta on the ground in Brazil; it's political and he just won't make that call."

"Well, hopefully we can handle anything Farbeaux can throw our way."

"That's problem number two; you have company headed your way besides the Frenchman."

"The boat and barge, we know about those. They're probably him," Jack countered.

"No, Jack. Boris and Natasha has picked up an armed group of about fifty men on foot, just entering the area of the falls. And I've more good news—your trailing boat and barge are nowhere to be found; I suspect they may have followed you into the tributary."

"Have you alerted Ryan to our backup? Operation Spoiled Sport will replace Conquistador?" Jack asked.

"Done, he's on full alert for plan two. The Delta team will act as security while Proteus is on the ground in Panama, but that's not a sure thing, Jack; they're having trouble getting the system online. Remember, the whole program is experimental and the whole damned platform could possibly explode over half of South America, so you be careful. Any rough stuff, get your team out of there, into the jungle if you have to. Are your orders clear enough, Major?"

"Got it; go get some sleep, Niles," Jack said and clicked off the satellite communication link. He patted Tommy Stiles on the back. "Thanks, it was clear as a bell."

"Is everything all right?" Sarah asked.

He winked. "Yeah, just cautionary. Inform everyone that from here on out we'll be going to fifty percent alert status, half on, half off."

CARL, SARAH, AND Danielle gathered close to study the computer-generated version of the Padilla map on the navigation table. Carl slid his finger along the shoreline of the tributary. Then he punched in the current coordinates on a small keypad, and the small blip that indicated *Teacher*'s position showed itself in red, underneath the deep tree canopy.

"According to the map, Padilla's Sincaro village was only about three klicks up the river. That would place the lagoon and valley not that far away."

"We can't even report our location since the sky disappeared," Sarah said.

"Yeah, I've never seen trees like these. How can they grow so much that they block out the entire sky?"

"Water, constant rain. They fight each other for the right to sunlight, making it a battle for supremacy," Danielle stated, "each one vying for the sun by reaching out over its neighbor, thus creating a giant umbrella effect that will allow nothing through."

The engines of *Teacher* were like the sad drone of a constant lullaby. Most of the team had sacked out as they entered the darkness of the rain forest, knowing sleep could be hard to come by in a few hours. Jenks was at the helm with Virginia. She was actually getting a kick out of his permitting her to use the toggle controls of the cockpit, as she had been amazed at how responsive the big boat was. As she copiloted the vessel, she laughed at almost everything Jenks had to say. The master chief had never smiled so much as during the time he was spending with Virginia.

Carl was still leaning over the navigation table with Sarah and Danielle when he heard the master chief and scientist erupt with laughter; he never knew Virginia had such a deep and reactive laugh. He stood up and looked at the two women at the table.

"Does anyone else find that disturbing?" he asked.

WASHINGTON, D.C.

Ambrose had received his marching orders. He didn't like it and knew the secretary was escalating the situation before he knew for a fact that there was even a need to. He picked up the phone and punched in the numbers he had memorized.

"Yes."

"General, how are you, my friend?"

The man in Brazil sat up straighter in his chair. He swallowed as he tried to find his voice.

"I am . . . I am well, *señor.*"

"Good. Are you prepared on your end to do what is necessary?"

"Yes. Yes, I am."

"Good. You may send your ground element onto the river to follow my countrymen now. If the area in question is found, you may set them loose. There will be no foreign element allowed out of your country, General, is that clear?"

"*Sí* . . . uh . . . yes, I understand."

"Are ten boats enough, General?"

"They are the best assault force in the private sector, *señor.* They will do their jobs."

"Good, good. Your reward will be handsome as we promised, both monetarily and politically. Your air force is ready in case?"

"This is an element I would rather not use—"

"It will only be used if something unforeseen arises; don't worry, my friend."

The connection was cut and the general was left holding the phone, aghast that he had gotten himself into this very dangerous game of treason.

BLACK WATER TRIBUTARY
TEN MILES ASTERN OF *TEACHER*

Mendez had bided his time. He was a patient man when it came to killing. That was where his former partners in the drug trade had failed on a monumental scale. Targets and places of assassination were to be chosen with expert precision and never, ever was the decision to be made hastily. Mendez and his operatives knew when the iron was hot enough to strike. Why place the blame of murder upon yourself, when you can make people believe the illusion of someone else's doing the dirty work?

In the darkness he could see the Frenchman in the wheelhouse talking with that fool of a captain. Santos was an annoyance that he would soon tire of, along with Farbeaux. He lit a cigar. The flare of the match momentarily illuminated his features as he caught Rosolo's eye. Mendez nodded and then turned away toward the stern of the boat.

Captain Rosolo made sure Farbeaux was still occupied by Santos, then he followed his boss to the gunwale at the far end of the boat. Once there, he removed a small cylinder from his coat pocket and found the trigger. He held the device up and out away from the *Rio Madonna* and aimed it through a small break in the overhead canopy where stars could be seen. To the rear, they could clearly make out the trailing barge as it silently cut the river into two white slices. Rosolo turned and gestured to one of his men just below the wheelhouse. The man held up a portable radio and switched it to the *Madonna*'s frequency. Then he pushed the squelch button, with the volume turned all the way up. Inside the wheelhouse, they heard the radio come to life with the most godawful squeal imaginable. At the same time, Rosolo pulled the string at the end of the tube and the bright flash of a flare shot out and through the small opening in the tree canopy. The light breeze quickly pulled the telltale smoke away from the boat and into the surrounding jungle, just as Farbeaux made an appearance on the bridge wing to admonish the man below for making so much noise with his radio. Rosolo smiled as the Frenchman didn't even look their way. He stepped back into the now silent bridge.

"Well done, my friend." Mendez puffed on his overly large cigar as the pop of the flare sounded three hundred feet above the canopy.

FIVE HUNDRED FEET above the trees and thick jungle, the lead pilot of a flight of two Aérospatiale Gazelle attack helicopters, once owned by the French army, circled. The bright flash of the red flare arched out of the forest below and the two pilots knew they had a mission. They were mercenaries hired by Mendez, and their specialty was airborne murder.

The pilot in the lead Gazelle had forgone the hiring of a weapons officer for this well-paying opportunity, out of greed. The two pilots would share their reward with no one. After all, they were only going after a slow-moving river craft. They could handle the attack themselves.

He called his wingman and gave his instructions. He reached out and turned on his FLIR radar. The forward-looking infrared system activated and showed the coolness of the jungle and trees below. Then as they crossed the winding and unseen tributary below, the target they were seeking came into full view. It was marked clearly through the canopy of trees as a long, very bright ambient red color as it churned away slowly below. The fools would never know what hit them. He pulled the safety cover from his trigger mounted on the control stick, and selected his guns. He had elected not to bring the missiles he had stored in Colombia because he felt it would be a waste; they would have trouble penetrating the trees below. But twenty-millimeter rounds wouldn't have that problem, as they would smash their way through any protecting wood surrounding their target.

The lead pilot smiled as he brought his Gazelle to full power and made his turn for the dark jungle below. His unsuspecting target didn't know it yet, but they were about to be destroyed by a lightning strike from heaven.

USS *TEACHER*

Jack stood up from the navigation table. A familiar noise had entered his train of thought and then vanished. He glanced over at Carl, who was staring at the cup of coffee that sat near the table's edge. A minute tremor was making the dark coffee inside shimmer in the dim lighting of the cabin. Jack reached out for the intercom.

"Chief, have you turned any systems on in the last thirty seconds?"

"It's late, Major, not the time to be using equipment we don't need." Jenks clicked off.

"Kill the engines," Jack said as he looked at Carl and then Sarah.

Suddenly the boat went dead quiet. As they listened with faces cast in varying colors from the navigation screens on the table, Jack tilted his head. He heard it immediately. He reached for the intercom again.

"Chief, restart the engines and wait for my word; we may have company."

"Goddammit, we're not a warship, Major; I told you that."

"Chief, shut up and be ready."

"What do you think, Jack? Brazilian?" Sarah asked.

Sarah finally heard the soft whine of engines from outside. She was amazed the two officers had noticed it above the sleep-inducing drone of *Teacher*.

"No, Brazil uses the Kiowas and old Hughies we sold them." Jack closed his eyes and leaned on the table, listening more intently. "These are Gazelles. French-built attack helicopters."

"Goddamn, are you sure?" Carl asked as he went over to the wall-mounted phone.

"I heard enough of the little bastards in Africa and Afghanistan to last a lifetime."

"Will, go to the arms locker and get a fire team on deck," Carl said into the phone.

He hung up the receiver just as forty twenty-millimeter rounds smashed into *Teacher*. Jack pulled Sarah to the floor as the red-hot bullets punctured the thin composite hull and passed through to the water below. Jack didn't bother to use the intercom this time as he shouted out toward the cockpit, "Get your ass moving, Chief!"

The order was redundant as Jenks had already slammed *Teacher*'s throttles to her stops. The large boat sluiced into the center of the tributary and then started evasive zigzagging. He knew exactly what was happening, and the way to beat some of the fire from above.

Around them they heard the screams of the doctors and professors as they were jolted awake by the sheer noise and terror of the large rounds hitting *Teacher*. The military personnel were trying their best to get them behind equipment and under tables as another assault slammed into them. The red tracer rounds passed through the thin hull easily and smashed equipment as it did so. The noise was absolutely horrifying.

"You stay here!" Jack yelled at Sarah. "Come on, Carl, we can't take much more of this."

Both men gained their feet and ran to the winding staircase in the next section, ducking when more steel-jacketed rounds slammed into them. The red phosphorus tracers ignited fires in the boat's interior as they went though the hull like a kid punching holes in a soda can. The sound of breaking glass and exploding fire extinguishers sounded throughout the boat as Jenks swerved from riverbank to riverbank.

Mendenhall, Sanchez, and even Professor Ellenshaw were already on deck. The professor, standing on the rubberized flooring, was reaching up to supply magazine after magazine for the two M-16s being used by the two security men as they fired blindly up into the trees toward the sound of the turbines passing overhead.

"Situation, Will?" Jack screamed as he tossed to Carl one of the M-16s Mendenhall had stacked on the deck. The lieutenant commander didn't waste time; he pulled the charging handle and opened up at one of the low-flying assault choppers. His own tracers stitched the sky and disappeared into the tree branches above them.

"I think there are two, can't be sure. Our return defensive fire ain't getting through the trees. We're going to get our asses kicked!" Mendenhall said as he inserted another magazine while more of the tracers slammed through the trees. They hit water at first and then the awful noise of rounds hitting the hull of *Teacher* sounded, as one of the science labs took heavy damage. He looked down as Ellenshaw, white hair flying in panic, reached up with another full magazine. "Goddammit, stay down, Professor, until I ask for one!" Mendenhall shouted as he used his foot to push the crazy bastard back onto the deck.

Jack heard the scream as one of the Gazelles came low. He pointed just ahead of where the chopper should be, and Carl, Mendenhall, and Sanchez opened up. Bright white-hot tracers arched up into the canopy, and with dawning horror Jack saw over 90 percent of the light 5.56-millimeter rounds ricochet off branches and tree trunks, not able to slam their way through to the sky and the attacking ships above them.

Damn!" he said. More tracer fire erupted around them as both Gazelles opened fire. The scene felt like something out of a science-fiction movie as lines of twenty-millimeter rounds resembling laser weapons struck the water and boat around them. The choppers were stitching the area with death and destruction even while they were, themselves, impervious to their return fire.

BELOW, THE MASTER chief knew he didn't have the time he needed to find adequate cover for his slow-moving target duck that was lined up as if in a carnival's shooting gallery. He howled in frustration as more thumps sounded throughout his boat.

"By God, that's just about enough of this!" he yelled as he reached out, took Virginia's slim hand, and thrust her fingers around the throttle and rudder control located on her chairs armrest. "Take the wheel, doll; keep zigzagging as much as possible; just don't slam the old girl into the riverbank. Keep her moving no matter what." He left his seat and, before exiting the cockpit, leaned over and kissed Virginia on the cheek. "Be right back, dollface, it's fucking time for the cavalry to show up."

Virginia didn't hear a word Jenks had said. Her eyes were wide and she was too busy shaking, which in the long run increased their survivability, as *Teacher* rocked from side to side when she shook the temperamental controls. She even failed to realize the master chief had pecked her on the cheek.

ABOVEDECKS THE SECURITY team knew they were fighting a losing battle. It was obvious to Jack and Carl that the shooters orbiting above the tree canopy had a FLIR system and were using the boat's own heat signature to track them through the trees.

"I'd give my right nut for a Stinger right about now," Carl said as he emptied a twenty-round magazine into the overhead branches, hoping at least three or four rounds could pop their way through.

Jack kicked himself for not including some kind of airborne defense in their small arsenal of mostly automatic weapons.

Suddenly, weapons fire opened up from the bow's upper deck as Sarah, Danielle, and a few of the scientists began shooting with arms from the forward locker. There were now nine M-16s firing blindly upward into the canopy.

"Good girl," Jack mumbled as he quickly inserted another magazine.

At that moment, a long line of twenty-millimeter red tracers broke through the trees and stitched a long line of holes across the bow. They heard a scream; one of the female assistants working with Professor Keating had cried out as one of the large rounds nicked her arm. Jack could hear the damage the shells were doing to the interior of *Teacher* as whoever was at the controls now directed the vessel toward the middle of the tributary.

A MERE HUNDRED feet above the tree line, the two Gazelle gunships swung around. Their target was far more evasive than they were led to believe. Mendez only said they would encounter a riverboat. But this craft was maneuvering as if it were a river patrol boat. And they were taking an inordinate amount of fire from below. So far the lead Gazelle had felt the distinctive thump of several small arms impacts against its aluminum fuselage. Whoever was below had organized a defense against the attack with lightning speed, and the volume of fire was amazing.

Mendez radioed the second Gazelle that they should make a scissoring maneuver and come at their target from two different directions, catching the boat below in a crossfire that should at the very least disable it. He would concentrate fire on the bow and his wingman would take the rear, possibly hitting the engine compartment, and bringing the evasive vessel to a stop. Then they could strafe the craft at their leisure.

The two French-built Gazelles climbed to an altitude of two hundred feet and then split apart. They would start their killing run in two minutes. They would line up the copters with the aid of the FLIR and start their assault as early as a thousand yards from target. Giving their ammunition a far better chance of slicing their enemy in two.

* * *

JENKS FOUGHT HIS way into the navigation and sonar section of the boat. Several heavy rounds had at one point almost ended his career as they slammed into the hull and rocked the galley area, sending pots and pans everywhere. He spotted three of the lab technicians, who were hiding behind one of the couches in the crew lounge. Instead of feeling sorry for the two women and one man, he started kicking at them as they tried to crawl away.

"Get you fucking asses out there and defend yourselves, you fuckin' idiots. Move, I said." He took a final swipe at the crawling techs and then turned and made his way to his seat at the navigating console.

The technicians quickly stood and ran for the spiral staircase that led to the upper deck. They must have figured that the odds of surviving the bullets outside were far better than they would get facing the master chief.

Jenks reached out and pulled up a clear red-tinted cover that had a flash symbol on it. Then he turned in his chair and hit several switches marked DWAEL. He watched as a monitor located above the sonar and communications panel flickered to life.

"Sons of bitches want to play with technology, *we'll* fuckin' play with technology," he grumbled as he hit the FLIR tracking system he had installed at the last minute when it had been offered to him by the Event Group technicians in New Orleans. It had been installed for use in detecting animal movement where thick cover foliage was blocking all other sensory systems. Now he would use the forward-looking infrared system and DWAEL to make a whole new weapon, a stinger for the old *Teacher*. The deep-water argon-enhanced laser was a new system that was to be used for getting precise readings on deep canyons of unknown waterways, such as the supposed lagoon they were heading for. But little did most of the public and military know, the laser itself, if turned to full power, could be used as a very efficient cutting instrument. The main problem was supplying the system with enough juice from *Teacher*'s generators to switch it from being a depth finder to a killing weapon. The master chief, though, knew his boat. He reached out and found the main power connection for *Teacher*'s many systems and then isolated the sonar console and generator stations. He pulled as hard as he could on the main conduit, breaking the line free from the cabinet, which in turn popped the emergency breakers for everything except the systems he had isolated, causing a major breakdown in the boat's power grid. In layman's terms, the master chief had basically pulled the plug.

ON THE UPPER deck, Jack and the others held their fire as they heard the screaming approach of the Gazelles' charging at *Teacher* from above. He encouraged everyone to aim at the noise. He knew it was a lost cause, but they had to try something.

Suddenly a warning horn blared and Jenks's voice came out over the loudspeaker on the tower.

"All hands, grab your socks and hold your cocks! Hit the deck and keep your eyes closed!"

Jack and Carl hollered for everyone to get down. They heard a motor engage and, before Jack threw himself to the rubber-matted deck, he saw a small section on the starboard side of *Teacher* rise. A long, cylindrical arm was hydraulically activated and swiveled its clear glass head around as the arm extended from the opening. It resembled a ballpoint pen with a lightbulb attached to the tip. Immediately recognition dawned in Jack's eyes as a memory flashed into his mind. He recalled his days at Aberdeen proving ground, specifically the Argon laser systems they had been working on, a larger version of what he had just seen come up from *Teacher*'s hull. But he knew that they were using it for many nonmilitary things like speed and radar enhancements, measuring tools that were accurate to the millimeter. What was the master chief up to?

He heard the generators below deck go full throttle just as Virginia brought *Teacher* to the center of the tributary again. Then the engines shut down. The hairs on Jack's arms began to tingle and he smelled ozone in the air as electricity was being put out at a monumental rate of power. The current was starting to escape containment and the hair of everyone on deck began to rise.

"Oh, shit, stay down!" Jack yelled just as the helicopters above the trees let loose with their cannon.

Rounds started striking the water three hundred yards from *Teacher.* The red tracers came down in a magnificent straight line as the two attacking Gazelles made their way to the stalled boat. Then suddenly a loud crack sounded from everywhere. *Teacher*'s bulk was slammed into the water as Jenks discharged the power that had built up in the laser, sending out a straight beam of white light that burned its way through the thick canopy of trees in a microsecond. As the beam reached out, the cutting began.

THE LEAD PILOT saw something explode from below; his target's being covered by trees, he thought sure he had hit one of the enemy's gas tanks. Then suddenly the trees disappeared in a bright flash. He was momentarily blinded as a brilliant white light shot up and out. The beam caught his wingman cleanly down the middle of the Gazelle, neatly slicing the helicopter into two distinct pieces and sending its spinning rotor blades off in all directions. The white-hot beam ignited the aviation fuel and the remains of the copter plunged neatly through the trees into the river below.

The leader immediately ceased his run and let up on the trigger as he turned his Gazelle away from whoever had just fired at them from below. The nature of that weapon he didn't know, nor did he care to remain and find out firsthand what had so suddenly ended the life of one of his employees. As he ventured a look behind him, the brightness of the beam of light lessened even while it still searched the area for its second target. The pilot turned the throttle on his collective all the way to the stops and tried to turn, but the beam, though faded in intensity, turned with him. It easily sliced through his tail boom. The helicopter started to spiral out of control. The trees rushed up and the pilot closed his eyes, waiting for the inevitable, crushing death that was waiting only seconds away.

JACK KNEW THEY were lucky. *Teacher*, still out of power and drifting, floated past some of the remains of the first Gazelle. As he watched the burning wreckage slide below the dark waters, he had his proof that someone was out to stop them at all costs from reaching the lagoon.

TEN MILES TO the stern of *Teacher*, Farbeaux had thought he saw the flash of gunfire through the canopy. He walked to the bow of the *Rio Madonna* and stared out into the darkness. He was soon joined by Captain Santos.

"You saw this thing also, *señor*?"

"I saw something."

"Ah, perhaps it was just heat lightning, a common thing on the river." Santos watched the Frenchman for a reaction. The captain was pleased to see the frown on his face.

"Perhaps." Farbeaux turned away and saw that Mendez and his pet killer hadn't moved from the fantail. They sat silently at their small table watching the night around them. The only visual evidence that they were there at all was the soft glow of Mendez's cigar, and even that hid the smile on his face.

15

IT took six hours to patch the holes in *Teacher*. Jenks had taken the pats he received on the back as well as expected as he supervised the repairs, grumbling about the slow reaction time of his crew, claiming they could have defended his boat faster than they had. If the truth be known, he had been stunned at how fast the major had organized the defense. Jenks now regarded the army officer with a little more respect.

The good news was the engines weren't hit. They started downriver as soon as the worst of the hull breaches had been fixed. The rest of the time was spent putting back the pieces of the boat's interior.

On watch abovedecks in the early morning hours after most of the major repairs had been made, Mendenhall, Sanchez, and Sarah watched the low-hanging branches slide eerily close to their heads. The antenna tower had been lowered again since they entered the rain forest, otherwise they would surely have lost it by this point. The drone of the engines, coupled with the anticollision strobe atop the deck fore and aft, lulled the lookouts as they fought to remain awake.

Sarah was alone in section three, just aft of the navigation section, when she saw a very low-hanging tree branch. Mendenhall momentarily illuminated it so Sarah could see it. Then he moved the light away and clicked it off to preserve his own night vision. Sarah leaned over as the large branch cleared her head by less than a foot. That was when she felt something touch her baseball cap and then remove it. She thought she hadn't lowered her head far enough, that it had been snagged by the branch, until she turned and saw the hat hanging there, the dark little fingers holding the bill and turning it. Sarah's eyes went wide as Mendenhall laughed.

"I think a monkey just stole your hat," he called from the top of section four.

As Mendenhall continued to laugh, the red cap was tossed back at Sarah, who caught it before it went over the gunwale.

"Must not have fit," the sergeant said with a chuckle.

Suddenly a small arm reached out and removed the bush hat from his own head and he instinctively ducked, but both arm and hat had disappeared into the trees.

"I guess it thought yours would be a better fit," Sarah said with a grin.

Mendenhall cursed. He clicked on the spotlight and aimed it at the trees. He shined the bright light behind him and then all around. Then he quickly shut it off.

"Sarah, now, this is no shit; there are about a hundred . . . things in the trees."

Sarah seated her cap back on her head, still smiling. "Monkeys?"

Before he could respond, the deck was inundated with small objects they immediately recognized as exotic flowers, bananas, and berries of every sort. Then the night erupted with chattering, not monkeylike at all in its sound, or maybe it *was*, Sarah thought, but it was as if the animals in the trees were laughing: their chatter was interrupted by short gasps of air. Sanchez immediately called out for Mendenhall to shine the spotlight his way, that something was in his hair. As he did so, his and Sarah's eyes widened when the light fell on a shiny-skinned four-limbed creature that had its tail firmly wrapped around the corporal's neck. It was running its small hands through his thick, dark hair, jabbering, and appeared to be petting Sanchez.

"What in the hell is this thing?" he called out, afraid to move. "It's kind of fishy smelling."

Sarah couldn't believe what it was she was looking at. The animal was about three feet in length and for all practical purposes did resemble a monkey, except it had not one hair on its body. Sarah started breathing a little heavier than before as she carefully and slowly reached out to push the intercom button.

"Chief, kill the engines," she said.

Without asking any questions, Jenks shut down the diesels and the night went silent. Sarah could now hear the lone creature sitting atop the head of the marine coo and chirp. It almost sounded as if it were singing as it groomed the hair of Sanchez.

Sarah still had the button depressed for the intercom and without removing her eyes from the bizarre scene three sections back, she found the button for the sciences lab. She hoped someone was still working down there.

"Anyone up in science?" she said in a barely audible voice.

There was no answer. Then the deck hatch above her opened and Virginia stuck her head up.

"The master chief wants to know if there's a problem; he said he can't get through your intercom," she said as she climbed out onto deck. Then she saw Sarah was still holding down the talk switch on the communication intercom. Virginia looked to where Sarah was looking and froze. "Oh my god," she whispered and then without turning, pried Sarah's finger from the button. "We have a visitor, Chief; everyone's all right."

"A visitor?" he asked.

"This thing has scales, and its fingers are wet and they're *webbed*," Sanchez said, still not moving.

"Hold it together, Corporal, I don't *think* it's aggressive," Sarah managed to say.

The small creature looked up at the sound of the humans' voices and tilted its head. It jabbered softly, and then it stood and reached for a passing branch and easily lifted itself free of the corporal's head and disappeared into the canopy. Its swinging tail was the last thing they saw as it vanished completely.

Sarah reached down and picked up a twig that had berries still attached to it. She pulled one off and ate it.

"Good," she said.

"That's not a very good thing to do, not very scientific, Sarah," Virginia said as she picked up a beautiful species of orchid she had never seen. She smelled it and then placed it in her hair, above her ear. "Have Corporal Sanchez fill out a written report on his description of what occurred, even his feelings on the matter. Okay, Sarah?" Virginia added in a distant voice. "What an amazing animal."

Sarah watched Virginia reenter the hatch and then looked at Mendenhall. As she watched, a small hand jutted from the trees and slammed his bush hat back onto his head. He

ducked as laughterlike chatter sounded all around the drifting boat.

The twin diesels fired back up and *Teacher* started forward again. This time, the three lookouts would have no
trouble staying awake.

MOST OF THE off-duty crew, twenty of them, were in the
cramped dining section of *Teacher* eating a breakfast of ham
and eggs as they listened to Mendenhall and Sarah tease
Sanchez about his strange encounter in the dark morning
hours.

"And these creatures weren't aggressive at all, or timid?"
Ellenshaw asked, his white hair looking as if a garden hoe
had churned it up.

"Well, ask the corporal, he had a little better view than
Will or I," Sarah said as she sipped her coffee with difficulty.
Even hours later, it was difficult not to laugh.

Sanchez shot her a look and then had to smile himself.
"No, I didn't exactly get the feeling they were timid," he
said as he took a bite of his toast.

"And they definitely looked aquatic in nature; you actually saw the webbing between its small fingers?" Heidi Rodriguez asked.

"Saw and felt it," the corporal said, losing his appetite for
his toast. "And it smelled to high heaven, like . . . well, fish."

As they talked, they heard *Teacher*'s engines shut down.

"All hands are asked to join Major Collins on the upper
sun deck," Jenks's voice said over the intercom.

Sarah looked out of the large window as she rose and saw
it first. "Jesus, look at that," she said as she hurried from the
dining section toward the nearest stairwell that led upward to
the deck above.

The others glanced out the windows and then hurriedly
followed Sarah.

JACK AND PROFESSORS Nathan and Pollock were on
deck with the rest of the first watch. Virginia was busy snap-

ping pictures and Nathan had a video camera out, documenting the amazing sight above them that had been illuminated by the boat's external floodlights.

Sarah joined Jack and shaded her eyes from the bright glare. "Beyond belief," was her simple statement.

"What in the hell are they supposed to be?" Jenks said as he joined them after placing *Teacher*'s automated systems online.

Towering above them, on both sides of the tributary, stood two eighty-foot statues. They were ancient with vines and other vegetation growing from age cracks in their stone.

"They're like no Incan gods I have ever seen," Nathan said as he continued to film with the camera.

"They are carved directly from the granite of the cliff," Virginia said as she turned to photograph the other one on the opposite bank. "They're identical depictions of the same . . . same deity," she said, snapping four quick pictures.

"Look at the hands," Jack said.

The large hands of the carvings were webbed, like those of the small creatures that were reported by Sarah and her night watch. The statues had scales like a fish and the body was humanlike, very massive, and depicted strength. The head was the most amazing thing of all. Its features were that of a fish, but in the shape of a human head. Several rows of finlike flaps extended downward from the neck and head and draped just over its broad shoulders. The lips were thick, pursed like those of a fish; the nose was but two small holes; and they could make out the gills that ran along each side of the jaw in four distinct lines. But the most amazing feature was the way in which the carvers of these ancient statues had depicted the eyes. Although human in shape, they had dead dark pupils like those of sharks.

"Lord, look what the left hand of each is carrying," Nathan said as he lowered his camera.

A small human skull was grasped in each statue's left hand. Long claws were sunk into the bone in a disturbing and vicious illustration by the stone carvers.

"What would you say the scale is on that, Charles?" Virginia asked Ellenshaw, who was staring wide-eyed.

"If that is an accurate-size skull of an adult human, I would say the gods depicted here would be at least eight and a half to nine feet tall, upright of course."

"It would have been one hell of a swimmer," Jack said. "Look at its feet."

The clawed feet were very long and wide, and they, too, were webbed. The powerful-looking legs had long fins down the back until they disappeared into the rock wall of the cliff. The arms also had fins, running along the back of the forearm to the wrists.

"All in all, not something I would care to run into either in the water, or out," Sarah said as she hugged herself. She remembered the fossilized hand, just as the others now recalled it.

"This must mean we're close to the valley and the lagoon," Professor Keating said.

"What makes you think that, Professor?" Jenks asked.

"Because these statues were placed here as a warning. They're guarding something," he said, looking at Jenks. "And I can't think of anything else they would be here to protect unless it was Padilla's lagoon, would you?"

The master chief placed back into his mouth the cigar he had been holding and clamped down with his teeth. "Well then, let's just go see what's so damned important that someone would carve a statue of their mother-in-law in the cliffs." He smiled at Virginia. "It must be good, whatever it is," he said as he turned and went below to get *Teacher* under way again.

The other thirty-plus members of her crew stayed on deck and watched the large statues slide past as they started downriver again. Most had to turn back for last looks as they just couldn't fathom why the Incan gods had never been cataloged or documented before; after all, there were lakes all over Peru, and her coastline was extensive. Why a water god way out here, and why one that was so different from the squat, rakish-looking gods of other Incan deities?

It was only Jack who noticed that the jungle and forest sounds had returned as they moved up river. What unnerved him was the fact that no one had noticed when they had ceased in the first place. Then he realized why: *Teacher*'s voyagers had been so awed by the giant statues that they hadn't noticed they had drifted into sunlight for the first time, when the canopy of trees had given way to the carvings. Now that they had reentered the tree-covered tributary, the sounds of life had returned. Why had the birds and animal sounds stopped when they were in front of the carvings?

Jack turned and went over to Carl, who was scanning the river ahead with binoculars.

"Carl, go to Mendenhall and get sidearms from the weapons locker. Issue them to all security personnel; give one to Jenks and Sarah also."

"You got it, Jack. See something you didn't like?" Carl asked, handing him the binoculars.

"Yeah, two somethings, both of them about eighty feet high and representing something we may have a part of in fossilized form, and those things didn't look like they were welcoming people to this part of the river."

16

TEACHER was still in semidarkness at noon. Every once in a while, dapples of bright sunlight would filter through in beams as bright as lasers. The oppressive heat and the sight of those strange carvings had unnerved the crew to the point that most were lost in their own thoughts. Before they had boarded, everyone had been briefed by each department on everything that was known about the original Padilla expedition, and now certain pages of those briefs were standing out like a lighted piece of artwork. Every man and woman onboard *Teacher* remembered the fossil and its estimated age from the carbon-14 tests that had been conducted. Although not official, the estimation of only five hundred years was now not just a curious fact, it was just a little scary, because the more one saw of this strange world, the more one could believe the existence of almost anything.

Jack was reading a tech manual on the operation of a small charge that could be used at depths up to two hundred feet, which was filled with Hydro-Rotenone, a tranquilizer used by research scientists and developed in Brazil for underwater catch-and-release programs. The hand grenade–size charges operated in exactly that fashion, except these silverish little eggs had a small switch that could be used to select certain depths to detonate a charge that would disperse the Hydro-Rotenone in a thirty-foot arch underwater.

"More toys?" Sarah asked as she sat next to Jack in the false twilight the canopy of trees had thrown them into.

He put the manual down and looked at Sarah, who was dressed in shorts and a sleeveless blue blouse. She was freshly showered and smelled strongly of bug repellent.

"Love that perfume," he said as he lightly placed a hand on her leg, then removed it.

"It's all the rage in New York these days." She watched his hand for a brief moment, saddened that he couldn't leave it on her leg.

Teacher had run up to six knots, and the breeze the extra speed created felt good. They heard laughter coming from a few sections down, where most of the science team was out on deck getting some air after lunch. Mendenhall was on duty with Jenks, and Sanchez and Carl were learning the fine points of the submersible operation in the engine room. Jack raised his head and wondered aloud were Danielle Serrate was.

"The last I saw, she was in the computer library doing something," Sarah said. "Why, are you starting to wonder what her motives are?"

"Yeah, it's hard to believe they're just ex-husband motivated, but with her being the head of her agency and being sanctioned by her government in the assistance she's shown, I wouldn't care to guess what her real motives would be."

"Does the fact that Carl is getting close to her affect your way of thinking?"

"Everett is a grown man; I think he knows how to handle himself. It's been over a year since he lost Lisa, and I think it's time he starts realizing there are other women in the world. Besides, have you ever in the last year heard him talk so much?"

"Yeah, I—"

They were interrupted by the very object of their conversation, as Danielle bounded up through the open hatch.

"Jack, look over the side!" she said as she made the deck and leaned over the gunwale.

The major stood and went to Danielle's side and Sarah to her other. Jack immediately saw what she was indicating and turned and ran for the boat's intercom, where he slammed down the proper button.

"Kill the engines, Chief," he said loudly as he again switched buttons and hit the one marked ENG.

"Carl, are you still in engineering?"

"Still here," he said.

"Get someone and get to the fantail; use a boat hook and snag those bodies," Jack said hurriedly.

Jack heard the engines shut down. He hurried to the hatch and made his way down the spiral stairs. He quickly ran aft to the engine room. The double rear doors were open to the fantail. One of the detachable chairs went flying as the men maneuvered to arrest the floating bodies with boat hooks. As Jack joined them, he saw the bodies were bloated.

"Goddammit!" he said as he reached out and opened the railing. The four men struggled, bringing the two bodies aboard over the fantail just above the black letters that spelled out *Teacher*.

"Oh," Carl said as the smell hit them. He gently rolled over the larger of the two and saw that it was a man clad in a diver's wetsuit. The neoprene was stretched beyond endurance and had split in the upper arm and thigh areas. The face was bloated and misshaped. But that didn't keep them from seeing the deep gouges that had been inflicted upon the man's face.

Jack heard noise behind them and saw Virginia and Dr. Allison Waltrip, the surgeon from the Group, as they hurried through the double doors. Virginia gasped but Waltrip immediately bent over the two still forms. The three marines backed away and turned to face the slow-flowing river. The doctor moved from the larger to the smaller of the two. She gently rolled it over and saw that it was a girl who couldn't have been more than twenty or twenty-one. This corpse was bloated like the other, but had no injuries that were readily apparent. Her eyes were wide in death and glazed over with a milky substance that made Virginia partially turn away before she remembered her professionalism. Dr. Waltrip started feeling around the body for a wound. The girl was dressed in shorts and a blouse; it reminded Jack of the very clothes Sarah was wearing. The doctor ran her fingers through the girl's hair and then stopped.

"Gunshot wound to her temple. My guess she was dead before she entered the water, but I can't be sure without an autopsy."

Then her attention was drawn back to the large man in the wetsuit. "His injuries are extensive. The face wounds wouldn't have been life threatening," she rolled the man over, "but these wounds are deep enough to have severed several arteries in his back and lungs." She probed the open wounds with her finger, making everyone cringe just a little. As she ran her fingers along one of the larger gouges, she extracted something and held it up to the deck light. It was rounded and ridged and it seemed to shine, giving off rainbow effects in the light.

"What is it, Doctor?" Carl asked.

"I don't know." She looked closer. "That almost looks like a hair follicle on the bottom, see?" She held it up for all to examine.

"I think I know what that is," Heidi said as she stepped up and took the object from the doctor.

"What?" Carl asked.

"It looks exactly like a fish scale—a damned big one, but a fish scale."

Jack walked to the railing and looked out on the water. "Dr. Waltrip, can you get a good picture in two hours of how they died?"

"I can try," she said.

Jack walked to the fantail intercom and informed Jenks that they would anchor in the middle of the tributary for two hours while autopsies were performed on the two bodies. Then he watched as the men moved the bodies to the section seven medical labs.

When they were gone, Jack looked at the rain forest canopy overhead and saw the dapples of light were fading from the sky. After hoping they would make the lagoon before nightfall, he had to reconsider under the circumstances. He might have to order them to anchor, as the thought of entering Padilla's lagoon in total darkness left little appeal. The bodies not withstanding, the urgency of arriving on site for possible survivors had become possibly a moot point. He would now have to consider the safety of *this* team his top priority now.

Jack couldn't shake the image of the young woman they had pulled from the river. When she had put on those clothes, she had never figured she would die in them. Just as he was sure Sarah would never have thought the same when she had put on her own similar clothing this morning.

Jack watched the water and the stillness of the shoreline in front of him. He touched the holstered nine-millimeter at his side. Of all the places in his career he had been assigned, this was the one that unnerved him the most. Was it the absence of direct sunlight? The cries of creatures that remained hidden in the vast canopy of giant trees? Jack knew himself never to be a man of premonition, yet he sensed beyond a doubt that men were never meant to be in this place.

As he turned to leave, motion on the riverbank caught his eye. He stood still and didn't turn to look, but used his peripheral vision to see. Standing back of the thick shrubbery that lined the bank, several small Indians stood and watched *Teacher* as she maintained her position in the middle of the river. The only sound he noticed was the almost silent hum of the vessel's thrusters as they fought to maintain their hold on the current. The noises of the rain forest had disappeared and silence filled the late afternoon. The faces of the Indians stood out palely in stark contrast to the darkness surrounding them. That was when Jack decided to let them know he was aware. He turned and held up a hand, but the gesture went unseen, as the Indians had vanished into the brush. As he stood there feeling silly, the cries of birds and even the scream of a large cat rushed to fill the air as sound returned around him.

SEVERAL PEOPLE WERE outside of the medical lab in section six waiting on the word from Dr. Waltrip. Heidi and Virginia had been drafted by the good doctor as her morgue assistants. Jack sat with Sarah, Danielle, Carl, Keating, and Dr. Nathan, who were all anxious to find out the results of the medical examination of the two corpses. Their conversation was muted.

Jack had not said anything about seeing the Indians along the riverbank, as he felt the information wasn't helpful to anyone. The discovery of the Sincaro's deity had already been the topic of conversation for almost a day and a half. One thing Jack did do was order not only sidearms to be issued to the military personnel, but two shotguns per watch. He had nothing against the little tribe of river natives, but until they found out about the reasons behind the disappearance, why take chances? He had a gut feeling that the people he saw weren't behind those two deaths; they seemed only curious. From prior discussions with Group historians, the professionals who had studied the legends, he had learned that the small people had every right to be at least suspicious of any strangers along their river.

The door opened and Virginia came out first. She was pale and seemed rattled as she asked for some coffee. Allison Waltrip came out, next pulling off her gloves and then placing them in a plastic bag. Then she held out the bag for Virginia to put hers in, and she complied with a shake of her head. Then she took her coffee from Danielle, who also offered a cup to Dr. Waltrip. The surgeon accepted it with a nod.

"Jack, we have to get those bodies into the ground," said Dr. Waltrip. "We don't have the facilities to store them here." She turned.

"Lieutenant Commander Everett, navy man, right?" she asked.

"Yes," Carl answered.

"This man," she held out a plastic specimen bag, "he was in the navy also, Kennedy, Kyle, M. A lieutenant."

"Doesn't ring a bell," Carl said as he took the plastic bag from Waltrip and examined the dog tags.

"He has a small seal juggling a beach ball tattooed on his right forearm."

Carl rolled up his sleeve. "Look like this?" he asked, showing his own SEAL tattoo.

"Exactly, except his had a four underneath, not a six," Dr. Waltrip said.

"SEAL team four, San Diego based; they are an excellent and well-trained assault force. But I've never heard of a Kennedy, and I know most of that team."

"Major, Virginia is aware of what your file contains and she said I can ask you, I understand you were in black operations and had trained for all kinds of—" she paused and looked at Virginia.

"Broken Arrow," Virginia answered.

"Yes, Broken Arrow scenarios, trained to deal with them, that sort of thing?"

Jack looked uncomfortable talking about it with so many in earshot, especially Danielle. "That's right, I am qualified to disarm or . . . why?" Jack only hoped everyone didn't know the term "Broken Arrow" was one used by the military for designating a lost nuclear weapon.

"Can you identify this?" Dr. Waltrip held out a second plastic bag. "It was clenched so tight in the lieutenant's right hand I had to pry it loose."

Jack took the bag and looked it over, glancing Carl's way once because he felt his eyes on him.

"M-2678 tactical warhead key," he said barely loud enough for anyone to hear.

"Jesus, Jack, what did those idiots bring with them?" Carl asked.

"I can't even venture to guess why they thought they needed a tactical nuke out here," Jack answered as the section grew silent.

"Just another mystery to add to our growing list," Dr. Waltrip said. "The girl was no older than nineteen. As I said out there, she died as a result of a possible self-inflicted gunshot to the left temple. There are gunpowder burns around the wound and powder particles embedded in her left hand, indication she was holding the gun that killed her. It was a nine-millimeter round." She handed another specimen bag to Jack.

"Could be military, but who knows."

Dr. Waltrip nodded her head. "Anyway, the bottoms of her feet were quite cut up, as if she had been running on a rough surface, and in her wounds on her feet I found this." She held up a small jar; inside were several cotton swabs. She held it up to the light and they all saw the glimmer. "Gold, I would say, found in her wounds, her hair, her clothes, her nostrils, and lungs. These samples represent a swab from almost every area of her body."

There were no questions, no talking. Carl handed the dog tags back to the surgeon.

"I'll place these in the ship's safe," she said. "Now, as I said, we need to bury these bodies very soon; they're deteriorating fast."

"The wounds, Doctor, the marks on the diver?" Jack asked.

"I was saving the best for last, Major," she said. "Virginia, show them the scale, please."

Virginia reached into her lab coat and pulled out a plastic case. She passed it to Jack.

"Without running a complete DNA sequencing, which Heidi is performing right now, I can't tell you much. It is a scale from a freshwater species, but according to every data bank we have, it belongs to nothing in the waters of the world. We don't even have a prehistoric record of a fossil's ever having scales like that. Look at the deep age ridges that run the length of the scale. I thought they would serve no purpose other than to show age, like the rings on a tree or the squares on a tortoise shell. But when I examined it, I found that scale to be almost impenetrable. I used a scalpel and couldn't cut it. The follicle that had attached the scale to its host is almost human. The minute sample of blood from that follicle is just like ours, I even typed it at O negative." She held up a hand when they all started protesting at once. "I don't have answers, people, none at all. Everything we have come across only raises more questions than we have answers for. It was Virginia who came up with something that makes me want to warn the major to take an armed team ashore when you bury the bodies—show them."

Virginia took the plastic case from Jack and held it up to the light. It, too, sparkled with gold.

"As you can see, it's covered, just like the girl, in gold particles, better known as gold dust. We examined both the gold from the scale and the girl, and found it to have been processed gold. Not gold in its natural state; it had already been heated and smelted. The electron microscope verified it," she said, still holding the scale to the light. "These particles came from bars or ingots, leftovers maybe from the molds that were used. But the scale—" she hesitated.

"What?" Sarah prompted.

"Hold on to your hats. It was also contaminated—with an enriched uranium source, most probably from a damaged tactical nuke that key represents and indicates may be down here. But there is a very strange factor at work here; the blood sample from the scale didn't show any long-term effects of it. Whatever creature this scale came from, it seems to even be impervious to radiation poisoning."

"That's impossible," Keating said at her side.

"It's my fucking field, Professor," she said quietly. "I am perfectly aware of what's possible and impossible, and radiation poisoning is an absolute; there are no immune species of animal. But if we could discover why this particular species is, or was, immune, it would be a find that would benefit mankind beyond belief."

"Why, so we could make nuclear war not only probable, but feasible, give governments the go-ahead to off everybody cleanly with no worries?" Keating argued.

Virginia lowered the scale and faced Dr. Keating. "No, not at all, I'm surprised that you would even think I would consider such an asinine theory," she said, staring Keating down until he looked away and shook his head. "But I was thinking, Professor, that maybe we could save hundreds of thousand of people suffering from cancer the indignity of the effects of radiation treatments. Maybe stop a little girl from throwing up every time modern science tries to help her, or keep her hair from falling out while stopping the pain of chemotherapy—not about making nuclear warfare feasible."

"My apologies, Virginia, stupid comment," Keating said, taking her right shoulder and squeezing.

"Show them the other item, Virginia, the reason why the burial team needs to be armed and watchful," Dr. Waltrip said.

Virginia closed her eyes for a moment and gathered her thoughts. Then she reached into her lab coat and brought out a photograph. "I enlarged this on the computer. I took it of the two statues the Inca had placed on the riverbank," she said as she again held the scale up to the light and then held out the picture for them to compare. "See the scales on the statues; they're lightly etched into the stone. Now look at the ridges on this scale," she held the plastic case back up to the light, "and compare them to what was carved hundreds or maybe thousands of years ago by a race that no longer exists."

"Oh, boy," Carl said.

"The ridges, they're identical. Why would the Incan stone carvers duplicate something on their statues that they could only know about by seeing it?" Sarah wondered.

"Maybe because they *were* carving from life experience, and the statues they carved were of a real animal," Virginia said as she passed around the scale and photograph.

"I guess Helen Zachary was onto something with that fossil," Jack said.

"Yeah, but it looks like she may not have lived to be congratulated," Danielle said, touching Carl's arm.

IT HAD TAKEN them another hour to land Jack and a shore party to bury the dead. The entire time it took, the sounds of the rain forest had ceased as if in respect for what was happening. The bodies were put deeply into the earth and covered quickly. Large rocks were placed over them to keep out predators and then Jack hastily hurried the shore party back. All the while, he felt the eyes of the Sincaro, or whoever the modern-day indigenous people were, upon them.

"Carl," Jack said, just before he reached the makeshift boat ramp.

The lieutenant commander stopped and looked around him in the semidarkness. Sweat rolled down his face as he looked from the forest to the major.

"That key," Jack said.

"Yeah, it's worrisome, Jack."

The thought didn't have to be voiced as Carl was just as well trained in theater-style nukes as was Jack. He knew when you turn an activation key on one of the warheads to arm it, the bottom half of the key snaps off; that's what connects the circuit, creates a bridge, thus allowing the warhead to be activated. Then all you have to do is set the timer, or push a button.

"The key is intact, isn't it, Jack?".

Collins reached in his pocket for the activation key. He held it up and Carl saw the bottom section had a rough edge, just as if it had been snapped off.

"Oh, shit."

"I hate to say it, but we have a live nuke someplace in that lagoon."

They both knew that once the activation circuit has been completed, it couldn't be commanded to just shut off; it would have to be disarmed manually.

"Okay, we both have Broken Arrow training; we can disarm this thing," Jack said.

"Yeah, but where in the hell is it? A pissed-off monkey could set the damned thing off just by looking at it too hard."

"Our priorities have shifted once again, swabby."

ONBOARD *TEACHER*, EVERYONE was still on deck save for Danielle Serrate. She was alone in the navigation section, just sitting there. The main screen on the table was dark and she was currently using it as a large coffee coaster. She was so deep in thought she didn't hear Sarah enter.

"So, how are you and Carl getting on?" Sarah asked as she slid into one of the couches next to the exterior bulkhead.

"You're a curious woman, aren't you?"

"Only because I like Carl and I'm cursed with that mothering instinct, especially about him. He needs looking after, like most men do, I guess," Sarah said.

Danielle looked at her for the longest time without comment. Then she smiled. "I don't have that mothering instinct. Other instincts? Yes. But not that particular one."

Sarah returned the smile and slid out from beside the table. "I bet you have other instincts, Mrs. Farbeaux . . . Damn, I'm sorry, I hate that," she said, shaking her head and gently tapping her forehead, "Ms. Serrate, I mean, but I do bet your instincts are more toward the survival kind."

"That and many other kinds, my dear Sarah," Danielle said as she watched Sarah leave. She stood up, knocking her coffee over in the process, and then she forced herself to calm down. She looked around for a rag and found none, so she glanced quickly into the cockpit area and silently stepped inside.

THE *RIO MADONNA,* THREE MILES DOWNRIVER

The large boat was cruising along at five knots, matching the last known speed of *Teacher.* It had taken the captain far longer than he thought it would to get his main mast and antennas up again after exiting the cave. Since then, he had numerous repairs to make as he had inadvertently gouged his hull on several occasions in the darkness of the cave. It was only his sheer ability as a river captain that had kept him from ramming one of the jagged-edged walls. The Frenchman had been a tremendous help, as he had assisted on the bridge, calling out depths and making course correction. The man was indeed very knowledgeable about surviving difficult situations. That fool Mendez and his men were a different story. They had cowered in the total darkness of the cave—a fact they would never live down in the captain's eyes. From here on out, the men from Colombia would have to be watched.

Thus far they had had one casualty on this bizarre journey. While making a physical sounding when the fathometer had failed for an hour, one of his men had entangled the sounding rope on the bow anchor and had reached into the water to free it as two men held on to his ankles while he dangled over the side. The water had suddenly erupted and the man had started screaming. As the men pulled him back aboard, a long trail of blood splashed the white paint as he was lifted up. His hand had been totally bitten off. One of the men, Indio Asana, a man raised in the heart of the Amazon basin, had said that the large fish that did it was unlike any he had ever seen on the river before, with a large jutting jaw and a tail that looked strong enough to snap a two-by-four in half. He said that it had fins on it unlike any he had ever seen, and since it was Indio who had said it, the captain had no doubt as to its truth.

"Capitán, I have received a ping from three miles ahead of us," his radio/sonar man said from his small desk in the back of the wheelhouse.

"Señor Farbeaux, a signal from the Americans: someone has pinged us with an active sonar search."

Farbeaux was amazed the captain had any notion as to what an active sonar search involved.

"Are you sure?"

"Yes, my equipment, while not state-of-the-art for the U.S. Navy, *señor*, is quite adequate for us South American rum runners," he said, smiling through his cigar smoke.

"I meant no disrespect, Captain. How far ahead would you say the search originated from?"

"My operator says three miles upriver, *señor*," he said as he turned the large wheel and started for the bank in anticipation of the Frenchman's order.

"We'd better delay a while; they may have stopped for some reason, maybe an accidental ping? Nonetheless, we better anchor for a while, would you agree, Captain?"

"*Sí, señor*, we are currently doing just that," the captain replied as he straightened the wheel and pulled the *Rio Madonna* alongside the south bank of the tributary.

Santos ordered the bow and stern anchors out and shut down his twin engines. Several men rushed aft and, with long poles, arrested the momentum of the large tow-barge that contained the Frenchman's equipment. When he was satisfied, he watched the sly Farbeaux as he went to the afterdeck to inform his majesty, Señor Mendez, of the delay. The shouting and tantrum at the unexpected layover would begin momentarily. The captain smiled as he wondered how long it would take for Farbeaux to put a bullet into that idiot's brain.

As he thought this, he wondered just who it had been to accidentally hit the active sonar button on the American boat, an accident that warned them the strange boat was stopped up ahead. *Convenient*, he thought and then laughed, happy that the Frenchman was on his side. But as he looked upriver his smile faded. Somewhere up ahead was a lagoon that was uncaring of laughter of any kind, rumored to be a place of sheer sorrow, and he was blindly following this Frenchman into the heart of that dark place. The captain removed a strange medal from inside the collar of his shirt, and kissed and replaced it. Then he turned off the overhead light and sat in the darkness, listening for the familiar sounds he had heard since his childhood. Ahead on the river, legends waited, as they had for thousands of years, to greet the greedy hands of man. Again, the captain reached for the medallion under his shirt and then crossed himself.

PART FIVE

THE LOST WORLD

Deep into that darkness peering, long I stood there, wondering, fearing, doubting, dreaming dreams no mortal ever dared to dream before . . .

—Edgar Allan Poe

17

WHEN *Teacher* slowly rounded a large bend, the calm waters suddenly angered and turned white with foam rapids. Jenks cursed and threw the two diesels into reverse. The crew, half on duty, half off and asleep in their bunks, were tossed forward. The ones on watch mostly lost their footing and fell to the deck, while the others cursed as they had heads slammed into overheads. A few even fell out of their tight bunks.

Jenks found he was fighting a losing battle as the river took hold of *Teacher* and thrust her forward as if she were on a wave. Whitewater was thrown over her bow glass as if she was submerging beneath the river. He cursed again when he felt a sudden blow underneath the hull and the boat rose two feet into the darkened space under the impenetrable canopy of trees. He found the emergency switches that controlled the underwater shields for the view ports and hit all as fast as he could. He couldn't hear the hydraulic whine that told him the steel shields were sliding into place.

Jack pulled himself along the sections until he reached the cockpit, and threw himself into the copilot's seat.

"What've we got here, Chief?" he asked as he placed his chair harness over his shoulders and tightened it down.

"Rapids out of nowhere, no warning at all; there wasn't a change in current indicating we had rough water ahead."

As they watched, *Teacher* slammed herself into a large rock outcropping and bounced back into the center of the now crazy tributary. She rocked twenty degrees to starboard and he could hear curses from the back as more people were slammed to the deck. Jack reached out, keyed the 1MC mic, and addressed those in the back.

"Everyone strap in," he shouted over the noise of the rapids.

Jenks pulled the joystick all the way to the right, trying to right *Teacher* as she again slammed into the far left bank. He could hear the twin jets at the stern as they caught mud and sand on the bank and shot it high into the air. Alarms started sounding on the console. There was a fire warning in the engineering section, and several hatch openings were reported. A damage alarm rang from section five, indicating she was taking on water.

"Son of a bitch! I hope those boys are standing by on that fire alarm," Jenks said as he throttled the engines into full reverse.

Teacher didn't respond as she ran for the center of the tributary.

"We're on a steep incline," Jack called out after looking at the level gauge.

"Impossible. There wasn't any current to speak of, unless we're falling into some sort of a damned hole," Jenks called back.

Other alarms sounded as *Teacher* was gouged somewhere in section eight.

"Chief, we have a major hole to the aft of section seven, between it and section eight," Carl called over the intercom.

"Handle it, Toad, we're a tad busy up here," Jenks said as the huge boat slammed into a rock in the center of the tributary and careened up into the air again before slamming back down into the white water with a giant splash, sending the cockpit ten feet beneath the swirling water. Again *Teacher* struck the right bank, this time encountering mostly rock. They all heard the sickening crunch of buckling composite material as she righted herself and rolled hard to port.

As suddenly as the white water had appeared it vanished, and *Teacher* was left spinning in a slow circle in the center of a much broader tributary. The floodlights picked out the twin banks as they spun toward the shoreline and then as they faced the river. Jenks hit the starboard jets and *Teacher* slowed her spin, but one of the jets must have sustained damage because she didn't slow fast enough. Finally the huge boat hit the sandy bank and that stopped her from spinning. He did the same on the aft-section jets and she stopped her spin off the rebound of the bank that would have sent her in the opposite direction. Jenks flipped the switch for automatic station keeping and hoped the system still functioned after the roller-coaster ride she had taken. *Teacher* was never designed for whitewater rafting. All was calm as he heard the jets engage in alternating blasts of water. Finally *Teacher* was at a complete standstill. The lights in all the aft sections had gone out and the crew was navigating by dull battery-driven emergency lighting only.

"Major, just aft of this section you'll find her lighting and instrumentation fuse box. Get that breaker back in so we can see how badly she's hurt, will ya?"

Jack unstrapped his safety harness and made his way aft. He quickly found the glass-covered panel and opened it. Three large breakers had popped. He pushed the first one and then the other two. The overheads came back on, and he could sense all hands breathed a sigh of relief. He heard Jenks on the intercom.

"Engineering, what's your status?" he asked.

"Give us a minute, Chief, we're still putting back some of the pieces here," Mendenhall called to him.

Jack went to check on the others. He encountered Sarah and Danielle, who were assisting the cook with a small fire that had broken out on the stove. The overhead fans were clearing out the smoke and he figured they had it under control, so he moved on. At section eight he saw that Carl, Sanchez, and Professors Ellenshaw and Keating were tightening the frame around one of the underwater viewing windows that sat below the waterline. There were about two inches of water around their ankles as they worked.

"Got it?" Jack asked.

Carl looked up and nodded. He had received quite a gash on his forehead.

"See to that, Carl," Jack said, pointing at his own forehead, and moved off again.

The rest of the science department was all right with only a few light injuries and equipment damage. It was in the engineering section that Jack became worried. Four feet of water was lapping at the two engine platforms. Mendenhall was kneeling in it, reaching around the number two engine.

"What've you got, Will?" Jack asked.

Mendenhall sat back in the water and looked up. "Engine two has broken clear off her motor mounts, Major. She won't be working for a while. Her shaft to the main jet is bent like a pretzel, and we're looking at atleast five days of repair time."

Jack walked over to the intercom and called Jenks.

"Chief, we've lost number two for extensive repairs. Number one looks all right, but we'll have to take it slow."

"We don't need her right at the moment," Jenks replied.

"Why? We can keep her at a few knots," Jack countered.

"We don't need her for a while. Tell the boys we'll work on number two in the next few days while you people find what you came to find."

"What are you talking about, Chief?"

"Major, we have found your goddamned lagoon," Jenks said calmly over the intercom.

THERE WERE FIFTEEN souls on the upper deck looking out on what could only be described as a lost world. The massive waterfall was just as the legend described. The water fell from a source several hundred feet in the air. The center of the large lagoon was dappled in the brightest sunlight any of them could remember ever seeing, while the fringes of the water remained in almost near darkness. The havoc created by the giant falls produced its own system of winds and drafts that cooled those on deck from the relentless heat and humidity. The shoreline around the lagoon had wide beaches that stretched away from the water like the sands one would find at only the most luxurious hotels on Waikiki. But, by far, the outstanding feature of the entire scene was the giant stone arch that ran up the sides of the waterfall as it disappeared under the falls. Two stone deities stood guard on either side, flanking the falls. These were similar to the strange statues they had seen before, but more ornate in their carving. Massive one-hundred-foot-long spears were clutched in the outsize hands of these deities.

"I have never in my life beheld anything as beautiful as this," Danielle said as she edged nearer to Carl.

"It is something."

"All right, I need security with me. Let's start getting our act together," Jack said. "In all of this natural beauty, I have failed to notice one thing. The Zachary boat isn't anywhere to be found."

The admiration for the lagoon and forested valley stopped as soon as Jack mentioned the missing craft. What had been a stunning view instantly became foreboding to everyone's eyes. Somewhere off in the jungle a cockatoo cried, and *Teacher* listed to starboard as she limped toward the open sunlight at the center of the lagoon.

MOST OF THE science teams broke into repair groups. The security team made ready a rubber Zodiac to scout out the shoreline, to search for anything that would possibly help them in locating Professor Zachary and her team. Jack had tried to get a satellite transmission out to Boris and Natasha but the transmitter dish had been knocked free of its mounting atop the main mast. Tommy Stiles had been tabbed to repair it.

Jack, Mendenhall, Carl, Sanchez, Jackson, and Shaw cast off the inflatable Zodiac. Carl was at the wheel and steered the boat into the darkness of the lagoon, heading toward the widest beach on the eastern side of the lagoon. The seventy-five horsepower Evinrude motor shattered the silence of the lagoon and the mountainous walls around it. He gunned the engine the last ten yards and ran the boat as far onto the sandy beach, raising the engine free of the water as the Zodiac hissed onto the sandy shoreline.

Jack was the first out, with his M-16 pointed toward the pitch blackness of the tree line. He was joined by the others, who followed suit. The extreme quiet was matched by their own silence as they scanned the area immediately around them. Jack looked back at the silhouette and interior lighting of *Teacher* as she remained in the center of the sunlit lagoon. He checked his watch; they had about an hour of daylight left. *If you could call this daylight*, he thought.

"Straight-line formation, gentlemen. Carl, you take up station at the rear."

Jack started forward along the shore and followed the waterline to the south. Every ten feet as they inspected the lagoon, Mendenhall reached into his pack and pulled out a small rod with what looked like a lightbulb on the end, and stuck it into the sand, sighting each one with its mate before and after, aligning the laser early-warning fence so they would have some security from something entering the water from the dry land side. As they went they heard the sounds of the forest as it came back to life. The screeching of birds and the chattering of monkeys allowed them to relax, as at least these were sounds they could identify.

They laid down their perimeter alarms for the next forty minutes. Although they had covered only half the perimeter of this eastern side of the lagoon, it would be a half they could basically ignore for the coming night, as nothing over a foot tall could breach the laser sighting that linked each pole with the one before and after it in the chain.

"Okay, let's head back for now," Jack said as the disappointment set in at not having seen anything, not one piece of evidence that anyone had ever been here.

Sanchez was looking about in the semidarkness when his foot hit something buried in the sand. He reached down and saw a rusted piece of metal jutting from the golden beach. He pulled on it but it wouldn't budge. Then he scraped out the sand along the sides of the rusted protrusion. Mendenhall joined him as the others stopped. The two men pulled and tugged. Finally the metal gave way and they both fell onto the sand as Sanchez held out a curved shape.

"Look at that," he said in astonishment.

The hilt was gone and they could see the remnants of braided fabric that had once covered the handle. The sword blade was mostly intact, but the once sharp edge had been totally eaten away by rust.

"God, how old do you think it is?" Sanchez asked.

"I would say it's about five hundred and seventy-odd years old," Jack answered. "Let's get the hell back; you can take your prize in and show the experts."

Sanchez lightly moved the Spanish sword through the air, amazed at his find.

As they made their way back, Jack and Carl in particular kept their eyes not only on the forest, but the lagoon, as well. But it was Mendenhall who saw it first.

"Oh, no."

Jack stopped and looked at the area just inside the tree line that Mendenhall was looking at. The major grimaced and made his way toward the area.

Strewn about was what was left of the Zachary expedition. Jack counted at least fourteen bodies. He gestured for his men to spread out and start checking the grotesque scene. The people appeared to have been mauled by an animal. The remains were cast about like torn dolls among the wreckage of tents and supplies. Boys and girls. That's the way Jack was seeing it. They were just children.

"Jesus, Major," was all Mendenhall could say.

Sanchez stared in horror at what lay before him. They had all seen casualties before in the Gulf conflicts, but nothing could measure up to this scene. Sanchez looked at the sword he had been holding like a prize and let it slide from his fingers.

"Before we bury them, we have to get the science people over here to look them over," said Jack. "Come on, let's move. The manifest says there are more than just these people. We may have survivors."

As authoritative as he sounded, Jack was losing confidence in finding anyone else alive.

JACK HAD ALREADY posted the roster for the night watch teams and kept the 50 percent alert status for the duration. Upon returning from the shore and turning over the Spanish sword to the sciences, the boat had been abuzz with the knowledge that Padilla had actually been in the valley, that the legend was no longer that, but reality. Jenks had sounded the loud navigation horn three times just in case there were survivors from the Zachary expedition hidden out in the jungle. It sounded in two-minute intervals but no one came forth. Since the loud intrusion of sound, the rain forest around the lagoon had grown unnaturally silent.

Virginia and the others had brought back the body of one of the students for a closer examination. The others had been hastily buried in the sand. Sarah had voiced the opinion that the bodies had not been disturbed by whatever animal had killed them because of the protection of the small creatures that inhabited the waters of the lagoon. The little monkeys had watched from the shadows of the trees where the men had done their grisly work of gathering up and burying the remains. Several mumbles and sighs were heard from the creatures as the bodies were covered with sand.

The repairs to *Teacher* progressed well through the evening. The only item that would remain after the night would be the repair to the number two engine. Remounting it and replacing the shaft would take most of three full days, but Jenks foresaw no problems in getting it back to 100 percent. They would need that engine to traverse the rapids outside of the lagoon. It was only sheer luck they had a backup shaft in ship's stores.

"Ready on ballast pumps," Jenks called as he flipped the switch and started filling *Teacher*'s ballast tanks to take her low into the water so her bottom windows could have a better view of the lagoon itself.

The crew heard the sound of the pumps as water was let into the four massive tanks lining the boat's inner hull. All hands watched the windows as the huge boat started to settle into the water. Now exactly half of her was below the surface of the strange lagoon. The fantail was only six inches above the waterline and her rear doors would remain closed for the duration of her stay here. The underwater floodlights did much to dispel the darkness around and under the boat. It also brought to life the majesty of what the lagoon held. Fish of every sort came and went through the lights, as curious of them as they were of the fish. Sarah watched over Carl's shoulder. Fish flashed in and out of her viewing range, coming right up to the large portholes, and she was amazed at their fearlessness of the strange craft in their midst.

"When do you plan to allow us into the mine, Jack?" Virginia asked, pulling a pair of rubber gloves from her hands as she entered the lounge.

"Not until we have *Teacher* back to one hundred percent in case we have to get the hell out of Dodge suddenly," he answered.

"But Jack . . ."

He looked at Virginia and she shrugged, knowing her argument would do no good.

"You're right; maybe tomorrow we can get some probes inside?" she asked.

"I want to check it out as much as everyone here, Virginia, but only because we may have people holed up in there. But I won't lose anyone because we didn't take the proper precautions. The satellite dish is still down, and yes, if we have to expend every probe we have, we will look for survivors tomorrow. What did you find in your autopsy?"

"Well," Virginia said as she sat in one of the large chairs, "the wounds are consistent with a wild animal attack. Large lacerations on the torso and head. Cause of death was massive bleeding. I'm afraid, without more equipment, we're limited to the tests we can run." She excused herself and left the table when she saw the master chief walk through the outer corridor.

Jack watched her go and shook his head. "I hope everyone understands that we can't go charging into that cave, or mine, until we know what in the hell we're dealing with here."

"Virginia's just anxious, as we all are, to find out about those kids. She knows you have to wait. I think it's you being hard on yourself. Waiting is the right thing," Sarah said.

Jack looked from Sarah to Carl, and Carl knew what he was considering. Carl nodded his head and Jack spoke. "Sarah, you know that tactical nuke key that was found?"

"What about it?"

"The key was used. Somewhere out there, or maybe inside the mine, we have a live nuke on our hands. I'm afraid our priorities have shifted. For reasons we don't know, someone was out to destroy this place. As much as the kids, if they're alive, need to be found, we now have an active nuclear weapon on our hands."

She didn't know if she liked knowing that little bit of information.

"Yeah, I see your point."

ON THE UPPER deck, Virginia joined Danielle and the master chief as they watched the stars come out directly above them. The night sounds had finally returned after the assault of the air horn. Insects and animal life allowed themselves to be heard again, which made the crew outside feel better. There was nothing worse than silence.

"Beautiful," Virginia said as she looked up into the void of space that the center of the lagoon afforded them.

"No smog or city lights to obscure them," Jenks said as he looked from the heavens to Virginia. He had shaved and put on a clean denim shirt for his night watch.

"I think I'll see what Sergeant Mendenhall is up to at the stern," Danielle said, excusing herself.

Jenks caught himself as he began instinctively to watch

Danielle's tightly fitted shorts while she moved away. He turned instead toward Virginia and removed his stub of cigar.

"Well, Doctor, I got you here—"

Virginia cut off his comment.

"I like you, too, Chief. And we'll take this up when we get home."

Jenks's eyes opened wide as he reappraised the tallish woman.

"I'll be goddamned and go to hell," he mumbled.

CORPORAL SANCHEZ HAD the tower watch and was lulled by the gentle movement of the boat. He rested his elbows on the railing just above the radar platform that extended outward from the sail. The gentle electrical hum also helped to induce the sleepiness he was feeling as he watched the white sands of the shoreline two hundred yards off in the distance. He slowly turned and examined the other side of the lagoon; it was still and quiet. He took a deep breath of air and was grateful for the cooling breeze that hit him. How it could penetrate such a thick canopy of trees, he didn't know. But it was nice nonetheless. He turned back toward the shore they had visited this afternoon and watched. He raised the night-vision scope to his eyes and scanned first the beach, then the tree line beyond. The laser fence they had placed was operating and glowed brightly in the scope. A light noise caught his attention. He swung the glasses around and looked to the immediate left of where they had landed the Zodiac. He saw nothing. Sanchez looked down at the early-warning alarm box that was linked via radio to the laser line. Of the thirty sensors, all the green lights were ablaze in a semicircle. Nothing had crossed the line from the jungle. But as he looked through the scope again, he failed to notice a large line of bubbles as something moved away from the waterfall side of the lagoon. It was rising from the deep and almost bottomless waters, and coming right at *Teacher.*

JACK AND CARL left Sarah and went aft to make ready the remote probes that would be used tomorrow for the mine excursion. Jack wanted to launch the probes tonight because of the pressure to find any surviving members of Zachary's team. But Jenks was right, daylight was best. No sense in losing whatever probes they had left by attempting a night-time search.

Upon entering the engineering spaces they saw Professor Ellenshaw and Nathan filling the emergency air tanks of the three-man diving bell, which sat motionless in its steel cradle next to the submersible. Its cable and air hoses were on a large steel drum above it. Tools were spread on a large cloth on the deck, as they had been in the process of working on the broken mounts of the engine. The boat's PA came to life.

"Major, this is Jackson in sonar. I have a target coming toward us at about three knots, seems to be about twenty, twenty-five feet in depth. Just came on the scope, and according to my reading, it's pretty big."

Jack was about to reach for the intercom when *Teacher* was rocked to her starboard side. Carl lost his footing and fell to the deck, and Ellenshaw was almost crushed by the diving bell as it broke loose from its steel cradle and swung outward into the walkway. Jack lunged and pushed the professor clear just as the bell struck the aft bulkhead with a loud clang. *Teacher* finally righted herself as the frantic calls started coming from the upper deck.

"Jesus!" Carl exclaimed as he looked out of the aft window.

Jack gained his footing and looked at what Carl was staring wide-eyed at. Almost blocking the entire five-foot-wide window was a dark undulating mass that was grayish white in color and appeared to have thinly placed fur covering a rough leathery skin. The window below water level was dark, meaning that the width of whatever had struck *Teacher* was enormous.

The boat rocked from side to side in a frenzy of motion.

"There's another over here—no, wait, two of them!" Ellenshaw gasped from his position on the deck where Jack had knocked him. "My god, this cannot be!"

"Hang on, it's going to hit us!" Carl shouted.

Jack braced himself as best he could and opened the double rear hatch. As the door swung open, water rushed in as *Teacher* was again rocked. This time, the hull came completely clear of the water on its stern end as the animal struck the bottom of the huge boat. Once again, everyone on deck was sent sprawling. Jack fell through the hatchway to the outer deck of the fantail as the angle of the boat became so extreme that he found himself suddenly underwater. The boat again calmed for a moment and he righted himself, taking a deep breath just as the stern of *Teacher* sprang out of the water after the impact.

"Secure that damned bell," Carl called out to Nathan and Ellenshaw.

As Jack turned back he could hear screams and several loud popping noises that could only be gunfire coming from the upper deck. The boat was slammed and rocked again. As he turned and secured the glass doors to limit the flooding in the engine room, he saw a tail, pointy and swift, slice by his face as it rammed into the deck of the fantail, smashing the aluminum railing that lined it. Then the tail vanished as it splashed back down into the water. He fought to reach the ladder that led to the deck above. Several shots more rang out on deck among the screams. Jack finally gained hold of the first rung and pulled himself upward as more shots and more yelling sounded.

Finally, Jack was able to see what was happening on the upper deck. The sight that greeted him was one taken from a nightmare. Mendenhall was standing erect and firing his M-16 over the gunnels, but the swiftness of the animals in the water afforded a terrible target. Danielle was on the deck at the staff sergeant's feet, trying to stand erect, as Jack gained the deck and drew his nine-millimeter from its holster.

An animal that resembled a presumably extinct plesiosaur moved its elongated neck quickly back and forth, snapping vicious-looking jaws at the people on the upper deck. The beast was small, at least compared with the fossils enshrined in museums. In Jack's hurried estimation, it looked to be no more than twenty feet long—most of that being neck. The body thrashed and the tail slammed into *Teacher* in an attempt to kill the large object in front of it. Jack saw smaller animals swimming and diving around the larger one. The obvious difference between these creatures and similar ones seen by people in most museums was the fact that it appeared to have a hardened shell on its torso. The shiny green shell glistened as water poured freely off it.

The fur-covered plesiosaur darted forward in the water with incredible speed. Jack heard another scream and more shots from somewhere in the bow.

"It's got the chief and Dr. Pollock cornered," Mendenhall yelled as he saw an open shot and took it. The sergeant's bullet grazed the dark skin of the beast and it hissed, its yellow eyes glancing away from its prey and toward the stern of the boat. Again it crashed its glistening body into *Teacher*, almost rolling her onto her side. They didn't think she would right herself after that heavy blow, but slowly she started leaning the right way.

"Look out!" Jack shouted as he pulled Mendenhall down and on top of Danielle. The thick, powerful tail of the animal had risen from the water and lashed out at the antagonists from behind.

Jack braced himself but he knew it was too late. The tail hit him across the chest and threw him six feet into the air and over the side.

SARAH WAS STILL in the galley and yelped when the overhead light shattered. She looked up as the lights were lost but could still see the hull as it buckled inward from the pressure the monster outside was forcing on it. The upper window buckled and cracked. Then she smelled fire as the interior of *Teacher* went black.

CARL FINALLY REACHED the upper deck from amidships after fighting his way through the darkness and flooding. When he first saw the beast his eyes widened, but it didn't stop him from firing his handgun at the swinging head of the plesiosaur. He was only two sections back of Jenks and Virginia as he heard her scream and the master chief curse. He saw the flash of three shots as Jenks fired from where he covered Virginia below the gunwale. High above, an M-16 opened fire with a three-round burst that caught one of the freshwater animals along the curvature of its body where its skin met *Teacher*, just above the waterline. Sanchez had opened fire from the crow's nest. The sergeant fired again, this time stitching a pattern in the water as he missed, and then guided the rounds across the body of one of the four smaller, shelled creatures.

The plesiosaur shook its massive head and slammed it into the section that Jenks was in, crushing the composite hull, causing the master chief to lose his weapon as he threw himself onto Virginia to protect her.

Suddenly Carl heard shots coming from the water. He saw the flashes about twenty yards from the boat. Several of the rounds struck the nightmarish beast just behind its head, jerking it violently. The dinosaur and its smaller companions turned their attention to their new antagonist as Carl turned on the battery-powered spotlight to see who had fired. It was Jack, treading water. Carl watched as the major fire twice more into the thick body of the creature. Its yellow eyes glowed with pure rage. It bowed its long neck and head, and immediately slammed its giant foreflippers into the water. Carl was astonished to see what looked like stubby fingers protruding from the flipperlike apertures as it dove away from the boat. The beast was going for Jack. Carl hurriedly fired several times, as did every armed hand on the upper deck. Even Jenks was now standing and fired wildly at the massive shape as it thrashed in the water.

"Goddammit!" Carl yelled. Sarah finally made it to the top deck as he emptied his nine-millimeter toward the prehistoric animal. "Swim for it, Jack!" he cried even though he saw Jack would never make it.

Sarah gasped when she saw one of the smaller animals

had made it to Jack first. He disappeared from sight as he was jerked under the water. Carl threw down his weapon, jumped clear of the upper rail, and dove headfirst into the roiling lagoon. Mendenhall did the same at the stern. Sarah couldn't help it, her legs gave out and she collapsed against the gunwale. Professor Keating came through the hatch and went to her side. The others watched in horrible dreamlike slowness as the water crashed and swirled around the small beast. They saw Carl surface and look around, and Mendenhall dive again. But as both men both went under, the thrashing stopped. The larger animal was now at the spot where Jack had been dragged down. As Jenks shined the large spotlight on the water, he saw a few bubbles and four long wakes leading away from an expanding circle of blood.

As the night became quiet all they could hear were the loud splashes of Carl and Mendenhall. Then even that sound ceased as the two men realized as one that Jack and the animals were gone. And then total silence swept across the water except for the gentle lapping of the lagoon at *Teacher*'s waterline.

IN LESS THAN twelve hours onsite, *Teacher* had sustained damage twice. The pounding she had endured from the family of plesiosaurs was substantial, but Jenks announced that it was not beyond repair. The report fell on deaf ears as the crew was laid low by the news that they had lost Jack. In the science lab, Virginia and Dr. Waltrip tried to convince Sarah that taking a sedative would by no means make her a lesser woman in anyone's eyes. Still, she refused and angrily left the lab.

She walked by everyone as if she were in a daze, to the spiral staircase amidships. Jenks headed her off and held her arm at the bottom step, then released it just as quickly when he saw her eyes.

"You watch yourself out there, young lady," he said, and handed her an M-16.

She took it and went up the stairs, then pushed open the

acrylic hatch bubble and stepped out into the night. She saw Mendenhall leaning against the gunwale and walked over. He was taken aback when he saw who had joined him. The black man studied her for a minute and then turned away to stare at the water.

"What you and Carl did, going into the water after Jack like that, I want . . . I want to say thank you for trying," she said as she steeled herself against the tears that threatened to form.

"I only did what he would have done if it were me in the water," he said without looking at her. "He trained us to react without thinking, but he never taught us how to act if we failed . . ." he said, trailing off.

Sarah placed her hand on Mendenhall's, suddenly realizing it was not only she who would be grieving for Jack. She knew the sergeant looked at Jack more as a father; and Carl, as his best friend. The lieutenant commander had buried himself in the task of repairing the ship, to take his mind away from what had happened. Sarah knew she needed to do her job, as well, and decided that it was time to get on with it. She patted Mendenhall on the shoulder and turned away.

IT WAS NEAR dawn when Carl was shaken awake by Shaw, who had pulled a double shift abovedecks on watch while the others repaired the boat. Carl saw the wide look of fear on the corporal's face and immediately rose from his bunk.

"What's wrong?"

"Sir, I think one of those animals has surfaced and is just floating around the boat. I felt something hit us a minute ago and when I looked down, there it was, big as life. We may have a chance at killing the bastard. I also repaired the laser warning system. Something set off the fence at some point during the night."

Carl leapt from the bunk, not bothering with his shoes, as he trotted for the arms locker. Jenks, who had been awake all night repairing the hull from the inside, saw him dash by and followed. Carl quickly removed a .50-caliber Barrett rifle from the locker and handed it to Jenks. Then he tossed two hand grenades to Shaw, and when he noticed Mendenhall come sleepily down the companionway he tossed him two grenades. He grabbed a white phosphorous canister and then ran for the amidships hatch. The rest of the boat was coming alive with the noise the men made as they ran up the steps.

Carl ran to the gunwale and was surprised to see the thick body of the large plesiosaur lounging up against the hull. It bobbed easily in the movement of the lagoon. His eyes followed the entire length of the beast. It disappeared into the darkness of the water toward the aft of *Teacher*.

"Fuck a preacher's daughter, she's one big son of a bitch," Jenks whispered.

Carl didn't answer. He was looking at something strange that seemed to be wrapped around the midsection of the long-necked animal. As he looked forward he saw the same thing toward the bow, where the head disappeared from view into the depths of the lagoon.

"It's dead." He handed Mendenhall the two grenades he was holding. Then with no explanation he jumped over the side, as all on board to a man reached out to try to stop him.

"Are you crazy, Toad, you fuckin' officer piece of shit!" Jenks said loudly.

As they watched in stunned horror, Carl surfaced and made his way toward the floating plesiosaur. His breast-strokes were slow and deliberate and although he suspected the giant beast was dead, he still looked up and made a gun motion with his hand. Jenks aimed the rifle down at the thickest part of the animal as Carl approached.

"You have company, Commander," Mendenhall shouted.

Carl pulled up short of the hull and watched as four of the smaller animals shot away from the corpse of the larger one. It had looked as though they had been intentionally staying close to it. Ellenshaw had explained earlier why he had thought the green-shelled animals were the larger one's offspring, and that not recognizing the boat for what it was, she had targeted *Teacher* as a threat to them. Thus, as he had lectured at them like a schoolmaster, why she had attacked the vessel.

Carl watched for a moment, but the smaller plesiosaurs didn't reappear. He resumed his approach toward the floating body. Slowly, he brought his hand up and touched the rough hide of the wondrous animal, then he slapped at it. It didn't move. Then he saw what had caught his attention from the deck above. The beast had been impaled onto the maneuvering water jets of *Teacher*, effectively holding it in place. He turned and swam toward the cockpit area, where it had been brutally attached at the forward thruster, as well.

"What in the hell, Toad?" Jenks asked. Other crew members had now come on deck to watch.

"It's been slammed so hard into the maneuvering jets that it's been impaled."

The conditions just under *Teacher* had deteriorated as revealed in the early morning's diffused light. The water was now murky. At last Carl found the long neck of the beast where it sank below the water. His hand traveled along it until it suddenly slid off. The head of the animal had been completely ripped off. Strings of meat protruded from the stump and long gouges deeply marred the plesiosaur's dark, lightly haired skin. Carl looked around him and suddenly felt as if he wasn't alone. He kicked upward toward the lagoon's surface. When he did so, he immediately swam for the ladder.

"What in the hell's going on, Toad?" Jenks repeated.

"Something wanted us to know this animal was dead. The head has been ripped off the body."

The others started speaking at once, but Sarah just looked away toward the falls and wondered who—or *what*—had avenged Jack's death.

THE SMALL HANDS worked and the jabbering was nonstop. Sand was thrown and even a few berries were forced into his mouth. The fruit was followed by cool water that not only splashed his face but started a choking reaction, as the water slid past the berries and into his throat. Jack sputtered and coughed as he fought his way back to consciousness. As he spat out the last of the overly sweet fruit and threw up about a glass of brackish water, he slowly looked around him. The forest surrounded him with darkness and it was loud with the noises he had come to be accustomed to. The screeching of monkeys and cries of the many different species of birds threatened to overwhelm his awakening senses.

As he stilled his heart he thought he could see through the trees to the lagoon beyond. He felt his chest and legs, and found no broken bones. His right ankle felt as though it may have been fractured until he attempted to stand and could put his full weight on it. That was when he noticed the damage to his boot and the puncture marks that lined the thick rubber sole. They looked like teeth marks. He was having the hardest time remembering what had happened to him. The only thing he could recall was drowning—being pulled under the water and not being able to come up for air. He remembered the feeling of being released and quickly grabbed again, and then a sense of speed, of being pulled through the depths and then just as suddenly being let go. Now he could recall the water becoming strangely and overly warm around him while there had been a tremendous explosion of motion around him. Then another vague memory of an animal that had no right to be in existence. The plesiosaur started to rematerialize in his confused mind. Now he remembered being thrown into the water and even firing at the great animal as it smashed into the boat.

Jack tested his sore ankle by taking a few steps. Then he remembered the berries being placed in his mouth, and saw where he had spat them out onto the grassy forest floor. He looked around and wondered who it had been who tried to feed him. He was deep in thought when a bunch of the small red berries hit him on the head and shoulders. He looked up in time to see a small, shiny arm shoot back into the tree branches. Keeping his eyes on the tree, he reached down and retrieved one of the berries and popped it into his mouth. He chewed and swallowed and continued to look upward. That was when he heard chattering along the ground in front of him, and he looked that way. As he watched, several of the small monkeylike creatures Sarah had said she had seen grooming poor Sanchez walked out of the underbrush. Jack felt as if he were hallucinating. He shook his head and stared as they advanced upright with a bowlegged gait. Their arms were longer than their legs, and they seemed to wobble as they walked. Their skin was perfectly smooth with not a hair visible. Scales covered their bodies and even in the dark he could see the fins that lined their forearms and legs. Small gills puffed in and out along their jawline, and their small lips were parted to show teeth that were short and pointy, not like a monkey's at all.

"Well, what have we here?" His own voice sounded strange to him.

The five small creatures stopped short when he spoke. They looked from one to the other as if the sound coming from this man amazed them.

Jack now noticed their small hands; and indeed, as Sarah had said, their fingers were joined by webbing, and the same went for their overly large feet. There was a finlike appendage on the top of their heads that flared up and down as they took in air through their small noses.

"I suppose I have you to thank for the berries and water?"

The creature closest to him turned to look at its companions and then back at Jack. It tilted its head and then suddenly ran the thirty or so feet to the trees and disappeared, immediately followed by the others. Jack watched them leave and wondered what had scared them off. He listened closely, and he heard splashing coming from the lagoon. He turned in that direction and that was when he saw the footprints. They were huge and came from the lagoon. There was another set going back the way they had come. The enormous webbed prints heading from the beach looked as if whatever they had belonged to had been dragging something.

"What in the hell?" he mumbled as he reached down to

touch one of the impressions. He picked up his nine-millimeter Beretta. Had it been him that had been dragged ashore?

He heard voices and looked again toward the lagoon. He followed the tracks of the large, fan-shaped footprints all the way to the water. In the bright spot of sunlight he saw the surreal vision of *Teacher* anchored in the center of the lagoon. Several people crowded the upper deck as they stared down at a man in the water. Jack stepped close to the water and called out.

ABOARD *TEACHER*, THE crew had just opened one of the lab windows to take Carl in when a shout startled all on deck. Sarah looked toward where the others were pointing and her heart almost leapt from her chest. Jack was standing on the small beach with his hands on his hips. Then he raised his hands to his face, to cup his mouth.

"Will someone get a boat and get me off this beach?" he hollered. Shouts and laughter erupted everywhere on the upper deck. Carl dove back and swam to the other side of *Teacher*, then pulled himself up into the rubber boat. He then quickly started the motor and cast off, sped around to the opposite side, and zoomed into the lagoon.

Running the Zodiac up on shore, Carl hopped out before it came to a complete stop. He shook Jack's hand and then guided him to the rubber boat. Sarah was so elated she didn't feel it as the others on deck patted her on the back and shoulders. Even Danielle Serrate gave her a smile.

AN HOUR LATER, Jack was cleaned up, his ankle taped and his stomach full of scrambled eggs and sausage supplied by Heidi Rodriguez. Sarah sat next to him and kept shoving food into his face while he told his strange story. Her happiness brought a mood of joy and a sense of reprieve to the rest of the crew.

"Not to break the mood here, but how in the hell has that animal survived?" Jack asked.

Keating started to reply but bowed to an excited Ellenshaw instead.

"Well, Major, one of the things we must consider is the fact that this lagoon, this valley, must now be considered as one would an island. A place that is separate from the rest of the world. And as on an island that has been left undisturbed, the animal life and even its ecosystem will evolve almost totally void of outside interference. The indigenous food supply would be the main key to any species and its growth. If this plesiosaur, or whatever it was, and its offspring has an ample supply of, let's say, monkey and fish, and both land and lagoon life is as abundant as I've ever seen in such a small environment, there would be less competition for that food supply. The same can be said of other life forms associated with this lagoon. Obviously, this species would be near the top of that food chain."

The others looked at Ellenshaw as if he had just spoken in Latin.

"Perhaps another example, Madagascar, off the coast of Africa. It was separated many, many thousands of years ago from the continent and in consequence the species on that island developed far differently from their cousins on the mainland. Why? Because they were isolated. Birds, for example, became flightless because they had nothing to fear in this new environment."

"Until man intervened on the island," Keating interjected. "Then many of these amazing new species went extinct, like the dodo bird, once found on Madagascar and now gone forever."

The group brooded quietly as Keating reminded them that although the mother animal that had attached *Teacher* had been a killer, still she couldn't compare to the relentlessness of man. The uncomfortable silence continued until Danielle broke in with questions.

"But how does an animal escape the very extinction that killed its land cousins? If I remember my biology classes correctly, wasn't the plesiosaur a saltwater species?"

"As for its escaping extinction, the argument has been made that many varieties of sea animal may have escaped the fate of their cousins by the simple fact of their enjoying a more abundant food chain in a particular location," Keating said as Ellenshaw agreed, aggressively bobbing his white head.

"And the fact that this variety of plesiosaur is clearly living in freshwater indicates that the creatures may have left the harsher, more competitive hunting grounds of the oceans for the less dangerous waterways to be found inland. We may never know. I have a new theory about the animal that attacked us, as I have looked at the carcass very closely. I believe one reason this beast didn't go along gracefully to extinction land is the fact—" Ellenshaw paused for dramatic effect, "I believe this particular species has turned into what we know today as the giant sea turtle."

"Oh, come on! How can you speculate so carelessly like that?"

With that, the argument was on between the two scientists.

Ignoring them, Sarah asked Jack, "How in the world did you kill the mother animal?"

"I didn't," he answered as he popped half a sausage into his mouth.

"Jack, *something* killed it. Tore its head right off and then staked its body to the side of the boat," Carl said.

The major turned around and looked out of the tinted side window. He opened it and breathed deeply. His eyes scanned the water and then the small beach he had been on only an hour before.

"Something saved me from the creature and dragged me up on that beach. It was something big," he said as he turned back to face the others. He took Sarah's hand in his own and didn't care who saw it. "I was as good as dead; the plesiosaur had me dead in her sights and there could have been no way I could have escaped on my own. I was pulled down by the smaller ones, hard enough to sprain my ankle. I was taken deep underwater. Every time I tried to fight to the surface, I was pulled even deeper. Then something came at the animal with incredible speed. I only saw a violent strike by something and then I was released. There was blood in the water; I could taste it. I didn't know if it was my blood or someone or something else's. Then before I could reach the surface, I was grabbed by my ankle and pulled away. All I remember after that was the feeling of being pulled along in the water. Then whatever saved me from the animal left me on the sand, and that is all I remember until I woke up with one of Sanchez's small monkey fishes trying to feed me."

"Then what was it in that water that saved you, Jack?" Virginia asked.

"I don't know, but according to the footprints that were left in the sand where I woke up, it's huge. Its feet resembled those on the couple of statues we came across."

"My god," cried Charles Hindershot Ellenshaw III. "It's real! The legend of a creature that walks upright is real!" His amazement was enough to interrupt his argument with Keating.

THE *RIO MADONNA* was at anchor, and Farbeaux thought the captain should count himself lucky for being that way. When the Americans went off the radar Farbeaux became curious as to why, when suddenly Captain Santos threw his engines in reverse and brought the *Rio Madonna* to a standstill in the middle of the river. There, the captain had sent a small party ahead to reconnoiter the river. They were gone but an hour when they reported the rapids lay in front of the ship. Santos had narrowly missed smashing the *Rio Madonna* to splinters. Of course Mendez was angry at this development, stomping the decks, threatening everyone who crossed his path. But the captain smiled and watched how coolly Farbeaux handled him, by not handling him at all. The Frenchman seemed content to wait and the captain was curious as to why.

"I'm afraid this perpetual false twilight is affecting your capacity to see my point, *señor*," Farbeaux said, "The Americans are there and we are not. Do you wish to charge in there with your guns blazing and take by force that which we can have with no risks by just waiting?"

Mendez stopped his pacing at the stern of the boat. He stared out at the anchored barge behind them and thought for a moment.

"I wish to do something, *anything*," he grumbled.

"As I would, but I am a patient man. The Americans cannot leave here without going through us; we have effectively cut off any retreat they may have. Besides, my friend, the minerals have been there since the beginning of time; they're not going anywhere."

Mendez made a decision. "As always, you are right; I must learn to be as you. But you must understand, it is hard for a man such as I." He turned to face Farbeaux. "What is your plan?"

"We will wait until the middle of the night and utilize our rebreather scuba equipment, which won't leave any telltale bubbles on the surface, and simply swim under or around the Americans and reconnoiter the mine. Are you ready for a swim, Señor Mendez?"

"Yes, this is a good plan. But I must ask as I am curious, why not just place a charge on the bottom of their boat and send her to the bottom of the lagoon?"

"And then if there are survivors, *señor*, what then? What if three or four of those highly capable men survive? I am prone to believe they wouldn't be in a very charitable mood because we tried to kill them, do you?"

Mendez just glared at Farbeaux. He hated having things explained to him as if he were a wayward schoolboy.

"I know these people you seem so quick to try and murder, *señor*. They are capable of cutting your men to pieces." Farbeaux glanced toward the sneering Rosolo. "Let's find out first if we even have a reason for such ruthlessness, shall we?"

Mendez relaxed and finally smiled. "That is why men such as I pay handsomely for men such as you, my friend; they think on another level."

Farbeaux nodded and then moved away toward the bridge.

As soon as his back was turned Mendez ceased to smile and addressed Rosolo.

"You will of course place the charge and send the people he admires so much to the bottom. Just make sure it won't detonate until we are well within the mine."

Captain Rosolo grinned. "*Sí, jefe.*"

"YOU LOOK LIKE a man who is concerned about a problem, *señor*," Santos said when Farbeaux closed the bridge door.

"There is no doubt about your ability to observe. And of course, I do have problems. Señor Mendez is a fool. But I have observed you, Captain Santos, and I don't believe you are one." Farbeaux held the captain's eyes. "And since you and *I* are not fools, tell me how a river captain, one who has said that he has never traveled this particular tributary before, knew there would be rapids ahead."

Santos smiled broadly. "I was born with a sense for danger, *señor*. My own mother, she was always crossing herself and telling me I was of Satan's villa. Proclaimed this until the day she sent me to Bogotá and the Catholic nuns there. Then when they couldn't figure me out, I was sent even farther away to study at the seminary. But, *señor,* the river, she was always calling for my return. So you see, I feel the river, I know the river and her many moods."

Farbeaux laughed. "You have a gift all right, *señor*, but it is a gift of storytelling. Be careful in the coming day or so, Captain, and hide this strange . . . ability of yours; someone other than myself may become suspicious."

Santos watched as Farbeaux left his bridge. He crossed himself and again kissed and then caressed his medal before dropping it back into his shirt. Then he went to the window and checked on the men on deck. He opened a drawer and removed a Colt .38 Police Special, all the while watching.

"*Sí, señor*, I will watch them very closely. But you, I will watch even closer," he said as he checked the loads in the pistol.

PANAMA CITY, PANAMA

Jason Ryan stood in the giant hangar and watched as the modified Boeing 747-400 aircraft taxied after landing in the hot afternoon sun. Ryan was dressed in casual clothes, as was his two-man Delta escort. Each was armed with a nine-millimeter Berretta. As the giant plane approached they heard the whine of her four large engines slowly throttling down. Her falsified camouflage had been painted on by the United States Air Force and was styled after the livery colors of blue, white, and red. The words FEDERAL EXPRESS were written across her side and the giant tail.

Ryan could see almost no variation from a regular civilian cargo carrier. But he did notice the strange protrusions on the nose of the 747. There were no windows; it was one long, sealed aircraft. The Boeing plane taxied slowly to the front of the hangar, where the engines shut down. A large yellow vehicle streaked forward, and a ground crew immediately hooked up the nose wheel and started pulling her in.

"So this is Proteus?" he said as he watched the plane being pulled inside. The large hangar door began to lower after the five-story tail section cleared the opening.

When the aircraft stopped, a gangway was driven forward just beneath the crew door and it opened. Several men scrambled down. They were air police and two came quickly forward. Four others remained in back with two lethal-looking MP-5 machine guns pointed toward the hangar offices and two others pointed somewhat toward Ryan and his men. Two advanced and asked for identification from Ryan and his men. He examined each, looking very doubtful about Ryan's navy card, enough to give him a nervous moment. Then the man quickly handed the cards back and then turned and waved toward the giant plane. Twenty U.S. Air Force personnel started down the gangway.

"Which one of you is Ryan?" asked the largest man the lieutenant had ever seen in a military uniform. He was a black full-bird colonel. His voice boomed throughout the hangar.

"Lieutenant, JG Ryan, sir," replied Ryan as he again handed over his military ID.

"So, I was told you have the targeting data? I hear it's a small one."

"Yes, sir, think you can hit it?" Ryan asked, putting his ID back into his wallet.

"Son, we haven't hit a goddamned thing yet in thirty-one attempts, and two of the test targets were an ocean, an ocean! Hell, the last time out we nearly blew the fucking tail off this thing," he said with half a smile.

Ryan looked over at the two Delta men and closed his eyes, "Be sure we bring the high-altitude chutes just in case, I have a feeling Operation Spoiled Sport may not work out."

18

JACK, Virginia, and Carl had come to the conclusion that, after an inspection of the mine, regardless of whether they found the lost students, the expedition would need to be terminated for reasons that included a possible Broken Arrow situation in the valley. Jack knew he would have to alert Niles and then get a full military team in here somehow to conduct a proper search for the weapon, *if* there was one. But between the discovery of a black operational unit that had been clandestinely attached to Zachary's team and the finding of an activated nuclear trigger key, the odds were soaring that this particular expedition could turn bad real quick. Jack would tell the others about the nuclear aspect only after the lagoon and the mine were checked for possible survivors of the lost expedition.

Before a party was sent under the falls and into the mine that Padilla's map indicated was indeed there, he first needed to know if there was another way out, in case of an emergency.

Thanks to sonar readings, the science team had determined that this whole valley was riddled with caves and tunnels because of ancient lava flows. Blow-out shafts were clearly indicated in their readings.

So Jack ordered the diving bell and submersible out to map the lagoon walls and try to discover any escape openings, as well as any possible wreckage of Zachary's chartered boat and barge. He urged the people to hurry as much as safety would allow. Even Jenks had cut short his very long list of checks of both craft.

The submersible, according to Jenks who would be piloting her, was fast and maneuverable. It could ride shotgun for the diving bell as that was lowered into place for the sonar soundings they needed to make. As for any aggressive life form they might encounter underwater, the master chief assured Jack that the submersible could handle it with its full magazine of pneumatic spearguns. Thirty-five in all had been placed in a swivel gun in front of the pilot and were operated from within the dry environment of the submersible.

Jack didn't want to seem overly protective, but he made Jenks give him assurances that the bell would be protected, because it was holding a cargo that was becoming more and more precious to him, Sarah herself. She was the logical choice for this probe, as she knew what to look for in the lava rock strata that made up the walls of the lagoon. For viewing the underwater life, "Crazy Charlie" Ellenshaw, as he had come to be known behind his back of course, would accompany Sarah—along with Professor Keating, who wouldn't let Ellenshaw out of his sight. Mendenhall had volunteered to go with Jenks in the two-man submersible.

Within his time constraints, Jenks had thoroughly checked out both systems and made sure they were operating right. The bell was the safer of the two, being attached by umbilicus to *Teacher* the whole time. The submersible was far more complex and dangerous, as it was totally free of the boat and could stay under for more than five hours with the oxygen it had on board. The torpedo-shaped craft was what was known as a dry diver; in other words, the crew would be totally enclosed with their own atmosphere. Jenks had named the diving bell *Yoyo One*, because it looked like a yoyo on a string. The submersible had the mighty name of *Turtle*.

"Well, I guess that does it," he said as he exited the *Yoyo One*. "Now you three keep those thermal suits on; as deep as you're going, it gets colder than a well digger's ass."

"A well what?" Ellenshaw asked, not understanding the comment.

Jenks looked at the crazy-haired professor and removed his stump of cigar to say something else, then thought better of it and just shook his head.

Jack was nervous as he and Carl listened to the master chief's banter. He knew everyone wasn't happy with his decision to delay the initial incursion into the mine itself. But he wanted all avenues of approach mapped before he risked losing his remaining probes and even a single life. They had conducted tests on the depths of the lagoon but had yet to discover a bottom. They thought they had discovered it once, but one of the softball-size probes had lodged momentarily on a jutting ledge and then rolled free, sinking into the inky blackness of the apparently bottomless lagoon.

Sarah had announced during one of the tests that after the initial coldness of the water at the 150-foot depth, the water started heating up at a fantastic rate. She dubbed it the lagoon's thermal layer, where volcanic activity was heating the water and forcing it through ancient steam vents. Virginia had also come in with her results from the five dropped probes. At the 200-foot level, the percentage of fluorides in the water increased by 500 percent—strange but still safe, even though she had never encountered amounts of fluorides in that high a degree before and was at a loss to explain the phenomenon.

"Major, you won't be able to see *Turtle*, but the interior of *Yoyo* will be on this monitor; you can switch from interior to exterior. But you and Toad keep your eyes on the pumps and power cables for the bell above all else, that clear?" asked Jenks.

"Clear," Jack said as he turned to Sarah and the two professors.

"A little out of my element here," Sarah commented.

"Nonsense, little lieutenant; it's just wet, otherwise it's like one of your caves," Jenks said as he adjusted her wetsuit. "Now climb aboard and take a seat. There's absolutely nothing for you to do but take in your soundings and snap your pictures and observe." He looked at Keating and Ellenshaw, who cowered back a step at his intense glare. "And I do mean *observe*, no turning of switches and no pushing of buttons, asking what's this, what's that. The little officer here is in charge down there, got it?"

"Yes, Chief, by all means, no buttons or switches," Ellenshaw said as he nodded his head slightly to the left toward Keating, indicating on the sly that it would be Keating who would indeed push buttons and turn switches, not him.

Jenks turned his glare exclusively on Keating for a moment, who flinched back another step. He didn't understand why he got the extra "chief" treatment because he hadn't seen the white-haired man indicate he was the troublemaker.

"All right, your chariot awaits, ladies." Jenks gestured and half bowed toward the open hatch.

Sarah and Jack exchanged a look, then she took the three steps up the small ladder and entered the bell. She was quickly followed by Keating and Ellenshaw, who were mumbling something about being called *ladies*. Jenks closed the hatch and turned a small wheel that tightened its seals. The passengers were out of sight below the collar that held *Yoyo* in place. Jenks slapped the rounded hull twice and then pulled a lever that freed the bell from its collar. Then he used a small hand pump to hydraulically open the large hatch below *Yoyo*, which when opened allowed a small rush of water into the space. It quickly drained and he used the winch controller to start lowering the bell. He stopped when the bell was completely awash, and put on his headphones.

"How are you reading, *Yoyo*?" he called.

"Loud and clear," Sarah called back.

"You'll remain there until *Turtle* is in the water, clear?"

"Clear."

The master chief removed the headphones and gave them to Carl and turned to a nervous-looking Mendenhall. "Okay, Sergeant, let's get into this highly experimental, uncertified, and probably the most dangerous submersible ever built, shall we?"

Mendenhall didn't respond; he just looked at Jack and Carl and then slowly followed Jenks toward the raised acrylic cockpit of the *Turtle*.

YOYO WAS LOWERED at fifteen feet per minute while *Turtle* zoomed around it in a spiral pattern, watching for telltale signs of leaking, which would be noticeable by small bubbles emanating from her titanium hull. Mendenhall momentarily felt dizzy as the fifteen-foot-long *Turtle* circled around the diving bell.

Sarah took active sonar soundings of the walls as they were lowered. The two professors watched out of their individual six-inch-thick portholes. They saw numerous fish, and took notes as to their species and the depth at which they were seen.

Sarah was writing down anomalies on her paper graph when she saw the sonar had picked up a large body of fish heading their way. She adjusted her headphones and placed the microphone close to her lips.

"*Yoyo* to *Turtle*, we have a large school of fish coming up on our starboard side, keep your eyes open," she said as she leaned back and pointed out Ellenshaw's window. She placed her hand over her mic. "Right out there," she whispered.

"Right, *Yoyo*, maybe we can bring back supper to fry up," Jenks called back.

Sarah didn't respond. She reached out and placed her sonar on active to track the school continuously. Suddenly Ellenshaw gasped out loudly and even the reserved Keating let out his breath.

"Those ain't no fish, they look like little scuba men," Jenks called over the radio.

Sarah leaned forward and saw the water around the bell was being inundated by the small, amphibious monkeys. There were close to a hundred as they darted in and out of the exterior lights. Sarah laughed as she watched them play. Keating jumped back when one came close to the window, held onto the frame for a moment, and then quickly darted away. Ellenshaw observed with utter fascination while writing frantically in his notebook. His mouth was wide open as he found himself in a world of his dreams.

"Jack, Carl, are you picking this up?"

"We are, we just piped your camera shots through to the labs," Jack called back.

"Should we snag one?" Jenks asked.

"NO!" Sarah and Jack said at the same time, almost cutting each other off.

"Chief, we're not here to antagonize anything, you're to observe only, are we clear on that?" Jack said.

"Clear, Major," the master chief answered sadly.

As he watched, a large group of the amphibians broke away from the main group and circled the *Turtle*. They kept pace easily by using their webbed hands and feet. Their tails were in constant motion as they whipped back and forth, supplying them with tremendous speed. Jenks laughed as one cut in front of the submersible and was bumped softly by the hull, then grasped the edge of the cockpit and stared inside at the two men. Mendenhall had to smile at the comical expression of the animal that clearly said it didn't know what had hit it. The monkey jabbered even while underwater, allowing a large flow of bubbles to escape its small mouth.

At the diving bell, the small creatures were hanging on in thick batches, trying to peer inside at the strangers to their underwater world. Sarah kept smiling and tapping on the glass, and the amphibians mimicked her action, in return tapping on the glass with their small claws.

A loud buzz sounded from her laptop. On the sonar graph

she saw that it had picked up an anomaly on the far wall of the lagoon far below the opening behind the falls. She quickly noted the cave on the graph and marked its coordinates. Then, as she was about to turn back to her porthole, the computer chirped again. The sweep of sonar revealed a red blip coming at them from about five hundred yards. At that exact moment the small amphibians broke ranks and scattered in all directions. She looked at the sonar again; it was awash with tiny blips as the creatures fled. Their hasty retreat covered the red blip that had been there.

"Hey, what did Ellenshaw do, let them see his hair?" Jenks called jokingly over the radio.

Sarah didn't answer, she had picked up the blip again at a hundred yards closer than it had been before. Whatever it was, it was fast.

"Chief, we have company coming, and coming fast from the northern part of the lagoon. I think it came from the area of the falls."

Jenks didn't respond as he stopped *Turtle*'s gentle spiral and turned her toward the possible threat.

Sarah continued to watch as the target blip suddenly plunged below them. It was coming upon them at over twenty-five knots, she calculated quickly.

"Jack, we may have the landlord coming at us here," she said nervously into her microphone. "Whatever it is, it just went deep on us, it's down below both vessels at three hundred feet and still diving. It's not large enough for one of the plesiosaurs."

The two professors unsnapped their lap belts and tried to peer though the portholes at what was below them, beyond the exterior floodlights.

"You two, strap yourselves back in!" she said louder than she'd intended.

"Major, start winching the bell back up," Jenks called as he swung *Turtle* around a hundred degrees. He brought her airplanelike flaps up and applied thrust. Her water jet engine responded immediately.

"Roger, bringing her up," Jack responded.

Sarah felt the winch engage. The depth of the bell started to decline, as indicated on her depth gauges. She saw the target was only a hundred yards away and now coming shallow. Jenks wouldn't possibly get into position in time.

As Keating watched for any movement outside of his porthole, it was suddenly filled with a horrific face. He jumped back as the creature looked inside the interior of the bell. Sarah froze for a moment when she saw what had frightened the professor through the glass.

"Oh, my!" Ellenshaw said under his breath. The animal had swum quickly to his porthole and now he was face to face with it.

The creature had large black eyes and looked in with what Sarah thought was mere curiosity. The scales that covered its body were thick and appeared to be an exact match of the sample found on the body of the SEAL. The mouth opened and closed as its gills worked on either side just below the jawline. The back lower half of its head had a long row of leathery spines that angled downward. When the strange row of finlike spines was activated, they fanned out like a protective shield. The creature's large handlike protrusions swirled back and forth in an effort to maintain its position in front of the porthole.

"Jesus Christ!" Jenks yelled into the radio. "What in the hell is that?"

"Stop and hold your position, Chief. Stay clear, it's not aggressive, *at least not yet*," Sarah called. "Jack, stop the winch," she said calmly. Just a moment later they felt a small jerk as the bell came to a stop just above the layer where they started receiving refracted light from the surface.

"Look at it, its part human! It has to be! You can just feel and see the intelligence," Ellenshaw said exuberantly.

"I agree, it's studying us." Keating was also mesmerized by the sight before him. "Professor, why would it have the spines running around the base of its head?"

"Your academic guess would be as good as mine, my

friend. Perhaps they are a protective apparatus or simply a mating tool used by this animal."

The creature suddenly moved away from the porthole and went deep. It reappeared in front of Sarah and she did her best not to react at its sudden arrival. The large head tilted, swinging the large spines that looked almost like braids. Being this close, Sarah could see the spines ended in clear, pointed spikes. The beast opened its mouth and she could see very small, almost clear teeth inside. The face had no scales to speak of. Its features were smooth and tinted a whitish light green color as compared to its body, which was a darker shade of green with swirling highlights of silver and gold.

"Jack, tell me you're filming this," she said.

"We got it. That has to be what pulled me from the water and killed that plesiosaur. Mendenhall, make sure you get some full body shots of this thing."

"Filming with the nose camera," the sergeant answered.

The creature swam from porthole to porthole, watching the bell's occupants with immense curiosity. It kept reaching out only to be stopped by the glass. Then it slowly started backing away first by swirling its webbed fingers, and then by kicking with its powerful legs. It came up to the bubble canopy of the *Turtle* and swam in circles around it.

"Easy, Chief," Sarah called. "It's just showing you the same curiosity."

"Yeah, you had a three-inch titanium fence around you, but this monstrosity could sink this aluminum coffin just by wishing real hard."

"Really?" Mendenhall asked, not moving as the beast stopped and looked at him, only inches away.

The creature rubbed a hand over the canopy and then jerked it away. The master chief reduced power and the *Turtle* came to a hover fifty yards from *Yoyo*. The monster again reached out and touched the glass canopy just above Mendenhall's head. It took all of the sergeant's discipline not to duck as the eight-foot-long animal reached out. Then as suddenly as it had appeared, it darted off into the inkiness of the lagoon.

"That thing is five times faster than *Turtle*, Major. Get the bell up and out of here. We'll stand by until she's pulled aboard. Be careful and take it slow," Jenks said.

Jack hit the switch again to bring *Yoyo* in, never so happy to obey an order from the crusty old master chief.

As *Turtle* slowly wound its way around the diving bell, *Yoyo* was slowly pulled up. Sarah plotted the downward-angled cave the sonar had picked up far below the falls. It might be a prehistoric lava vent, but without seeing it first-hand she couldn't be sure. But the water that flowed out of that particular vent was thirty degrees cooler than that of the lagoon at that depth.

The two professors were debating the existence of the animal they had just witnessed when a shudder coursed through the bell. Sarah held onto her clipboard full of calculations, and Ellenshaw and Keating stopped their bickering long enough to look above them at the rounded ceiling.

"Our visitor's back. Goddammit, it's messing with the umbilical lines!" the master chief called.

The creature first pulled on the steel cable, then on the rubber oxygen line, and then the electrical and oxygen lines together. It shook them lightly at first, then harder.

Sarah and the two professors were rocked in their seats as the bell was pulled from side to side. Then suddenly they stopped moving.

"It's coming down the line toward the bell," Jenks called.

The creature appeared at Ellenshaw's window and then quickly darted away. Then Keating made a frightened puppy sound as the thing suddenly came up in front of him. The half-man, half-animal placed a hand on the glass and tilted its large head. The thick lips parted as its gills worked. The black eyes narrowed and blinked three sets of clear eyelids.

"I don't care for this," Ellenshaw said. "This behavior is not common to an animal in the wild. It should exhibit curiosity and then move on."

"I agree, this is not right," Keating said.

"Oh, now you agree. Jesus!" Sarah said in exasperation as

the beast raised a webbed hand and struck the glass in front of Ellenshaw.

"Uh-oh," Sarah said just as the beast struck the glass. "Jack, get us out of here!"

The bell immediately started to climb.

"It's bashing the hull!" Jenks hollered.

The creature swiped at the glass, then the titanium bell, and quickly kicked out with its legs. It rose to the umbilicus again and started pulling and swiping at the cables in a maddened frenzy.

"That does it, it's going to kill them," Jenks said as he applied forward thrust to *Turtle*.

Mendenhall grabbed for the two handholds along the top of the canopy, pushed back in his seat by their sudden acceleration as they rushed toward *Yoyo* at full speed.

The beast pulled up suddenly as it was struck by the pressure wave sent out from the advancing *Turtle*. It stopped its attack and hovered for a moment, eyeing the threat coming at it. Then it swam back toward the bell, going from window to window to look into the interior. Then an explosion of bubbles came from its mouth as it reached out toward the window Ellenshaw was close to and struck it hard, rocking the bell from side to side. Finally it suddenly broke off the attack and vanished into the darkness in a swirl of bubbles.

"Beats the hell out of looking for Bigfoot, doesn't it?" the shaking Keating said with a nervous chuckle.

Ellenshaw ignored the slight and continued to alternate between his window and the monitor mounted on the bell, trying desperately to find the beast once again.

"Okay, Jack, it's off the scope, bring us up," Sarah said as she slowly pulled off her headset and sank down into her seat.

TWENTY MINUTES LATER, Sarah was back in *Teacher*, in navigation, plotting the underwater cave the sonar had picked up.

"It may just be an extinct lava vent, but look at this," she pointed at the graph laid out on the large map table. They saw that her hand was still shaking slightly from their encounter in the water. "See how perfectly round this is? It's about fifteen feet in diameter, I would say. I don't know, Jack, but if I were forced to guess at this point, I would say that cave is man-made and not a lava vent at all."

"Lieutenant, if I may point out, the depth on your graph indicates that vent is over four hundred feet below the surface of the lagoon. A task quite impossible for man to have carved it out," Danielle said as she looked from Sarah to Carl and finally to Jack.

"Not if at one time this lagoon wasn't here," Sarah countered, holding the Frenchwoman's eyes.

"What are you saying?" Jack asked.

"I have a theory, and it's just a theory," she said, "that maybe this used to be an open pit mine, a natural formation that was discovered and used by the Inca, or maybe another civilization. I had time to think about it and I think this lagoon is a natural geological feature. A caldera—a creater— of a volcano that isn't quite extinct, but stable enough because the lava flow and steam vents act as a natural pressure relief valve, never allowing the volcanic pressures to build up to the point where it could erupt. My guess is a rough one, but I don't think this once-active site has erupted for close to twelve or fifteen million years. And maybe, just maybe, the tributary and the river above the lagoon that creates the falls were once flowing in other directions. I think that at some later time they were diverted here to fill a man-made lake, this very lagoon."

"What evidence is there that even hints at such an outrageous theory?"

Sarah didn't answer Danielle's question at first. She reached over and placed a CD into one of the networked players beside the navigation table. She hit a button and an underwater picture appeared.

"Now the absence of light hurts the quality of the video taken, but we got these on the way down before our visitor appeared. See this far wall—its about a hundred feet below the waterfall and two hundred above the cave opening, or lava vent. Now look at this," she said as she used a pencil to trace a line that at first only she could see. The pencil point zigzagged as she moved it down the screen.

Jack and Carl didn't see it at first. But then Jack noticed a formation that nature could never duplicate on its own. "A staircase?"

"Bingo."

"Damn," Carl and Danielle said at the same time at a pattern that was too precise *not* to be man-made.

"I must apologize, Lieutenant. You have a valid theory going here," Danielle said as she studied the rock wall. "But why would men build a staircase underneath the water?"

"I need to go back down, Jack," said Sarah.

Jack straightened and scratched his forehead. "Let's just assume you're right, that this vent is a man-made portal of some kind. I think we have enough to go on."

"But if you were hesitant about going into the mine without an escape route, why does an underwater cave reassure you?" Danielle asked.

"I'll make a wager that the cave is a viable exit from the mines. Ancient man had a habit of doing impossible things, Ms. Serrate. For all we know, there is a pressure area just beyond that opening that holds the water back and keeps the shaft beyond dry."

"Like a diver's trunk on undersea platforms," Carl volunteered.

Jack just nodded and looked at his watch. It was already well after three in the afternoon, but he wanted a few more answers now. He hit the intercom.

"Chief?"

"Yeah," Jenks answered from engineering.

"You ready to take Snoopy for a walk to see what the hoopla was about for all these centuries?"

FARBEAUX WATCHED AS Mendez squeezed his fat body into the wetsuit and as Rosolo placed a rubberized nylon bag on his dive belt and made sure it was secured properly. The other men sat about with their wetsuits on and checked their rebreathers. There were sixteen men in all, including him. *Enough*, Farbeaux thought, *to almost guarantee a foul-up while traveling that long a distance underwater to the mine.*

Santos was leaning out of the bridge window with his large cigar tucked into the corner of his smiling mouth. Farbeaux walked to the opposite side of the boat, where the remaining crew was bringing over some of the packed supplies from the anchored barge. He thought he saw something flash out of the corner of his eye. As he strained to see, the movement didn't recur.

THE COMMANDER OF the assault element had been following the *Rio Madonna* for days. The track had been difficult to follow, but the colonel had been raised in the thick canopied forests of Brazil. He watched as his men performed their preparations deep inside the jungle.

"Are you ready?"

The small man walked up to the colonel but remained in the shadows. "We are ready."

"The radios will have no trouble operating underneath this cursed tree canopy, so have it monitored closely. I will signal when it is time for you to move the men in force into the lagoon, are you clear on this?"

"Yes, but my men, they are not used to water travel. We are at home on the land; our training has been for land assault."

The colonel looked angry for a moment but then quickly calmed. "My orders were to get your men to the assault point and let you do what you were paid to do; you will inflate your boats past the rapids and enter the lagoon. I expect you will only have to face a third of the Americans, the rest will be inside the mine by now."

"What about these fools on the boat? They pose a threat to my men, yes?"

The colonel looked through the darkness at the *Rio*

Madonna. The men onboard were loud as they prepared to enter the river.

"They may make your assault all the more easy. I suspect they are at cross-purposes to our American friends. In any case, they must be eliminated also. No one leaves this valley alive; those are my orders and thus, your orders. Your employers will be very unforgiving if you fail in this."

"We do as we are paid to do. I have worked many times for your general and have never failed him. We will kill every person in the lagoon and then seal the others in the mine. But the situation has changed, hasn't it? We were told about the Americans, but your general never said anything about this second group. This will double the price, otherwise you can use your own military for these murders."

The colonel looked about in exasperation. "Your price will be met. But I will be with you to ensure your contract is fulfilled."

The mercenary nodded and ordered his men forward with the rubber boats. "Soon your general will have many dead Americans."

ONBOARD THE *RIO Madonna*, Farbeaux went to the fantail and started situating his equipment. He still had the strange feeling that they weren't alone. The jungle opposite the boat was quiet but he still glanced up every few moments to examine the area as far as his limited sightlines permitted.

The rebreather he held was large and bulky but he would only have to carry it beyond the rapids. Then at that point, he and Mendez's men would enter the lagoon unnoticed. As he placed his nine-millimeter and five extra clips into a plastic satchel, his hand brushed against the large cross in his pack. He took a breath and curled his fingers around it. He brought it up into the fantail's weak deck light. It had been stolen by a contact who had known the item had been lifted by the U.S. government in the 1930s. How they had come into possession of it, Farbeaux had no idea. But it was his, and that included the unusual items *inside* the cross. The reason he was here. He rattled the large object and was satisfied when he heard the two samples inside slide up and down in the false bottom. It had been an ingenious design by none other than Father Corinth himself, the very same man who was responsible for one of the very first political cover-ups in the New World. As he held the cross and felt its internal warmth, he knew the priest of the Pizarro incursion had been beyond his years in wisdom. With what he held in his hand, Farbeaux knew beyond doubt that he could change the balance of world power forever. But it would be he who had that choice, not some banking bloodsucker that was far more evil than the men he once served.

PART SIX
PADILLA'S HELL

Abandon all hope ye who enter here.

—Dante's *Inferno*

19

THE WHITE HOUSE

THE president listened with difficulty to Niles as he gave the latest update on the Group's incursion into the Amazon tributary. He was finding it harder and harder to concentrate on the words the director was saying. He had informed the First Lady about the predicament their daughter was in; he couldn't keep it from her any longer, unable to lie about something that was clearly showing on his face every time he saw her.

"The latest coordinates have been passed onto Proteus so they will have a general idea where they will need to orbit." Niles repeated the longitude and latitude.

"Anything else?"

"Not yet, Mr. President, Pete Golding and I have been assembling a timeline and historical record for everything we have on Padilla and the subsequent expeditions to that area. A most important bit of intelligence should be in our hands soon. A man in his nineties, Dr. Allan Freeman, a retired professor from the University of Chicago, will be able to finally tell us what it was he was doing down there in 1942."

The president could hardly pay attention to these details. "When is Collins going into the mine?"

"They are starting now."

THE NATIONAL SECURITY advisor sat with the president on one of the two couches arranged in front of his desk, waiting for the president to continue. But the man sat silently, the fingers of his right hand rubbing his right temple.

"Sir, you were saying?" prodded Nathan Ambrose.

The president looked up and seemed lost for a moment, not recognizing the face looking at him. Then he shook his head as if startled awake.

"I'm sorry, Nathan. Caught me there, didn't you?"

"Is there something happening that you're not telling me about?"

The president looked at him and said nothing.

Ambrose tossed his notebook onto the coffee table and leaned forward on the couch.

"Has the secretary of state made any headway with your request for assistance from Brazil?"

"No, for some reason Brazil is acting as though the Zachary expedition was a cover for something else. They're stonewalling the secretary."

"Have you spoken with the Brazilian president yourself?"

"No, Secretary Nussbaum informed me that the president will not speak to me directly, but only through the secretary's official office. He's even threatened to go to the UN Security Council."

Ambrose had to admire the secretary; he did have the balls it took to run this country. Keeping the leaders of both countries at arm's length could only cloud an already confusing state.

The door from the outer office opened and a Secret Service officer stepped in.

"Sir, the First Lady is on her way down for the reception."

The president stood and walked to his desk as he pulled up the knot of his tie and buttoned his jacket.

"Sorry, we'll pick this up later."

"Sir, I'm your national security advisor. You have to tell me what's happening here."

The president straightened his tie and then brushed at his

lapels. "It's being handled. But if things become more active, I'll get you up to date."

"Sir, you're moving whole carrier groups around the Pacific. You shut down Panamanian airspace for three hours without any official explanation, and the secretary of state is trying hard to avert a conflict with a friendly neighbor where there wasn't a conflict this morning."

"Later, Nathan," the president said, clenching his teeth. His jaw muscles worked visibly beneath his skin as he glared at his advisor, then he brushed passed him.

Ambrose watched his boss leave and then counted to three. He moved quickly to the president's phone, then quickly looked up to make sure the doors were closed. He had decided to take a very dangerous but necessary chance three hours earlier while the president was with the First Lady. He had placed a small bug inside the cap of the receiver, a small gift from a friend across the river. He deftly unscrewed the cap, transferred the small device to his pocket, then replaced the cap. He then moved swiftly away from the desk. None too soon, as the outer door opened and a Secret Service agent stepped through.

"Mr. Ambrose, you know this area is off limits when the president isn't in."

"Yes, I was just gathering my briefing materials; the president left rather abruptly." The national security advisor made a show of reaching for his case as the agent reached out and held the door open for him, the move so sudden it made Ambrose nervous.

ONCE IN HIS own office, Ambrose decided that the information on the miniature recorder couldn't wait. He had to know what was going on. He removed the small round object from his pocket and placed it inside a small device that resembled an iPod. He quickly tapped the play button as he put on his headphone. A voice he didn't recognize explained to the president a plan Ambrose just couldn't believe. As he listened, he jotted down the coordinates Niles Compton had given in his last phone conversation. This information had to be placed in the hands of the secretary as soon as possible. The national security advisor had to stop this mission at all costs. How had the military sneaked Proteus by him?

TEN MINUTES LATER, after he had used several sources in the military to confirm the existence of Proteus and its abilities, he placed a call to the U.S. embassy in Brazil. The private cell phone number was answered by the American secretary of state.

"I hope you've come through for us, Mr. Top Advisor."

Ambrose didn't like the tone the secretary was taking with him lately. They would have to discuss their roles in this melodrama at a later date.

"You believe the president already has people on the ground in Brazil. Well, I may have just confirmed it."

"Imagine that, the national security advisor to the president of the United States has come up with something concerning the military he was supposed to be overseeing in the first place. I'm stunned. I'll have you know, I also have people on the ground, thanks to our Brazilian Air Force friend."

Ambrose closed his eyes and waited for the secretary's sarcasm to run its course. Lying to both presidents must be taking its toll, and it was coming through in the cabinet member's temper.

The advisor continued, "I can't confirm the rescue attempt, but I believe I may have come across their security blanket against your mercenaries. And it's right up the road you wanted to go. To protect the ground unit in the Amazon Basin, the president has ordered up a Proteus scenario."

"That Star Wars crap the air force has? I thought that project had been shelved."

"It was. But the air force flexed its muscle and got one prototype built before the cancellation."

"So, what's this to do with what I need?"

"Think, Mr. Secretary. In order for Proteus to be of any value, they have to be on station."

There was silence on the other end of the phone and Ambrose couldn't resist a smirk. Having the upper hand in talking with the secretary was a situation he liked very much.

The national security advisor decided to spell it out. "They'll have to intrude on Brazilian airspace to accomplish their mission against the force you arrayed. However, I am now in possession of the coordinates where Proteus will be taking up station. I'm sure the president of Brazil would be none too happy over having their sovereign territory not only invaded but their airspace compromised. Down that plane and there will be no helping the ground team when they need it most. Let's see the president talk his way out of *that* one. I think you may say that he has pulled the rug out from under your diplomatic efforts, wouldn't you?"

"Yes, I believe you have indeed earned your spot in my new cabinet, Mr. Ambrose. I will contact our friend in the Brazilian government and get his guarantee of action."

"Not too hard to do with what you have hanging over his head already."

"Remember, Mr. Advisor, we're still talking about American men in that aircraft and the people on the ground. I just hope we haven't gone too far."

"By my estimation, Mr. Secretary, we've gone just far enough already. We have covered exactly thirteen steps up the gallow's staircase. And with your official statements to both sides confusing the issue of a rescue, I would think its safe to say that the few remaining steps to the hangman's rope are already in the bank. I see no other choice here."

"Give me the coordinates."

BLACK WATER TRIBUTARY

Jack had several operations going at once: Charles Ray Jackson was on the sonar in a constant watch for their underwater friend. Tom Stiles was atop the main mast finishing up the repairs to the satellite communications dish, and Mendenhall and Sanchez were working on Operation Spoiled Sport: In the darkness surrounding the lagoon, they were attaching small battery-operated heat cells to nylon line attached to semitransparent Mylar balloons, which would be raised with the help of the helium tank Sanchez had carried in a backpack as the men made their way nervously around the perimeter of the lagoon. The balloons would raise a package that emitted a high-temperature signature through the use of heating coils in the foot-long cylinder.

"I hope those monkeys don't try and mess with these. The major seemed pretty adamant about having them in place and operating on time," Mendenhall said as he nervously eyed the trees around them.

Sanchez pressed the release valve on the hose and the large balloon filled with helium. Then the heat transponder was attached, and he slowly allowed the nylon line to play out through his fingers. They were on their thirteenth one; each one had to be placed as close to the tree canopy as they could get it. By the time they were finished they would have fifty balloons raised to a height of two hundred feet above the highest of the trees. Once that was done, the team would use the Zodiac to travel to the shore and tie every balloon to the roots of trees. Thus the entire lagoon would be lined with the heat-emitting elements.

INSIDE THE ENGINEERING section, Jenks was preparing Snoopy 3 for her journey into the mine. The probe was five and a half feet long and had a pop-up floodlight and camera on each of four points. But the problem with using that much power for the illumination and cameras was that Snoopy 3 had a battery lifespan of less than an hour.

He reached for the intercom. "Okay, you in there?"

"This is Everett in sonar. Anytime you want, Chief."

"Go ahead, Toad, blast the hell out of the water and get

me some readings to feed into Snoopy—and give it full amplitude."

OUTSIDE IN THE water, a sound wave was created by the loud sonar ping. The signal bounced off the rock walls and bounced around until it found its way back to *Teacher*, where the size of and distance to all underwater obstructions were recorded. Again the ping sounded, and again. Fifteen times at ten-second intervals, the sound bounced around the lagoon and even into the mine itself.

BLACK WATER TRIBUTARY

Robby watched the animal from within an enclosure in the cave as it moved around the darkened central cavern. He could see the amphibian turn and stare at him. Robby knew the beast was aware of its being observed. It had seemed agitated when it had returned only minutes before to herd several more members of the expedition team into the cave: two students who were carrying a third between them. In the semidarkness he couldn't make out who they were. He'd heard a lot of screaming by the animal but it had finally got its point across, and the three women had gone inside another of the dug-out slave enclosures. Then Robby had heard cries of relief from the people already inside, at the sudden reunion.

But now the beast traversed the floor of the cave. Every now and then it would raise its face toward the ceiling and then cock its head to one side. It seemed to be listening for something. Afterward, it would lower its head and look directly at Robby, stabbing him with its eyes across a hundred feet of cave. It would growl and shake its head and half swipe in his direction, as if it was he who was causing whatever distress it was obviously feeling.

"Did you see who they brought in?" Kelly whispered from behind him.

Robby didn't move his eyes from the animal. "No, they were pushed into the enclosure too fast. Look, it's acting strange. Something must be going on."

Kelly studied the beast as it just stood there. It tilted its head again and again, from one side to the other, and raised its right hand into the air as if trying to grasp something that wasn't there.

"My god, it's hearing something and is confused by it. Either that or the sound is making it uncomfortable. See how it's snapping its hand? Sound waves."

The creature suddenly placed both enormous hands over the sides of its head. It emitted a roar that echoed off the walls of the cave. It looked straight at Robby and Kelly, roared again, and took a menacing step toward them. Then abruptly it turned and awkwardly walked toward the grotto and fell in. There was a quick splash and the animal vanished under the clear water.

Rob walked around in the cave but could hear nothing. Kelly, on her hands and knees, began to crawl out of the enclosure, after the animal. "Robby, do you feel that?"

Robby stood stock still, but still didn't feel or hear anything.

Kelly crawled all the way out and stood. She ran as fast as the darkness would permit to the edge of the grotto, then went down on her hands and knees once again. Her palms were spread out on the floor of the cave.

"What are—"

"Shhh—"

"Come on, what's—"

"Come down here and feel," Kelly said as she felt around closer to the water. Then she suddenly placed her right ear to the wet stone. Robby finally joined her and pressed his ear to the ground.

"Don't you hear that?" she asked. Robby couldn't figure out what she was listening to.

Kelly, smiling, sat back up.

"What are you smiling about?" he asked.

"I think we have company in the lagoon, maybe our rescuers."

He looked from Kelly back to the floor of the cave. Whatever she had felt or heard had eluded him. There was a steady sound but he didn't know what it was.

"Active sonar. Someone out there is pinging the lagoon!"

Now Robby understood. The feeling through his fingertips, and the steady beat of sound that he had felt, was the sound of sonar as it pulsed through the lagoon outside and was acoustically transferred to the grotto through the best conducting material there was: water.

"What's wrong?" Kelly asked when she saw his face.

"That animal didn't look too happy when it left here. It was feeling the sonar pulses, too."

"Damn!" she exclaimed.

"Yeah, I hope whoever is out there is paying attention, because our slave master is about to pay them a visit."

"WELL, SHE'S READY," Jenks said into the intercom as he reached out for the lever that opened the small two-door hatch at the bottom near the bilges. He winched Snoopy 3 into the murky lagoon, then made his way back to the main lounge, where everyone had gathered for their first glimpse into the mine. Even in the radar and communications room, Jackson leaned forward in his seat to watch, and accidentally hit the Sonar Contact Alarm switch, an audible warning system that allowed the operator to be warned of the approach of something moving toward *Teacher*. When the switch was accidentally thrown, it effectively converted the sonar's programmed task to an ordinary eyes-only sweep.

TWENTY FEET BENEATH the keel of *Teacher*, the creature was now swimming on its back, kicking easily as it stared upward at the bottom of the boat. Every few minutes it would rise and run a hand along the hull and then quickly dart away. When Snoopy 3 was lowered into the water, the beast swam quickly toward the opened hatch but came up short when the doors silently closed. The hand slowly reached out and touched Snoopy's smooth, torpedolike shape. When the probe did nothing but sit there at zero buoyancy, the amphibian gently slapped at it, then struck it again as the device dipped its nose and then righted level. The beast became bored with the small craft and swam once again along the bottom, every once in a while rising and quickly peering through the underwater windows of *Teacher.* Finally it came to a window where several people sat on the opposite side of the clear acrylic. It closely examined all the faces within its view, slowly becoming agitated by what it saw. A second, smaller animal approached and was quickly chased away by the larger, more aggressive one. Even several of the plesiosaurs' came close, out of curiosity, and were abruptly swiped at. They shot off into the lower extremities of the lagoon.

THERE WAS A buzz of excitement as Jenks made his way to the additional control panel he had installed in the lounge. Virginia was already there and he smiled at her as he sat down next to her. Jack was leaning against the bulkhead, Sarah sitting in front of him, by the large underwater window. Carl and Danielle were seated next to her. When Jack nodded, Jenks turned to the controls and threw a switch. The four monitors arrayed around the lounge came to life, along with the six-inch screen in front of Jenks. The probe's nose camera came on at the same time as the lights did, and they saw the bright green waters of the lagoon illuminate in a twelve-foot diameter around Snoopy 3 as the small craft bobbed just below the surface.

"Here we go," the master chief said as he toggled Snoopy forward and down into the depths. Virginia patted his leg and then placed her hands in her lap.

Snoopy made a half circle under the boat and came out the opposite side, then made for a compass heading of magnetic north, toward the falls. As it approached, the water became choppier, but the master chief held it on course and depth, only adjusting the speed as he advanced the throttle to compensate for a current that was starting to push the probe back toward the center of the lagoon. Then Snoopy started forward again, its thruster started to gain a foothold in the current. To conserve power, Jenks kept only the forward light and camera on, the latter now picking up white water ahead as the two-hundred-foot falls struck the lagoon's surface. He lowered Snoopy's nose as the water became rough. He sent the device deep to smooth out its ride beneath the catarata. Ellenshaw was so nervous during this that he began ringing his hands together until Heidi reached and stilled them.

Despite its depth, Snoopy 3 was in tumult as it reached the cascading falls. Its nose dipped again as the free-falling water above the device created turbulence as deep as thirty-five feet. Snoopy rolled to the right as the nose came up, only to immediately lose buoyancy as the full weight of the falls struck its hardened plastic body. On camera, it almost looked as if the probe were being manhandled by otherworldly forces as it was tossed by the natural falls. Jenks wasn't too concerned, as his concentration was centered on the panel in front of him, where he had readouts showing speed, depth, and power usage. He held steady, then throttled back as the vortex of water pressure started to lessen. Most everyone in the room breathed a sigh of relief as Snoopy edged its way past the extreme edge of the waterfall and into calmer waters.

"Chief, can we get a fathometer reading on the depth of the water where she's at right now," Sarah asked.

Jenks toggled a switch. The readout on his remote control panel went from passive to active sonar. "I can only use this a few times, so this will be a quick scan of her surroundings. Just watch the monitors and the readout will appear there."

From within the confines of the ship, everyone in the boat felt as well as heard the powerful sonar ping that coursed through the water.

OUTSIDE, BELOW THE boat, the animal brought its large hands up to its head and started thrashing about as the loud underwater noise struck. Then it settled down, shaking its head from side to side, as the sound dwindled to nothing.

"THERE YOU GO. It looks like we have twenty-five on the starboard side, thirty-seven on the port and . . . well, she's a deep channel, numbers are still going up," Jenks said.

The numbers from the sonar reading resembled those they had received from *Teacher* when they had probed the bottom of the lagoon. The body of water looked to be bottomless, with the exception of two large shelves on either side of Snoopy. Other than that small anomaly, the sheer rock walls appeared to extend down infinitely.

"I am convinced this is a caldera—what we're looking at is a lava shaft that runs hundreds of thousands of feet below the surface here," Sarah said. "There's no other explanation."

"Maybe we just found the front door and long hallway to hell," Jenks joked.

The poorly timed joke was met with deathly silence by everyone. Caldera or underworld, the question remained whether any of the missing students were still alive.

FARBEAUX AND MENDEZ faced their men, on the far side of the rapids. The lagoon lay just beyond the bend, and the Frenchman had just seen the American craft sitting at the center of the lagoon, well lit and inviting within this hidden wonder.

"Now am I clear—we are to use the shoreline as cover as we skirt the Americans. We will be lost among the shore clutter if they are actively using sonar as security."

The men nodded. Even Rosolo admired the Frenchman's approach. It was just too bad he would not be following him. He had a detour to make.

Mendez, rotund and ridiculous in his shiny wetsuit, went from man to man speaking Spanish to each. Farbeaux caught a phrase or two. The Colombian was promising they would have riches beyond belief if they succeeded in their mission.

Farbeaux suspected the mines were indeed full of gold, but how much could be removed before the Brazilian government moved in to take their find? That fool Mendez thought he could buy off anyone, any government. But why should a government accept his pitiful payout when they could have the entirety of the greatest gold find in history? The greedy Colombian couldn't be allowed to live once they reached El Dorado. The Frenchman didn't need the Brazilian authorities to ever gain full knowledge of the other treasures that were hidden in veins underneath the ground here, which the gold would lead them to. No, he could not allow that.

Farbeaux placed his face mask over his head and made sure his rebreather was operating properly. He held his hand in the air, then slowly lowered it toward the water and started off. He was followed by Mendez and his men. The last to enter the water was Captain Rosolo, who would swim as far as the boat with them.

"IT LOOKS LIKE a very wide shelf on the right, about thirty-five feet I would say," Jenks said as Snoopy entered the cave behind the falls. The light picked up the calm water and the master chief proclaimed loudly that there was indeed a current inside, of about three knots.

"That means the waters in here must empty out somewhere," Sarah surmised.

Snoopy shallowed as Jenks pulled upward on the toggle. The camera went from showing a solid green frame of water to a darker variant of the same as it aimed the camera up through the surface of the canal.

"Turning to the right," Jenks called as he angled Snoopy in that direction just as the probe came shallow to fifteen feet.

Carl pointed at the screen. "Look at that! The shelf you were talking about has actually been carved out—"

"Are those steps?" Virginia interrupted.

On the monitor, the camera picked out first one, then two steps that went off into the distance on either side of Snoopy.

These first two stone steps led to a third, then a fourth, and on and on.

Jack leaned in closer to the monitor. "Chief, can you get me a shot of the upper areas of the cavern?"

"Yeah, you see something?"

Jack just looked at him and didn't answer.

Jenks adjusted the right-side camera and brought three pounds of ballast into the small probe, tilting it to the left and raising the angle of the camera. As the lights disappeared into the darkness, the camera caught another sight that made everyone's mouth drop. Once again, a strained silence filled the cabin. Onscreen were level upon level of pillars and, beyond them, ornately carved walls.

"Look at those walls, how they angle inward toward the waterfall at the top," Virginia observed with awe.

"A pyramid," Keating said as he studied the camera's moving image. "It's a damned stepped pyramid."

"It's like we're looking at it inside out," Heidi said, moving closer.

Each level of the interior became smaller the farther toward the top they went. Each pillar lining its respective level served as a load-bearing strut, strengthening each story as they climbed higher toward the source of falls. Giant openings were visible beyond the pillars, indicating that there were portals into the mine itself.

"This is an impossible engineering feat," said Keating.

"The Inca must have turned the inside of a natural cave, or lava vent, into a more recognizable architectural interior. After all, they couldn't take anything out of here without praying and having their god Supay sanction the removal of his treasure," Sarah said and then looked around her at everyone. "I'm just guessing, of course." A silence followed.

"I think it's as good a theory as we have at the moment," Virginia finally said.

The camera continued to send back images of the vast expanse of the mine. Because of Snoopy's depth in the water and its being only the right-side lens that poked free of the surface, their view was limited. But to Jack, this information, along with what Sarah had gathered in the diving bell earlier, indicated that the mine shafts not only rose with the pyramid, but also would lead down into the earth, far beyond the level of the lagoon.

"Surfacing," Jenks finally called, anxious to see the pyramid in a better light. He and everyone in the section again leaned forward in their seats, as Snoopy broke the surface. "Turning on all her lights and cameras," he said, and quickly flipped the switches on the other three cameras and three sets of lights.

On the monitor, the screen image separated into four separate camera angles. One showed the long staircase as it rose out of the water and continued another fifteen or twenty steps above the surface of the entrance canal. The steps terminated at what looked like a giant flat rock, about two hundred feet in length.

"A platform?" Heidi wondered aloud.

"Close, Heidi," Jack said, uncrossing his arms. "Do you want to tell them, swabby?" He turned to Carl.

The lieutenant commander rose from his seat next to Danielle and pointed along the image on one of the wall-mounted monitors. "See how this rises out of the water as a solid square of stone with steps petering out in the middle, and then they start up again on either side of this platform? Now, look along the edge of this giant stone— see these?" He pointed to ten different protrusions that lined the edge of the platform. They looked like a set of longhorns, each horn branching out left and right about three feet each. "They're cleats, and what we're looking at here is a dock."

Everyone finally saw it. It was a two-hundred-foot-wide docking area, with two-pronged projections used for tying off boats. The stairs came up from either side of the dock, for swimmers to go to and from the canal.

"Think we can tie up there, Chief?" Jack asked.

"Be awful rough heading through those falls, not like the

smaller ones we went through earlier. I don't think so, Major. My bet would be she would be battered to pieces."

"I suspect there may be a mechanism inside that place, which can alter the direction and force of the falls, to draw the fury of the water away from entering and exiting boats," Heidi ventured. "That's how the ancients collected their treasure."

Jack just nodded. On the screen he saw Snoopy back away from the dock, giving the four bright lights a chance to take in more higher up. Several darkened objects became visible on the top of the platform, shapes that the voyagers had come to know intimately. Two towering statues of Supay, the Incan god of the underworld, rose majestically on either side of the huge dock. The stone carvings stared down on Snoopy with belligerent eyes that were heavily lidded and appeared to be made of solid gold as the light from the probe played on it. The artwork was far more meticulous than on the two statues they had passed at the tributary entrance. The stone was studded with gemstones of all shapes and sizes; rubies and emeralds lined the arms and wrists of the giants. The trident and ax were also made of gold, and looked even more lethal than the ones outside. Then the light picked up something on one deity's belly. The statue on the right had been vandalized. Professor Keating loudly voiced his outrage, making everyone else in the lounge jump.

"What kind of a hoax is this?" he shouted as he went to the nearest monitor and raised his glasses. As the others looked at the image closely, just more than one jaw dropped. Curses erupted throughout the lounge. If Jack hadn't been so taken aback he would have laughed. Etched in paint on the belly of the giant deity was a graffito that had traveled from the docks of the Brooklyn shipyards in New York to Africa and through all of Europe and Japan during World War II, once used as a universal marker in all the places where American troops had already been:

"So, how long will you need to decipher this message?" Jenks laughed, but inside he was just as stunned as everyone else.

"After the days and the danger our people faced in finding the Padilla route, we find *this*?" Heidi said angrily.

"Someone in our government has known all along that this was here," Virginia said, standing up. "What were they after, gold?"

Jack reached out and selected the proper switch on the intercom. "Stiles?"

"Yes, sir?"

"How's the transmitter coming?"

"Been online for five minutes Major; just finished up," Stiles answered from the main mast.

"Good. Get in here and get me Group, ASAP," Jack said as he watched the bobbing and unstable picture from Snoopy 3.

"On my way," was the quick answer.

"This can't be about gold," was all Jack said as he turned toward the radio room.

ROSOLO HAD LEFT the long line of men as they continued on past the American boat. He had easily swerved away without being noticed and swam toward the large hull, which was aglow with bright light emanating from the interior. He would have to be careful to avoid the underwater windows. He reached the stern, slowly made his way to the halfway point amidships, then studied the design. He placed his hand against the hull. He could feel the activity inside even through his gloves. He didn't need a flashlight, as the water was lit up as if he were inside a giant emerald. He reached into his bag and brought out a three-pound limpet charge. He placed it against the hull and pushed, engaging the large suction cups on the back of the mine. Then he traveled down toward the stern, where he'd estimated the boat's engines would be, and placed another charge there. As he set the timers for three minutes, he felt movement around him. It was as if something had swum by at a very fast speed, but as he turned he saw nothing.

JACKSON HAD TURNED back from the window to his sonar when the major had called for a situation report on the repairs for the radio. He was no longer looking outside, to see the approach of Rosolo or that of the creature. He even failed to notice that he had unintentionally changed the setting of the sonar alarm, the very specialized piece of naval equipment that had been previously activated to warn of the proximity of an underwater threat.

"THIS IS TEACHER Actual one, on the line for Group Director Compton," Stiles said into the large handheld phone, then he set the instrument down and switched the communications to the speaker, to enable the voyagers to hold a conference call.

"Jack, where in the hell have you been?" Niles asked.

"Well, we had a bit of wildlife trouble here; knocked out our transmitter."

"Boris and Natasha had your visual for most of the day, and then we had a circuit failure on her and we lost picture. But before the old girl went down we saw who we thought was Stiles on the main mast working on your dish. Any luck finding those kids, Jack?"

"Negative, but we have discovered something we need you to check on."

"What's that?"

With just those two words Jack heard how some of the hope had drained from Niles's voice. Finding no survivors was not what the director had wanted to hear.

"Stand by to receive a fax of a still photo. I think you'll find it interesting."

Stiles placed an eight-by-ten of the graffito painted on the belly of the eighty-foot statue of Supay into the scanner and then hit send.

Several moments later Niles came back on, furious.

"All right, I want you and Carl to disembark *Teacher* and go it alone in the search. Get everyone else out of there, Jack. We've been had by someone. Either the president is lying outright to me or someone is lying to him, but I'm not taking any chances. Someone knew what was there and didn't warn us—or Helen. Get your people out now!"

"I haven't had a chance to tell you about the two bodies we discovered on the way in," he said.

"What bodies?"

Jack took the next few minutes and explained about Kennedy and the tactical release key. Needless to say, Niles Compton was about to explode, without any nuclear key being inserted.

THE CREATURE WAS watching the shipboard activity through the port window. Sarah entered the lounge area after Jack had gone out to contact Niles. The animal became still as it recognized her face from the diving bell. It then saw Sarah turn and leave, disappearing through the hatch. The creature became agitated once again as it shook its massive head. Then it dove and streaked to the other side of the boat by swiftly passing beneath it. The animal was by no means enraptured by Sarah; on the contrary, it was interested in her because it couldn't figure out how she had transferred from the diving bell into *Teacher*.

Sudden movement caught the beast's eye at the stern section of the hull. A black form was barely visible there. The beast could see it was alive—an intruder. It kicked out with its legs, and the mighty fins of its feet stirred an invisible vortex through the water as it was propelled at a fantastic speed through the lagoon.

The man felt movement as it passed by and turned, but the creature was already around him and turning back. The animal stilled its actions for a moment. It watched as the intruder rose two feet in the water until he could see inside one of the submerged windows. That was when the amphibian charged through the water straight at Rosolo, who was blessed with a thief's instincts to know when something wasn't right. He turned just before the beast struck. His eyes wide, he tried desperately to swim away.

"THE SEAL, KENNEDY, had a tactical nuclear arming key on his body, Niles, and he was contaminated with radioactivity, according to the autopsy. So whoever ordered them in here with a tactical weapon more than likely gave them orders to blow up the mine. I need you to find out why they would risk these kids like that."

"I've been on the Kennedy investigation for hours, and so far Pete and I are drawing a blank."

"It has something to do with whatever else is in that mine. I can't believe they would risk a nuclear incident just to protect gold. Find out whose game we're involved in and get it stopped, sir, or we may be up a creek here."

"I'll do my best, but for right now, get our people out of there, Jack; do you understand, get them out. But I have to ask that you and Carl stay to get Helen's team out if at all possible."

Sarah, who had listened in on this part of the conversation, patted Jack on the back and left the communications center to go aft into the lounge once again.

Jackson suddenly noticed the sonar was on the wrong setting. "Major, we have contact, bearing two nine-seven and coming on fast, thirty-two knots and closing!" he said as he reached out and turned the audio alarm back on.

"Niles, we may have a situation here; I'll try and get back to you. It seems our animal friend may be paying us another visit."

"Animal? You mean the goddamned stories are real? That breaks it, Jack, get the hell—"

Niles was cut off as *Teacher* was jolted by a massive explosion amidships. The detonation sent everyone sprawling to the floor. *Teacher* immediately started listing to port, taking on two tons of water a minute as her composite hull split and buckled in the very section where everyone else had gathered. The lounge.

THE CREATURE TOOK Rosolo by the neck and rammed him straight into the water jet of engine number two, momentarily knocking him senseless. He tried to gather his panicked thoughts when he felt the beast's webbed fingers close once again over his head. Just as his attacker drew back to slam Rosolo's head into the stanchion, the underwater world was rocked by a violence the animal had never encountered before. It released the Colombian and sped away, grasping its head against the pressure wave that slammed into it. Rosolo, lucky beyond measure, was tossed about like a twig in the roiling currents that gripped the waters surrounding *Teacher*. His very own bombs had saved his life. He shook his head and made for the shore and the mine beyond.

MENDENHALL AND CORPORAL Shaw had been working on the damaged engine when the explosion knocked them from their feet. A large piece of composite hull exploded into the engine room and caught Shaw in the chest. Acting like a buzz saw, it sank through his body to his backbone. Mendenhall raised his head out of the water that was quickly filling the bilges and rising above the grated floor. He looked around for Shaw and saw he was dead. The sergeant had been protected from flying debris by the damaged engine they had been working on. However, although he shook his head to clear it, he knew he was partially deaf, as he had heard nothing after the loud roar of the explosion. He looked for the source of the blast and saw a six-foot-diameter hole blown in the aft side, half above and half below the waterline.

"Help me before we sink!" he shouted.

At that moment Sanchez entered quickly through the hatch and then sealed it closed. Looking around, he saw Shaw's body floating and Mendenhall struggling with the diving bell, which had come loose from its cradle.

"Help me!" Mendenhall repeated.

Sanchez moved quickly through the rising water and helped the sergeant, as he realized in an instant what it was he was trying to do.

The bell was swinging back and forth in front of the damaged hull. Sanchez and Mendenhall needed literally to cram the round bell into the smaller hole in the boat's side to stop the flooding. Sanchez knew immediately that the sergeant wasn't going to have enough play on the umbilicus to reach the damaged area, and splashed though the water to the main control.

Mendenhall doubled his efforts to keep the one-ton bell swinging while Sanchez tried to time its movement. It would come close to the hole and then swing backward, always about a foot short of wedging itself in. When he thought he had it timed, Sanchez hit the descend switch that operated the winch, but nothing happened. Then he realized the winch was moving, but very slowly. The bell swung back out again and this time as it started forward, with Mendenhall pushing, he hit the emergency release for the winch. It broke free from the umbilical lines and slammed hard into the hull. The hole exploded with water one last time as the bell settled and successfully blocked most of the damaged area.

"It worked!" Mendenhall screamed for all he was worth. Then he saw Sanchez start stuffing everything he could find into the gaps where the bell hadn't blocked the inrushing water.

They were still sinking, but now they would have an extended life of maybe twenty minutes if they could get under way.

* * *

AMIDSHIPS, ALL HELL had broken loose. Jenks fought to get his head above water but his foot was trapped underneath one of the couches. The master chief thought his leg might also be broken from having been hit sharply by a fallen monitor. He cried out and swore when Professor Keating floated by, face down, in the rising waters. He knew his beloved boat had been dealt a death blow and that he would more than likely go down with it. He struggled but his foot was wedged in good. Every time he moved his leg, he screamed in pain and frustration.

Three feet away, Virginia surfaced. Blood was flowing freely from a broken nose, and at first she thought her left arm was gone. She felt relief when she raised it and saw it still attached, although cut very deeply. She felt a hand on her other arm and saw Danielle surface, choking and coughing up water. Virginia saw crew members' bodies were being tossed like bathtub toys by the incoming tidal wave that was rushing through the damaged hull. Three of the lab technicians were clearly dead; they had been standing right where the explosion had disintegrated the composite material. Then she panicked as her eyes fell on Jenks just as the water started to cover his head.

"Chief!" she yelled, and pushed Danielle forward. "Help me with him!"

They both dove under and were instantly grateful that the lights had remained on. Virginia went low and Danielle high as they both pulled on Jenks's broken leg. He screamed but his foot came out from under the couch and they all surfaced.

As the master chief came up, spitting out dirty water, he saw immediately to what degree they were in trouble. The water was coming in too fast, which told him that whatever had happened had mostly occurred below the water line. He saw Ellenshaw was trying to open the latch to the next compartment.

"No, Professor, no!" Jenks screamed loudly over the

noise of the incoming flood. "Stop him! We can't flood the aft areas; we may already be taking in water!"

Danielle broke free and quickly swam over to grab the old man. He turned to her in shock, and for a moment could only point mutely toward the glass porthole of the hatch.

"That section is taking on water, Sarah's in there!" he finally croaked.

Danielle threw the professor aside and looked through the port. Sarah was lying against one of the underwater viewing ports where the damage was sustained; it was cracked and shooting water into that section. Sarah looked unconscious; the water, though not filling that section as fast as the lounge area, was slowly creeping up to the level of her neck.

"Chief, we have to get in there," Danielle said.

The master chief, in much pain and assisted by Virginia, inched his way through the chest-high water to look for himself through the porthole into the next section.

"Okay, the hatch on the far side of that section is sealed; we'll flood only that area. Go ahead, get her!"

The Frenchwoman pulled up on the handle and the hatch exploded outward. The room flooded immediately and Sarah went under. Danielle swam her way over and reached for the young second lieutenant. Her hand came into contact with Sarah's hair and she pulled. Then Danielle pulled Sarah free of the aft section and dragged her into the lounge.

Jenks yelled for Virginia and Ellenshaw to get him to the cockpit.

"What about the rest of them?" Virginia asked.

"They're dead, Doctor, can't you see that? Now move or we're going to go down. Look at the list!"

As Virginia followed his eyes, she could see that *Teacher* was leaning at least forty degrees to port. That sight was enough to start her pulling the master chief forward toward the sealed hatch that led into communications.

As Danielle reached the lounge area, holding the young woman under the arms as she treaded water, she saw Sarah's chest rise and fall more rapidly as she started to awaken. At that moment, the hull section split along the area already heavily damaged by the explosion. Danielle was pelted by sharp-edged pieces as the creature breached the hull and came up through the neck-high water. She screamed. Virginia, Ellenshaw, and Jenks turned just as the beast reached for Danielle and Sarah. Danielle kicked out at the creature but lost her hold on Sarah as she did so. She then watched helplessly as the beast took Sarah by one arm and raised her up out of the water. The animal roared, swiping at Danielle and making a grab for her also. The sound was hoarse, but loud enough to shock them all as the overhead light caught its greenish and gold features. Unable to reach Danielle, it took Sarah below the surface of the flood and then out through the split in the hull.

Jenks felt absolutely helpless as Sarah was dragged out. Virginia screamed with rage as she ineffectually shoved the master chief forward with her good arm. Danielle could only stare at the spot where the beast had been only a moment before.

JACK FOUGHT HIS way out of the communications room after quickly tending to the injuries of Stiles. Jackson had been killed when an overhead power box had ripped free of its mountings and struck him in the head, but Stiles was still moaning from an electrical shock that coursed through his body when the radio blew up. His face had been struck by several large pieces of glass and steel.

Jack next made it into the companionway and saw Carl, or at least his legs. The lieutenant commander was struggling, trapped underneath the overturned navigation table. Jack told him to hold still.

"Hurry, Jack, this thing is about to snap both of my legs!"

Jack reached the large table and lifted as much as he could, but one corner had been blown off its mountings and had sunk deep into the deck where water was oozing around the steel frame. Then another loud groaning sound was heard as *Teacher* suddenly shifted and then listed crazily ten more degrees, making the weight of the table shift just enough for Carl to hurriedly pull his legs free.

"Drop it!" he yelled as he backed his way to the bulkhead.

Jack let go of the heavy table and jumped back quickly onto dry, nonconductive floor as it shorted out when the electronic package hit the puddle of water. Then he began to make his way toward Carl, when he heard pounding coming from the closed hatchway behind him.

"The lounge, Jack. There's people trapped in there!" Carl said as he struggled to his feet by himself. Jack splashed to the door as the incoming water beneath the table rapidly spread.

A woman's hand was pounding at the port glass set inside the aluminum door. Jack saw it was Virginia; on the other side of the door, the water was lapping at her chin. Caught in the crook of her arm was the master chief, just barely keeping his head above the surface.

"Carl, make your way into the cockpit and get ready to slam that door," the major yelled over his shoulder. "I have an idea. Call engineering and see if the engines are still above the waterline."

Carl limped as fast as he could toward the cockpit and tried the intercom on the bulkhead. It started shorting out as soon as he hit the plastic button. On the overhead speakers he could barely make out a shouting voice; he thought it might be Will Mendenhall, but he wasn't sure. Then the intercom shorted out one last time and died. All he knew now was someone was alive back there and hadn't drowned yet. He quickly looked out of the cockpit and saw that the nose of *Teacher* was starting to rise out of the water.

"Jack, were going down. I don't know if it's the stern or if we have so much flooding amidships that she's bending at her gaskets!"

Jack thought he heard Carl hollering but ignored it as he fought with the latch for the lounge section. Virginia was pushed aside and then the master chief's angry face appeared at the glass. He was shaking his head no and pointing behind Jack, who could barely make out Jenks's voice as he shouted, *"Beach her!"* The old seaman quickly pointed at the hole the explosion had made and made a swimming motion. Jack finally understood: the survivors in the lounge should escape through the damaged section and swim for it. He grimaced, not liking the plan, but the master chief was right; he wouldn't be able to close the hatch because of the pressure of the water behind it, and, even if he could open it, the cockpit would be flooded and that would ensure that *Teacher* foundered. He quickly turned away and started for the cockpit.

"YOU AND ELLENSHAW swim for the breach, Frenchie," the master chief yelled at Danielle. The professor was having a hard time keeping his head above water, but obeyed. "Okay, sweet cheeks," Jenks winked at Virginia, "I hope you can hold your breath, because this section is now below the surface of the lagoon and she's bending like a fishing pole!"

"I'm not going without you, Jenks," Virginia said, taking a mouthful of water as her reward for speaking.

"You watch too many movies; I'm not the hero type. Follow me, doll," he ordered, as he dove under just as the flooding reached the overhead lights, shorting them out and sending a cascade of sparks over the surface of the undulating water.

Virginia dove with the master chief. She accidentally took in another mouthful of foul-tasting water when she ran into the torn body of Professor Keating. Then she shoved him out of the way and swam, trying desperately to get out of the nightmare she now found herself in.

JACK PUSHED PAST Carl, who was leaning heavily on the bulkhead and trying to figure out what Jack was doing.

"What about those people?" Carl yelled, pointing toward the flooded lounge.

"They're going out another way. The chief said for us to beach *Teacher* before she founders." Jack reached for the start switch and prayed the engine would fire. As he turned it, he heard a soft rumble course through *Teacher* and he throttled her forward. She was heavy as at least one, maybe two, or even three sections were fully flooded. Then he tried to turn her by using the rudder control on the armrest. Nothing happened; *Teacher* continued straight on toward the right side of the falls.

"She's not turning!" Jack said frustratedly as he again pulled the hand toggle to the left but *Teacher* continued going right.

"The main jets must have been damaged; they're frozen in position. We've got to get this thing grounded somewhere, Jack."

The major thought quickly. "The mine! We can get her into the mine and beach her there, it's our only chance!"

"Shit," Carl exclaimed as he rolled into the copilot's chair and quickly buckled his harness. "Go, Jack, go," he yelled as he braced himself against the glass.

Jack pushed the throttle all the way to its stops and *Teacher* struggled forward, her midsection below water and her aft end sticking up, her water jets and damaged rudder barely beneath the surface. He had a hard time seeing, as the boat was bowing up at both ends. *Teacher* started to gather forward momentum and Jack felt her start leaning to the right as the water in her flooded sections shifted.

"Oh, shit; can you at least center her with the middle of the falls?" Everett asked as calmly as he could.

"We have no steering at all!"

Jack pulled back the throttles but it was too late. *Teacher* was under the crushing falls, and the weight and fierceness of the water forced her nose down beneath the foaming tumult. Then they felt the impact as *Teacher* slammed into the outside wall of the cave opening, tearing the right-side cockpit glass away and sending a ton of water into the bridge, hitting Carl so hard it momentarily stunned him. Suddenly there was a wrenching impact abovedecks as the mainmast was torn out of its mountings. Jack could only pray that there had been no one on or near it. The fall of the tower was heard as it struck the upper deck of the last five sections, ripping a massive gash in the superstructure as the weight of the aluminum tower rocked her from side to side. Then *Teacher* shot through the falls and into the dark interior of the mine. She immediately rammed the solid rock wall inside the cave, tearing a section fifty feet long along her right side.

Jack felt the engine go, and then the control panel in front of him went with a shower of sparks. Still, by sheer momentum alone, *Teacher* sped along through the opening, hitting the stone wall again, knocking Jack into the center console. Then he felt the keel strike solid bottom and her nose rose into the air as *Teacher* hit the first of the stone steps on the right side of the ancient dock. She glanced off at first and then the weight of her flooded sections turned her again, slamming her bottom into the steps. This time her momentum sent her violently up and out of the water. For a moment Jack thought the twenty-one-ton *Teacher* was going to shoot out over the top of the stone steps and onto the dock, but when she slammed back down she slid backward fifty feet to finally lodge onto the steps with only her stern section in the water.

"Oh, that's going to leave a mark," Carl said as he removed his harness.

Jack sat back to catch his breath; as he did, he felt a cool draft coming through the torn window frames on the right side.

"The chief and navy can take it out of my check," he said as he reached down and unbuckled his seat harness. "Come on, Commander Everett; let's see how many people I killed with my driving."

FARBEAUX HAD JUST entered the falls when he heard the two explosions underwater. He dove deep until the water had calmed, and then he surfaced. Now he, Mendez, and the Colombian's fourteen men watched from above as the American boat came to rest on the steps that led from the canal at a point just beneath the mammoth statue. He gritted his teeth and knew exactly what had happened.

"When your man Rosolo arrives, I am going to kill him,"

he said as he slowly brought up a nine-millimeter pistol and pointed it at Mendez.

His men saw this and brought up their own weapons.

"Please, please," Mendez said, holding his hands out from both sides of his rotund body. "There is no need for this. If my man Rosolo did this thing, you can have him, but we can only fail to do what we came here for if we can't think clearly," he lied. He turned to his men, "Lower your weapons. That is an order."

Farbeaux kept his pistol up. "You cannot tell me he acted without orders from his master."

"I believe killing them would have to have been done eventually. But I did not order it at this time. Besides, the Americans are finished; they will now be far too busy just surviving to interfere with us."

Farbeaux saw from their high vantage point that the American boat still had some power. He holstered his handgun and then reached down and picked up a small satchel, angrily kicking his wetsuit against his rebreathing unit.

"Follow me, and keep strict noise discipline until we are well within this upper shaft. No flashlights until I say so. I have to discover if we need to go down into the mine, or up."

As Farbeaux turned his back, Mendez sneered and then waved his men forward. Rosolo would have to find them on his own. But then again, if Mendez knew his man, he would finish the job he had started, possibly before he met up with them again.

For now, El Dorado waited and Mendez could not wait for his just rewards.

20

RYAN took the offered phone from one of the Delta operatives who were now assigned as security for Operation Spoiled Sport.

"This is Ryan."

"Lieutenant, we've had a major problem with the expedition; they no longer appear to be in the lagoon. Boris and Natasha is picking up an empty space where *Teacher* had been. She also picked out those fifty-plus men making their way past the rapids. It looks like they intend to enter the lagoon. Listen, Mr. Ryan, Jack did manage to get the heat emitters placed before this happened, so you will have an illuminated target area. Is your team ready to deploy?" Niles asked.

"Sir, we really should consider sending our team in on the ground. There's glitch after glitch with this billion-dollar boondoggle."

"Get it to work, Ryan. The president says absolutely no ground incursion, so it's Spoiled Sport or nothing. We have got to keep this unknown ground element off their back."

"Yes, sir," he replied.

"Now look, CIA has confirmed that there are no Peruvian or Brazilian units out there, so they have to be bad guys headed their way. Zap 'em, Mr. Ryan, you hear me? Protect our people. Get in the air!" Niles hung up.

Ryan handed the phone back and looked at the Delta sergeant. And then he jumped when he heard an alarm sound.

Two men ran up the stairway and into the converted 747, carrying fire extinguishers.

"Goddammit, what now?" he asked as smoke started billowing out of the large double doorway of the aircraft.

EVENT GROUP CENTER
NELLIS AFB, NEVADA

Niles sat at his desk and rubbed his temples. He removed his glasses and then slammed his hand on the table.

"Are you sure you heard an explosion just before communications were lost?" Pete Golding asked.

Niles didn't look up. He just nodded, not caring to use his voice. He took a deep breath and shoved the still picture of the giant statue and its graffito-marked belly toward Pete, whose eyes widened.

"This whole thing is a hoax?"

"Pete, we need Europa to do some digging, and I mean *dig*. Someone knows about Padilla's lagoon, and I want to know who lied to us and why. Can you help me?"

Pete studied the photo from *Teacher* once again and then something clicked in his mind about the familiar caption on the cartoon that everyone who had looked at the still had missed. He looked up. "Yeah, I can help."

"I have a man flying out to interview the lone survivor of the 1942 expedition. He should be able to at least tell us what it was they were after out there."

"Then let's get to it; we can cover a lot of ground until he checks in."

Niles jumped at the chance to be doing something, anything. But the feeling remained that an ancient trap had been set, and that Jack and the others had walked right into it.

TEACHER WAS SITTING high on the stone steps. Her flooded compartments were draining due to the fifty-degree lean to her port side as she had come to rest on the staircase.

The towering statue loomed above the diminutive boat that lay broken at its feet.

The major crawled out of the cockpit through the broken windowframe and then helped Carl through. They climbed slowly down the nose and slid to the stone beneath. Jack turned on his flashlight and shined it around. Carl did the same as they hurried back toward the stern. Their light was seemingly absorbed by the blackness surrounding *Teacher*. As they looked around, an unfamiliar rustling noise sounded from what seemed a great distance, and could be heard even over the waterfall that fell in the center of the pyramid.

"What's that?" Everett asked as he shined his flashlight into the air.

"Uh-oh," Jack said.

Suddenly the air was alive around them. Giant bats had decided the intrusion of noise and vibration *Teacher* had made was quite enough. They swarmed like angry bees as they circled Jack and Carl, who dove for their lives, hitting the wet steps and covering their heads as bats grazed them in their frenzy. If just one of the large animals struck them solidly, it would have been bone crushing. Then as suddenly as the raid had started, the bats were gone.

"I can live without that!" Carl said as he stood up again. "Where did they go," he said as he shined his flashlight upward once more.

"The falls, I guess. There must be another opening up there that comes out through the river that creates the falls. Come on; let's get our people out of *Teacher*."

WHEN JACK SHINED his light into the communications section, he saw that Stiles was on his feet, trying to revive the clearly unrevivable Jackson. He shook his head and moved on silently. Carl flashed his own light on the glass and looked in and cursed when he saw the dead navy man. He then followed Jack down the row of windows. No one appeared to be in the navigation section, as they suspected there wouldn't be. Then they came to the lounge. Their lights immediately picked out three bodies floating in the waist-high water. Jack recognized Keating immediately. He was floating faceup and was actually in a slow spin as the water drained from the damaged section. By the looks of his body he had been caught dead center of the explosion; his right arm was missing, and half of his head. Jack moved the light and saw that Dr. Waltrip was lying crumpled on top of Sergeant Larry Ito, who looked as if he had tried to shield her. But the explosion had killed them both. Jack swallowed hard when he didn't see Sarah. He hoped she was with the master chief and others who had made it out.

Carl looked inside the lounge and cried out when he saw the bodies. He shined the light around, hoping to see someone else, or someone breathing.

"We're one hell of a rescue team, Jack."

The major didn't respond. His light was now trained on the opening of the mine. The water churned and rolled in the violence of the falls, and in that maelstrom of foam he saw no one. The survivors from *Teacher* were alone and in the dark.

SARAH AWOKE AND immediately started choking. She fought her way back through a dark unconsciousness that threatened to overwhelm her just like an induced coma. She rolled over and threw up a stomachful of water, then heaved and then vomited more foul-tasting fluid. She tried to push herself up from the overly hot and wet floor but fell back down. She knew she was hurt somewhere but couldn't for the life of her think straight enough to find out where. Then she pushed up again and collapsed, screaming in pain, when she realized her right wrist was broken. It was then that she thought clearly enough to remember it hadn't been broken in the initial violence of whatever it was that had happened in the boat; it had snapped as she was being pulled down through the water.

She used her other hand to push herself up off the hot stone. As she peered around in the darkness she could barely make out long, hot wisps of steam coming through the stone floor and the walls. Some strange luminescence was also emanating from those walls, providing enough light that she could see her hand as she held it up, almost as if she were viewing things through the green-tinted lense of a night scope. She brought her wrist closer to her face; the damaged section was already swelling. It was broken, all right.

Then she noticed she could hear running water and smell fresh vegetation. Then she heard a hoarse growl. She shot back against a wall using her ass and good hand, the fingers of which touched an object not made of stone. She grasped it; it was a pole of some kind. But as she tried to use leverage against it to stand, it started to tilt off balance. She let go but too late, the pole crashed to the ground with a loud clang and the sound of breaking glass. She looked down and did a double take. Unless Padilla was centuries ahead of his time, someone had indeed beaten even Helen Zachary to El Dorado. Lying at her feet was a light stand. Old, rusty, and three legged, with six high-powered lamps. Her eyes followed a power cord to another stand, this one upright. The cord led from that to still another.

"What the . . . ?" she mumbled as she saw in the unnatural green light that there were six stands in all. They had been arranged in a semicircle facing inward from the ninety-foot perimeter they had been placed in. Now the graffito picked up by the camera on Snoopy 3 was starting to make sense.

Sarah glanced around her but could see no generator that the light stands had been connected to. She followed one thick cable to a wall, and from there to an opening that was about seven feet in diameter. It looked as if it had been burrowed out of solid rock. She tentatively reached out with her foot and touched a raised step, then another and another. She slowly backed down the several steps she had taken, not knowing if she wanted to head that way in the darkness. At least here she had that strange phosphorescence to see by. Curious, she ran her hand along the wall and then brought it to her face. Her fingers were covered in some sort of natural tritium. Her entire hand glowed softly as she quickly wiped it on her pant leg.

"What in the hell is going on here?" she blurted out.

She looked closer and could see that the glowing particles were actually ancient writings of some kind; indeed, the whole wall was imbedded with the mineral but only parts of it were carved, creating a relief. Possibly an ancient people had spelled out their history. She wondered if the writings were Incan.

Her eyes caught on a darker object that had been stuck into one wall. As she approached she could see that it was a torch. She felt it and determined that it was made of some kind of metal, a rough iron perhaps. She tried to pull it free of its mounting but it was stuck with hundreds of years of grime. She doubled her efforts. As it finally came loose she almost lost her balance with the sudden change of momentum. Some sort of fuel substance was still embedded in its end. She felt in her pockets and found the lighter she always carried for the one chance, she had always joked, where she might find herself deep in an underground cave with no flashlight. She used her thumb to bring the lighter to life and she raised it to the tip of the old iron torch. It flamed to life. She held the torch away from her and examined her surroundings more fully.

All around her were strange images and hieroglyphs. Drawings of animals lined the walls, and images of small people. She could see the people were in chains as they toiled, bearing heavy loads on their heads and shoulders, while Incan taskmasters stood by with menacing whips and clubs. Far more menacing were the skulls. They lined the entire chamber at about head height. There were at least a thousand that had been inlaid into the solid rock. The torchlight also revealed stone slabs, like bunks, covering the floor. The cavern held room upon room with large seating areas. Around her, ancient chains lined the walls, most broken but a few looking as if they had been used only yesterday. Sarah picked out evidence of fire pits, long dead, in the center of the cavern, lining a deep grotto. The ancient stone flooring was worn smooth by the countless footsteps of slaves long dead.

Sarah moved the torch around, following the long history along the walls of what had to have been the Sincaro Indians and their Peruvian slave masters. Some images depicted load upon load of gold being mined from this site. Others were pictographs of strange green minerals being pulled from the depths of giant pits. She was studying one such rendering when a burst of steam erupted from the wall twenty feet to her right. She leaned down and felt the wet floor, and was amazed at how hot it was. She pulled her hand back and then touched the floor again, this time lightly. She knew then that, indeed, there was underground seismic activity here. That explained the difference in water temperature the deeper into the lagoon one went.

She held the torch up once again to examine the walls. There were depictions of many of the creatures she had seen in the diving bell. They stood like guards before the images of small men and women. *These must be the Sincaro*, she thought as she lightly touched one of the reliefs.

A clear picture was emerging: The beasts were trained in these lower levels to watch and feed the Sincaro. Whatever was mined here was too dangerous for the Inca to supervise. So they trained these beasts to be the Sincaro's overseers.

Sarah turned her attention to the skulls lining the walls. Not only were they small, presumably of the Sincaro, but there were also larger bones and skulls belonging to the strange creatures. So the fate of the overseers was the same as slave. Death.

Turning from the wall, she shined the torch along the center canal. It, too, was carved from the stone and looked to be twenty or thirty feet deep. Sarah suspected that these canals ran from the top of the pyramid, originating from the river that fed the interior falls, all the way through from level to level, transporting the ore from one level to another.

She even saw crumbling block and tackle used to fight the gravity of the canal as ore was shipped up, indicating that she was in the very deepest part of El Dorado. The whole mine must have been inundated with these canals. It was the most ingenious method of moving ore from place to place that she had ever heard of.

Something grunted in the darkness beside the moving water and Sarah held up the torch in that direction. Her eyes widened when she saw the large creature rise from the man-made canal and swim easily into the large grotto that took up the entire center of the huge cave. It came to shallow water and stood, fully eight feet tall. The large, powerful-looking arms were laid easily at its side.

Sarah swallowed and looked up at the creature. She remembered its huge black eyes from the diving bell incident. She winced as she moved her broken wrist and then a memory returned.

"You pulled me out of the boat, didn't you?"

The beast moved its legs as it shifted weight from one leg to the other. Its gills on either side of it jawline moved in and out as its mouth opened and closed, obviously trying to breathe in enough air to have strength on land. She realized that although the creature was amphibious at the very least, its underdeveloped lungs must not be capable of sustaining it for long periods out of the water.

"Wouldn't Ellenshaw love to get a look at you? I think he would crap himself," she muttered.

Viewing the animal close up, without the color-deluding dark waters of the lagoon interfering, she could see that it was really just an enormous mutation of a freshwater cichlid, a mild-mannered species one could buy in any aquarium-supplies store in the States.

Sarah studied the swaying creature as it studied her, more than just intrigued, but that still didn't mean that this magnificent being didn't scare the hell out of her.

The beast barked hoarsely twice and then slowly began to move off toward the deeper water. Trusting it not to attack her, Sarah turned back to the pictures that seemed to glow against the light, and reexamined the ancient drawings. She looked closely at the mineral that the creatures brought from deep in the mine and wondered what it was. *Emeralds, maybe?* She held the torch closer to the wall and saw the spot that depicted the area where the dead were placed. She saw that both Sincaro and the creatures were buried side by side, as if they were equals in their misery and finally their deaths.

"Bastards," she said under her breath as she thought about the riches the Inca had brought out of here on the labor and pain of others.

Sarah turned away and saw the bubbles of the beast's underwater retreat from the chamber.

"I'm not a slave and you're not going to keep me here," she called as she turned toward the opening with the steps.

She suddenly stopped, as she thought she heard a gasp and then a sigh. She turned to trace the sound to its source. It came from the far wall. She held up the torch and could make out a small opening at the base of the excavated chamber. The light revealed discarded fish bones and rotted things strewn about the floor of the cave. Then she saw what she thought was a flick of fire emanating from one of the larger of the small caves. The light seemed to be coming from behind what looked like fabric of some sort.

Sarah grimaced at the smell coming from the wall of cave openings. She raised her damp shirt up to cover her nose and mouth, and walked toward the largest of the rooms. She slowly and carefully pulled the rotted flap of animal skin aside and leaned in, holding out the torch before her. Her eyes widened. There, lying and sitting around a natural pool of magma boiling in a small caldera that smelled strongly of sulphur, were the tattered remains of the Zachary expedition.

"Oh my god," said Sarah.

FARBEUX STOPPED THE men as the shaft started to spiral at a much steeper angle. He held up his light and shined it along the hot and sweating walls. Then he focused it on Mendez, who stood there breathing heavy. His men were just as sweaty and out of breath. They had been moving for only twenty minutes when they stopped for the first time.

"Tell me, are you tired, *señor*?" Farbeaux asked, smiling.

"Tired, hot, and beginning to believe that there is nothing more than old statues in this mine," Mendez answered angrily.

"Then maybe you wouldn't be interested in this," he said as he shined his large flashlight toward a three-inch vein of gold that streaked like a lightning bolt through the wet stone of the shaft.

Mendez's eyes widened as he dropped his small pack and ran toward the vein. He rubbed it with his fingers lovingly. His men, too, immediately totally lost any fatigue they had shown earlier.

Farbeaux lifted his small satchel and quickly noted the reading on the small device he had inside. He smiled and looked up.

"Now, you can be satisfied with this small deposit, or we can go to the place were El Dorado really begins."

Mendez beamed, totally rejuvenated. He reached down, removed his canteen from his belt, and swallowed some water.

"Lead the way, my friend. Where you go, we will follow."

21

EVENT GROUP CENTER
NELLIS AFB, NEVADA

ONCE again Niles was in a clean suit alongside Pete Golding in the clean room where the mainframe for the Cray supercomputer Europa was housed. They had been searching U.S. Army and Corps of Engineer databases for the past hour, hitting dead end after dead end.

"Gold—the army wouldn't have been after gold with World

War Two breaking out all over the globe; it just doesn't add up. So what else would send a specialist team down there?" Pete asked, leaning back in his chair and stretching.

"I agree, to expend time and effort, and using the military and OSS to save gold prospectors—I just don't buy it. Not with the way the war was going in 1942; we were still losing, remember?"

"Okay, so let's try to go through the back door. The senator said he had no names for the people the OSS pulled out in 1942, right? But he did say where they were from: Chicago and Princeton. Let's start there."

Niles leaned forward. "Okay, Pete, go ahead."

"Europa, query. In the war years 1940 through 1942, was there any American university-sponsored expeditions to Brazil or the Amazon Basin?"

Formulating, said the female voice of Europa, then as quickly, *During years 1940 to '42, there was no American scholastic sponsorship of any South American excursions.*

"Great start," Pete said.

Niles shook his head but continued the line of questioning. "Europa, query. Were there any missing persons reports on University of Chicago or Princeton filed in those same years? Correction; expand search to 1945."

Formulating, she said as she started to penetrate the security of not only university records but those of police departments and federal agencies throughout the nation.

Twenty-two records of missing persons reported from both universities during target years. Twenty-one were later reported as solved. One remained open, filed at Princeton, June 1945.

"Too late for filing," Niles said.

Both men sat and thought. They were at a brick wall and they didn't know how to penetrate it.

Europa has detected a pattern in your queries. Query: Do your current search parameters include accidental death of university personnel on foreign territory?

Niles looked at Pete. The Cray was designed to interact

with its operators and advise if there might have been something overlooked in the search they were conducting.

"It does now, thanks to you, Europa. Continue please," Pete said.

In calendar year 1942, a chartered aircraft leased by the University of Chicago was reported missing in the Brazilian rain forest south of the Amazon River. There were two University of Chicago survivors and one reported survivor from Princeton University.

"Wait a minute; didn't you say there were no university-sponsored expeditions in Brazil during those years?" Pete asked.

The incident upon which the report was filed was not a university-sponsored action.

"Come on, who sponsored it?" Niles asked, losing patience.

Pete looked at Niles as if he had lost his mind. "Name the sponsor, Europa," Pete commanded, still looking at Niles.

The aircraft in question was leased through the United States Army Air Corps and geographical survey sponsored by the U.S. Army and U.S. Army Corp of Engineers.

"What in the hell is this?" Pete asked.

Europa does not understand the question.

"Not you. Niles?"

"Query. Can Europa identify the departments involved in this charter at the University of Chicago?" Niles asked.

Formulating, she said.

Niles stood as something distant and forgotten started to flirt with his memory.

The University of Chicago Department of Physics and Theoretical Sciences at Princeton University, Europa answered quickly.

Niles realized what picture was starting to form from the puzzle pieces being laid before him. And now the past came flooding back to him as Europa started putting the pieces of that puzzle together—something he did not want to think about. He rubbed his hands across his face in vexation but continued his line of questioning nonetheless.

"Query. Who were the heads of these departments at the two universities from UAO through 1942?"

Chairperson for the University of Chicago's Department of Sciences and Physics for years in question was Professor Enrico Fermi. Director of Theoretical Sciences, Princeton University, and departmental chairperson for years in question was Professor Albert Einstein."

"What have I done?" Niles asked.

"What are you saying here, Niles?" Pete asked while looking incredulously at the printed names.

"I may have killed everyone on that rescue mission, Pete."

On the screen, spelled out in big blue letters, was Europa's answer to the mystery of Padilla's lost expedition: EN-RICO FERMI and ALBERT EINSTEIN.

PART SEVEN
SPECIES OF GOD

The release of atom power has changed everything except our way of thinking . . . the solution to this problem lies in the heart of mankind. If only I had known, I should have become a watchmaker.

—Albert Einstein

22

IT took thirty minutes to pry Mendenhall and Sanchez out of the engine room. They found the body of Lebowitz pinned underneath the mainmast where it had crashed onto the deck. Professor Ellenshaw had been trapped beneath one of the bunks in section six and it had taken a hacksaw to free him. Heidi Rodriguez had a nasty wound on her forehead and they had thought she wouldn't wake up until she suddenly sat straight up and screamed that she was drowning. She had been found in section seven under an overturned stainless-steel table amid broken beakers and tech equipment. The bright floodlights from what remained of the deck lights lit the opening and surrounding dock and stairs that *Teacher* sat upon.

There was no sign of Jenks or Virginia. Danielle and Ellenshaw had shown up after they had freed the engineering section, and said they had been separated from the other two. Ellenshaw excitedly explained how Danielle had saved his life and almost killed him at the same time, by making him dive deep beneath the falls to keep from being crushed.

Danielle was now wrapping Heidi's forehead with gauze from sickbay and talking softly to her. Jack took stock of the many bodies they had pulled out of the lounge and science sections, twenty-four in all. Ellenshaw's two young assistants were lined up on the dock along with five of the Group's security people, including Shaw and Jackson. Carl came up behind Jack and placed a hand on his shoulder.

"Jack, I checked the holes that were punched into us. Two separate charges, definitely explosive devices. We have scorching on the hull and it was bent inward. I would say a three- or four-pound charge, the same with the engineering section."

The major continued to stare at the covered bodies and didn't answer at first. Carl was about to speak again when they were approached by Danielle.

"I hope Sarah is safe," she said.

Jack turned on her, his gaze demanding to know what she knew.

"Major, the beast took her when our section was flooded. She and I both were grabbed. I struggled free, but Sarah didn't. I'm sorry."

"Why would the animal come into the ship?"

"This may sound strange to you, but I had the distinct feeling it was trying to help Sarah and me; don't ask me why, it's just a intuition." She turned away.

"Jack, are you all right?" Carl asked, rubbing his bruised legs.

"Will," Jack called out, ignoring the question.

"Yes, Major," Mendenhall answered from where he was helping to tend the wounds of Ellenshaw and Stiles.

Jack walked over to one of the glass windows that now had a crazy line of cracks through it. Using a flashlight, he smashed out the remaining glass. He reached in and pulled out two handheld radios from the communications compartment, and quickly checked the settings and charge. He tossed one to Mendenhall.

"I have a job for you, and it's damned well dangerous."

Mendenhall looked from Jack to Carl and smiled. "Yes, sir."

Jack just nodded, never more proud of the man he had sworn to make an officer, then a thought struck him. "Staff Sergeant Mendenhall, you are hereby promoted to the temporary rank of second lieutenant, United States Army, as witnessed this day by—"

"Lieutenant Commander Carl A. Everett, United States Navy," Carl said in all seriousness.

"And based upon pending approval and recommendation of the director of Department Fifty-six fifty-six, Dr. Niles Compton, you are hereby notified of said field promotion. Is that understood, Lieutenant Mendenhall?"

Mendenhall frowned. "Yes, sir, understood. Now, you've given me the sugar, so I guess I'm ready for the medicine."

Jack took Mendenhall by the shoulder and steered him away from the others.

"Look, Will, I need you to go out there and get to high ground. That means finding some way out of the lagoon, and climbing out and up beside the falls. I don't know if the radio will reach me in here but, once in position, you are to watch the lagoon. Dig up a set of night-vision goggles and report on secure channel seventy-eight; you'll be speaking with a mutual friend of ours who's call sign is Night Rider One and your call sign is Conquistador. You are to tell him that Operation Spoiled Sport is on and to fire at will, if and when you see an armed element reach the lagoon, either on land or by boat. We hope it's by boat. You tell Night Rider to execute, execute, execute. Three times, you got that, Will?"

"Yes sir, three times, and then what?"

"And then what? Get your ass behind a big rock and hope that Mr. Ryan's burned-up body doesn't land in your lap."

Mendenhall just looked at the major.

"Seriously, if Operation Spoiled Sport works, you stay down until you know it's safe, and, believe me, you'll know when that is."

"Major, who are these men coming?"

"We have to assume they're bad guys. Boris and Natasha picked them up yesterday, heading our way. They're heavily armed, and Niles and the president can't account for 'em."

"Yes, sir, I'll do my best."

"Good luck, Lieutenant."

The major was joined by Carl, as they watched their new

officer load his radio into a large plastic bag and stuff it in his shirt.

"All right, Commander Everett, let's get ready and see if we can find anyone alive in here."

SARAH WAS JUST entering the small cave when the sound of splashing water sounded behind her, and she quickly backed out in time to see first Virginia, then Jenks, as they were lifted out of the water by the creature. It started walking, dragging the choking and puking duo across the hard rock. It deposited them in front of Sarah, then turned away and walked slowly back to the water, where it disappeared.

Sarah helped Virginia to her feet and hugged her. Then she helped Jenks struggle to one leg before he shook off her assistance and sat back down.

"God, am I glad to see you two," she said, crying. "Come on, Virginia, I've got something to show you."

"Don't worry about me; it's only broken in two places. Ain't shit," Jenks said, looking at his leg.

Virginia ignored the master chief for the moment and followed Sarah to the largest of the cave openings. Sarah pulled back the cover as she again held the torch inside. Virginia immediately rushed inside, careful to avoid the bubbling magma caldera in the center of the room.

"Helen Zachary?" She went to her knees and placed her hand on the burned and scarred face of her old Event Group colleague. "My god, what happened?"

The young man next to her moved and his eyes fluttered open. He reached down to place a hand in the small running creek that coursed through the wall of the cave, and then wiped his face. Then he started to sob, waking up the other nine people that were sleeping along the rough-hewn walls.

"Thank god," he said through his tears.

"What happened, why are you here?" Sarah asked.

"The . . . creature, it brought us here. It's been . . . feeding us, keeping us alive."

"What's your name?" Virginia asked.

"Rob, I mean Robert Hanson, I was . . . am, Professor Zachary's assistant."

"Well, you've done well in keeping your people together," Sarah said.

"Kelly, Kelly, come here," Robby said into the darkness of the cave.

As Sarah watched, a young woman eased forward and sat next to the crying assistant. She smiled at Sarah.

"God, are we happy to see you," she said with tears welling up in her own eyes.

"We have to get her out of here," said Robby.

"We're here to get everyone out," Sarah said.

"You don't understand." He reached out and took Kelly's hand. "This is the daughter of the president."

"What?" Sarah asked loudly, startling all those that had awakened and were inching toward their rescuers to make sure they were real.

"Knock it off, Robby; I'm no more important than anyone else here."

"All right, all right, you can explain this little tale later," said Sarah. "Right now, we plan on getting all of you out."

Meanwhile, Virginia gave Helen a quick examination, not liking what she saw. The professor's face was covered in lesions, and there had been massive hair loss. Her fever was so high that Virginia instinctively pulled her hand away after touching her forehead. There were black marks on her face and neck, and it looked almost as if her left eyelid had melted down over her eye.

"Good god, if I didn't know any better, I would say this is—"

"Radiation poisoning," Robby said as he failed miserably to be as brave as he wanted to be in front of the others and resumed crying softly while touching Helen's hand.

"Radiation poisoning?" Sarah asked.

"The mine is full of uranium, enriched uranium, damned close to extremely hot plutonium. God, her fever is out of control," he said as he felt Helen's forehead for himself.

"These others, are they all right?" Virginia asked.

"Yes, scratches and frightened to death mostly. There are these animals that bring us plenty of fish to eat. But it's as if they were keeping us here for a reason," he sobbed. "At least the smaller one seems to keep the other creature away from us."

"Other creature?" Sarah asked.

"Yeah, this one's big, has no human characteristics like the smaller one. It hates anything that breathes air, the professor thinks." Kelly looked down at Helen. "She thinks the smaller animal is wild, and lives in the lagoon, while the big one was bred from the creatures that worked the mine, worked at bringing the ore up. She thought they were used to keep the slaves in line. Keep them corralled in here. The damn Inca used both the Sincaro and animals to do what they knew they couldn't—mine the hot uranium."

"There is no such element in the natural world as enriched uranium ore; it's an impossibility in the natural order of elements," Virginia said as she checked Helen's pulse. She closed her eyes and thought a moment, trying desperately to make sense out of this highly unusual moment.

"Okay, I admit the elements and the situation would seem to contradict the natural assumption of improbability," she conceded as she reached out and took a palmful of water and spread it on Helen's forehead. "We have uranium ore, heated to an extreme temperature by the seismic activity of the caldera . . . and remember, Sarah, we picked up unusually high concentrations of fluorides in the water of the lagoon, obviously released through the clay or other soil in this valley; thus, it is possible to breed that ore into—"

"Weapons-grade plutonium, free for the taking," Sarah finished for her, remembering the light stands in the cave behind her and the graffito on the belly of Supay. "Jesus, everyone who entered this level of the mine is contaminated. If we don't get out of here soon, especially them," she nodded toward Rob and the others, "we're all screwed."

"That's just about what the professor thought," Kelly said, locking eyes with Sarah.

JACK AND THE others began hurriedly removing supplies from *Teacher* because she would never see the water again without Jenks here to supervise her much-needed repairs. She was too unsteady on the stone steps to delay in getting the supplies out.

Although they were eager to get moving into El Dorado to look for survivors, Jack and Carl set up some makeshift lighting on the massive dock the Inca had carved out of solid stone. The wonders it revealed were beyond belief. All the Incan gods were represented along the high walls and many columns. The tunnels and shafts were stacked one upon the other in a never-ending spiral heading toward the top of a giant indoor falls that cascaded toward the floor in the center of the great mine, its spray keeping the interior of the mine constantly damp. The pillars that lined each level were carved from solid rock. How many hundreds of years, or possibly thousands this shaft had taken to be excavated boggled their minds.

As they ventured deeper into the vast expanse of the pavilion and beyond the powerful lights and into shadow, they saw crate upon crate of stacked K rations, fuel drums, crated equipment, and other supplies. Each wooden crate was stenciled in black lettering.

"United States Army."

Jack looked at Carl and raised his eyebrows. "Look at this."

Arrayed against the stone outer wall of the main chamber were what looked like graves. Heavy stones were laid layer upon layer, creating a large bulge in the stone floor. There were twenty-three in all. Jutting stone markers protruded from the rocks at the head of each. On each was looped a small chain and on each chain was a single dogtag. Jack raised one and shined a light on it.

"Technical Sergeant Royce H. Peavey."

"Well, I guess that explains who the Kilroy artists were. But what in the hell were they doing here, Jack?"

"This whole damn thing smells to high heaven. But we can't speculate here; we have to get moving." Jack took a last look at a group of Americans that had come pretty far to be left in a horrible place.

"I figure we start at the bottom of the mine first and then work our way up," Carl said as he turned away from the seventy-year-old cache of military supplies and the men they were meant to feed.

"The canals?" Jack asked, as he started following Carl back to the smashed *Teacher*.

"I figure we can scrape up the scuba gear we need if you're game, ground pounder."

"You're on, Commander Everett, after you."

"You think Sarah is still alive?"

"I do, and I'm betting Jenks and Virginia are also."

Carl glanced back toward the long-lost graves.

"Good thing you have the navy here, Jack; from the looks of it, you army types didn't fare too well around here in the past."

FARBEAUX HALTED THE group when he heard voices. He cocked his head to the right and then listened again. Nothing but silence greeted him as he hushed the men behind him. It had been over an hour since he had started the group down a steep slope in the tunnels. Farbeaux had figured the ramp used to be a slide of some sort that had been possibly used for removing slag and other unwanted material from the mine. The ramp, as steep as it was, connected with almost every sublevel as it coursed down through the mine.

Mendez and his men were really starting to grumble as they had passed vein after vein of gold, each deposit larger and wider than the one before it. He knew each of the fools, including Mendez himself, had taken their own samples and pocketed them.

Farbeaux saw their bulging pockets in his night-vision

goggles and smiled, then brought out his satchel again to take another reading. The men behind him didn't notice what he was doing because of their avarice. They were intent on picking up as much of the gold ore as possible.

He turned the machine off and then removed his goggles. He shocked the men behind by turning on a broad-beam lamp and shining the light on a very wide and very green-looking vein of ore that ran side by side with another of gold. He turned the miniature Geiger counter back on again, held out a probe, and the machine went crazy. It emitted what sounded like the clicking of a cricket. Farbeaux closed his eyes and then shut off the machine once again. He had found what he had come for deep inside the mine. After years of waiting and receiving the ore samples from his man at the Vatican, the chase and search for the diary of Padilla, suddenly now the lode was here, ready to be torn from the earth and sold to the highest bidder.

"What was that instrument you were just using, *señor*?" Mendez asked as he wiped sweat from his brow with a filthy handkerchief.

"This?" Farbeaux held up his satchel. "Well, let's say it's pointing me to the richest find of all, something you wouldn't be interested in. But I will explain shortly; right now, let's find that which excites you my friend, your gold."

"But we have found enough gold to last a lifetime just on this winding ramp you discovered. Why even proceed further?"

"My friend, you can stuff your pockets until the very weight crushes your bones, or you can follow me into the lowest reaches and find it already mined, smelted, and possibly even stacked for you, ready to be shipped out. But I leave it to you—take what you have now and wait months while you try to get more equipment in here to mine the gold and possibly watch the Brazilian government take it before you have a chance to steal it, or you can follow me and find it all ready to take out. My way, you will at least have what you can ship out now. Not what you can stuff in your pockets."

He looked again at the meandering ramp, then faced Mendez again. "Which looks quite ridiculous, by the way."

Mendez didn't know how to react to the mild rebuke. He was beginning to hate the Frenchman. Farbeaux's attitude since entering the mine had changed; it was as if he had received what he had sought and now treated his benefactor with disdain. As he emptied his pockets of the gold he had collected, Mendez watched Farbeaux continue down the steep refuse ramp. He would see to it that the man learned respect for him, as had many who had crossed him did in the past.

Farbeaux found the exit he wanted from the refuse ramp. The reading of his counter was almost pegged in the red. The ore was strongest down a wide hall that was marked by two columns, indicating an entryway into a broad corridor. The twin columns had the same carvings of the strange creatures that had marked those at the tributary's entrance, but these gods were depicted in a squatting posture, as their massive arms and legs held up the top of the stone frame that guarded the entrance into the actual passageway used to remove the gold and other ores from the lowest levels.

The group continued down into the great shaft past the ancient trail as laid down by the Sincaro as they labored among whip lashes to bring the Inca their treasure. The canal running the length of the shaft had obviously been used to carry small boats attached by ropes, and used as an ancient conveying system. The men even found remnants of the small boats in areas of the excavation from shaft to shaft, very ingenious for the ancient time and efficient in their way.

One room just inside the stone entry that had been dug into the side of the shaft smelled of danger. Farbeaux shined his light inside and saw that the room held a small deposit of white sacks. One sack had disintegrated over the years and had fallen to the stone floor and broken open. The gold dust was unmistakable in the light as it gleamed and sparkled. He looked around the room and saw what appeared to be a fulcrum release. He also noticed small holes that lined the doorway which were currently dripping water. It was extremely hot in there. He once again shined the light on the lever, a small handle that jutted from the wall just inside the room, within arm's length of the doorway.

"Have your men stay clear of this room," he said, turning to face Mendez.

"I see what's in there, *señor.* This is exactly the find we are here to exploit," the Colombian challenged the Frenchman. "Jesús, Hucha, proceed inside and retrieve one of those bags for me," he ordered.

Farbeaux stepped aside. "You have been warned, *señor.*"

Two men in the center of the long line stepped up to the doorway. Jesús stepped though tentatively and while Farbeaux watched, silently his left foot hit the false floor directly in front of the doorway as his companion followed him through. The stone at his foot slid down only a half an inch, barely perceptible even to Farbeaux who knew what to look for. The rectangle of stone settling into the floor triggered a small bronze pipe inside the thick tile. Small stone caps burst free from the doorway and several other spots inside the carved-out room with a loud pop, making everyone in the tunnel outside flinch at the gunshot-type reports. Jesús and Hucha were suddenly caught in a steaming-hot shower of water that must have run straight up through the magma chamber buried deeply inside the pyramid. They instantly fell to the stone floor, screaming and writhing. They rolled, but everywhere they tried to escape the roaring, searing steam, it found them from the many ancient nozzles inside. Farbeaux finally reached inside as his point was made about following his orders, and pulled down on the fulcrum release. The steam dwindled almost immediately to nothing.

"You knew the room was booby-trapped?" Mendez said accusingly.

"Yes, that was why I said for no one to enter."

Jesús and Hucha were dead. One of the bodies didn't seem to believe it, as yet it rolled over on its back, leaving the man's face sticking to the floor. Their boots were melted off, and in several areas bone protruded from clothing.

"You have gone too far, you should have said something!"

"I did, I said 'do not enter this room.'" The Frenchman looked down the line of Mendez's men. "Please do as instructed and you will not end up like your compatriots. There are many pitfalls here that can and will kill you in many horrible ways." Farbeaux glanced into the room at the now red and fleshless bodies; only their clothing had survived the liquid inferno that had engulfed them. "I believe seeing is the best teacher we can have. You have seen, now follow instructions," he said coldly as he turned and continued down the trail.

The Colombians didn't say a word because they could all still smell the boiled skin.

Mendez watched as Farbeaux stopped and studied the deep canal for a moment. He was very weary of the imperious way this man was acting within the mine. He was doubly worried because Rosolo had not caught up with them. He waved his men forward, not taking his eyes from the Frenchman.

JACK FOLLOWED THE more experienced Carl into the canal and out through the falls, looking around wildly for any sign of the animal that took Sarah. They followed the wall for almost sixty feet, started looking for a way in. They knew Sarah had detected several openings using the diving bell's sonar track. Jack almost ran straight into Carl when he stopped suddenly. There, just a few feet ahead in the black water, Carl's light was illuminating the creature. It was holding station in the lagoon by swirling its webbed hands in the water and lightly kicking with its feet. The dark eyes studied them for a moment and then it suddenly turned and sped off toward the wall. Jack grabbed Carl and pointed to where the beast had vanished into a small opening in the rock. They started kicking with their fins and made for the spot the animal had vanished into.

Unbeknownst to them both, another set of eyes had

watched the creature and the officers as they made for the lower opening of the mine.

Captain Rosolo, having survived the attack by the very beast he had watched a moment before, turned and kicked in the opposite direction. Since the twin explosions of his limpet mines, he had taken his time to study the underwater layout of the lagoon. Now that he was finishing, he had become aware of company in the water and had watched as two of the Americans entered the lagoon from the falls.

Now he swam for the opening of El Dorado. He figured it was time to take out an insurance policy against both the American group and the Frenchman, which he would deliver with extreme delight.

HELEN ZACHARY AWAKENED and tried to open her eyes, but they were sealed shut with infection; additionally, her left eye was seared closed because of the extreme nature of the ore she had handled.

Jenks was having his leg tended to by three of the young women from the expedition who were happy just to be doing anything at all. The master chief kept smiling and reassuring the girls that others were there and undoubtedly looking for them, even through the horrible pain as they tried clumsily to set his leg. Every once in a while he would take a deep breath against the excruciating waves their touch produced, and then he would look up and wink at Virginia, who was proud of the way he tried to reassure all of them in the cave.

"That man, Kennedy," Robby babbled and cried, "he came here because someone wanted him to make sure nothing like that ore was brought out of here. But it was he who took samples. It was Kennedy's people that set off the dark one, the creature that lives in the pyramid; it attacked his team and then us when we tried to help. I don't know why, but that thing acted as though it was here to stop anything from leaving this mine. I mean the ore; it wasn't concerned with gold, just that damned ore. And then it was Professor

Zachary who discovered why. She was actually communi-
cating, well, in a rudimentary way with the smaller one, the
one that's hidden us since the other went berserk."

"Why . . . not, we're . . . related."

Sarah and Virginia saw Helen was trying to sit up.

"Oh, don't do that, Helen, don't move, you're very sick,"
Virginia said, placing her hand on Helen's chest and easing
her back down.

"Virginia?" she whispered. "Do . . . you and . . . still . . .
hate me?"

"Stop that, no one at Group—" She caught herself before
she said it. "No one ever hated you, Helen, no one."

A tear slowly trickled from Helen's right eye and forced
its way down her swollen cheek. "Niles," she whispered.

"Dear, it was Niles who sent us," Virginia whispered in
her ear.

A sad smile came to Helen's features as she lost consciousness.

"What did she mean when she said the creature and us
are related?" asked Sarah.

Robby placed a wet cloth on Helen's forehead and then sat
back and explained. "Before the dark beast sank the boat and
barge out of anger over those guys' taking ore samples, Dr.
Zachary ran a complete DNA sequencing on both of the creatures. There was not one difference between them, or us."

"That's impossible. From what I saw, that thing is an amphibian," Virginia challenged.

Robby shrugged. "Doesn't matter what you believe;
those animals were once us. The doc said it *chose* to go back
to the water, whereas we chose to stay on land."

"You say she communicated with it?" Sarah asked.

"According to a wall diary of sorts, painted by the Sincaro, which the beast and its kind saved once upon a time
from a bleak future, the darker species and its kind used to
be slaves alongside the Indians. And they were the only
creatures, human or otherwise, who could mine the uranium
without becoming sick. The smaller ones, the doc figured,

were wild, never tamed by the Inca, that's why they have more tolerance for us than the dark one. The doc said the animals had a natural resistance but not a complete immunity to the ore. It had something to do with total immersion therapy, a natural way to fight radiation sickness. Since the creatures mined the ore underwater, they didn't die as rapidly as us land walkers."

"But what did the Inca need or even want the ore for?" Virginia asked.

"The doc said they used it to heat their giant smelting pots. She says they discovered it was more efficient than trying to use the natural volcanic aspects of the mine. No telling how many people were killed during their reign over this area. Pizarro might have had the right idea; who's to say who screwed who?" he said bitterly. "The Sincaro weren't sad their masters were conquered; I bet those creatures have been a sight happier also."

"How many are there?" Sarah asked, actually concerned.

"Kelly, you were there when the professor transcribed her notes. What did she say about the number of animals?"

Kelly was haggard like the rest but she gave a smile that told Sarah she had a lot of courage. "She said that the animals are a long-lived species, but Helen thinks these two may be the last of their kind. The wild one, the green and gold creature, is very protective of all things in this valley. It saved us from starving to death."

"But what—"

"Any further questions can be asked out here," a deep, French-accented voice said from the cave opening, cutting off the question Virginia was about to ask. "So please, come out quickly, as my associate has stupidly pulled the pin on a hand grenade and is quite prepared to throw it in among you," Farbeaux said as he stared at the stupidity of the move by Mendez.

They all stood with the exception of the injured professor and Jenks, who could only look around in frustration for a weapon.

"These guys aren't with you?" Robby asked as he started to follow the rest from the enclosure.

"No, they're not," Sarah answered.

"Please, *señor*, find the pin and replace it in the grenade, quickly," Farbeaux ordered, flicking his eyes from the motley group of survivors to the sour countenance of the Colombian.

Mendez scowled as he placed the silver pin back in the grenade. He tossed it back to one of his men and then faced the twelve raggedy people before him.

"Colonel Farbeaux, I take it?" Sarah asked.

"At your service." The Frenchman actually looked pleased for a moment as he took in Sarah. "Ms. McIntire, isn't it? How was Okinawa, my dear? A learning experience, perhaps?" He turned and told several of the men in Spanish to light a few of the torches that lined the wall.

Sarah didn't answer, but she did wonder how this maniac had known she had been to Japan recently, then she thought she knew the answer. In her estimation, it didn't take a brain like Niles Compton's to figure it out.

Farbeaux smiled as he walked past Sarah and Virginia and leaned into the small cave opening. He frowned at the sight of Helen, then he straightened and returned to the group. Mendez and his men had found other torches and the area was alight with illumination that brought out the wall paintings and carvings into stark relief.

"Helen is seriously ill?" he asked.

"She's dying, Colonel, so surely you don't intend to hold us up here. We must get her to a hospital," Virginia said, lowering her hands.

Farbeaux looked from the Americans to Mendez and closed his eyes.

"Please keep your hands in the air, *señora*," Mendez growled.

"I will not," Virginia stated flatly.

"Do as he says," Jenks hissed from his place just inside

the small cave. He was watching through the opening while lying on his side on the cave floor.

"Shut up, Chief, these people have been through too damned much; we're taking them out of here," Virginia announced.

"I'm afraid no one can leave here," Mendez said as he waved his men forward.

Farbeaux reached into his satchel, removed a small bottle, and tossed it to Virginia. She looked at him quizzically.

"Potassium and iodine. It will slow the spread of infection, but I'm afraid by the looks of the professor's condition it will do no good, though no harm, either. She must have received over five thousand rads, a rather massive exposure."

Virginia angrily tossed the pill bottle back to Farbeaux.

"Shove them up your—"

"It's far too late for Professor Zachary," Sarah said, stepping quickly in between Virginia and the Frenchman. "But I'm curious to know why you thought to bring the one pharmaceutical that could help with a lesser exposure, Colonel."

Farbeaux raised his left eyebrow at Sarah and then with the corner of his eye saw Mendez tense up.

"I suppose you wouldn't accept it was a lucky guess, perhaps?"

"Not likely, Colonel."

"I should also like to know why you would take such a medicinal precaution without informing your financier, señor," Mendez said as he pulled a nine-millimeter Beretta from its holster and pointed it at Farbeaux. His men followed suit with their Ingram submachine guns. "Now I insist you tell me why it is you are really here."

The Frenchman was about to respond when he saw the disturbance in the water. The wake was traveling very fast, obviously created by something just beneath the surface of the canal. Mendez saw his eyes flick from himself to something the Colombian could not detect.

The creature was suddenly there. It had exploded out of

the water like a shot from a cannon. The first two of Mendez's mercenaries never knew they were being attacked. Being the closest to the grotto, they were taken unawares backward into the roiling waters, as everyone present saw just a spray of water and a fine mist of red swirling where the two men had been only moments before.

Farbeaux didn't hesitate as the mercenaries were snatched from the land of the living in a microsecond. He made a dash for the opening in the far wall that Sarah had discovered earlier. Too late, Mendez saw what Farbeaux was attempting. His slow reaction time seemed even slower in sharp contrast to the quick and violent death of two of his men. He fired wildly at the retreating Frenchman. Three nine-millimeter bullets hit to the right of the opening, missing Farbeaux by mere inches as he disappeared up the steep steps.

Just then, the beast came from the grotto again. A sudden swath of water accompanied the creature as it cleared the grotto wall by six feet, landing inside the circle of gunmen, who began firing. Sarah ignored the noise and gunfire as she seized this opportunity to grab for the Ingram of the man to her left. But just as she thought she would succeed at catching him by surprise, the Colombian sensed her movement and turned toward her.

Jenks tried desperately to maneuver his bad leg. The pain was so intense that he knew he only had a moment to react and help the diminutive army officer. As gunfire erupted only feet away from Mendez and his men as they defended themselves against the maniacal creature in their midst, Master Chief Jenks grabbed his shattered leg with both hands and with a howl lashed out in a sideways kicking motion that caught the armed man beside Sarah by both of his ankles. Jolted by the unexpected blow, the man fired his Ingram, sending rounds into the stone ceiling.

Sarah reacted almost as quickly, slamming her fist into the man's upturned face as he was knocked off balance. He hit the floor right in front of the small cave opening, and

Sarah let her forward momentum carry her down on top of him. Jenks was still screaming in pain as the two rolled into him.

As Mendez watched in horror, the beast before him swiped with long powerful arms at his men. Seven-inch claws ripped into their flesh and bone, and the heated air was instantly corrupted with blood and sinew. In shock at what he was witnessing, he blindly turned his Beretta on the bloody scene. He fired twice, hitting one of his men in the back. Then he panicked and ran for the doorway that he had just watched the Frenchman disappear into a moment before. Three of his men quickly followed their boss into the far wall.

Sarah had managed to gain control of the Ingram but the Colombian, merely stunned, was quick to recover from the blow of landing on the stone. As Sarah raised the weapon and tried to gain some semblance of aim from where she lay, another scream and a unlaced boot heel came crashing down into the mercenary's face. Jenks started shaking badly after he had smashed his broken leg once again into the man. He passed out from the pain as Sarah screamed a shout of triumph and rolled free of the unconscious Colombian.

Robby, Kelly, and Virginia were trying their best to get the rest of the students out of harm's way as bullets started flying in every direction from the firing of panicked men. Several rounds found their mark as the beast screamed and roared in pain. But that didn't stop the huge creature as it reached out and grabbed the closest man still standing in its midst. It easily raised him above its head and tossed him like a stuffed doll into four others.

From her position on the ground, Sarah saw one of the men near her had expended his magazine and drawn a large, very lethal-looking machete from a long scabbard and raised it above his head. As it came down, Sarah pulled the trigger. Later she would be grateful for the three-round-burst-of-fire setting on the Ingram because in her haste she depressed and held the trigger down. Two of the three rounds caught the man in the back as his machete came crashing down into the chest of the animal. The blade sank deep as the man's forward momentum carried him into the enraged creature. Blood spewed out of the animal as it grabbed for the man that had hurt it so, and jumped with him into the grotto.

Sarah quickly sighted on the next man, concerned that her slowness might have killed the creature that had suddenly come to their rescue. As she was about to depress the trigger again a large boot slammed down on the short barrel of the weapon, knocking it onto the wet stone floor. She looked up; another of the remaining mercenaries was standing over her with his own smoking weapon pointed right at her head. Now that the animal appeared to be disposed of, the man clearly relished the power of holding the struggling Sarah beneath his boot.

Robby saw what was about to happen and came at the two. Another of the surviving men quickly swiped at Robby and sent him sprawling to the floor. Several of the panicked girls screamed as he skidded along the stone.

Sarah knew the master chief wasn't likely to throw this man off his feet. But instead of being scared at her imminent death, she became angry as her attacker brought his hot gun barrel up to her face. Suddenly he jerked as a look of consternation crossed his face. His body quickly jerked again and then he fell forward, slamming face first into the cave opening and rolling dead onto the floor. Sarah felt the fine spray of his blood as it misted down her face. But her horror turned to amazement when two figures rose from the grotto. They were dressed in black wetsuits and advanced with two XM-8 light machine guns at an aiming position.

Now 5.56-millimeter rounds started to slam into the remaining men. Five of them went down without ever knowing they were hit, bullets neatly parting their foreheads. Three others besides the one that had almost dispatched Sarah managed to at least turn toward their sudden executioners. Going from a frightening animal attack to this new threat overwhelmed them; more XM-8 rounds easily found their mark. One man withdrew a hand grenade from his belt, pulled the pin, and was in the act of throwing it toward the new, human demons to attack them when he was also hit, the round glancing off his skull that sent him sprawling. The grenade hit the slick flooring and Virginia, thinking quickly, picked it up and threw it toward the canal opening to the outside. It hit the floor and bounded into the arched opening, where it detonated next to the right-side arch. The shrapnel burrowed into the soft, water-soaked stone.

Sarah, thirty feet from Virginia and the others, realized what was happening. They had been saved! The two figures rising from the water were close to being the best marksmen in the world. Jack Collins and Carl Everett were methodical as they went from man to man, dispatching all with neat shots to the head. Sarah knew they would take no chances in the environment around them and with the students in such close proximity, even while they would be ruthless in dealing with the remaining threat. Jack and Carl would never allow an enemy to survive to harm people again, especially where kids were concerned. The four remaining men who tried to run for the wall opening only knew the sudden slug of impact on the back of their heads as their bodies came crashing down to the ground.

"Clear!" the smaller of the two men shouted in the echoing and sudden silence.

"Clear!" the taller answered.

Jack and Carl moved their silenced weapons from side to side as they visually covered the interior of the cave around them. Everywhere their eyes went, the barrel followed. Several of the girls of the Zachary expedition screamed as one of the smoking barrels slowly pointed at them and then moved on.

"That's it, Jack, they're all down! The bad guys are down!" Sarah called out as she held one arm in the air.

Slowly the two men stepped from the shallows of the grotto. They had entered from the lagoon side right into the melee of the animal attack. They had watched the violence explode above them as the beast swiped and moved like greased lightning. They couldn't tell who was being attacked or who was inside the large chamber they had surfaced into. After the beast disappeared, they quickly assessed the situation and Jack communicated with hand gestures what the plan would be. The former Special Forces operative and ex-navy SEAL had understood exactly how to proceed. Now they stepped onto the hot floor and surveyed the devastation around them.

"GODDAMN, TOAD, IT took you assholes long enough!" Jenks said, grimacing in anguish as Virginia again tried to straighten out the mangled broken right leg.

"Chief, we thought that fish man may have got you," Carl said as he examined the first mercenary Sarah had wrestled with. The man was surely dead.

The lieutenant commander stood as Jack and Sarah came back to the group. Carl safed his XM-8 and placed it on a snap hook on his weight belt. He unzipped the top half of his black wetsuit because of the extreme heat.

"I see you found some of the kids that we saw on the milk cartons, Chief," he said as he took in the haggard group before him.

"Jack, Helen's with them; she's in there." Sarah pointed.

Jack slowly removed his wetsuit hood, then went toward the small cave and bent down. He shined his light on the lone person inside. Helen Zachary moved, rolling her head toward him.

"Professor Zachary, I'm Major Jack Collins. Niles sends his regards and wants you to come home now," he said as he stepped into the enclosure. He kneeled down and took her hand. Jack immediately recognized the nature of the sickness afflicting Helen.

She attempted to smile but failed through her obvious pain. "Give Niles . . . my apologies, I . . . don't think I'll be able to . . . promise anything," she murmured and Jack squeezed her hand.

"I'll tell him that you did what you set out to do, Professor. You proved your theory about a species unknown to us."

This time she managed to smile, as Virginia entered the cave. The heat inside because of the lava vent made it almost unbearable, but still Helen shivered with cold.

"Don't harm the creatures . . . they are the last of their . . . kind, there are . . . no more . . . mysteries left . . . let them be."

Virginia quickly reached down and touched Helen's head. The sad, trembling smile remained as the professor felt her touch.

"Tell . . . Niles . . . I love him . . . and . . . I'm—"

Helen stopped breathing and lay still. The smile had left her face as her last thought had been to try to apologize to Niles Compton.

"She's gone," Virginia said as she released Helen's wrist. She took a deep breath and swiped angrily at a tear as it slid down her face.

Jack took Virginia's hand and held it for a brief moment.

"How many of these animals are we dealing with, Virginia? Carl and I think there was one in the lagoon; it couldn't have been two places at once."

"I don't know, maybe just two."

"There are two of them?" Jack said, releasing her hand.

"Helen believed one is wild, but the other one saved us and attacked those assholes. The professor discovered its ancestors had worked the mine as slaves; the Inca may have bred insanity along the way to increase the beasts' cruelty," Robby said as he and Kelly entered the enclosure. His eyes welled up when he saw that Helen was dead.

"Hang in there, kid, this isn't over yet," Jack said as he drew his nine-millimeter from inside his wetsuit and tossed it to Robby, who caught it and looked inquiringly at the major.

Carl withdrew his own handgun and gave it to Sarah. "Collect a couple of those Ingrams and a few magazines; those guys won't need them."

Jack stood and made his way out of the ancient slave quarters. He was followed by Robby and the others. The major looked at the face of each student; these kids had been through so much. His eyes locked on Kelly; clearly she was all right. He took a deep breath, relieved that was one major concern out of the way.

"The professor would want you to be tougher for just a little while longer," he said as he watched Sarah gather weapons from the dead men around them. "She died happy, so you remember what she did here in this place. Tell others about what she found, and make them believe with the same zeal and commitment she had. Make her proud. Now, before we attempt to get out of here, we need to know what's happening, I and Lieutenant Commander Everett here don't take kindly to surprises."

Robby fought back tears as he left the small cave. "This place, it's bad; no one can ever find this mine."

Jack's eyes went from Robby to Virginia, who moved to the master chief's side.

"This place is contaminated, Jack. Its walls are shot through with uranium that has been naturally enriched, tons and tons of it. It's very close to weapons grade," Virginia said as she gestured around her at the gleaming walls filled with tritium. "It's as if it came from a breeder reactor— impossible, I know, but Jack, it's here and it's starting to kill us all even as we speak."

Jack quickly pulled Carl aside and they took a few steps away from the group. He whispered, "If that bomb is inside this mine at the ore level and it goes off, it'll be the largest dirty bomb in the world. It would kill half of this hemisphere if it's ignited by a thermal nuclear device."

"And the hits just keep coming," Carl whispered back.

Jack turned and found the face he was looking for.

"You, your name is Robby, right?"

"Yes, sir," he said, stepping forward.

"Kennedy, the name rings a bell?

"Yes, sir. I think he knew about this place before we ever got here, don't ask me how, but somehow he knew."

"Son, did he have a case he brought along, about four feet long, three deep? It may have had a flotation device attached since you were going to be working near water. The case was more than likely yellow in color."

"Yeah, he practically killed us looking for it after the larger creature sank the boat and barge."

Jack reached into his wetsuit. He pulled out the release key that was attached to his dogtag, and showed Robby and the others. He didn't have to ask as Robby's eyes widened. Jack knew then that at least the professor's assistant had seen the key before.

"This is an arm key for a military weapon. I can tell it's been used because, once the key is turned in the device, a small, bulbous end breaks off and allows an electrical connection. Your Mr. Kennedy found the device and armed it. Now think, son. Do you or the others know where he did this?"

"We were separated; we never saw the case after the boat and barge were sunk." Robby was starting to look desperate as he stepped forward with Kelly in tow and whispered to the major. "Sir, this is Kelly." He looked around at the staring faces. "She's the presi—"

"The president's daughter; we know, son. Right now we have to get everyone out of here." Jack looked deeply into the boy's eyes. "Okay?"

"Yes, sir."

"Now we have—"

Jack's words were cut short as a loud cracking sound rumbled through the flooring of the enclosure.

The shrapnel from the grenade had penetrated the water-soaked limestone of the underwater opening and had created several faults that had slowly expanded over the last few minutes to the breaking point, until the pressure from the outside lagoon was too much for the ancient engineering to bear. The wall and arched opening gave way as one, and a torrent of water rushed into the quickly overwhelmed canal.

"Jack, that opening was engineered by the Inca to hold the lagoon at bay by a precise measuring of the opening against the pressure of the outside depth. The system has failed and can no longer hold the water back. Judging by the walls' thickness, we have about three minutes before there's no way out of here," Sarah said as she started to push everyone toward the same opening Farbeaux had vanished into.

Jack leaned inside the smaller enclosure after tossing Virginia his XM-8. Then he grabbed the master chief and threw him over his shoulder.

As Carl and Sarah started to run with the others toward the stairs just inside the small archway, a loud crack could be heard. They watched in horror while a long fissure opened at the center of the wall, right through the ancient drawings carved by the Sincaro, effectively cutting the images right in two. The crack widened as it hit the small arch and, in a split second, it collapsed. Large stones from the opening's interior rolled and crashed into the main chamber, making their attempted escape impossible. They all came to a sudden stop when the water slammed into their legs as it breached the top of the canal.

"Jesus Christ, this doesn't look good," Jenks hissed as he and Jack saw what had just happened.

For an exclamation mark to his comment, the grotto erupted, as the floor beneath cracked open and a geyser of lagoon water shot straight up, adding its volume to that of the failed canal opening. The group led by Carl and Sarah backed into Jack, Jenks, and Virginia.

Jack was shocked to see Sarah throw down the two weapons she was carrying and run toward the back wall of the excavated cavern. He saw her start to slide her hands along the wall as if searching for something. The water was hitting Jack's knees and was rising fast.

"You didn't happen to bring scuba gear for everyone did

you, Major?" Jenks said upside down from his position slumped over Jack's shoulder.

"Carl, give me that torch!" Sarah called out as the others looked on in utter confusion. Between Sarah's yelling, the unbearable roar of onrushing water, and their imminent death, the students stood frozen is terror.

Carl grabbed one of the wall torches and tossed it to Sarah, who caught it deftly in one hand and then turned back to continue feeling the wall. It had taken her only a moment to realize they only had one hope of escape, and she was praying she wasn't wrong. It had been the memory of her last classroom discussion that had spurred her to action.

Jack felt helpless as he watched, the weight of Jenks across his shoulder growing heavier by the moment. "Robby, you and Kelly and the others get over there and help her do whatever she's doing!" he ordered.

Robby and ten others, including Kelly, ran for the back wall. They only had to wait a moment for Sarah to explain. The water was now at waist level, and Jack had to adjust the position of Jenks as the master chief's head was momentarily dunked under the swirling onslaught.

"A depression, a varying thickness of stone, something that looks out of place on the wall," Sarah shouted to the students over the sound of rushing water.

All ten of Helen Zachary's grad students, now joined by Virginia and Everett, started feeling the wall, working their way around, some even ducking beneath the surface of the swirling rise to feel the stones underneath. Their time was dwindling rapidly. The water was now at Jack's lower chest. The master chief had maneuvered up and was bracing himself by holding onto the neoprene rubber of the major's wetsuit.

"Oh, boy, someone needs to pull something out of their tight ass, or we're going to spend a long time here!" Jenks yelled out to the students.

Jack was following the students' search when his eyes fell on an iron torch. It was lit but that wasn't what caught his attention. It was somewhat larger than the others surrounding the chamber, and it had deep etchings around the base. As his eyes adjusted to its intense light, Jack made out the image of an eagle, or was it a hawk? Clutched in this large bird's talons was the carved image of a man.

"Sarah, the torch!" he called.

Sarah looked up, momentarily confused as she turned toward the torch she was holding next to the wall. Jack, his hands full of the master chief, nodded toward the larger torch ` on the wall. She located what he was pointing at immediately and went to it. The water was now at Sarah's shoulders, as it was some of the smaller students, as well. She quickly examined the carvings. Without warning, she reached up and pulled down on the iron torch. Nothing.

"Carl, here! Pull down on the torch. I think it's a fulcrum release!"

"A what?" he asked as he waded toward Sarah, quickly followed by Robby.

"Pull, damn it, pull!" Sarah yelled as she hopped to keep her head above the water.

Carl reached up and pulled. Still nothing. Robby added his weight to it and yet the torch didn't budge. Sarah was beginning to think she was wrong when, in a second effort by Robby and Carl, the torch swung down, its lit head dipping into the water with a sizzle. Sarah saw the stone just to the right of the levered torch suddenly slide up about three feet into the wall. She quickly swam over and pulled herself up.

"Carl, there should be a stone handle in the cavity. It only moves one way—pull it!" she said as her head slipped under the water.

He was torn between getting Sarah to the surface and doing what he was told. He reached for the opening in the wall just as water started entering the cavity. He felt around and his fingers hit on a slab that was sticking up. It was about ten inches in height and about six wide, and was made of stone, as Sarah had said.

"What in the hell . . . ?" he said as Sarah came up from behind and held onto his shoulder.

"Pull!"

Carl pulled and the ancient fulcrum release handle moved easily, as if it had been greased only yesterday.

A tremendous rumbling was heard even over the roar of water as a ten-by-eight-foot section of wall opened to their left. It was immediately filled with water. Sarah shouted for everyone to enter the new, larger cavity. Carl helped the students inside, while Jack and Virginia struggled with Jenks as they slowly moved toward the wall. As they did, an eruption shattered the flooring as one of the caldera vents, ruptured by the cold water, exploded with a crushing thunder. Another vent farther away popped when the elements of fire and water could no longer tolerate each other.

Jack struggled and finally entered the opening just as Sarah started smashing a small stone to the opening's right side. It was smaller than its surrounding neighbors, and Sarah hoped beyond prayer it was the right one.

Carl was telling the students to brace themselves against the far wall of the twenty-by-twenty-foot dead end they were now trapped in, and to rise with the water, just as Sarah screamed in frustration and stopped using her small hand. She pulled the Beretta Carl had given her.

"Hold your ears!" she shouted as she fired into the stone. The bullet struck and cracked it, and it fell into the swirling water. She dropped the gun and braced herself against the small opening she had created. "Thank God!" she yelled as she reached in. She quickly found the second fulcrum release and said a silent prayer that the Inca were as efficient at their engineering as she had always heard. She pulled the release.

Suddenly to the shock of all inside, they were hurled into blackness as the wall above the door frame slid down with crushing weight. The parting waters of the impact sent a torrent of water rushing at everyone, smashing them against walls and floor. Some, Jack and Jenks included, lost their hold and went under. In a split second, the world became quiet as they came to the surface sputtering and spitting. The waters inside the chamber soon settled and they were all left in the dark.

"Disneyland would love this little ride," Carl said as he helped one of the smaller girls stay afloat.

"Everyone all right?" Jack called out.

There were yes and no answers but the major figured, if they could talk, they were alive.

"The ride's not over, people. Let's hope everything still works, or we just went from drowning to being entombed forever."

As they listened the floor beneath their submerged feet began to rumble. Then a soft green glow started to illuminate the interior of the room. Chunks of tritium touched off by the brightness of the torchlight before the door slammed down had started the reaction it needed to gather its internal energy and start to brighten. Jack quickly found Sarah as the rumbling below grew to a fever pitch.

"This isn't going to be pleasant," she said as she locked eyes with him.

"What's happening?" Virginia asked. She started to feel that the floor and the water around her were heating up. "What is this thing?"

"It's what the ancient Inca used as an escape route in case of collapse. The mine must be sprinkled with them."

"I don't like the sound of this," the badly injured Jenks said.

"Sprinkled with what?" Carl asked as he took the floating Sarah and held onto her.

"I think we're in an elevator."

"A what?" several people asked at once.

"An elevator!" Sarah shouted.

At just that moment the rumbling stopped and suddenly they heard a great hissing as the water around them became almost unbearable with heat. Then in an instant, an explosion rocked the chamber and all inside were pressed underwater as centrifugal force sent them all to the bottom.

Five thousand years ago, the Inca had feared being trapped in cave-ins far more than they dreaded any other possible disaster. Consequently, they had engineered the most ingenious escape platform the ancient world had ever devised. They had taken a naturally formed shaft that ran up and outward to the top of their excavated pyramid and had drilled a shaft beneath the flooring of the lowest cavern. Once reaching the boiling lava flow two thousand feet below, the Inca had capped the well at the cost of over a thousand slaves' lives. The chamber had been fitted to precise specifications inside the naturally formed shaft, which had been smoothed to a finish that would have made any future stonemason proud. The seal formed a natural tube that was as close to airtight as humanly possible at the time. Sarah had heard a rumor of the technology advanced by the University of Southern California, following a large dig inside the ruins of the northern Yucatán site of Chichén Itzá. She had remembered the specifications—and now had prayed the Inca had gotten it right. They had.

The chamber was propelled up through the interior of the giant pyramid at eighty miles an hour, and was gradually building speed. The pressure buildup under the chamber had been unleashed when Sarah had activated the fulcrum release, and that in turn had brought down ten tons of iron weight onto the stone caps that had been sealed five thousand years before by the elevators' original designers. The immediate release of so much pressure and steam just beneath the designed escape apparatus had no difficulty in forcing the stone chamber up and into the smoothed shaft. The only problem the Inca had failed to see was that of stopping. Even Sarah, the professor who taught her, and many others who had studied the system in classrooms across the globe were unable to figure out the problem. It was assumed that since the shaft and the chamber itself weren't perfect, the pressure would eventually bleed off. But there was controversy in that lone theory. No one had been able to see any logical explanation as to how this could be controlled. In essence, they could be traveling in an express train with no brakes.

As the centrifugal force increased, all inside sputtered to

the surface of the rapidly shallowing water as it was forced out of the minute cracks in the chamber. They could feel the speed gathering as the elevator roared upward into the unknown parts of the pyramid.

"Oh, shit," Kelly said as she hugged Robby.

"I hate this!" the master chief announced.

Suddenly the chamber tilted, as the elevator started to climb the steep, inverted slope of the inside of the great pyramid. Everyone screamed as the angle changed and they lost their footing. Jenks screamed in agony as Jack lost his balance and fell, crashing them both to the floor. The angle of ascent finally stabilized as the enclosure made its way up toward the uppermost reaches of El Dorado.

"We're slowing!" Sarah shouted.

Beneath the flooring of the chamber, the pressure was bleeding off the higher they climbed. The Incan engineers had calculated the length of the escape against the distance the pressurized wave could travel through the shaft, a simple formula that most would have considered impossible. And it would have been, even by the Inca, if several hundred Sincaro hadn't been used as guinea pigs in its weight-to-pressure-ratio experimental development.

Without warning, a tremendous hissing exploded with ear-hurting sound through the stone walls of the chamber. Outside, as the elevator passed the third level from the top, another fulcrum release was ripped that opened a series of stone valves in the shaft. Steam and pressure was rapidly bled off in a calculated feat of engineering that was designed to evacuate the shaft of pressure that was left over after the push to the top. At the same time as the bone-crushing stop on the upper level slammed everyone once again to the floor, the passing chamber tripped a series of stone nubs that broke away and allowed spring-loaded logs, hewn and covered with amber thousands of years before as a preservative, to pop free of the shaft through drilled holes. Six of these shot out under the chamber and arrested it just as it rebounded off the stone ceiling.

The wall that had closed to seal them in broke free and crashed into a large chamber where the elevator had come to rest. Dust swirled about as coughing and crying could be heard. From somewhere high above, natural light filtered into the highest chamber of the pyramid as Jack quickly stood and pulled Jenks out.

"Quick, Carl, get everyone out!" the major shouted.

Now the others heard what he had, the splintering of wood coming from the shaft. There was a general panic as the students rushed, were pulled, or crawled out of the elevator as the popping and cracking became louder. Just as Sarah cleared the doorway, the elevator gave a huge lurch and then it quickly vanished back down the shaft in the swirl and vacuum of the air.

As they all looked at one another in turn, most still in shock at their double narrow escape, the silence seemed to be a blessing.

"I guess the brakes gave out," Sarah said weakly as she turned over and lay on her back to stare upward at the intricately carved pyramid top two hundred feet up.

But of course it was the gruffness of the man in the most pain who broke the ice of terror that shrouded the company. Jenks sat up on one elbow and looked around.

"Goddamned Incans can't design worth a shit!"

23

THE dim light at the top of the pyramid had faded to nothing as Jack gathered torches and relit them and passed them around.

The new level they were in was fresher than anything they had come across since their arrival inside El Dorado. Jack had surveyed the extreme topmost of the apex and found the main vents that gravity fed the canal system throughout the mine. The point of the pyramid must have protruded from the river above, as its windows were above the surface. The torrent of water came down inside a culvert from the falls above and emptied into another large grotto at the center of the floor. The speed of the current was adjustable, he could see, by a system of floodgates controlled from this room. A large handle was set into one stone wall, and that in turn was attached to a dam door. The flow of water into the grotto was smooth and even, creating a current of a gentle five or six miles an hour down the gravity-fed canal system.

"There must be close to three hundred miles of interior canals inside the mine. The structure is unlike anything uncovered in history. A team could spend a lifetime in here and never uncover anything," said a woman's voice.

Jack turned and saw Sarah as she came up behind him. She was also admiring the dam engineering inside the wall.

"Well, you discovered enough to save our asses down there," he said as he turned back to the wall and held a hand to it.

"Lucky guess," she said as she, too, placed a hand on the dam. "There must be thousands and thousands of gallons of water inside that wall. In its heyday, the Inca may have had several hundred treasure boats traversing this system."

"There's eight of them right there," Jack said, moving his torch so Sarah could see the strangely crafted boats near the canal. "More over there, although they don't look in as good a shape."

Sarah observed that several of the boats had been laid along the far wall, and had been damaged severely.

"But I think with a little luck, these may hold up," Jack continued.

"Are you thinking of using the canals to get back down to *Teacher*?"

"You and the others are, but Carl and I have some searching to do."

"The bomb?"

"Yeah," was all he said as he made his way back to the group.

The interior was now well lit by at least thirty torches that were either in the hands of people or arrayed in their holders around the room.

"I think this room was nothing more than a way to control the water in the canals. We have to get down. The only way is to use what we have," Jack announced. "It may take hours, or maybe days, to get out on foot. But with the canals we can be assured of going one way, and that's down. *Teacher* is down there and the way out is also. We haven't a choice."

The students looked at one another. They nodded their agreement that it might be the only way.

"Everyone get over here and select the most structurally sound of these boats. They're large enough to fit everybody."

Carl wasn't paying any attention, as he was looking around the giant water room with Virginia in tow. The cavernous area had several doorways sliced into the stone walls. He would run the torch inside one and then quickly bring up the XM-8 and look inside. He was tired of being surprised and wanted to know his surroundings a little bit better.

"Carl?"

"Yeah," he answered Virginia as he backed out of the fifth room he had looked into.

"This place is giving me the creeps."

He looked at the strained features on Virginia's face in the torchlight.

"You mean more than just the mere fact that we're stuck in probably a ten-thousand-year-old pyramid that was reverse engineered and constructed inside a mountain surrounded by a lagoon that seems to be torn from the pages of a Jurassic history book. Why would that be less creepy than being here in the penthouse of a place that probably killed thousands of innocent Indians?"

Virginia rolled her eyes. "Smart-ass," she said, but she still looked about nervously. "I mean, can't you feel it? It's like we stepped into a cemetery here."

"Look, go on back with the master chief, he seems to become half human when you're around, Doctor. I'll take a look at these other rooms."

"Don't treat me like a child, Carl," she said, as she turned and led the way to the next room.

As Carl smiled and followed, his nose did pick something up that had not been there only moments before. He extended the torch into a room with downward spiraling stone steps. He thought for a moment that he heard something. He listened closely but then figured it had only been the sound of the canal echoing off the walls the deeper he went on this level.

"This must be the peasant's way down," he said.

Virginia didn't answer. Carl leaned back out of the opening and held up the torch. He saw Virginia's back as she stood frozen in the stone archway of the next small chamber. Carl raised his weapon and moved forward. He gently moved the doctor out of the way and brought the torch inside. His eyes took in the sight and he swallowed. Virginia had been right; this level was creepy for a reason. He stepped into the room and shined the torch around. He had entered a mausoleum.

"Go get Jack and Sarah."

THE MAJOR STEPPED into the room and saw what had stopped Carl short. The navy man had lit several of the interior torches and was bent low, examining some of the treasure in the room. Not the treasure of El Dorado, but treasure that marked the march of time throughout history.

"Oh my god," Sarah said, as she squeezed by Jack.

In every conceivable position, bodies, skeletal remains actually, were laid out across the floor. Artifacts from the history of El Dorado accompanied these humans from the past in their journey to wherever each soul's journey took them. There were breastplates of conquistador armor, stacked next to a case of old World War II K rations. A rusty Thompson submachine gun was lying across the case. Swords were strewn about. Spears, stone axes. But by far the strangest and most bizarre artifacts were the bodies. They were arrayed in all positions, but Jack noticed one very puzzling thing: all were chained to the wall with bronze manacles.

"The animal."

He turned toward Virginia. Carl and Sarah glanced at her with quizzical curiosity, then Sarah looked down at a sixty-plus-year-old body of an American soldier. The remains were in remarkably good condition because of the dryness of this particular chamber. Both bony arms were raised in mock surrender as the chains held them up. The body next to it was that of a conquistador, the red shirt still clinging to the bony frame, the empty eye sockets staring blankly at the intruders.

"The bodies were brought here postmortem. Their blood has stained the stones around them. The beast brought them here and actually chained them to keep them from escaping the mine, still doing its job after centuries and centuries."

"That's a stretch, Doctor," Carl said.

"It is still an animal, Commander; it hasn't a concept of death, impending or otherwise, its own or another animal's. It just does what it was trained to do."

"Bring back escaped slaves," Sarah said as she went over to another set of bones. "Major, here's a fellow soldier, look."

As Jack and the others stepped to a far corner where Sarah was standing, they could see a skeleton that was chained by only one arm. The man, centuries before when still alive, had worked his right hand free of the manacle that dangled above him. In the torchlight Jack could see that the dying man had used a lead ball, a musket round, which now lay by the bony fingers, to etch something in the stone flooring. Sarah had seen the first few letters and already guessed at the rest. Jack leaned over and blew some of the layers of dust away from the remaining letters.

"I'll be damned," Carl said over Jack's shoulder.

" 'Captain Hernando Padilla, 1534,' " the major read aloud.

"What does the rest say?" Virginia asked.

As Jack lightly and reverently moved the bony fingers of the long-dead conquistador away from his final words, the musket ball rolled away and lodged in a flooring crack and stayed. He again took a breath and blew air over the remaining words.

" '*Perdóneme*,' " Sarah murmured, and then stood and walked away. "Even though he was dying, he was ashamed of what he had done."

"What does the word mean?" Carl asked.

Jack patted him on the shoulder and walked away, sad for a fellow soldier lost long ago and in a place he didn't want to be. No different than any man in the world.

" 'Forgive me,' " Jack answered. "It says simply 'forgive me.' "

Carl looked back down at the skeleton and then the armor lying next to it. The scratch marks, the dents. He couldn't fathom the remarkable journey this man had made, the horror of losing everyone in his command. He shook his head and straightened up just as he heard Virginia intake breath sharply. She had begun slowly backing away from something in a far corner.

"Major, that item you were looking for, what color case was it in again?"

"It should be yellow and—"

Jack's words were cut short when he heard a soft beep coming from the far corner that Virginia was backing away from. Then he saw the case. The weapon was lying in a pile of other items from the Zachary expedition. The beast must have deposited it here along with its other finds. It was as if the animal simply brought anything of shiny or colorful material to its nest, its home. It was a scavenger.

The lieutenant commander joined the major, and they both looked down on the case that protected the five-kiloton nuclear weapon.

"Jack, I think we've found what we were looking for."

JACK LEANED OVER and easily unlatched the lid of the protective case. He had sent Sarah and Virginia back to hurry the others in their preparations for getting out of there.

"Damn," he said as he saw the LED readout on the aluminum facing of the weapon.

"Looks like we finally caught a break," Carl said as he looked over Jack's shoulder.

"Countdown's frozen at thirty minutes. Yeah, we may have. Kennedy turned the key but didn't initiate the countdown. I think we may have that creature to thank for that."

"Yeah, remind me to thank him if we run into him," Carl joked.

Jack closed the case and nodded for Carl to take the other end. They both gently lifted it off the stone floor. As they made their way out of the room, they paused and looked at the remains of the soldiers from the past. Then Jack looked at Carl and shook his head.

"Let's be sure not to join these fellas."

"I always liked the way you think, Jack."

They made their way out of the lighted chamber and into the darker passageway. They had gone just past the opening with the descending staircase when they were suddenly flanked by two men with automatic weapons. One came from the main chamber, the other was hidden in the dark opening and came out after they had passed. The man in the back gestured for them to continue on into the main chamber.

As they entered the lighted main water room, Jack saw that Sarah was there with Virginia and the students. They all looked dejected and terrified.

"Ah, this is like old home week. Major Jack Collins and the resourceful Commander Everett, I am but truly amazed. You two are like the taste of bad wine; I can't seem to get rid of you."

"I'm sorry, Jack," Sarah said.

"Do not speak again, *señora*," Mendez said as he raised his hand with the gun in it, ready to strike Sarah.

Jack tensed and was about to drop the warhead when Farbeaux's words stopped him and Mendez.

"Stop! You do not strike a lady for being concerned, Señor Mendez."

Mendez's hand was stayed in midair. He turned toward the Frenchman and saw to his bemusement that Farbeaux was looking not at him but at the American major.

Jack looked his way and their eyes locked. They remained fixed like that for a full thirty seconds.

"What is in the case, gold?" Mendez asked as he gestured for his remaining three men to take the case from the Americans.

"I wouldn't do that, mate," Carl said as he was relieved of the weight of the warhead.

Jack continued to look at the Frenchman as he allowed the handle of the case to be pried from his grip.

The two men, the third continuing to hold a gun on the two Americans, took the case over to Mendez. The greedy look in the heavy man's face was one that history had seen millions of times as men of avarice thought they were about to gaze upon a mother lode of riches.

"Gold, artifacts? What is in it?" he asked as he leaned over the yellow aluminum container. He reached out for the heavy-duty clasps.

"Don't!"

Mendez looked up into the face of Farbeaux, who said to Jack, "Explain why he shouldn't open the case, Major."

"By your temperament, I can see you've guessed at it. I prefer not to say anything to the pig," Jack said calmly. He caught Mendez's sneer out of the corner of his eye and just hoped the fat man would make a move in his direction.

"I believe what you have there is a means to seal El Dorado for all time. Am I correct?" Farbeaux reached into his satchel, placed a heavy glove on his hand, then reached inside again and pulled out a greenish lump of stone. It was coursed through with a white, chalky substance. He held it out toward Jack. "To rid the world of the source, *this* source." The room became silent as everyone stared at the same.

"Mass murder doesn't seem to be a part of your résumé, Colonel," Jack finally said.

"The selling of material has always been my way of making ends meet. As you Americans say, I have to keep up with the Joneses."

Farbeaux replaced the enriched sample of uranium in his satchel and removed the glove.

"What you are looking at in the aluminum case, *señor*, is a five-megaton nuclear warhead. What the Americans fondly call a Backpack Nuke. It's manufactured by the Hanford Nuclear Weapons Facility in Washington State. It is designed for minor troop arrest in a battlefield theater. But would do nicely in bringing down, oh, say a pyramid."

Mendez quickly backed away from the case.

"My Colombian friend may be slow on the uptake, Major, but the man truly does understand death and all its forms. Now as I was saying, this source material is very valuable; even in its rough form, it is capable of creating a weapon of—"

"A dirty bomb, a poor man's nuclear device, I'm still not buying it, Colonel. It's not—you."

"You will share in this also, and you will—" Mendez furiously started to say.

"*Señor*, please be quiet while we adults speak." Farbeaux smiled as he looked from Mendez to Collins. "Being a supplier of such material to others does not a murderer make. But I admit you're right to a certain degree, Major Collins. Commander Everett, your reputation has preceded you, sir; please do not move another inch toward that fool's weapon," Farbeaux said as he removed his own nine-millimeter and pointed it toward the commander.

Carl stopped inching toward one of the Colombians who, still taking in the situation, hadn't noticed him moving. The man snapped to and shoved him backward.

"As I was saying," Farbeaux's eyes lingered for a moment on Carl and then slowly moved to Jack, "The material has been bought and paid for by a former employer of mine, and his cause is the same as your country's: the elimination of certain terrorist cells across the world. An untraceable source of dirty material that can be sent into mountains and valleys in far-off barbaric places. So you see, our ends are the same."

"I'm afraid you have misjudged Americans, Colonel; we still do things the hard way, and some would say the stupid way. But to introduce radiation into the atmosphere to kill everything along with terrorists, well, the line has to be drawn somewhere."

Farbeaux saw the flick of Jack's eyes toward the darkened corridor from where they had come. He grimaced when he realized the major was playing for time. And Jack had indeed seen something that was sure to occupy Mendez and his men in the next few minutes.

"You're beyond belief!" Farbeaux shouted just as the creature burst from the deep shadows of the corridor.

Farbeaux fired twice as the animal took down the first Colombian by slashing at him with its claws. The Frenchman's bullets did little to slow the beast as it advanced into the chamber.

"Get them in the boat!" Jack shouted toward Carl who had taken out the man he had initially set his sights on—he had simply reached out and snapped the mercenary's neck. Picking up the man's fallen Ingram, he ran toward the cowering students and started to help Sarah and Virginia as they pushed the first boat they came to into the canal.

Several more rounds struck the creature and it roared in pain. It fell to one knee as it grew weak from this and the earlier attack.

Jack quickly ran to the case and opened it. The brightly glowing numbers were still locked at thirty minutes. He reached down, pulled his knife from its scabbard, and was about to smash the readout face, stopping the timer forever, when a stray bullet hit the case in the side. A momentary array of sparks shot from the housing of the weapon. Now a second set of numbers appeared to the right of the minutes. The seconds started tumbling down as the minutes digits went to twenty-nine. The countdown had been activated. The designers of the weapon had placed a fail-safe in the warhead that would not allow an enemy to try to destroy it by doing what had just happened. A bullet in the case would start any command previously placed into the central computer.

The major quickly rolled away from the case and gained his feet as the Colombians stopped firing at the animal and turned their weapons on him. Rounds ricocheted off the floor and walls as Jack ran toward the waiting boat. As he did, he gathered up an XM-8 and quickly fired into the stone-faced dam that held the flow of water at bay. The bullets struck, producing nothing but chips at first, then as the magazine of the XM-8 emptied the stone with the large handle in it cracked and disintegrated. Then, in quick succession, the dam split inside the wall and a torrent of water escaped into the canal system.

Farbeaux watched in horror as the first wave of water smashed into the aluminum case before it reached the canal. The weapon was washed away and was carried by the rush of the water into the canal ahead of the Americans as they shoved off in one of the boats.

Jack jumped into the boat with the fourteen people inside, and of course he fell on Jenks, who screamed out in pain.

"I can't take any more of these roller-coaster rides!" Jenks yelled as the students around him yelled in terror. The large treasure boat sped into the main shaft and disappeared into the darkness.

BRASÍLIA
CAPITAL OF BRAZIL

The Brazilian military chief of staff hung up the phone. He stood and paced to the open window of his residence. The man he had just spoken to had called his private line. His soul had been sold to the devil, the American who would soon become the president of the United States. His future was being planned by others outside of his country. But the deal he had made with the foreign devil was struck, and he had to keep his word. Now there was a supplemental order to the one that sent fifty mercenaries into the valley to stop the American rescue effort—he had to kill to protect his assault force.

He walked back to the nightstand, picked up the phone, and called the Força Aérea Brasileira (FAB), the Brazilian Air Force; he said he wanted fighters scrambled immediately. He gave the duty officer the orders and the coordinates that had been given to him by his American caller. That done, he placed the phone in its cradle and then picked up the presidential line, to inform the president that the airspace above Brazil was being invaded by military forces of the United States and that he was duty bound to shoot them down.

ANÁPOLIS AIR FORCE BASE
BRAZIL

Two Dassault Mirage 2000C fighters lifted into the sky and headed west. Used to attacking ground targets consisting of production and distribution sites for the cocaine trade, the two pilots were stunned to learn they had been ordered to intercept and down an aircraft that had been identified as a civilian airliner that had invaded Brazilian airspace. It wasn't until ten minutes after they went to afterburner that they were informed by the chief of staff personally that the invader in question was actually a military variant of the American Boeing 747, and that the aircraft's intentions were hostile.

THE WHITE HOUSE

The president had been upstairs with the First Lady, awaiting any word from Nevada, when the national security advisor called. The president went downstairs in his white shirt and went directly to Ambrose's office in the West

Wing, but was met by him in the hallway before he could reach the office.

"Mr. President, maybe you'd better inform me what operation is running in Brazil, since it seems to no longer be a secret."

"What do you mean?" he asked as he took a piece of paper from Ambrose.

"The Brazilian Air Force has scrambled two Mirage fighters, and they are heading in a westerly direction. Fort Huachuca in Arizona has picked up radio chatter that says they have orders to shoot down a 747 overflying their airspace with hostile intent."

The president read the handwritten note Ambrose had jotted down while talking with the intelligence-gathering station in Arizona. He closed his eyes and took a deep breath.

"Get me the secretary of state."

"He's already on the line, sir."

The president walked past Ambrose and into his office. He picked up the receiver and the secretary was waiting.

"Get to the presidential residence and get him to rescind that order, now!" the president said angrily, not bowing to diplomatic formality. His patience was starting to wear thin after hours of consoling his wife about their daughter.

"Mr. President, Brazil insists it has every right to down that aircraft, and will do so if it doesn't turn away from their airspace."

"To hell with it. Tell him that aircraft is there to support a rescue operation and has no intention of harming any Brazilian nationals. They are support only."

"I will try once again to get through," the secretary lied. He knew the president had ordered the fighter groups onboard *Nimitz* and *John C. Stennis* to stand down and and that they should in no way come to the aid of Proteus.

The president hung up the phone and addressed Ambrose. "How did the Brazilian Air Force get the information on Proteus?"

"The weapons platform?" Ambrose asked, acting innocent of the knowledge.

"Someone passed them information. Find out who, and do it yesterday! Also, get me a direct line to COMMSUR-PAC; I can't leave them boys hanging out there with nothing to protect them."

Ambrose had never seen the man lose his temper before. He watched as the president turned and walked quickly to the Oval Office. If he called in protection for Proteus, there would be hell to pay, and their tracks would be covered by an overt act of war.

Ambrose relaxed as he saw the secretary's makeshift plan take shape.

BLACK WATER TRIBUTARY

Newly appointed Second Lieutenant Will Mendenhall swallowed when he adjusted the magnification on his night-vision scope. Ten Zodiac-type rubber rafts entered the lagoon on the opposite side of the falls from where he had set up position. He removed his right hand and shook it, trying to get some feeling back into it after the long climb up the side of the falls. He had used the rough-hewn archway that covered the falls most of the way, and then he had to use the natural features of the terrain to ascend the rest. His hands had been severely cut and scraped from the jagged rocks and bushes. But he had finally made it only five minutes before he spied the first boat. He lowered the goggles and looked at his watch; it was 0515 in the morning. He hoped Ryan was in place, or else the team below in the mine was about to have a shitload of company. Neither Night Rider nor the major had answered his first three calls.

Mendenhall quickly removed the radio from his belt and made sure the frequency was set on channel 78, and then he took a deep breath.

"Night Rider, Night Rider, this is Conquistador, do you copy? Over!"

OPERATION SPOILED SPORT
SOMEWHERE OVER BRAZIL

The converted 747-400 was cruising at twenty-eight thousand feet in clear skies. The pilot had been on the radio for the past hour talking with the Brazilian civil authorities and explaining that they had rudder difficulties and were circling while their flight engineer checked out their hydraulic systems. They were screaming bloody murder but what else could they do, allow an air cargo plane for an influential international company like Federal Express to crash because they couldn't allow some extra time over their airspace?

Inside technicians were cursing and shouting at one another as they furiously worked on the system that wasn't supposed to be fully operational for three more years. The megawatt-class, high-energy chemical oxygen iodine laser system had malfunctioned four different times that day, causing fires in two of those incidents.

Ryan was watching the fiasco develop alongside two of his six-man Delta team when an air force major tapped him on the shoulder.

"We have Conquistador on the horn; he's asking for Night Rider One," the major said over the noise in the cargo bay.

Ryan nodded and followed him. "Tell those monkeys they're on," he said to the Delta sergeant, indicating the laser technicians. "And remind them that American lives are at stake."

Ryan entered a separate area that was closed off and quiet. He leaned over the radio operator's ejection seat, careful to avoid the ejection handle looped at the top. He picked up a headset and pushed the button on the long cord.

"Conquistador, this is Night Rider actual, over."

"Night Rider, we have bandits approaching our pos, are you tracking, over."

Ryan leaned over and whispered to the satellite officer, a lieutenant colonel who was looking at a real-time infrared image downloaded from Boris and Natasha.

"We currently count fifty-four targets and ten craft. The information has already been fed to the targeting computer," the lieutenant colonel said.

"Roger, Conquistador, we are tracking, over."

"Start the music, Night Rider, they are in our laps. Operation Spoiled Sport is on! Execute, execute, execute!"

Ryan knew it was Will Mendenhall on the radio so he decided to chance it. "Conquistador, you find a safe location. I don't trust this thing. Over."

"Been warned already, Night Rider, just get the bad guys. Conquistador is beating feet. Out."

Ryan nodded to the lieutenant colonel who was in charge of the operation and also that of targeting. His system relied on Boris and Natasha, whose infrared cameras locked onto the ring of balloon-carried heat emitters that circled the lagoon. Once that location and exact coordinates were fed into the targeting data, the KH-11 locked in on the individual heat sources of the men inside that target area or, more precisely, their body heat. The chemical oxygen iodine laser (COIL) would use the reaction of chlorine gas with liquid basic hydrogen peroxide to produce electronically excited gas-phase oxygen molecules. The oxygen would then transfer its energy to iodine atoms, which would emit radiation at 1.315 microns, producing a beam that would cleanly slice through solid steel. Assuming it worked.

The lieutenant colonel alerted the laser technicians—who actually worked for Northrop-Grumman—to activate in thirty seconds. Then he casually adjusted the mirror based inside the open barrel to disperse fifty-four separate high-energy beams that would target even moving objects—the mirror would separate and bounce the one main beam and split it into the individual killing lasers—all in theory, of course.

"Stand by to initiate," he said into his headset.

Ryan frowned as he watched the targets getting closer to the falls. "*Stand by to initiate*" *usually meant "stand by with the fire extinguishers,"* he thought, as he closed his eyes in silent prayer for his friends.

Outside of the command center, the power grid went to maximum as the main generators kicked in. They reached 100 percent power without exploding, at least this time. At the same time on the targeting screen, ten illuminated circles centered around each individual target on the surface of the lagoon.

Outside the 747, a large port spiraled open fifteen feet below the cockpit. The pilot closed a specially made blind that would protect them from the intense light that would escape the port just feet from where he and his copilot sat.

"Stand by, system at one hundred three percent power and targets are acquired. *FIRE COIL!*"

Jason Ryan flinched as nothing happened.

"Wasn't there supposed to be a power surge about right now?" he shouted angrily.

Outside the soundproof cabin and in the cockpit, the pilot saw thirteen alarms all start flashing at once. The red blinking lights showed power loss in the 747's main power systems. The four massive engines were powering down as if the pilot had slid the throttles back, and the nose of the giant 747-400 started dipping. The pilot immediately announced an emergency.

.Ryan held onto one of the computer consoles and threw off his headset.

"Goddammit! We're going to lose people down there!"

The lieutenant colonel in charge of the COIL called, "We're about to lose the aircraft, Mr. Ryan!"

"This piece of shit needs to be lost! Goddamned technology, we can make fantastic video games but we can't get one piece of military hardware to work as fucking designed!"

Ryan's words were drowned out by the whine as the giant Boeing aircraft started to fall out of the sky.

MENDENHALL WAS ABOUT to try the radio to raise Ryan again when suddenly the night around him lit up with large-caliber tracer fire from the lagoon. Someone in one of the Zodiacs had caught him on night-vision. Fifty-caliber rounds struck the rocks and bushes around him as he raised his nine-millimeter with one hand and tried the radio with the other. He fired down into the lagoon as he attempted to raise Night Rider.

RYAN WAS HOLDING onto the same console, only now it was at an angle that clearly said the 747 was heading for the deck. He was calm as he had been though a similar situation before during his last days in the navy. *You just had to know how to handle it,* he thought.

One of the Northrop-Grumman technicians in the bay knew what had happened. He suspected it during the last test and was prepared for it. The main command console was patched into the Boeing power grid and when the targeting computer sent the command electronically to the COIL itself, the entire system shorted out. He pulled open the panel and found the wires he needed, and jerked on them. They came free and then he pulled the command wire and routed it through another power circuit. He quickly reattached the cockpit throttle input cable. Immediately, he was rewarded with the increasing whine of the four General Electric engines as they sparked back up to full power. The technician leaned over and struck the intercom.

"Power restored to aircraft systems. Power restored to COIL targeting!" The tech slid down along one of the interior bulkheads. *Man, are heads going to roll when they find out they had routed one of the weapons systems through the platform power systems. Shit!*

Ryan felt the nose come up as the power from the engines clearly indicated they were once again climbing.

"Rider, we're taking heavy fire, over!" Ryan finally heard Mendenhall's firm but harried call.

He was about to initiate the order to fire once again when the radar intercept officer at the front of the 747 called over the headsets: "We have two inbound bogies at fifty miles and closing fast. They snuck up on us. They're squawking Brazilian Air Force and they are ordering us out of their airspace or they will open fire."

"Time to firing sequence on Proteus?" Ryan asked loudly into the radio.

"Five minutes to bring up power," the lieutenant colonel said as he quickly retargeted the scattered boats.

"Damn it, we'll be a fireball in two minutes!"

THE TWO MIRAGE 2000 fighters finally saw the anticollision lights of the 747 after the giant plane made a sudden dive for the jungle below. They adjusted their pattern to take up station one mile behind the large jet. The lead fighter armed his weapons. His orders were clear: down the Americans.

He used his thumb to select his weapon, two South African–made MAA-1 Piranhas, a short-range air-to-air missile relying on infrared passive guidance, which seeks the target's heat emissions coming primarily from the engines. He immediately received guidance lock from the seeker heads of the two missiles themselves, which were poised on the launch rails beneath both wings just waiting for the electrical signal that would send them on their deadly way.

"GODDAMMIT, THEY HAVE missile lock on us, Ryan!" the pilot called over the radio.

"I don't give a damn, we have our orders! Now get us back into position and fire the damned weapon before we lose those people down there!"

THE BRAZILIAN FIGHTER pilots were relieved to see the giant aircraft start a slow turn back to the east. Then they watched and followed the 747, hoping they were about to leave the area from the direction they had come. They didn't know it was only starting to make a long and slow circle as their targets were reacquired. When the lead pilot saw they were commencing another attack run, he became angered at the perceived deception and quickly spurred the French-built fighter back into its optimum firing position. He knew the 747 was ten minutes away from a sure death as it slowly turned.

THE WHITE HOUSE

Ambrose nodded to the Secret Service agent outside the Oval Office and then walked in. The president was standing at his desk with his hands placed firmly on its top.

"What's happening?"

The president didn't answer. He was looking down in thought as the muscles in his jaw were clenching and unclenching. Then the phone buzzed.

"The president of Brazil is returning your call," his secretary said from the outer office.

"Mr. President, what are you doing?" Ambrose asked nervously.

"Something I should have done from the beginning," he said as he picked up the phone.

Ambrose froze. The man was calling the president of Brazil personally, circumventing the secretary of state.

"Mr. President, thank you for taking my call. I need to ask you to stand down your forces. The aircraft in question is on a mission to support a rescue operation only. There is no hostile intent on their part."

Ambrose slowly tossed a file folder on the coffee table in the front of one of the couches and sat. He closed his eyes as he felt his career, even his freedom, slipping out of his grasp.

"Yes, Secretary Nussbaum has undoubtedly explained to you the circumstances surrounding the—"

The president fell silent as the conversation became one-sided. He listened intently for three minutes and then angrily pounded his fist on his desk. He thanked the president of Brazil and hung up. He then pressed the button on his intercom. "Get me Admiral Handley at COMSURPAC headquarters in Pearl Harbor, now!"

* * *

THE TONE EMANATING from the seeker heads of the Piranhas once again told the pilot his missiles had locked onto the 747 heat signature. He was moments away from triggering the weapon when his wingman called out frantically.

"We have two inbound targets closing in from the west! They are at mach two point two and coming on fast from low altitude; they must have been orbiting in our airspace somewhere!"

The flight lead removed his finger from the trigger and started looking to the west. It took him a moment to find the afterburner glare of the two hostile aircraft, but when he saw them he knew they had covered their approach by flying at tree canopy level. As he thought this he heard the telltale warning that his fighter was being painted by the enemy weapons radar. Then a split second later, the tone became louder and steady, and that was when he knew his Mirage had been locked onto by an enemy missile.

"Brazilian fighter planes, this is United States Navy fighter aircraft to your west. We ask that you alter your approach to United States experimental aircraft that is currently off course. Their overflight is an accident, repeat, it is accidental. We have orders to protect United States property at all costs. Do you read, Brazilian flight leader?"

A CHEER ROSE inside the spacious area inside Proteus as the announcement was made that the Brazilian fighters had turned away. Ryan listened as the communications operator informed them that the attacking fighters had been called off by the Brazilian chief of staff, calling out of Brasília.

"Goddamn!" one of the Delta men said, shaking his head. "Someone told someone else we're the good guys!"

"Colonel, how long until you have a firing solution?" Ryan asked.

"We have one now, but it looks like our targets are awful close to your no-fire area; they are almost clear of the heat signature pattern."

"Fire, goddammit, FIRE!"

The 747 started to shake and vibrate. They heard the main generator kick over to full power. And that was when Ryan just knew the whole platform was going to explode.

BLACK WATER TRIBUTARY

Mendenhall heard the click as his weapons firing pin hit an empty chamber. He had just hoped he had poked a few holes in a few Zodiacs below. With that thought of devious hope came twenty heavy-caliber rounds. Their tracers phosphorous red and horrible to behold, they slammed into his position.

He lay back and fumbled for another magazine when the sky lit up with a green blaze that shocked him into stillness. As he watched upward in amazement, fifty-two fluorescent laser beams coursed through the clear night air with deadly silence. It looked as if they formed the spokes of a wheel as they struck and then moved like giant stirrers mixing a drink.

The lead Zodiacs exploded as the COIL made adjustments in her targeting. Men were sliced in two by the green mirror-enhanced lasers as they struck them and punctured easily though their clothes and flesh. They didn't even have time to react as the airborne laser killed half of the assault element in a matter of 1.327 seconds.

The sky had formed into a giant pinwheel of green light, taking out the first twenty-five-plus men before they knew they had even been attacked. Will Mendenhall was in shock as the attack ended even before he had finished flinching. He rubbed his eyes from the sudden flash, then looked out over the water. He saw nothing but floating rubber and dead men. However, the last five Zodiacs had turned and tried desperately to make for the far end of the lagoon. After seeing the deaths of their comrades at the hands of something they would never understand, they thought a more stealthy attack might be in order.

Mendenhall turned away and sat down hard on the small outcropping of rock. He watched as the last remains of the lead boats of the assault element sank beneath the calm waters of the lagoon, never suspecting that there were survivors.

THE SYSTEM HAD performed nearly flawlessly. With the exception of the short firing cycle, which allowed the rear attack boats to escape, the laser performed as intended for the first time after over three hundred laboratory and field tests. The technicians knew they would pay for it later because the generator had shorted out (causing another fire) and the thirty-five-inch mirrored barrel had melted under the intense heat. But right now, the largest assemblage of American nerds in the air ever were jumping for joy and giving high fives until the lieutenant colonel burst out of the targeting room and yelled for them to knock it off.

"In case you just forgot, you just killed one hell of a lot of men with this fucking thing; now let's see if maybe we can still help them by getting this damned system back online to get the rest of the bad guys!"

The technicians immediately silenced as he angrily stepped back inside.

Ryan went over to the twenty field techs from Northrop-Grumman.

"Listen, they were men, but they were also bad guys and they were on their way to kill some friends of mine, and possibly a bunch of students. So take *that* with you when you go home. You did *real* good," he said and walked away.

The loudspeaker over their heads crackled. It was the commander in targeting speaking: "Okay, we had a malfunction in the fire sequence and half of the assault element was missed. They are currently grounding their craft on the far bank of the lagoon. Satellite imagery indicates they are regrouping. All our systems are down and—"

The explosion erupted out of the thickly protected generator systems room. A fireball outgassed through the thin aluminum of the 747 in a horrendous fireball. The giant air-craft was rocked as it first slammed the crew to the floor and then those that weren't strapped in into the air, as the Boeing jet lost and then gained altitude. Roaring wind swept through the interior of the aircraft as its integrity failed at al-most twenty-five thousand feet, the sudden depressurization pulling fifteen of the unsecured technicians to their death through the ten-foot diameter hole.

Ryan was stunned and was close to passing out, first from hitting the floor and then from his flight to the roof of the 747 as the impact knocked the remaining oxygen from his lungs. As his eyes fluttered he could hear men shouting as they fought to control the dying aircraft and others as they reached for men sliding away toward the massive tear. Ryan's slide toward the breach was halted by a strong arm.

Suddenly he felt an oxygen mask slip over his bleeding head, and the first trickle of air as it coursed down into his windpipe while the arms were securing him to the matted flooring. He shook his head and tried to focus his eyes. The Delta sergeant was there, shaking him and trying to make the navy man stand up.

The 747 was going down. Ryan felt the nose of the great plane was at an angle that didn't lie. He saw at least two more technicians sucked out of the damaged generator sec-tion, along with papers and equipment, as the tremendous pressure bled the air out of the fuselage.

"All personnel, stand by to eject. We have a total vital systems failure of the aircraft. Delta element, when we call, 'eject, eject, eject,' blow the cargo hatch!"

"Oh, shit!" the sergeant holding up Ryan said into his oxygen mask. "Delta equipment up, prepare for HALO!"

"Oh, no," Ryan said as he staggered to his feet.

As the plane passed below 18,000 feet and the interior of the 747 stabilized somewhat, the sergeant yelled at him, "What the hell, you wanted our element on the ground any-way. Did you plan on living forever?"

Ryan started to struggle into his chute. "Well, maybe living just another year would have been nice."

MENDENHALL WAS JUST starting to make his way down the steep incline when he saw the flash in the night sky above him. His jaw dropped when he saw an expanse of flame streak outward from an unseen object as it started falling from high altitude. He closed his eyes and prayed it wasn't Lieutenant Ryan and the rest of Proteus.

AS THE REMAINING crew ejection seats exploded out of the doomed 747 one and two at a time, the Delta team, with Ryan in tow, pushed the panic button of the large cargo door on the right side of the aircraft. After the brief explosion of the door, they strained and braced themselves against the blast of passing air and lined up by twos for HALO—high-altitude low-open—parachute egress. The only problem was they were becoming a low-altitude jump very fast, as the steep dive of the giant 747 became even steeper.

"Jesus Christ, what about the tail?"

"Oh, yeah, Mr. Ryan, don't hit the tail," the sergeant said loudly behind his mask. He pulled the lieutenant out of the door and into the painful slipstream.

They flew out and down like discarded paper from a fast-moving automobile. The first two-man team out of the cargo hatch flew up and over the swept-back rear stabilizer. The rest went below, luckily missing the fast-moving tonnage of aluminum. The crew, jumping with their ejection seats attached, had a much smoother exit from the plane. The Delta element would watch below and try their best to follow the 747's air force crew and remaining civilian technicians to the ground.

As they fell toward the black jungle below, they knew to a man they would land at least a half mile from the lagoon. The now fully engulfed 747, flames licking its frame like a falling meteor, slammed into the jungle three miles away, ripping a gash in the dark countryside.

Ryan watched as the top canopies of the trees rushed at him. The sergeant had explained at what altitude they would pop their chutes, but he had lost his wrist altimeter sometime during the commotion of getting the hell out of the burning plane. His gloves had been ripped from his hands in the slipstream and his fingers were frozen Popsicles. As he reached for his ripcord he knew he wasn't going to be able to pull it in time, as the ground was coming at him like an oncoming freight train and his fingers just couldn't feel the damned thing.

He closed his eyes as he waited for the bone-crushing impact that was only moments away, when he felt someone slamming a fist into his black jumpsuit. Then he heard his parachute pop, and he suddenly slowed as the black silk caught the dense air. He struggled to look above him, knowing that it had been the sergeant who had reached out and saved his life.

RYAN OPENED HIS eyes and tried desperately to get the headgear and mask off his face. The world had become a foggy, strange place from his new vantage point. He knew he was upside down because the flow of blood in his ears was pounding away as if his heart were in overdrive. The cold oxygen flowing into his mask was enough to fog the glass of his mask, and that terrified him more than anything: not being able to see just what kind of danger he was truly in.

He struggled and felt something give way above his feet where they were tangled in the black chute. He didn't want to chance using the radio that was still attached to his mask, for fear he might not be in friendly territory, which he wholeheartedly doubted he was. He heard a sharp tear in the fabric of the chute. He felt his stomach lurch as he dropped two feet farther toward the ground. He finally freed his right hand and arm, and tore the oxygen mask from his face.

Ryan breathed in the hot and humid air of the small valley. He turned his head as somewhere off in the distance he heard the call of birds and the sound of a waterfall. Then he ventured a look down and closed his eyes. He was no more than three feet off the forest floor. It was a miracle—he had hit one of the few open spots within a quarter mile of the lagoon. He quickly fought out of his harness and released himself from his upside-down personal hell. He hit ground on his shoulders as his feet tangled in the harness at the last moment, and he managed to knock the wind from his lungs.

"Nice one, Mr. Ryan." The whispered voice came out of the darkness somewhere to his front.

Ryan eased his hand to his holstered nine-millimeter Berretta.

"Easy, Lieutenant, easy, I'm a good guy. But be careful, there are some of the other fellas around here; I saw them as we came in. Now come on, we got some friends we have to get out of some trees."

Ryan watched as Sergeant Jim Flannery slowly came out of the bush, rubbing greasepaint on his exposed features. He finished and tossed the tube to Ryan.

"Black up, Lieutenant."

"Have you seen anyone else?" Ryan asked as he painted his face.

"Not yet, but when we do I sure as hell hope they came down with more equipment than I did. I lost everything except my peashooter."

Ryan knew he was talking about the same weapon he himself had, a lousy nine-millimeter, which wasn't too damned good for fending off heavy weapons.

The Delta sergeant easily placed his chute harness and helmet within the bush and left them. He placed a black and green do-rag on his head and winked at Ryan.

"Well, I guess we start our defense of the lagoon from here. Let's get the rest of the cavalry."

Ryan nodded; his eyes were the only part of his body visible in the darkness of the jungle surrounding them.

"Right, I guess Proteus has just gone back to Operation Conquistador," he mumbled as he took up station behind the more experienced Delta man.

"I guess you can say that. Let's just hope we find one hell of a lot more conquistadors than we have right now."

"Yeah, like maybe a couple with real weapons."

The sergeant nodded in agreement, and the two men set out to find the rest of the doomed Operation Proteus team.

24

THE PYRAMID

THE first turn in the canal almost did them in as the boat slammed hard into the wall and the fifteen souls inside careened around in the large treasure boat. The current was picking up speed as more and more water slammed them from behind. The dam had completely broken free above them, and they now found themselves traveling at breakneck speed toward a dark and unknown death.

As Jack tried to focus as water cascaded over him, he ventured a look up from the front of the boat. The darkness was once again becoming shaded green. The Incan designers had embedded large stones of tritium ore in the walls to illuminate the treasure trail. At least now he could vaguely see the turn in the system that would smash them to splinters. Jack knew they had to try and control their descent somehow.

He addressed the panicked faces. "Look, we have to start shifting weight in this—" The boat careered against another turn and Jack was awash with water as the boat bounced into another canal and slipped down an even steeper causeway. He regained his sitting position and held onto the sides. "Watch me. When I raise my right hand, everyone crowd to the right side and vice versa, or we're going to wind up hitting a wall at fifty miles an hour."

He didn't wait for anyone to nod or comment; he just turned and faced the front. Carl would have to control them in the back.

In the dim light, the major saw another turn coming and

this one went left. He held up his left arm and yelled, although over the roar of water no one could hear him: "Shift, now!"

Carl jumped to the left side and pulled Robby along with him. The others upon seeing this repeated the movement; most seemed to fall on the master chief, who again howled.

Jack braced himself as the boat started to slide to the left, too late he saw the weight wasn't sufficient enough to make the turn. The boat slipped and slid into the curving wall. It hit with such force that he was tossed from the boat. He hung on to its side for dear life as it started to gather momentum once again. Sarah was there in an instant and was joined by Kelly. Together, they helped the major back into the vessel.

"Thanks, I—"

The canal shaft was brilliantly lit up by the flare of gunfire as rounds slammed into the walls around them. Jack looked back and saw Farbeaux had jumped into another boat along with Mendez and one other man. They were traveling light, so they had less weight to control. Another burst of fire nearly caught him before Jack had time to get into the bottom of the boat.

With no control, the boat gathered speed and slammed into the next turn. It struck the wall so hard that it tipped to the right and then spun on its blunt bow. Now they were traveling backward. More bullets were fired and Jack heard one of the students cry out in pain.

He rose and fired his nine-millimeter back toward the onrushing boat. He saw Farbeaux's eyes widen before the Frenchman slammed himself into the bottom. One of Jack's rounds caught Mendez in the shoulder, and he saw him spin and collapse below the gunwale. Just as he took aim again, another turn rocked him to the side. This time they all heard the crack of wood as the boat began to split in two. Water started rushing through the gap as it started to come apart.

"We've had it, Jack!" Carl called out.

"Everyone grab onto someone and—" It was too late, as he started to speak the boat broke into two pieces and all fifteen people went into the roaring canal.

The water was deep and unlike rapids. Jack knew they could survive if they just paid attention. Another turn was quickly upon them as the water brought them around a corner. A young woman sped by Jack and went under. He quickly reached out and grabbed a handful of hair and pulled her up and back to him, as they both hit the wall and were raised up into the air as it curled around the curve.

Farbeaux held on as his own boat made the curve and came out in the midst of the current-tossed survivors. He watched in horror as the remaining Colombian in the front of his boat took aim at two students struggling to stay afloat to his right. He knew he couldn't react in time.

"Save your ammunition for those who can fight back, fool!" he shouted.

He could see the man was going to shoot anyway. Farbeaux was furious but was also powerless to stop him as a sudden roar, louder than even the rushing water, sounded in the canal shaft. The man was pulled into the water by a large webbed hand, and then the vessel seemed to hit a submerged object. Farbeaux and Mendez found themselves airborne. They hit the water. Both were close to panic as they realized one of the animals was in the canal with them.

Together seventeen men and women were on a ride none of them could have ever imagined. The canal system was becoming steeper and the turns not as numerous as they traveled down the pyramid that got wider at its base.

Jack tried to rein in as many as he could, yelling for each to hang on to the next, to form a chain that would allow them to travel the current together. Without notice, the water spilled over a small fall and now they were all airborne. Carl held the master chief one moment and then lost him as Jenks's own weight tore him from his grasp. They hit the water on the next level and all went under. When Carl surfaced he saw the master chief only feet away, grimacing in pain as Virginia splashed toward them. It was that movement that told Carl they had passed into light. As he looked back he saw that the fall of water they had come over had sent them into a tunnel, a tunnel that led them to a place they had been before.

"Look!" cried one of the sputtering students.

They were entering the main chamber. *Teacher* was there, still smashed on the staircase leading from this very canal.

"I'll be damned," Carl said and slapped the slowing current as he watched Jack ahead, already helping students out of the water and onto the stone staircase. "That was one hell of a ride!"

"What did you do to my boat!" the master chief cried out as he floated out of the cave.

THE SOUTH SHORE OF THE LAGOON

The Delta team was complete. It had taken close to twenty minutes to locate them all and another ten to get four Delta and air force personnel down and out of the high trees where they'd landed. At least they had been able to hang onto three coils of rope. They took stock as they reached the lagoon's south end. The five Zodiacs were just starting out. Altogether, to stop them, the men had at their disposal thirteen nine-millimeter Beretta handguns, two Ingram assault weapons with only one extra thirty-round clip, and one M-14 sniper rifle with no extra ammunition.

"Hope you boys have a plan that calls for throwing rocks when we run out of boom-boom," the air force colonel said as he knelt beside two injured airmen.

"Even with what we have, it won't be much against those fifties mounted in those Zodiacs," the Delta sergeant said.

"Come on, guys, we have to make sure those boats don't get to the other side," Ryan said anxiously.

"That's what we plan on doing, Mr. Ryan, but we only have so much firepower to accomplish that mission," Delta Sergeant Melendez said. "Look, I hate to say this, but our opening salvo can't be kill shots; we have to first slow and then stop the Zodiacs. Punch as many holes in 'em as we can. We're going to take one hell of a lot of return fire. Discipline, gentlemen, discipline."

The thirteen men gathered around nodded their understanding.

"Okay, two-man firing teams: my people pair up with the blue birds and I'll take Ryan. Boats first, assholes second, got it? Wait till my fire, then let all hell break loose."

The men paired up without comment and started to file into the dense terrain.

As the makeshift rescue force moved out, they failed to see the small Indian who went right to the spot the men had been only moments before. The mud-covered man raised a small whistle to his bone-pierced lips and lightly tooted, imitating one of the many Amazonian birds perfectly. As he did, the jungle started filling with the not-so-lost tribe of Sincaro, and they moved off silently, following the Americans.

EL DORADO

Everett swam to the right side of the cave opening. He waved at Jack and the two men made eye contact. The major knew exactly what Carl was up to. Jack shot the lieutenant commander a sloppy salute, then reached out and helped the others pull the master chief from the water and onto the stone steps.

"Look at my boat," Jenks wailed.

Carl waited. As he did so, he pulled his last clip of ammunition from his rear pocket and ejected the empty from the Berretta. He inserted the new one with no time to spare as the two men came sputtering out of the cave. Farbeaux was first as he tried to hold the heavier Mendez up. The fat man wasn't trying to assist the Frenchman in the least; he only held his wounded arm. Farbeaux saw Carl immediately and continued on. Carl followed.

Jack was there with the rest of the survivors and even helped Mendez to the steps. As the Colombian collapsed, Jack held out a hand to Farbeaux and the Frenchman took it.

"Major, you amaze me no end. Your calculated risk seemed to have paid off; unfortunately, I'm afraid it was for nothing, unless of course you managed among your other miraculous activities to have disarmed a certain warhead in your mad rush down the feeder canals."

"Afraid not, Colonel."

Farbeaux found footing on the steps and collapsed in exhaustion. "A shame," was all he said as he lay back against the stone beneath the legs of Supay.

CARL HELD FARBEAUX and Mendez at gunpoint. The Colombian had offered the American everything this side of the moon to set him free. But Carl and even Farbeaux laughed at the attempt. They followed Jack and the others up the stone stairway and into the brighter chamber lights they had set up before.

Jack and Virginia found a smooth spot in the floor and lay the grumbling master chief down. He immediately slapped Jack's hands away. The major stood up, wondering where Sanchez, Danielle, and Ellenshaw were. He didn't have to wait long. He heard a sound and the professor stumbled out from behind the wall of supplies. Jack reached for his nine-millimeter just as Heidi, her head bandaged and still bleeding, came next, supported by Danielle and Sanchez. Then came a man Jack didn't know. He was dressed in a wetsuit, the same as himself and Carl. The stranger had a lethal-looking handgun pointed at the head of Heidi Rodriguez.

"You will release Señor Mendez, or this woman will be the first to be blown apart," the man said menacingly in accented English.

"I would do as he says, Major; he is rather an unsavory character," Farbeaux said as he advanced and slowly removed Jack's handgun.

With his good arm, Mendez relieved the lieutenant commander of his weapon and then slammed Carl in the face. The navy man didn't go down; he just wiped the blood from his nose and mouth, and gave the fat man a strange smile.

The others reacted with cries to the assault on Carl but Jack held up a hand, stopping them from moving. Robby was pulled back by Kelly, who watched the scene with dawning horror.

"Sorry, Major, this dick came out of nowhere," Sanchez said as he was silenced by a shove in the back.

The man motioned for Carl to get closer to Jack so he could keep them both in his line of sight.

"Why don't you let Sanchez help Dr. Rodriguez, Danielle, so you can join your partner?" Jack said as Sarah and Carl raised their eyebrows.

Danielle looked at Jack, and then at Carl, knowing it was he who had found her out.

"You three knew?" she asked as she let Heidi's arm drop. Robby rushed over to help Sanchez as Ellenshaw sat hard on the floor.

Jack looked at his watch and remained silent. Twenty minutes.

"Yes, our boss is just a tad smarter than you gave him credit for. Director Compton never believed your story for one minute, especially after Commander Everett here saw your tan line on the *George Washington*, which sent Dr. Compton off investigating."

Danielle closed her eyes, then reached down and fingered the spot on her ring finger. It had once held her wedding ring, whose recent presence had left a clear mark of untanned skin beneath.

Farbeaux laughed. He stepped forward and put his arm around Danielle and brought her close to him.

"I told you they would be hard to fool, my dear."

She shrugged out of his embrace and looked at Captain Rosolo.

"It took everything I had to convince this maniac not to murder us all," she said as she took a menacing step toward Rosolo.

Mendez, still holding his arm, stepped forward and aimed the gun he had taken from Carl at the French couple. "Stop or I will shoot you," said Mendez to Farbeaux. "Now I have two reasons to kill you, *señor*, for lying to me about the dangerous mineral, and now to find your supposed ex-wife, who seems to still be very much connected to you, very devious."

Jack was watching Rosolo. The weapon he held was of an obscure Russian make, a Malfutrov fifty-caliber. There was a running joke in American Special Forces that named the weapon the Malfunction for its proclivity to misfire after being dunked in water. As Jack watched, a small drop of water fell from the handgrip where the weapon's ammunition clip was stored. It was something that gave him hope.

"It is time to leave this place," Farbeaux said as he turned Danielle toward the stairs. "In case you have forgotten, there's a rather nasty little device floating around somewhere."

"I agree, *señor*. But you will remain here with the Americans."

Farbeaux turned to look at Mendez. The barrel of the Berretta was pointed right at him.

"Please remove the gun from your belt," commanded Mendez.

Farbeaux flashed a significant look at Carl, who began to prepare himself.

"My man, Captain Rosolo, will shoot everyone here if you do not comply." Mendez looked over at the major. "I'm sure he would very much like to complete what he failed to do in Montana."

Jack half smiled and asked Rosolo, "That was you?"

"Yes, you can be assured the mission would not have failed if I had been on the ground and not in the air," the thin man said as he took a quick step over to his left. He snatched Sarah away from Jack's side and placed the gun to her head and fired.

BLACK WATER TRIBUTARY

Captain Santos chomped on his cigar as he throttled the *Rio Madonna* forward. He knew certain places where the shallow draft riverboat could penetrate the rapids, and he steered toward the first. His men were hung onto the gunwales and surveyed the rushing waters out ahead of them as he steered the large boat to the left. He had released the equipment barge back on the river and beached it as he had started his run. He cursed as the bottom came out of nowhere; the *Rio Madonna* lifted free of the water momentarily and then slammed back down.

The moment to act was upon him and his boat, and it was time to earn his rather bloated financial rewards. He knew he would only have moments to get to the lagoon and stop the people he was being paid to stop.

As he successfully turned away from one of the more hazardous rocks in the rapids, he ventured a hand from the old wheel and felt for the necklace in his shirt. He pressed his fingers around the round object inside just as the *Rio Madonna* smashed into another hidden rock along her run for the lagoon.

EL DORADO

The firing pin clicked and Sarah flinched at the suddenness of her nondeath. Jack reacted first, Carl and Farbeaux next. The latter grabbed the failed weapon at the same time Sarah realized she was still alive and swerved away. Farbeaux dove and at the same time tossed Carl the weapon he had removed from his waistband. He fired and took Mendez in the head. The fat man fell to the floor, right on top of the master chief.

Jack had the gun before Rosolo knew what had happened. The captain took a swing at him with the side of his palm and missed, as the major ducked away, came up a foot to Rosolo's left, and cuffed him in the side of the head.

Carl extended Farbeaux's gun toward him and Danielle. The lieutenant commander didn't bother to look at the struggle between Jack and Rosolo. In his opinion, the outcome was a foregone conclusion. Rosolo had made a very serious mistake with Jack: he had tried to kill Sarah.

Rosolo had gone into a jujitsu stance and Jack smiled. The students who didn't know his capabilities started hollering for Jack as the two men squared off. As Rosolo brought his palms up, Jack did just the opposite; he lowered his arms and circled the captain. As Rosolo lunged, Jack easily sidestepped the open palm and then elbowed Rosolo across the bridge of his nose, shattering the bone and sending an explosive arch of shrapnel made up of cartilage and bone fragments into the captain's brain, dropping him to the stone floor like a rag doll.

The students were stunned. Everett tilted his head at Farbeaux and Danielle. "Doesn't pay to piss Jack off, does it?"

Virginia was just standing and watching. Never in her life had she witnessed such a quick death as what she had just seen.

Jack turned and faced everyone. His eyes were mere slits and it took a moment for him to come out of the semitrance he was in. Then all at once his vision cleared and he saw Sarah.

"You all right?" he asked as he broke his self-induced spell and started forward toward the group of students.

Sarah didn't move at first, she just swallowed and nodded her head, stunned at the sudden change of predicament.

"Come on, people, move, we have to get out of here. Sanchez, get Heidi into the water. Commander Everett, cut those two loose, we don't have time right now."

Carl lowered the weapon but was tempted to raise it again and put a bullet in Farbeaux's brain. But he was stayed by the fact that he didn't murder.

"Until the next time, Henri," he said as he left the couple and ran to help get the late Mendez off the master chief.

Farbeaux pulled Danielle roughly, for some reason angry at himself for doing what he was about to do. He thought he must be insane for feeling this way.

"Come, my dear, time to leave."

"We cannot let them live—they know about us. I could never go home again."

"That doesn't matter; their director knows about you anyway and, if I know Compton, he'll hunt you down for our small deceit. Now, we must get out."

Danielle was shocked beyond measure as she stumbled along in his hard grip. If she didn't know any better, she could swear she saw remorse on his face. Or was it guilt?

As Farbeaux approached the spot on the staircase just below the height of the dock where *Teacher* lay grounded, the rising water had belched up one more surprise. There, floating against her stern where the water was starting to lap, was the aluminum case. The weapon had survived intact its journey down the canal. Farbeaux slid to a stop, losing his footing and dragging Danielle down on top of him.

"What are you doing?" she screamed.

"The weapon."

She looked and saw the container as the rising water around *Teacher* bumped it again and again between its twin thrusters.

"We have to get out!" Danielle cried.

Farbeaux quickly made a decision. He reached around and removed his satchel; the strap holding it slid off his shoulder. He opened it and took out the heavy Geiger counter, which he tossed away to smash against the stone steps. He then took the satchel and crossed the strap over Danielle's head.

"Take it and go. I'll meet you on the river, by the rapids." He leaned over and kissed her on the mouth. "Now go."

"What . . . what are you doing?"

"I can't live with the fact that I helped kill those young people, I have to help this Collins get rid of the device." He roughly pushed her away as he stood and ran for the rapidly disappearing *Teacher*.

Danielle watched him for a moment, then stood and made for the canal and the now-vanishing opening that led out of El Dorado. She took a last look at her husband, adjusted the satchel that contained the plutonium, and then turned and dove into the rushing water.

* * *

AS JACK HELPED Sanchez with Heidi, Ellenshaw was the first to see the Frenchman as they breached the top of the dock and staircase.

"Look," he said, pointing.

Jack saw it immediately: Farbeaux was struggling with a yellow anodized aluminum case that could only be one thing, the nuclear weapon. He was trying to bring it to the vanishing staircase but couldn't get the momentum he needed to fight the speedy current.

"Professor, take Heidi and make for the opening," Jack said as he handed Heidi off and ran down the stone steps. He jumped feet first into the current, splashed his way to the Frenchman, and helped get the case to the first step out of the water.

"You wanna steal this, too," Jack quipped as they collapsed against the case.

"Do you always joke upon the moment of your imminent death, Major?"

Jack didn't answer, as he was watching everyone dive into the water and start swimming toward the falls. He saw Robby try to help Kelly, and her slap his hands away and dive into the water. Virginia and two of the students had the master chief around the neck and were dogpaddling toward the now-submerged opening. Then he noticed a shadow fall on him.

"You two get the hell out of here," he said, looking up into the faces of Carl and Sarah.

"Not happening, Jack. I think we've been through this before," Carl said as he reached down and pulled the major up. Then he grimaced and helped Farbeaux also.

Sarah just held up a hand when Jack turned on her. "Save it, Jack, we're wasting time."

"The thing is, Lieutenant, I'm all out of ideas," Jack said as he looked down at the case.

They heard shouts and looked up and toward the canal. Just before the master chief's head went under the water they heard him.

"Did I hear right?" Farbeaux asked.

Sarah, Carl, and Jack looked at each other and said it at the same time.

"Turtle!"

THE LAGOON

Delta Sergeant Melendez unscrewed the cylindrical silencer mounted on the barrel of his nine-millimeter. He patted Ryan's shoulder and winked at him. Then he raised the weapon and took aim on the lead Zodiac that was already twenty feet from shore. The black rubber glimmered with wetness just as the first brightness of morning turned the blackness of the night into an almost even blacker sunrise as it filtered through the canopy at the center of the lagoon.

Just as the sergeant started to squeeze the trigger, screams and shouts filled the night air from the direction of the falls. The lead boat opened up with the heavy thump of its fifty-caliber machine gun, momentarily blinding the men taking aim on shore. Melendez took a deep breath and fired five times in quick succession. The first four bullets found the hard rubber of the first Zodiac, and the fifth struck the man operating the heavy weapon, dropping him into the murky water. Because of the people in the water, Melendez had disobeyed his own orders about boats first, bad guys second.

"Oops, last one missed the fucking boat," the sergeant said as the other teams opened fire.

Ryan wanted to smile at the remark but didn't as bullets flew out of the jungle and caught the assault teams in the boats off guard. Several men, more than likely Delta, let fly and hit several of the other machine gunners, dropping them also. One of the heavy-caliber weapons managed to swing around and open fire. It was like hell opened up around the men onshore. They dove to take cover as the large rounds struck trees and plants around them, forcing them down. One airmen and one of the Delta men cried out as large pieces of tree trunk and bark struck them. It wasn't long before another of the attackers' fifties found them and started laying waste to their hiding places. Ryan figured it would only be a matter of moments before their protective cover was down to nothing.

The men, each in turn, would stand and fire quickly and then duck. Ryan heard the M-14 sniper weapon open fire with six quick and sure shots, dropping four of the men that were arrogantly standing inside the rear craft. Then another loud burst of two more fifty-calibers strafed the area immediately to their right, and this time there were accompanying screams of pain as some of the deadly projectiles found their mark.

Ryan was following Melendez when he suddenly reached out and grabbed the soldier's boot.

"Listen," he said loudly.

As the sergeant stopped and tried to hear over the continuous gun battle, he thought he heard a long blow of a ship's whistle.

"It's an engine," Ryan yelled over the din. He quickly ventured a look up and over some elephant ear plants. "Goddamn, look at that!"

As both men looked on, an ancient-looking river tug came careering down the rapids and then entered the calmer lagoon as if its pilot had done it a hundred times before.

"I think the bad guys just got reinforced," the sergeant said, as he placed his last clip of nine-millimeter rounds into his automatic.

As Ryan grimaced, looking down at his own handgun with the slide all the way back, indicating it was empty, a bright red flare fired from the boat. His momentary hopes had been dashed by the sergeant. He had hoped it was some navy fellas coming to their rescue.

As the flare hit its apex, over a hundred arrows suddenly arched into the sky with a sound none of the Americans had ever heard before. Then they heard the thumping of large sticks as they pounded against hollow logs, a deep drumming that was absolutely frightening. Then the attackers in the Zodiacs started screaming as the volley of arrows hit them. As Jason Ryan started to stand up, he felt the sharpened end of a stick press against his back as the screams of the dying filled the darkened air around the killing field.

The Sincaro had arrived to take back their Garden of Eden.

EL DORADO

As they struggled with the yellow case, trying desperately to get it inside *Teacher*, the very canal shaft they had come down earlier had filled to the point where it could no longer withstand the pressure. The outer walls lining the cave opening gave way. Ten million gallons of water that could no longer be restrained by mere stone cascaded into the open chamber. The rush smashed into *Teacher* and sent her sideways, slamming into the dock. Jack, Carl, Sarah, and Farbeaux were almost snatched away, but all held on thanks to a jagged opening they had the container wedged into. *Teacher* once again began to take on water as she settled hard, awash against the legs of the great statue of Supay.

"Push it in; we have five minutes till detonation," Jack called out as he doubled his efforts at trying to fit a square peg into a round opening. They were all losing footing as the chamber filled. None could touch the staircase as they and *Teacher* rose above the dock.

The ancient stone supporting Supay started to crumble from the wash of water. It was Carl who heard the first loud crack and rumble as part of the left leg of the great statue gave way and fell into the swirling water.

"Oh great, come on, come on," he said as they shoved harder.

"Damn!" Jack shouted as he stopped shoving suddenly and started pulling.

"What are you doing, Major?" Farbeaux cried as he tried to restrain Jack.

The major didn't answer, and finally pulled the case free. As it hit the water, another loud crack was sounded inside the chamber as the entire left leg of Supay crumbled into the race of water. *Teacher* was floating on a prayer as her forward spaces took on more and more water. Sarah screamed. The giant statue had started to fall backward toward the canal.

"Oh, this isn't happening," Carl called out as he saw what was going to be the result.

The statue hit the water with the force of an exploding fifteen-inch naval gun. *Teacher*, along with the four people, was pushed farther into the interior of El Dorado. Then Supay did what Carl had hoped it wouldn't. It plugged the opening to the falls like a cork in a bottle. Once the great stone statue had settled, wedged into the canal, the water started rising at a tremendous rate.

Jack had lost Sarah when *Teacher* had been picked up by the crashing wave, and Carl was no longer with him and Farbeaux. He could only hope they hadn't been crushed by the boat's heavy hull. Instead of worrying about it, he grabbed the case he had hung on to for dear life and snapped open the latches. He opened the container and he saw they had three minutes left. He removed the weapon from the case and not too gently tossed it into the damaged space in *Teacher*'s engineering compartment.

"Damn, why didn't I think of taking it out of the case!" said the Frenchman.

Jack didn't hear the question as he quickly swam into the opening and disappeared. Farbeaux quickly followed.

Outside the hull, Sarah finally surfaced after being pummeled by the wave left in Supay's wake. She bumped into Carl as he, too, surfaced not two feet from her. They both swam for the stern of *Teacher*, which had begun to stick up in the air. She was going down by the bow at a fast rate of speed. Carl got to the opening first, and reached up and grabbed on. He tried in vain to pull himself up but the part of the composite hull he was hanging on to gave way and he went back down into the water, narrowly missing Sarah.

"Forget it, her ass is riding too high," he shouted over the roar of the water. The chamber was filling quickly. "Jack, we're losing her!" Carl just hoped the major heard him.

Inside *Teacher*, Jack was not only fighting with the bomb to get it inside the now-dangling *Turtle*, he was fighting with *Teacher* herself as gravity started to take effect. The boat now started to go down by the nose.

"Hold the canopy up, Colonel," Jack shouted.

Farbeaux grabbed the Plexiglas canopy and held it in place as Jack fitted the stainless-steel weapon into the front seat. The major then pulled himself toward the back, reached into the cockpit, and gave a quick prayer that the electrical system hadn't shorted out. He flipped the switch and was rewarded with the control lights coming on like a Christmas tree. He didn't hesitate as he reached for the keyboard on the small computer set deep inside the panel. He quickly switched on the autopilot, activated the computer, and tapped in a depth of ten feet, which was what he estimated the cave opening to now be under water by. When he was prompted, he set a speed of forty-five knots, the maximum speed of the small craft. He ignored the computer prompts for oxygen output and other nonessentials. A warning flashed that told him at the speed setting he had selected the maximum amount of dive time was only three minutes. He ignored that, as well, and programmed his course, praying that he had the setting right or the damned thing would come back on them. He closed the canopy and it snapped shut.

"Carl!"

"Yeah," the lieutenant commander answered from outside.

"This thing's going to fall free; make sure her nose is pointed in the right direction when she hits the water."

Jack didn't wait for an answer as he reached over and hit *Turtle*'s cradle release. As he did so, the doors beneath it swung open with an explosive sound. When *Turtle* was released, the men cringed as its angle smashed the small craft into the opening on her way out of *Teacher*. Jack and Farbeaux sighed with relief as the sub cleared the doors.

"We'd better go, Colonel."

"I agree," was all the Frenchman said in answer as he quickly swam for the hole in *Teacher*'s hull.

TURTLE **HIT THE** water, almost decapitating Sarah as its high-speed jets started up before it hit the water. Carl braved death by reaching out and pushing *Turtle*'s nose toward the canal and the spot where the inner cave had been before it had gone under. The water jets pushed against the water and *Turtle* shot outward toward what looked like a solid rock wall. Then it slowly went beneath the surface.

"Okay, let's swim for it," Carl shouted at Sarah just as Jack and Farbeaux surfaced beside them.

As one, they broke for the Supay statue that had totally clogged the opening. They dove deeply. Farbeaux was the first to see the small gap where Supay's pointed ear lay against the stone opening. There was a gap of about two and a half feet. He just hoped they had the time to squeeze through.

Meanwhile, *Turtle* hurtled through the cave's opening. The setting for her depth had been miscalculated; the canopy struck the top of the mouth of the cave and cracked. As water started to seep in, the aroma of electrical ozone and smoke began to fill the unoccupied compartment of *Turtle*. The sub entered the canal system and started to climb.

FARBEAUX SURFACED FIRST and looked around for the others. Sarah popped up, and then Carl.

Jack felt himself grabbed from below and pushed upward. He was grateful for the help as he started to rise. When he broke free to the surface of the lagoon he looked over and had to smile as Will Mendenhall came up next to him, sputtering and spitting out water.

"Good to see you, Lieutenant," Jack said.

"Saw you were a little slow coming up there, Major."

The new second lieutenant had just reached the level of the lagoon after climbing down from the cliff face, when he saw the others come to the surface but not Jack. He dove in after him.

"Let's get the hell out of here!"

Just as Jack said the words, a deep rumbling sounded from all directions. High up where the falls originated, a massive waterspout shot straight up into the air and then the side of the cliff face exploded outward. All the survivors still in the water ducked under, in the hope that the tremendous quantity of debris would somehow miss them. Jack stayed afloat as missiles shot in all directions, but he just had to see, to make sure. He felt Farbeaux next to him.

As they watched, the giant Incan pyramid of El Dorado began to collapse from the inside. The falls, mountainside, and cliff face started to fall inward as the thermonuclear weapon melted stone from within. The weakened stone walls dissolved under the massive attack of gamma rays and fell in.

The witnesses to the death of the legendary El Dorado would never forget how the mine died with an ear-shattering bellow, as the entire northern end of the lagoon collapsed in on itself. The bomb took down a pyramid that had been constructed by ancient man to withstand a tremendous force equal to up to ten tons of TNT.

Farbeaux looked at Jack and not a word was uttered. The Frenchman raised his hand in a halfhearted salute, then turned and swam away. The major watched him go, more confused than ever about the Event Group's most-feared adversary.

"We let him go, Jack."

Collins turned toward Carl, Mendenhall, and Sarah, who were treading water close by.

"This time, he earned it. We'll see him again."

Carl was about to say something when a new sound entered his ears. They turned as one to see a most welcome sight.

It was large and looked like the boat they had seen the day the marines had dropped them off at the tributary, which seemed like years ago now. The men who now lined the rails were beginning to pull the survivors of *Teacher* and the Zachary expedition from the lagoon. At the bow, a large, heavy-set man in a filthy white shirt, and with a thick five- or six-day growth of beard, stood with a leg propped up on the gunwale. Even from their poor vantage point they could see he was looking straight at them. Jack, Mendenhall, Everett, and Sarah started to swim toward the oncoming boat.

As the boat's engine chugged to a stop only feet from the four swimmers, the man at the bow smiled and removed his cigar.

"You are in distress, gentlemen, oh, and lady?" he asked, a smile evident on his dark features.

Jack spit out a mouthful of water. "Nah, just . . ." He stopped. He didn't feel like joking; he was beat and worried about his people. He remembered this man's picture from the list of qualified river captains he had originally gazed over, back at the Group complex. He knew what to call him because most of the captains on the list had the same last name. "Captain Santos, isn't it?"

"*Sí*, Capitán Ernesto Santos at your service," he said as he replaced the cigar in his mouth and half bowed toward the four floating Americans.

"Pull us up, Captain, and let's talk business," Jack said as he swam the last few feet to the boat and helped the others secure the dangling cargo net.

FARBEAUX GINGERLY PULLED himself out of the water and looked back at the spot where the students and event personnel were being rescued.

The Frenchman saw large bubbles as something swam toward shore and then quickly turned away. He watched as the bubbles diminished. Whatever it was turned around and swam back toward the center of the lagoon, then Farbeaux wanted to look no more. He weighed his options as he watched Santos and his men start picking up the Americans. He decided he and Danielle would take their chances in the forest after the rapids.

As he started to turn away, he saw something floating at the lagoon's edge. He blinked when he recognized what it was. His vision blurred as his heart sank at the sight. He stepped to the water's edge and pulled out the satchel he had strapped onto Danielle. He turned the weightless bag over. His eyes widened when he saw the claw marks that had shredded the thick material. He touched the edges and saw that the marks had wicked up fresh blood. He slowly let the empty satchel fall from his hands as he went to his knees in the fine sand of the lagoon's bank.

He stayed that way, kneeling and looking at the water, for many moments, beating himself. His wife had been killed. Why had he helped the Americans? He closed his eyes and then looked at the now-collapsed El Dorado. Then his eyes went to the *Rio Madonna* as it picked out the last of the survivors. His eyes narrowed as they focused on the last man pulled out. Jack Collins.

At that moment, the mind of Henri Farbeaux snapped as he took in Collins. He no longer blamed himself for his momentary burst of generosity that had cost his dear wife's life. The person responsible was right there in front of him. Major Jack Collins.

Farbeaux slowly stood and turned toward the jungle. He started walking. Walking and thinking of how he was going to get even with the people who had fooled him into thinking he was human.

Colonel Henri Farbeaux walked into the jungle where he would be as one with the other animals, because that was what he had become in his instantaneous insanity. An animal.

JACK WAS THE last to be manhandled off the cargo net as Captain Santos ordered the *Rio Madonna* to the opposite shore. Sarah, Carl, and Mendenhall were safe among the others. The students all looked his way in silent thanks; that was as much as their sorrow and fatigue would allow them. They knew it had been the four people before them who had saved everyone from being stranded in the mine just as Helen Zachary and a lot of their friends had been.

The major now located Virginia—and a scowling master

chief, sitting by the wheelhouse in silence. Then he reached out to Sarah and half smiled as he took her hand.

"I didn't exactly get them all out, did I . . ." he began.

Sarah turned on him and looked him right in the eye. "Don't even start with that crap, Jack. You did all you could; the result is right before your eyes. Ten kids will see home again because of you."

Just beyond her, Carl nodded his head, agreeing with Sarah.

JACK, SARAH, VIRGINIA, and Carl stood at the bow and looked at the falls, which had been reduced to only sixty feet from their tumble to the lagoon. Three hundred feet of mountaintop had collapsed in on El Dorado, enough tonnage to keep the plutonium and gold away from the hands of man for many decades.

The lagoon itself was silent again as life sounds returned to the rain forest around them.

"I guess Farbeaux would have made off with enough uranium to guarantee we would all be scared to death for the next fifty years," Virginia said, as the captain of *Rio Madonna* gave orders for getting under way.

"No, his plan would have ended right here," Jack said.

· "What do you mean?" she asked, as Santos turned and smiled at the gathered Americans, his cigar freshly lit.

"Our friend here," said Jack, nodding toward Captain Santos, "would have killed anyone involved with the mine as soon as they returned to his boat. Hell, he may still be planning to kill everyone."

Sarah didn't follow this. "What makes you say that?"

"Because it's his job," Jack answered, staring at Santos. "Captain, would you mind joining us, please?"

Santos stepped over and removed his cigar from his mouth. "*Sí, señor?*"

"Captain, you can knock off the peasant act now and show these ladies your jewelry," Jack said, smiling.

"Act? No, *señor*, I am a peasant of the river," he said as he reached into his shirt and drew out his necklace. He kissed the object on it, as he always did. Then he smiled and held it out so the two women could see his proudest possession.

"A papal medal of the Order of St. Patrick," Virginia said, astonished.

"*Sí*, it has been mine for twenty-three years. Starting with my ancestors many years ago; our passion for the pope has continued through my bloodline. It has been our responsibility to ensure that the world shall never benefit from Padilla's discoveries. To make sure no one ever goes beyond the borders of the river and her surrounding sisters," he said as he dropped the medal back into his sweat-stained shirt, then he struck a match to his dead cigar. "My pleasure in life has been safeguarding Eden from men and women such as . . ."

"Us," Sarah said, comprehending at last.

Santos smiled as his cigar glowed to life. "*Sí, señora*, people such as you."

"Captain Santos and his family were listed by Europa as having been awarded the first medals back in 1865, your great-great-grandfather, I believe," Jack said as he remembered the papal medalist list he had studied after Niles had hit on Keogh's name in Virginia.

"*Sí*, this is true. You are surely a man with great knowledge, and I must assume you would not be easily disposed of, *señor*?"

"No need; we are going to make sure El Dorado remains just a myth, a place where legends go to die," Jack said, looking the captain straight in the eye.

Santos didn't say anything, but just nodded and puffed on his cigar. Then he briefly looked toward the collapsed mine that was hidden behind the waterfalls. The waters allowed only wisps of smoke to escape from the devastation inside.

"It must get tiresome out here all alone," Virginia said.

Santos laughed heartily as the *Rio Madonna*'s engines came to life and the old boat made for the far shoreline. "Alone? No, I have my loyal crew and all of this," he said. He looked up into the bridge and gave an up-and-down motion with his fist. The boat's whistle sounded loudly in the silence of the valley.

Santos laughed as he looked up along the lip of the extinct volcano. Then Jack and the others heard chanting, almost a gentle song as sung by hundreds of people. They looked at the spot Santos was indicating and saw that the edge of the caldera was lined with Sincaro who stood watching the boat as it chugged its way out of the center of the lagoon.

Professor Charles Hindershot Ellenshaw III broke away from the other survivors and held a hand to his bandaged head when he saw the ancient people of this lost valley. He began to cry for Professor Keating, who had died before he could see the prehistoric success story now unfolding before them. The Sincaro had taken everything the outside world could throw at them, be they Inca, Spanish, or modern man, and it was they who God allowed the sole ownership of Eden.

"It is a hard life, but my friends up there and not El Dorado is why we have always done this service for our pope. Not gold, not strange minerals." He turned and looked at the major. "This place is truly Eden, but it does have a few snakes that will protect it at all costs."

A large group of Sincaro watched from the sandy beach as the *Rio Madonna* dropped anchor on the eastern shore of the lagoon. Santos hummed the very tune of the Sincaro as he stepped to the gunwale. He gestured for Jack, Carl, Sarah, and Mendenhall to join him.

"I have it in my power to kill all of you. It is within my right to do so," he slowly explained without one iota of accent to his English. He turned away from the shore and the jungle beyond, to address the Americans, his face a death mask of seriousness. Then he smiled a sad sort of smile, replaced his cigar in the corner of his mouth, and tilted his filthy saucer cap back on his black hair. "But I think you have acted honorably in this place, as others have not. Those that have not are now a part of the legend of the valley, *sí*?"

"Yes," Jack answered as he heard noise coming from the bush.

"Good. Now, I think you may have lost something of yours in the jungle, *señor.* You may have them back. My friends the Sincaro are quite finished with them."

As Jack and the others followed his eyes to the shore of the lagoon, the bushes parted and an even larger party of Sincaro came forward, marching in a straight line. Jack smiled when he saw who they had in tow, tied with hands behind his back and strung along like a dog on a leash, but very much unharmed.

"Hey, guys, what's up?" Jason Ryan asked with his boyish grin. It quickly became a grimace when a small spear was probed into his lower back. The Sincaro chattered something in their own tongue as they herded him and the thirteen survivors from Operation Proteus forward. "Think we could get a lift out of here?" Ryan flinched and looked back at the miniature man pointing the stick behind him.

HALF AN HOUR later, after Ryan and the Delta and air force personnel had been pulled aboard and the *Rio Madonna* began to make its way out of the lagoon, the lone creature breached the surface and stared at the departing boat. Then the beast slowly sank beneath the surface as the small monkeylike creatures came out of the trees and started jabbering and jumping into the water. And so life returned to normal in the Garden of Eden, which returned to serenity in front of a collapsed legendary treasure that would continue to tease the mind of greedy men the world over—the lost mines of El Dorado.

25

PETE Golding paced outside Niles Compton's office. Alice watched him walk by her desk for the twentieth time. She shook her head, wondering when people would learn that you can wear the carpet down to fibers pacing and worrying, but that still couldn't change the speed at which things happened.

She had learned this after her ten-thousandth mile of doing exactly what Pete was doing now.

Pete stopped as the door finally opened. Niles was finished with his phone call to Scottsdale, Arizona.

"Well?" Pete asked.

Niles had spoken directly to the surviving member of the 1942 expedition to Brazil. Charles Kauffman, an associate professor under Enrico Fermi at the time, was still very cognizant of what they had achieved back in the war years. His mind was sharp and he remembered everything.

"The Army Corps of Engineers, along with the U.S. Navy and Army, removed one hundred and two pounds of enriched uranium from El Dorado." Niles sat on the edge of Alice's desk as he spoke. "They had discovered information from a spy in 1941 that the ore samples were indeed real and were stored in the archives, the same samples and cross Farbeaux got his hands on in just the last few years. Anyway, Mr. Kauffman explained to me that Fermi and the effort at the University of Chicago had yet to achieve that which they had been theorizing since Einstein had said it was possible—"

"A sustained chain reaction," Pete said for him.

"That's right. They needed something that they did not have, a source of enriched uranium. Well, we now know the source fell directly into their laps, thrown there by the U.S. military and Corps of Engineers when they confirmed the existence of Padilla's lagoon and samples. It was never about the gold. It was always the uranium."

"Let me guess from my memory of the dates," Pete said. "By the time the expedition had met its ill-fated end, Fermi and his team had achieved their reaction in the States?"

"Yes."

"And the material?"

"It was placed in storage in Utah by the Army Corps of Engineers, and forgotten about until just recently."

"Is that it?" Pete asked.

It was Alice who guessed at it.

"The material has come up missing, hasn't it?"

"Yes, it has. And you will never guess who the beneficiary of this unusual find was."

"Well, who was it?" Pete asked when Niles didn't say anything more.

SIXTY MILES SOUTH OF BAGHDAD, REPUBLIC OF IRAQ

They owned the night. There wasn't a team in the world better at operations that called for sheer audacity than the Blue Light element of Delta, the highly secretive commando and antiterrorist unit of the U.S. Army.

They had been briefed on their mission by the secretary of defense, himself. The plan called for a twelve-man incursion into the most unlikely weapons storage facility they had ever been called upon to strike. The storage unit was placed three stories below ground level in an area the Iraqis knew no one would ever suspect.

The HALO parachute jump had gone off without incident and the twelve Blue Light commandos settled easily to the desert scrub just outside of the ancient ruins. The facility had been hastily constructed and was lightly guarded and the strike team took advantage of the close in intelligence supplied to them from Iraqi informants inside their military.

The target: the ancient ruins of the city of Babylon.

The material was stored in an underground bunker originally built by Saddam Hussein during his tyrannical rule of Iraq. Since no one but the topmost chiefs of the Iraqi military knew what the material was, the area was virtually unsecured. The bunker's few guards were easily dispatched with regret toward their innocence. Five soldiers in all silently, quickly killed without a warning being sounded.

Thirteen minutes later, the material had been found and tested, verifying the fact that it was indeed the same ore that had been removed from Brazil almost seventy years before.

An hour after the mission had started it was over and news relayed to the president of the United States that Iraq was no longer in possession of material that would enable that country to manufacture the world's largest "dirty bomb." The Iraqi government would have to defend themselves from Iran with the aid of a few well-chosen friendly nations instead.

BOGOTÁ, COLOMBIA

The Brazilian chief of staff had just made a withdrawal from his protected accounts at the Banco de Juarez. Señor Mendez, his benefactor, was out of the country, or so he was told when he asked for him. He smiled to himself; it did not matter as he would never see him again, as his military career was over at any rate due to his final act of treachery to his country.

As he stepped from the suite of offices he looked at his watch; plenty of time to make his charter flight to Venezuela. As he strolled casually toward the elevator, his briefcase pleasantly heavy with more than six million American dollars in payoff money earned over the years from various cartels, to allow drug overflights of his country, he was appreciative of the attractive twenty-something woman who joined him as he waited for the elevator. As the express car arrived he smiled and gestured for her to enter first. As the door closed, the general removed his sunglasses and turned, smiling. His smile faded quickly as the silenced Glock nine-millimeter pistol went off in his face. The woman placed the smoking weapon in her handbag and waited for the elevator to arrive at the private lobby on the first floor. Before the door opened, she reached down and removed the briefcase from the dead hand of the general, then popped its latches and poured the money out, onto his prone body.

The president of Brazil did not care to be made a fool in front of the Americans.

THE WHITE HOUSE

The crowded pressroom was deathly still as the secretary of state slowly unfolded his prepared statement. He scanned those assembled and saw the president standing well away from any prying camera lenses. Secretary Nussbaum closed his eyes and then opened them, and tried in vain to smile.

"Good afternoon. For the many months of campaigning to succeed the president into this very office, I have been blessed with many letters of support from our party. Thus it is with a sad heart that I must now decline the upcoming nomination for the presidency due to health reasons I won't go into here—"

THE PRESIDENT LISTENED for a moment and then turned away. He had never been so tempted in his many years in public life to throttle a man he had considered a close friend and advisor. A man who found it easy to lie, cheat, and murder his way into the highest office of the country.

"Hi, Daddy," Kelly said as she joined him on his way back to the Oval Office.

He smiled and placed his arm around her. "Hi there, yourself."

"What's going to happen to that jerk and his buddies now?" she asked, thinking about Robby, Professor Zachary, and the others, and the horrible fate handed to them from these men her father had trusted.

"They are all being retired from public life."

"That's all? After what they did?" she asked incredulously.

He would have loved to explain the real inner workings of the world to his daughter, because she and the other survivors deserved at least that much. But what good would it do to tell them and his countrymen that, on his watch, trusted men were able to get their hands on the most deadly material in the world and use it for their own gains? None.

Passing enriched uranium to a foreign nation and allowing them to use that material as a possible means of detonating a dirty bomb over the forces of an aggressive Iran was not legally treason. No U.S. law existed to forbid it. And so, the military men involved in the conspiracy were simply reassigned for their failure to foresee the Iranian threat of invasion. *At least officially.* They would be quietly retired, and their despicable lives would go on with only a look back at the positions they might have held in the secretary's new government.

As for the secretary, he would die quietly in his sleep from something resembling a massive coronary. That would be the only justice handed down for the man who had cost the lives of over seventy Americans. Kelly did not need to know the details.

"That's just the way of it, baby." He stopped and turned her toward him. "I'm sorry. So, are you heading back to California to visit your friend, Robby?"

"Yes."

"You tell him to get well, and we'll talk about certain aspects of his summer with you when he's better," he said. He kissed her on the cheek and sent her upstairs to her mother. Then he turned and entered the Oval Office.

The four Secret Service agents and three FBI were standing around a lone man sitting on the couch. The director of the FBI sat facing the man, who held his head down. The president walked past them and sat at his desk. He looked up and shook his head. The ex-national security advisor slowly looked up into the eyes of his former boss.

"Now, what am I supposed to do with you?" the president asked no one in particular as he glared at his own personal Judas.

The Secret Service agent by the door reached out and closed it.

It had been a surreal experience since the moment the team had stepped off the transport until the time they had finally been called to final debrief by Niles. The invitees didn't include any of the regular Event Group hierarchies, with the exception of Virginia and Jack. Pete Golding was even missing. Heidi Rodriguez was there, sitting next to Sarah, and so was Professor Ellenshaw. Alice smiled as she took in the small group. Carl came in late and apologized. Only Niles was yet to enter the room.

"This isn't a normal debrief," Virginia said, looking at her watch.

"No, its not," Alice said, knowing full well that Virginia was anxious to get out of the meeting and fly back to Los Angeles to see Master Chief Jenks, who was laid up in the hospital there. The Stanford graduate students had been debriefed by members of the FBI and told that the others on their trip had met with a boating disaster—a story they all wholeheartedly agreed to proliferate if asked. Three of the Zachary team was in for much harder times, including Helen's assistant and Kelly's fiancé, Robby, who had taken in enough rads to assure him of some form of dreadful illness before he reached old age. The other two kids wouldn't make it through the month.

As for the Event Team that had been under Jack's command, including the Proteus Operation, they had lost thirty-three people, all brilliant men and women, friends that couldn't easily be replaced—Keating, Jackson, Larry Ito, Dr. Waltrip, and many others. Losses Jack would have a hard time getting over.

The door opened and Niles walked in. He stepped aside and allowed Senator Garrison Lee, the former director of the Group, to enter. Lee was followed by the president of the United States, who was supposed to be on a fund-raising tour of Arizona, Nevada, and California in support of the newest party candidate, a former general in the U.S. Army whose campaign was starting to steamroll after the secretary of state's abrupt resignation.

The Group started to stand, but the president waved them back down.

"Don't do that, please," he said. He couldn't meet their eyes.

He waited for Senator Lee to be seated out of respect for the old gentleman, and then he sat at the far end of the conference table. Alice smiled at her former boss and current roommate, and Lee patted her hand.

The president spoke first, catching Niles off guard.

"No," he said looking up from the tabletop toward Niles. "I will not accept it, so don't even try."

Niles angrily removed his jacket and looked at Lee, who didn't flinch from his gaze.

"My right; I was lied to at every step," Niles calmly said.

"Not by me," the president countered brusquely.

Alice closed her eyes and stopped taking the minutes of the meeting.

The president took a deep breath and then finally looked at the people around the conference table.

"The United States government has known about Padilla's valley since early in 1941. The information was discovered by an American agent working in the Vatican. He gave the information to his controller in Army Intelligence, who knew beyond a doubt what ore was in his possession. That agent was able to retrieve the route from the diary, with the official sanction of the Catholic Church and the Archdiocese of Madrid. They deemed that we Americans would be able to use the material wisely in the end. So, the route and ore found its way to the University of Chicago, whose experiments in building a reactor underneath Stagg Field in Chicago had been an unadulterated failure to that point. Enrico Fermi was allowed to examine Padilla's ore samples firsthand. He came away convinced the samples were as close to weapons grade as they could ever achieve artificially. Naturally, he continued work on his atomic pile in Chicago. But they wanted to use the Padilla samples as a fallback material, so they went after it."

Niles had refrained from telling everyone in the room. The president insisted he be the one to take full and ultimate responsibility for the lives lost.

He swallowed and looked from face to face. "You know the rest. His friend at Princeton, Albert Einstein, sent ten of his closest and most trusted people, along with Fermi's chosen few. He dubbed them the Chicago Mining Association. Unfortunately, he never saw most of them again and the ones he did would live only three months, with the exception of Professor Kauffman in Arizona. Needless to say, Fermi was more competent than he believed himself to be, and was successful in producing a chain reaction the very same month his expedition was destroyed."

"And then the world became a better place," Lee interjected with sarcasm.

"The material from El Dorado had been kept and filed away for years and years. Then it was accidentally discovered by the head of the Army Corps of Engineers, and that information was shared with several friends of his, including my own national security advisor and the former secretary of state. Together, they found a worthwhile cause for the use of the weapons-grade material. An event that would make one man look good enough to hold this very office, and for the others to have high new positions afterward as a reward for stopping the threat of invasion from an aggressor nation."

Niles still looked angry.

The president looked at Compton and said, "Resignation not accepted, Mr. Director, simply for the reason you are too valuable to the American people."

Niles swallowed and allowed himself to feel for the first time in days.

"I withdraw my resignation request," Niles said and allowed Alice to take his hand and for Lee to reach over and pat both of theirs.

The president sat a moment, looking tired. "Now, Major Collins, I understand you believe you have the right to award battlefield commissions to sergeants?"

Jack grinned. He was prepared for the argument with the president. "Not only sergeants, but navy junior grades also." He nodded toward Virginia, who stood and made her way to the double doors and pulled them open.

Second Lieutenant (temporary grade) William Mendenhall stepped in dressed in his U.S. Army dress blues that still had his gold, staff sergeant's stripes on the sleeve. He was followed in by Lieutenant JG Jason Ryan, USN, who was dressed in shorts and a Hawaiian shirt of multiple colors. They both stood at attention.

"Glad to be home, Mr. Ryan? I understand Delta wants you back, and the Proteus program also wants you. So tell me, are you done flying for the air force?" the president asked.

Ryan glanced at Collins before answering the president.

"I think the major knew that laser platform would try to kill me, sir."

"Well, it's his right to do so. After meeting you and seeing you again, Mr. Ryan," he looked pointedly at the shorts and Hawaiian shirt, "I can't blame him."

"Mr. President," Jack said, standing, "I officially request that Sergeant William Mendenhall be given assignment to the very next class at OCS. He will make a fine officer in the army. As for Mr. Ryan here, either we need to promote him for duties above and beyond, or kick his ass out of here completely, if you'll pardon the expression—your choice."

The president stood and shook both men's hands, and nodded his agreement.

"I suppose *you* would have also tried to resign if I didn't give in?" he asked the major.

"Me, Mr. President? Not a chance, I was hoping for Niles's job until you talked him out of quitting."

The president smiled and then slid two small cases along the conference table toward Niles. "Do the honors, Mr. Director, please."

Niles, with as much pomp and circumstance as he could muster, simply tossed one box to Jack and the other to Carl.

The director then opened a flimsy paper and read. "Major Jack Collins, as befitting a military liaison to an agency outside of his own, you are hereby promoted to the rank of lieutenant colonel, with pay grade adjustment commensurate of said rank, minus one hundred dollars per month, which is to be deducted toward the repayment of monies to the United States Navy, stemming from charges brought about by Master Chief Archibald Jenks, United States Navy, for the destruction of U.S. government property, namely the commissioned river transport, USS *Teacher*. Lieutenant Commander Carl Everett is hereby promoted to the rank of captain, United States Navy, with pay grade increase for same, plus a monthly deduction of pay amounting to one hundred dollars, as aforementioned compensation for property recently destroyed."

Jack and Carl looked at each other and couldn't gather the words.

"You are also hereby officially reprimanded by the president of the United States and said reprimand will be placed in both 201 files. In addition, both officers will immediately fly to Los Angeles and formally apologize to Retired Master Chief Archibald Jenks, whom I must say is quite anxious to see you," the president finished for Niles. "Now, you're officially dismissed."

Jack Collins and Carl Everett walked from the conference room stunned at what they had just happened. As the doors closed behind them, they heard the life of the Event Group return to normal as the director and president started their yearly argument.

"Now, Mr. Director, we need to discuss this outrageous budget you've turned in for the next fiscal year; it just won't do. I won't be in office the next time around, and the next guy may not be so generous."

ANCIENTS

KATONAH
WESTCHESTER COUNTY, NEW YORK

THE mansion was surrounded by immense manicured lawns and gardens, which belied the fact that hidden among imported shrubs and trees was the most sophisticated security system ever installed within the confines of a private estate. It had taken Special Agent Monroe only hours, with the help of his Europa link, to track the owner's business expenses, and the discovery of the advanced security system told the agent that the man had something to hide within the walls of the estate. The eight-million-dollar system had drawn scrutiny and been cross-referenced with the owner's identity. From there it had been only a matter of digging a little further to find the truth behind the wealthy world traveler.

The team had decided to travel over a mile overland to reach the outer gate at the rear of the property in lieu of using a helicopter. Nothing would have been more conspicuous than the taletell thump of rotor blades after dark in quiet Westchester County, New York.

The ten-man assault element watched as one of three security trucks negotiated the long driveway from the front of the mansion. They were nearly invisible in the dark, blending in well with the cloudy night in their Nomex clothing and hoods. The team was armed with MP-5s—lightweight, short-barreled automatic weapons.

The dark figure squatting beside a tree raised his hand as the small pickup truck cruised by, its spotlight swinging toward them but missing the ten men. He then held up two fingers and made a scissoring motion.

A large man in the middle of the line came forward after the truck had vanished around a curve. He removed a small black box and held it as close to the steel fence as he could without touching it, then he switched on the power to the box. The soft glow of the gauge was covered by the big man's hand as he studied the LED readout. He nodded and held up his left hand. He splayed his fingers wide, indicating five, then closed his hand again and spread them once more: ten. The man in the lead nodded, easily seeing the signal with his ambient-light-vision goggles, bringing the team into a silhouetted ghostly image of greens, blacks, and grays. The large man lowered his hand and removed the twin electrical leads. He was hearing the soft hum of ten thousand volts of electricity as it passed through the chain-link fence.

Another of the team duck-walked forward and brought out the insulated wire cutters, then he waited while the larger man ran rubber-coated wires from one link of the fence to another. He did this until he had a four-foot circle woven into and connecting the chain links. Then he held out his hand and took the cutters from the second man. Then he started snipping the thick wire of the fence.

The wiring he had woven into the fence was an electric-free corral, designed to isolate an electrical current and keep a connection of the fence to fool any alarm that would sound as the links were severed. With the last of the links cut, the man pulled free the circle of wire, and the team moved in.

Two three-man teams went left and right, hunkering low as they went. The leader took the last three and went straight ahead.

On the left, that team would make first contact, so they lowered themselves to the ground and waited. They were rewarded a moment later when headlights came around the corner from the back of the house. This was the second security truck. As it approached, one of the three men removed a small ball bearing from his armored vest and waited until the truck was ten yards away on the other side of the slope.

The first man in line crawled the last three feet to the top of the rise and pulled a funny-looking pistol from a holster at his side; then he aimed. The other drew back and threw the lightweight ball bearing in a nicely tossed arc. It struck the side of the truck, making a louder-than-expected crack as the vehicle came quickly to a stop, its driver curious as to the cause of impact. As soon as he stepped from the small truck and walked three steps to its hood, and looked to see what had struck the vehicle, the compressed-air dart caught him in the left side of his neck. The security guard yelped and then tried to make it to the driver's-side door, but he made only two steps before his legs refused to cooperate and gave out completely. He fell with a muffled thud. He would be that way for several hours, awakening with the worst headache of his life.

The three other vehicles and the three foot-patrol officers were dispatched just as easily. Only one had given the team a fright, as he had actually had the physical strength to get his hand on the radio clipped to his shoulder before giving up the ghost.

The team spread out into their designated entry points and waited for the signal. The large man who had cut the fence found the telephone and power boxes on the outside of the house near the basement door and placed a small, circular object against the incoming phone and power lines that ran in from the county grid. He set the timer for ten seconds and then backed away. A small electrical charge sent power racing back into both lines, popping the circuit breakers somewhere inside the house. The phone line would be useless until the phone company discovered that the fiberoptic line had been fused and clouded from the electrical charge.

The lights around the compound went out: that was the signal for step three in the structure assault. At that exact same instant, the front and rear doors, along with the center panel of French doors beside the pool, exploded inward with a shower of wood splinters and glass. The black-operations team entered with weapons held high.

On the ground floor, the unseen and invisible assailants roughly pushed several shrieking servants to the ground. They were expertly bound with plastic ties and then the men moved off quickly. The raid took exactly three minutes and twenty-two seconds from the time the first guard had been taken down.

The leader of the team stepped forward after counting heads and looking at each face. He came to a man who was looking up into the hooded face above him arrogantly.

"Your name is Talbot?" the man with the funny goggles asked.

The man only stared up into the darkness, not as arrogant now as he'd been before the man called him by name.

"Are you Talbot, the butler, the man in charge?" the man asked quietly again, this time kneeling down, bringing his science-fiction-looking outfit closer for inspection. For emphasis, he adjusted the MP-5 weapon on its strap menacingly.

"Yes, yes," the man said quickly.

"Where is William Krueger?"

"He . . . he . . . was upstairs when we retired for the night. . . . I swear." '

The menacing figure glanced up at another even larger team member coming down the stairs. This man shook his head, negative, and then the man kneeling beside the butler unsafed his weapon, and everyone in the room, even the maids and cooks, knew a menacing click when they heard one.

"I'll ask one more time, and if I don't get the answer I want, you'll be serving your next high-paying master with a limp, because I will shoot you right through the kneecap—understood?" The threat was delivered with a menacingly cool voice.

"You can't do this . . . you're . . . you're police officers!"

The man chuckled and looked at the big man above him. "Who in the world ever said we were police officers? This is what you would call a home invasion, and we're the invaders. I'm also running out of patience."

The calm and sensible demeanor of the man wearing the strange goggles terrified the butler.

"For God's sake, Albert, tell them what they want to know!"

The man calmly looked over at the belly-down servants and saw an arrogant-looking woman trying to peer at him through the darkness. Then he remembered the detailed pictures shown to him by the recon team. She was Anita McMillan, the estate's chef.

"All right, all right. There's a panel in the library behind the desk. It's a false front, there are stairs behind it. Just slide it, it'll open right up. That's the only place Mr. Krueger can be."

The leader nodded toward the larger man and he and three others went to the library.

"Thank you, Albert. Your cooperation has been noted." The man gestured for another of his team and soon all the servants were blinded by black bags that were placed over their heads.

The leader joined the three men inside the library and watched as the paneled wall was probed. Then he heard the panel slide into the wall. He gestured for the middleman, the best rifleman on the team, to take point. As he did, the others waited until he was ten steps down the flight of stairs before they followed.

The men removed their night-vision scopes as there was a soft light coming from below. They were halfway down when the point man held up his hand with splayed fingers, and they stopped. As they watched him take another step, they were surprised by the sound of a pistol shot as it glanced off the stone wall, just missing the man in the lead position. They saw him grimace as stone chips struck the side of his face. Then he took a determined stance, braced himself against the stairwell's railing, and fired a ten-shot burst of 5.56-millimeter rounds into the basement. Then he waited another split second and fired ten more. The men behind him knew his routine and prayed it would work.

"Now, that was a warning! The next burst is going to chew your ass up. You have three seconds to surrender that popgun you have. Oh, hell, forget it. I'm not waiting." The point man fired a three-round burst into the stairwell and the basement below. The men behind him on the stairs smiled as he did so.

"Okay, okay, you son of a bitch. You didn't have to do that. Give a man time to think, goddammit!"

"You're all out of time, fuckhead! You took a shot at the wrong goddamn black man!"

"Who in the hell are you?"

"That's of no concern to you at the moment!" Another three-round burst was sent into the basement, close to but not near enough to the unseen man below to cause him any harm. "I didn't hear that cap gun hit the floor yet, asshole!"

"Goddamn maniacs!" The whimpering voice answered from below, but that was quickly followed by the clatter of metal hitting concrete.

The point man didn't hesitate. He took the stairs quickly and the others behind him made as much noise as possible to tell the man below that the maniac had a lot of company. They heard the commands before they reached the bottom of the stairs.

"On your belly, Rockefeller. Hands spread out in front. *Now*, dammit! Put those silk pajamas on the cold-ass floor!"

The others arrived and watched as a plastic wire tie was placed on the wrists of a very large, rotund man. The man's breathing seemed distressed, and the leader of the assault team gestured for the point man to get him on his feet.

"Who . . . who . . . who are you? What do you want?" the man rasped in halting words.

The team leader found a large chair behind an even larger desk and pushed it toward him with his black boot.

"You're not going to die on us, are you?"

The fat man took several deep breaths and finally color began to run back into his face. The lighting was sufficient in the spacious basement to see that he was recovering from his initial shock.

"As for who we are, we're the people that have come to

ke back the things you have stolen over the years and to
nake you account for the lost lives of innocent archaeology
students in Ethiopia. That's who we are."

The owner of the mansion watched from his chair as the
black hood was removed. The three other men did the same.
The angry black man to his front was staring a hole through
him. He shied away, leaning as far back in the chair as possible, when he realized that it was the man he had taken the
shot at.

"I don't know what you're talking about. I'm an invest-
ment banker and commodities trader," he said, still looking
at Mendenhall.

Colonel Jack Collins stepped forward, tossing his hood to
Carl Everett, standing at his side.

"Mr. Krueger, do we look like men who have been misin-
formed? Do you think we came here on a whim, or do you
think we may have a purpose?"

Krueger looked from face to face. There was no identify-
ing insignia on their clothing and each man had his face set,
and it was a determined look.

"No . . . I mean yes, you look as if you have a purpose."

"We know about your collection, so, if you would like to
leave this house in one piece, you'll show it to us right now.
I'm sure you don't want the authorities involved here, do
you?"

Krueger looked as if he had accepted his fate in one fell
swoop. His head lay to the side and he started to cry. His
large frame shook with his sobbing as Will Mendenhall helped
him to his feet.

Colonel Collins looked over at Everett, who nodded and
then walked over and assisted in getting the overweight
Krueger to a standing position. Collins waited while the
art-and-antiquities thief, not to say murderer, composed himself. He heard a click in his earpiece. He thumbed a small
switch at his throat that activated his transmitter. He turned
away from Krueger.

"Recovery One," he said softly into his throat microphone.

"This is Eagle Eye. All palace guards are cooperating ar
we have Ernie's Fix-it Shop and Recovery Three on propert,
and moving toward your pos, over."

Collins heard the whispered voice from his outside security. Instead of answering, he reached down and manually
clicked his mic twice.

Everett also heard the report. All the security guards had
been rounded up and placed in a safe location, still out from
the tranquilizers, and now the three-man outside security element reported another Event team approaching the house.
Carl rolled back his black glove and looked at his watch. *Not
bad*, he thought; Ryan and his team were right on schedule.
Not bad for a flyboy.

"Okay, Krueger, the artifacts," Collins said, stepping toward the man.

"Take me over to my desk, please."

Jack nodded, and Mendenhall and Everett walked him
over to a large, ornate desk in the far corner of the basement
office. The large man reached out for the top drawer.

"Ah-ah-ah, we'll open it for you," the black man said.
Mendenhall leaned forward and gently pulled out the top
drawer. He gave Krueger a mock-disappointed look and removed the snub-nosed .38 Police Special and tossed it over
to Collins.

"That was not my intent. There's a button just under the
lip of the desk. Push it once."

Mendenhall felt around until he found it and then pushed it.

At first, there was nothing. They could hear only the activity upstairs as Ernie's Fix-it Shop, an Event Group maintenance team, went to work with subdued hammering and
electric-tool sounds. Then battery-powered floodlights joined
those few emergency lights and illuminated the room
brightly. In the harsh glare, the team could see nothing but
barren walls. There were a few things like diplomas and family pictures, but other than that, they were white and empty.

"Push the button one more time," Krueger said with his
chin almost touching his chest in despair.

Mendenhall repeated the process and they heard an electric motor, obviously battery-operated also, start to hum, and then the far eighty-foot-long wall parted in the center and slowly slid back in two sections on hidden tracks.

Instead of watching the false wall divulge its secrets, Collins watched Krueger. He sniffled and wiped a hand across his sweating face, but his eyes weren't concerned about the secret door. Jack watched as the man's eyes quickly darted to the desk once more and then just as quickly looked away. Collins saw that the desk sat in front of one of the basement walls, and beyond that wall one would assume was dirt and rock. As he looked back, Krueger was again sobbing, but once again he saw the man's dark eyes glance at the desk.

"Jesus, you've been a busy little thief, haven't you?" Mendenhall said as spotlights illuminated a treasure trove of ancient and not-so-ancient artifacts.

Collins and Everett stepped forward and looked at the commodity trader's extensive collection. There were special pieces sitting atop pedestals from the third and fifth dynasties of Egypt. Lights shone down on armor dating back to the days of Alexander. There were oil paintings from the Renaissance. Others displayed jewelry had been stolen from collections around the world. Crowns of kings long dead. Collins activated his com link.

"Recovery Three, you can bring the trucks in now."

Jack turned to Krueger, who was still being held by Will. He stepped up to him, raised his double chin, and looked him in his watery eyes.

"Your cooperation will be noted and the prosecuting authorities will be notified."

"But you're thieves! Why . . . what—"

"To further enhance the chances your team of defense attorneys have of getting you acquitted, do wish to tell us about the second room now?"

The man's face drained of blood right before their eyes. His thick lips started to tremble and his eyes widened. All at once, he wasn't timid or frightened any longer; he was mad.

"You bastards, you're dealing with things beyond your concept!"

"Seems you hit a nerve, Jack," Everett said.

"Will, reach in and push the same button again. I think our friend is hiding his real treasure in another location. This room here is nice, but X doesn't mark the right spot, does it, Mr. Krueger?"

As instructed, Mendenhall pushed the button again. This time there was a loud whine of an overgeared motor, and as they watched in amazement, a large circle in the center of the floor separated from the surrounding concrete and started to corkscrew down into the earth. The opening was about sixteen feet in diameter and started spinning faster as they watched. They could see the threads of the giant screw-type elevator as it spun and descended farther and farther. Jack could see that a man would use those threads as a winding staircase to enter the real treasure room.

"Now we know why his security system was so expensive," Jack said as the whine of the large motor stopped.

"Jesus," Everett said, looking from Krueger to Jack. "This guy and his engineers should have been working for us."

"You don't know what you're doing. You've just killed us all."

Everett feigned shock at Krueger. "Now that's a scary statement. Care to expand on it?"

Krueger closed his mouth into a tight line and looked away. His eyes did not follow Jack as he walked to the opening in the floor. Everett caught up with Collins and they both went down into the true light of the ancient past.

When they reached the bottom of the screwlike stairs, they couldn't believe what they were looking at. Row upon row and stack upon stack, layered a hundred thick, were scrolls of every shape and size. They had been neatly placed on specially designed mounts in hermetically sealed glass cabinets. As if they had entered an old library, Jack and Carl took in the most amazing collection of ancient writings they had ever seen.

The room was temperature and humidity controlled and they saw plastic clean-room suits, of the sort they had used on occasion when working with Europa, hanging on pegs in the corner. There were examination tables and viewing

.ands. In a clean area fifty feet to the rear was what Jack recognized as an electron microscope. There was a rolled-out scroll on the glass top in the process of examination; it was covered in thick plastic to protect it from any dust particles that filtered into the room.

Also lining the walls were a hundred different flags. Some were emblazoned with a symbol reminiscent of the swastika, different only in small and varying ways. The one constant symbol on every flag was the shape of a large golden eagle. Some had straight and unyielding outstretched wings, and others had the wings turned down.

"Holy shit—is this guy Krueger for real?" Everett asked, staring at the strange banners.

Jack shook his head as he moved on. Also arrayed on one of the walls were several large relief maps from ancient times, sealed in the same manner as the scrolls. There were signs beneath each, warning of severe shock if the frame was touched. Jack stepped up to one and examined it more closely. It was an ancient depiction of Africa before the continent of Antarctica had separated from it. The rest of the world's continents had just broken away from one another and were in the process of moving as depicted in the next four wall-mounted maps.

Everett turned to the rear wall and looked at a strange chart that had millions of lines running through a mosaic relief of the African, European, and even North American continents. The strange lines wiggled through the Atlantic and Pacific oceans. Beneath this ancient diagram was a small table with a computer and a stack of research materials laid out upon it. Everett quickly rifled through it and then turned to face Jack.

"It looks like someone was trying to interpret this chart. Just what in the hell is this?"

Collins didn't answer. He was standing at the farthest end of the chamber, looking up at a giant glass-enclosed map that was by far the largest object in the room. A large spotlight shone upon it and illuminated the frame's meticulous construction, which showed specially designed nitrogen and air evacuation hoses built into it.

"Jesus," Carl hissed as he saw the huge map.

Everett walked over to where Jack was standing and staring upward. He saw what looked to be the ancient Mediterranean. The map looked as if it had been painted on some form of exotic paper. He could also see the age-induced crumbling around the edges and corners. While the obvious age of the map was a striking feature, it was not the one that held the colonel's attention. Everett had to take a step back when he saw the ancient depiction. It showed a large island, made up of four distinct circles of land radiating outward from a center island, that was surrounded by the great inland sea that was one day to be known as the Mediterranean Ocean.

"What in the hell?"

"Mr. Everett, contact Group and inform them that we will be bringing some things back to the complex. We cannot let the FBI have these. I will let Agent Monroe know he'll have to prosecute Mr. Krueger with what stolen items he finds upstairs. I'm sure there is enough."

"Right. Uh, by the way, Jack, are you thinking what I'm thinking?" he asked as his eyes centered on the island that should not have been in the middle of the sea that would someday be known as an ocean.

"You don't have to just think it," he said as he reached out and touched the gold plate beneath the twenty-by-fifteen-foot map of a world long gone. "I think this spells it out quite clearly."

Everett stepped closer as Collins moved away so that he could read the plaque. Carl closed his eyes and shook his head.

"Yeah, I don't think the FBI would truly appreciate the value of this room as much as our people would."

The gold plaque glittered in the illuminating spotlight and both men looked at it and felt numb inside.

Engraved on the plaque was only one word: *Atlantis*.

CPSIA information can be obtained
at www.ICGtesting.com
Printed in the USA
LVOW11s1157080517
533702LV00002B/366/P